D1569521

I CAN SEE
CLEARLY

Also by James A. Cusumano

<u>Fiction</u>

The Fallen: As Above, So Below

Twin Terror: Good Seed, Bad Seed

The Dialogue: A Journey to Universal Truth

<u>Nonfiction</u>

Freedom from Mid-East Oil
(with coauthors Jerry B. Brown and Rinaldo S. Brutoco)

Cosmic Consciousness:
A Journey to Well-being, Happiness and Success

Balance: The Business-Life Connection

Life Is Beautiful: 12 Universal Rules

JAMES A. CUSUMANO

I CAN SEE CLEARLY

RISE OF A SUPERNATURAL HERO

— BOOK ONE —

Waterside Productions
Cardiff-by-the-Sea, California

First Printing, 2020

Printed in the United States of America

ISBN-13: 978-1-941768-52-5 print edition
ISBN-13: 978-1-941768-53-2 ebook edition
ISBN-13: 978-1-665025-59-1 audiobook edition

Waterside Productions
2055 Oxford Avenue
Cardiff-by-the-Sea, CA 92007
www.waterside.com

For Julia,
our talented young storyteller

CONTENTS

Who looks outside, dreams;
who looks inside, awakes.

—Carl Jung

AUTHOR'S NOTE

When reading a nonfiction book, I often find it instructive and sometimes even entertaining when the author occasionally inserts a personal story or relevant real-world information concerning and supporting the book's premise. Similarly, I thought that in a work of fiction, it could be of interest, and at times, illuminating, to have access to this kind of supporting material.

For several chapters of *I Can See Clearly*, I wanted to take a similar approach, especially during narratives on the effects of super-consciousness. However, discussions on the potential for elevated states of consciousness to enable access to superpowers was a bit lengthy to be part of the main text. Therefore, for those interested, I've placed this material in supplemental endnotes at the conclusion of the book.

My intent is to provide the reader with complementary, and hopefully instructive, material about certain concepts addressed in the storyline. I hope this moves the novel toward the Wisdom Fiction genre—that is, providing useful knowledge and a valuable perspective in addition to entertainment. A suggestion: for optimal continuity, consider reading the novel straight through and the supplemental endnotes afterward. To distinguish these comments from footnotes, they're designated by a number followed by the letter s—for example, Luc.[1s]

Last point—regarding the use of profanity, I doubt that any of us have ever met any 20th- or 21st-century teenagers who don't use their share of it. And so it is with our protagonist, Luc Ponti. But Luc is not your typical teen wise guy, where every other sentence is decorated with common curse words. Furthermore, he has a peculiarity about him, something that started in early grammar school. Although a third-generation Italian, he's proud of his Sicilian heritage. As a young boy, he learned some Italian from his parents. While they eventually let their Italian go as they strived to be perceived as "full-bred Americans," Luc expanded his linguistic frontier and became well versed in Sicilian profanity, which he learned from his paternal grandfather, who lived with the Ponti family for a couple of years after his wife died. Luc became quite adept at making profane wisecracks in the Sicilian dialect to those he held in disdain.

As a youngster, and when angry at someone with authority, like a teacher he would smile and curse at them in Italian. With his quaint gestures and melodic presentation, he almost always got away with it when confronting what he irreverently called *stupidi Americani*. For your information and convenience, whenever Luc swears in Italian, the translation is footnoted on the same page, but only the first time it appears. If you forget the translation and it appears again on a subsequent page, you can find it in the glossary at the end of the book. My purpose is not to tutor you in the art of Italian profanity, but to prevent you from missing the sense and nuance of Luc's thoughts. I hope you find this useful.

Godere![1]

James A. Cusumano
Prague, November 2020

---

[1] *Godere!*—"Enjoy!"

PROLOGUE

*"The mystery of human existence lies in finding
something to live for."*

—FYODOR DOSTOYEVSKY

December 24, 2017—Lhasa, Tibet

THE SNOWS CAME EARLY. By December, the snowpack was deep, and although the afternoon sun felt comfortably warm, evening subzero temperatures and biting winds were a challenge for the uninitiated in the 12,000-foot *Forbidden City*. But this didn't stop 14-year-old Ananda from venturing from his home in the center of Lhasa on a steep five-kilometer trek to Drepung Monastery at the foot of Mount Gephel in the Himalayas. The Chinese government allowed it to reopen in 2013 after ordering it closed in 2008 because of a monk-led protest against China's occupation of Tibet.

Ananda's spiritual teacher had told him that a wise spiritual guide named Dawa had just arrived at the monastery for a short stay while on his way to Nepal. Dawa was world renowned for his *Siddhi* powers—that is, clairvoyance, levitation, viewing the future, and memories of past lives.

Ananda's aspirations to become a Buddhist monk were fading, and he wasn't sure he should continue on this path. He needed clarity that he wasn't getting from his teacher on how to think about the seemingly impossible challenges facing the people of Tibet, Nepal, India, Kashmir, and, in fact—the rest of the world. Ananda thought, *Were these the acts of a vindictive God?* If there was any reasonable amount of goodness in the world, none of this made any sense to him.

Ananda arrived at Drepung late that evening, nearly frozen to the bone. Although he was a stranger to the monks, in their usual compassionate manner they welcomed him with hot matcha tea and a simple meal of lentils and steamed vegetables. They even provided him with a comfortable place to sleep for the evening. The abbot agreed to allow him one hour with Dawa the next day after breakfast.

And so, the next morning, the meeting came to pass. Ananda entered Dawa's monastic cell in silence and sat lotus-style opposite him on a worn carpet next to the spiritual guide's sleeping cot. The contrast was quite amusing—Dawa, a tall, thin septuagenarian with sharp, dark, angular facial features, intense brown eyes, and silver hair pulled back in a ponytail, dressed in traditional robes and simple sandals—and Ananda, a young, fleshy teen, his cherubic face recovering from a mild case of acne. He was dressed in torn jeans and a much-too-small, tattered "New York City" sweatshirt his father had bought used at the Lhasa market.

卐 卐 卐

Dawa smiled at Ananda and opened the dialogue.

Dawa

"Namaste, Ananda. It is my pleasure to meet you. I heard from the abbot that you traveled up here from Lhasa last evening through wind and snow just to visit with me. I am impressed—and I should say, honored!"

Ananda

He sat with folded hands in front of his chest and a deeply bowed head. "Namaste, Bhante[2] Dawa. When I heard from my teacher that you would be here, I had to speak with you."

---

[2] *Bhante*—a Sanskrit-derived title of respect meaning "Venerable Sir."

Dawa

"It must be important if you came on foot last evening during that frigid weather. What is it you want to discuss with me?"

Ananda

"I know you're busy, and our time is short, so I'll answer you immediately and not waste your time." Ananda took a deep breath and shared his thoughts. "Even though my parents and teacher will be concerned when I tell them, I no longer think I want to become a monk. I don't want to disappoint them, so I need to understand if I'm thinking clearly and making the right decision. I thought you could help me."

Dawa

"I see . . . that is a big decision. And it is wise of you to seek outside counsel from people you trust—your parents, teacher, and perhaps even close relatives or friends. But then you alone must decide what to do. First, let me say that in a moment of truth, *your* truth—namely, what seems right for you—if you decide that becoming a monk is not what you want, then do not do it. Perhaps, a more important question for us today is: Why are you hesitating? Why are you changing your mind?"

Ananda

"That's easy. I've wanted to become a monk as long as I can remember, but the last couple of years, as I've listened to what my mother and father discuss about what's happening in Tibet, Nepal, India, Pakistan, Afghanistan, and, in fact, in much of the world, I'm not sure I want to do anything—especially become a monk. I don't even like getting out of bed in the morning anymore. My mother thinks I'm depressed, and I just need to pray and meditate more. But that hasn't helped so far."

Dawa

"I see. I agree that many of the things happening now in the world can be frightening and disturbing. Perhaps I can share some lessons from history that may help you understand and give you some hope for a better future. Do you think that might help you?"

Ananda
"Absolutely!"

Dawa
"Okay, Ananda. Let me consider the best way to relate this to your young, inquisitive mind." He closed his eyes for several moments of meditation and then continued. "I want to take you back about 5,000 years. It was a vastly different millennium then. A handful of enlightened mystics made a profound discovery that has continued to affect us to this day and will do so into the future for as long as there is a universe."

Ananda
"Bhante Dawa, it must have been a really big discovery if it's lasted this long and will go on for what seems like forever."

Dawa
"It was—and it *will* last forever."
Dawa could tell by the look on Ananda's face that he was perplexed. "I will explain, and maybe it will help, but in the end, only *you* can decide if it feels right for you. After all, we are talking about something particularly important—your life purpose. Shall we proceed?"

Ananda
He said with enthusiasm, "Yes, yes, please."

Dawa
"Fine. I will try to put it in today's terms. Thousands of years ago, seekers had much more quality time to experiment and think about big questions—more time than people have today. The world was slower then and much less chaotic. One of the most significant discoveries was that every thought, word, deed, and event that has ever occurred or ever will occur throughout the

entire universe—whether it's a massive black hole 600 million light-years away violently birthing new stars, an ancient galaxy flickering toward extinction, or even your thoughts about what you will have for dinner tonight—all of it—absolutely all of it— is recorded in an infinite, eternal ethereal plane separate from, yet connected to, our three-dimensional world. These wise sages called this infinite cosmic knowledge the *Akashic Record*, today also known as the *Akashic Field*.

Ananda
"That's amazing, but how could they be so sure they were correct? How could they test what they found?"

Dawa
"As I said, they had lots of time to think and experiment. They made their discoveries while they were at deep levels of meditation, which created high levels of consciousness, and in that state of being, they were able to closely connect with Cosmic Consciousness and therefore, with what Einstein often called the 'Mind of God'—total knowledge, past, present, and future. In doing so, they could consistently and accurately predict numerous, specific future events, so they knew that what they had uncovered was real, correct, and useful."

Ananda
"That's unbelievable! Have others since then been able to do this?"

Dawa
"Yes, some, but only by doing much work in learning how to reach high levels of altered consciousness, almost always through intense, deep meditation."

Ananda
"Why did they call it the Akashic Record?"

Dawa

"In Sanskrit, *Akashic* means the 'Fifth Element,' a subtle yet powerful force immensely greater than the four fundamental elements of alchemy—Earth, Fire, Water, and Air. In fact, the scientific laws governing the Akashic Record are well beyond those of classical and quantum physics. The ancient Wisdom Seekers called this ultimate science *Manasa Bhautazastra*, meaning 'spiritual physics.' They used the word *spiritual*—not in a religious or theological sense—but to emphasize that this was a science of nonmaterial things."

Ananda

"I don't understand. Why isn't this well known today . . . or is it?"

Dawa

"You are correct; it is not well known. Even after thousands of years, few people have knowledge of this amazing discovery. You could say that we humans have been slow to recognize and understand our connection to the creative power of Cosmic Intelligence and our access to its infinite and eternal reservoir of knowledge, and more important, wisdom—the extent to do so depending strictly on the level of consciousness we choose to achieve."

Dawa could see that Ananda was in awe of what he was hearing. But Dawa wasn't sure the boy completely grasped everything. He wanted to share more so that Ananda had a clear understanding of what Dawa was sharing with him so that it could help the young man make his decision.

Dawa continued. "Those wise sages discovered that the total consciousness of the universe—what they called Unity Consciousness—eternally evolves toward perfection, providing access to increasing powers—eventually what have become known as *superpowers*. But sometimes this path of evolution requires a correction. However, unlike physical evolution, which makes corrections by effectively responding through what Darwin called 'natural selection' or a 'survival of the fittest' strategy, conscious evolution requires nearly the opposite. It creates cooperative concern for all, and seeks broad prosperity through greater intimate access to the Akashic Record."

Ananda

"Does that mean that everyone can have this access and have superpowers?"

Dawa

"To varying degrees, yes, depending on the level of consciousness they can achieve. But few people want to make the effort required. Also, to make the correction in Unity Consciousness, it requires someone who has complete access to the Akashic Record and its unlimited information and wisdom. This person generally comes into this world with a natural, innate, high level of consciousness and therefore does not have to work so hard to access the superpowers necessary to make a difference. Or, alternatively, something happens to these people—usually a serious physical event—after which their constant level of consciousness is incredibly high, and they begin to demonstrate various superpowers—powers they will need along their future path and life purpose."

Ananda

"That *must* be a special person. How does that happen?"

Dawa

"Yes, it is a special person, and how it happens, no one knows or understands for sure. We just know that it *does* happen and seems to be an important part of the *Cosmic Plan*.

Ananda

"Oh, Bhante Dawa, please, please tell me more."

Dawa

"Very well. Spread across a vast time frame, rarely and seemingly unpredictably, a superconscious human is born. As this person matures into an adult, his or her role, at first unbeknownst and often even strongly repelled by them, is to guide the evolutionary course of global consciousness, perhaps even *Cosmic Consciousness*—toward perfection. Known as an Avatar, this spiritual-human entity is a magician at unlocking and accessing the complete wisdom and knowledge of the Akashic Record to assist in the evolution of the Unity Consciousness of the universe.

"Although there likely have been several Avatars throughout history, we are aware of two in the last 2,500 years. The first was born circa 500 B.C.E. He arrived in the form of Siddhartha Gautama in the lush gardens of ancient Lumbini, which to this day remains one of the most spiritual sites on Earth, located in what we now know as the Terai plains of southern Nepal. Born a prince to a wealthy family, he eventually gave up all material possessions, and as you know, ultimately became known as the Buddha."

Ananda

Nearly beside himself, Ananda could no longer control his emotions and questions. "Oh, dear Bhante, please tell me, who was the second one?"

Dawa

"The second was born just over 2,000 years ago in the town of Bethlehem to a poor family and resided most of his life in Nazareth, Galilee, now part of Israel. He as you know, was known as Jesus of Nazareth.

"Neither Jesus nor the Buddha had any interest in forming an organized religion like those that exist throughout the world today. Both felt the frustration, pain, and hopelessness of the downtrodden masses. To show them a path to higher levels of consciousness and personal fulfillment, they brought forth in their teachings a philosophy of spiritual tools to ease their pain and enable even the most spiritually bereft persons to find purpose and fulfillment."

Ananda

"Most holy Bhante, what you have told me is so beautiful. But how can this help me with my decision to become a monk?"

Dawa

"Ah, that's the right question at the right time. The answer is that the world is about to begin to change in ways that will address your concerns. It will not be an easy journey, and there will still be many difficulties along the way. But in the end, Unity Consciousness will rise around the world, and all will be much better than it is along our current path. And as a result, there will be many possibilities and opportunities for you as a monk to contribute to this change and make an important difference."

Ananda

"Oh, dear Bhante, how do you know this?"

Dawa

"All I can tell you is that I know this with absolute certainty. You see, the world had to wait more than 2,000 years—until 2018—when an Avatar would begin to take form and evolve here on Earth, halfway around the world—in Palo Alto, California. As was the case with his two predecessors, his social position, initial demeanor, and behavior will be quite out of character as far as what we might expect for an Avatar. But he will soon learn of his powers and begin his struggle with what they mean, how best to use them, and what the world needs from him. And, like other Avatars before him, he will find his way. It will not be an easy path for him, but in the end, it will be a deeply fulfilling life purpose."

Ananda did not say another word. He smiled at Dawa, thanked him, and left the monastery on his trek back to his home in Lhasa. The morning sun was high, warm, and shining bright. Somehow he felt like he was going in the right direction.

THAT DAY

I'LL REMEMBER JANUARY 13, 2018, in agonizing detail for as long as I live. My life hasn't been the same since then. I now know that it never will be.

Chapter Two

A PERFECT SHOT

MADRA MIA![3] THEY'RE GONNA BLOW THE ROOF OFF THIS DAMN PLACE!

"Hey, hey, are you ready? Are you ready to strut your stuff?"

"Hey, hey, are you ready? Are you ready to fire up?"

"Fire up, Vikings! Fire up!"

There are only five players on a high school basketball team, but those incredible cheerleaders—they were our "sixth" players. It felt like they were on the court with us, and God, were they really rockin'. In the bleachers our diehard Viking fans chanted back and forth with our cheerleaders:

"We are!"

"VIKINGS!"

"We can't hear you!"

"VIKINGS!"

"Louder!"

"VIKINGS!"

"We're number one!"

The scoreboard said it all—fourth quarter, seven seconds left in the game—us, the Palo Alto Vikings, 79; our cross-town rivals,

---

[3] *Madra mia!*— "My mother!"

the Bellarmine Bells, 80. The Bells, or as we like to call them, the Dumb-Bells, had never kicked our butts in basketball. Ever.

Mike Zielinski, our team captain, and Coach Ralston had just called a time-out. *Thank God*, I thought to myself. The rest of the guys looked worn out too, but I was the only one with my shoulders hunched over, head drooped, hands planted on my knees, panting to catch my wind—*more oxygen, God, please—and make it quick*! I hadn't stopped running for the entire quarter—not a single break until now. It was do-or-die time if we were gonna take this one home after coming from behind. Now, standing up straight with my hands on my hips, sweating like a pig, I was getting ready to listen to Coach like the rest of the team, wondering what the hell our last play should be to pull off this win. *Gesu Cristo*[4]—our fans were going wild!

"Hey! Hey! How do ya feel?"

Like James Brown's famous line "I FEEELLL . . . GOOD!"

"Everywhere we go!"

"People wanna know!"

"Who we are!"

"VIKINGS, VIKINGS!"

"THE MIGHTY, MIGHTY VIKINGS!"

"Hey! How do ya feel?"

"I FEEELLL . . . GOOD!" James Brown's soul was vibrating through the bleachers.

The gym was pulsating, oscillating, resonating—it was about to explode!

Equally ferocious, those damn Bells fans countered, "De-fense! De-fense! De-fense!"

Both sets of fans were about to lose their collective minds. Neither team had ever played a game like this one. Coach had made it clear when we were down by six points at the end of the third quarter that this had to be our win if we wanted to go to the championships. So we all busted our tired asses to get to this point. But by the looks of it, the Bells had decided it would be theirs—or so they thought—*those schmucks*!

---

[4] *Gesu Cristo!*—"Jesus Christ!"

No way we're gonna let them win—no way! I thought to myself. Thought it loud enough to hear myself over the thunderous fans.

I could see Dad near courtside. At times like this, it was usual for him to get insanely intense—and much too often, involved. He'd come down from the bleachers, stand right next to my team-mates, like he was our coach or whatever. It had been more than 25 years since he'd graduated from Princeton as their NCAA star point guard. Yeah, he had talent, lots of it. Princeton recruited him from St. Benedict's Prep in Newark, New Jersey. He had the two winning "As": A student and All-State. He'd been the perfect point guard, cut from the same mold as the Utah Jazz's John Stockton. I was sure he totally regretted turning down those offers to go pro.

Instead, he completed his ROTC military commitment at Princeton, graduated as a second lieutenant, and was quickly pro-moted to first lieutenant. He entered combat training and became a platoon leader in the Special Forces during the Iraq War. He almost died in the "Mile of Death" battle on Highway 80—not at the hands of the Iraqis, but in a freak accident of friendly fire, or at least that's what he said it was. He didn't like to talk about it, and I knew enough not to make myself a target of *family* fire—friendly fire, except that the one shooting at me would be dear ol' dad.

Too critically injured to stay, he was discharged and did his MBA at the University of Chicago, where he met and married Mom. Both were first-generation Sicilians, but what a match—she a beautiful, refined young lady from an upper-class San Francisco family, and he a reaching-for-refinement tough guy from Newark. After Mom finished her PhD in psychology, they moved to Palo Alto. She became a psychology professor at Stanford, and he ended up as an executive at Bank of America in Silicon Valley.

I just knew he must have looked back, wondering what his life could have been like if he'd dropped out of ROTC and gone pro. He said he'd done the right thing, but if anyone was fooled by his words, it sure as hell wasn't me. I wanted to tell him, but never did: "Too late, Dad! *Fatti una vita!*[5] Stop trying to replay your life

[5] *Fatti una vita!*—"Get a life!"

through me, for God's sake. You've been on my case for as long as I can remember." *You made your choice and paid the price. Now get off my back. Let me make mine.*

I got used to him coming to nearly every one of our games, and Coach probably got used to his uninvited two cents' worth of strategy, which sometimes, I gotta admit, was good advice—especially when the chips were down. I guess Coach had come to the same realization. But he could sometimes be a real *dolor nell'as.*[6] In those crunch times, just like now, I could see his laser-sharp eyes screaming at me: "Luc, do it, damn it! Just do it!"

Minchia![7] *Gimme a break, will ya?* I looked away silently.

The roar of the cheerleaders and our fans brought me back.

"Stand up on your feet!"

"Palo Alto Vikings!"

"We won't be beat!"

"Yeah!"

Coach had gone over to speak with the ref.

My friend Mike came over to me. "Thought you were gonna puke in the locker room today. Still think you should have said something to Coach, even though it seems like you're playing great, as usual."

"Nah, I'm good. It went away—too many waffles and too much greasy bacon for breakfast. If I'd said anything, he would have told my father, and then I'd still be here. I don't need him telling me to 'tough it out.'"

"Yeah, I hear ya."

Coach finished with the ref and was on his way to our team huddle, when Dad pushed his way through the guys on the bench and whispered something in Coach's ear. Coach acknowledged it with a smile and a positive shake of his head, then hustled to join us.

Che diavolo?[8]

---

[6] *Dolor nell'as*—"Pain in the ass."
[7] *Minchia!*—"Shit!" or "Damn!" or "Hell!"
[8] *Che diavolo?*—"What the hell?"

Coach laid out the plan. "Luc's dad had an excellent idea. We're gonna use his strategy, you know, the one that won us last year's championship against Mountain View. Remember?"

Gesu Cristo, Dad—che palle![9] *Why don't you come out here and I'll give you the damn ball? Yeah, of course I remember. He's always taking credit for that win, so how could I forget that he's such a genius?*

"Billy will take the ball out and pass it to Jimmy. Jimbo, you'll be on the sideline at left court. You'll make like you're driving to the basket, and then push back to center court behind the three-point line. Fake a pass to Mike, who'll be running up the left baseline, but instead fire the ball high to Luc, who'll be just behind the three-point line. Luc, the Bells know you've got an 80 percent hit rate from the three-point range, so they'll start charging you. Wait to draw them out. Billy and Mike will come around to set a screen, then Luc, you'll drive hard right to the basket. Jump those long, beefy *Dago* legs of yours, and slam that sucker down for two points."

There it was: "Bend those long, beefy *Dago* legs of yours." Christ, he never calls Mike a *Polack*, or Jimmy a *Mick*. Coach was straight outta Dad's era, born and bred Boston Irish, at a time when the Irish were always trying to upstage the Italians—but never could. And, of course, he'd never admit to the slightest hint of prejudice. Yeah, I'm 6'7", but does he think only Italians and blacks can play above the rim? Hell, there are more Larry Birds in this world than he'll ever admit to. *Gesu Cristo, Coach, you're still a real Boston Mick!*

I was pissed and couldn't hold it in. "Look, Coach, I can win this damn game. If I have an open three-pointer, I should take it!"

"Hell no, Luc! Don't even think about it! Even with your 80 percent hit rate, we can't risk it. Your two-point layup is more than 95 percent. An excellent percentage shot. Got it? Now go out there and do it! Make it happen!"

Shit! The pressure's always on me in tight spots. But I get no say in it. I was looking at Coach, but my eyes were glazing over. For some crazy reason, I felt disconnected from him, the team, the

[9] *Che palle!*— "What balls!"

16

crowd, the last shot of the game for a win, wondering, *What the hell am I doing with my life?*

"Luc, come alive! You okay? Got the picture?"

Coming back to reality, as usual, I surrendered. "Yeah, Coach, I got it. Real clear."

What was even more clear was my Dad running every god-damn thing in my life, right down to the shots I take on the court—unbelievably clear. *May I take a 15-footer, dear Dad? No, son, make it 14 feet and 11 inches instead.*

I took a deep breath and wiped the sweat from my face.

The buzzer sounded, and we went back out on the floor. Billy had the ball off left court. Jimmy was on the left side in front of the foul line.

The crowd was wired higher than if everybody in the stands had drunk three Red Bulls each. The noise was deafening. With just a little bit of room, I knew I could make the three-pointer. *Why waste myself on a two-pointer when I absolutely know I can get us three? Besides, there's a scout from Duke here. Coach just doesn't get it. I'm lookin' to get into a good college. If I only have the balls to pull it off.* My legs were shaking. I took a deep breath. Had to get my shit together.

Okay, I can do this. Focus, focus, focus!

The waxed floor squealed with its own pain under my shifting Nikes as Billy nervously danced back and forth waiting to make the inbound pass. He shot me a piercing look. I nodded back to him. Good, fairly sure the Bells' point guard saw it too. He's thinking we'll drive to the basket, just like in last year's championship game. Hell, the whole conference would probably bet on it. Well, it didn't matter. I had a better plan. I just needed a little bit of breathing room and *grandi palle*.[10] *This is my time, damn it. It's my time!*

The ref blew a short, sharp blast on his whistle. The clock was on. The crowd faded into a slo-mo dream. I waved my arms up high at the foul line, faking for the ball from Billy, but as planned, he passed it to Jimmy—the game clock was in its death march

---

[10]*Grandi palle*—"Big balls."

down: seven . . . six . . . five—who in turn faked it to Mike running up the right court line. I hustled from the foul line and pushed back to just behind the three-point line. Jimmy, then, as planned, fired the ball to me, but it was way too high—a crazy pass from a kid cracking under pressure. I jumped and barely caught it, tipping it with only a few fingers before juggling and then bringing it into my palms. *Shit!* Did that sting!

The Dumb-Bells didn't bite! I knew it! They thought we were going to cut and run up the right lane for a layup, so I'd had a nearly clear three-point jump shot. For less than a split second, I thought of Coach and of Dad—one and the same in that instant—I was sure they were wondering, *What the hell is he doing?*

Mike and Billy set a screen, and I started my drive up the right side. Then I stopped, stepped back—the clock winding down . . . four . . . three . . . I planted my feet just inches behind the three-point line, the Bells still convinced of our drive to the basket for a layup shot. Their guys defending both lanes like towering citadels, sensed a change and raced out to block my shot. Two . . . one . . . I jumped as high as I ever had in my life—you know, with those "long, beefy *Dago* legs."

Just as the ball was leaving my hands, Brian Banning, the Bells' point guard, not having enough height to block my shot, crashed into me full force, driving me backward. I fell to the floor hard. Couldn't breathe. Everything was out of focus, but I could faintly hear: "Luc." Then at last, the full familiar chant: "Luc! Luc! Luc!" The crowd roared.

What the hell? The ball must have gone in. What if that crazy Banning hadn't fouled me? Would it have still gone in? I could see the scoreboard now: Palo Alto Vikings, 82. Bellarmine Bells, 80, with no time left on the clock. *Shit, I knew I could do this!*

Coach and Dad must have been going apeshit when I took the three-pointer. Still struggling to catch my breath and get up off the floor, I was suddenly surrounded by my teammates, who were jumping up and down with excitement. I could barely hear Jimmy's voice. "Shit! Sorry, Luc. Didn't mean to throw it that high. I don't know how you caught it—but you did—thanks, man."

"No prob, Jimmy."

Coach pushed his way through. His voice hovered over me: "You okay?"

"Yeah, I am now. Just got the wind knocked out of me."

Somewhat recovered, I stood up and faced the crowd with both arms outstretched in victory.

"Luc! Luc! Luc!" I could feel their energy beating into my chest. I felt jubilant as they serenaded me. I hoped the Duke scout was watching and liking it too.

Then, from over my left shoulder, I heard, "Luc, what the hell was that?"

I didn't have to turn around to know it was my father. Not just by his voice, but only a hard-driving fool would say somethin' like that after that kinda winning shot.

"We had a play drawn up, for God's sake! You risked it all by hotdogging? That wasn't the plan, goddamn it!"

What he really meant in his macho, military, commando tone was: "Orders are orders! Never, ever break them—no matter what!" I didn't say a word, but my whole body tightened up. I stared at the floor. At 6'5", and built like a prizefighter, except for his salt-and-pepper hair, Dad was not unlike *The Godfather*'s Sonny Corleone: a muscular, overconfident, tough guy. Except he was a helluva lot smarter than Sonny. Nobody messed with him, least of all me.

Coach saved me. "Luc, I have no idea why the hell you did what you did out there, but we won the game. No argument with that. Listen, you've got two foul shots for that flagrant foul, but you're in no shape to take them. How 'bout I let Jimmy do the honors?"

"Yeah, sure, Coach."

I looked over my shoulder at my father. He was fuming, clenching his teeth and his fists at the same time, staring at me with every muscle in his face constricted in anger. That's when I decided, what the hell, slam-dunk it on him. Besides, Jimmy was probably still regretting throwing the ball too high. "Coach. Hold on. Give me half a minute. I'll take the foul shots."

"Fine. Your call."

I walked slowly to the foul line. My abdomen was burning from the hit. "Luc! Luc! Luc!" The crowd was going bananas. "Lu . . . c." They trailed off, and all went silent as the ref gave me the ball. I dribbled a few times before caressing it between my hands, eyeing the basket.

Then, a perfect arc, swish—like a circus lion jumping through a hoop—and it never touched the rim: 83-80.

The crowd was stomping in the bleachers, yelling my name. They quieted down again, and the second shot was just like the first: 84-80. We won by three more points than Coach and Dad had planned. And, *minchia*—they didn't like my strategy? I wondered for just the briefest moment: *Will I ever be good enough?*

As our team walked off the floor to the crowd's cheers, suddenly, from out of nowhere, an unbearable pain drilled into me. It felt like a red-hot knife stabbing into the lower-right side of my stomach. *No tears, goddammit! No tears!* That was the last thing I remembered.

LIFE OR DEATH

IT SMELLED LIKE BLEACH. I barely woke up, feeling like I was about to die—little did I know. I was barely able to move, as a throbbing pain was pounding my stomach like a jackhammer. I strained to open my eyes. They were glued shut with all kinds of crud. One crusty eye popped partially open, then the other. My mouth was parched. I felt a fire raging through my body.

I tried desperately to get my bearings, but my brain wasn't working right. Just a dim light on the wall across the room barely peeked through the darkness. *Where the hell am I? What's happened to me?* I felt like I'd been drugged. Or run over, or both. Whatever it was, I'd never felt anywhere close to that bad before.

Straining with what little energy I had, I tried to raise my head but could only lift it a few inches before it crashed back down on the pillow. My sight began to clear. I noticed tubes in my arm, and another one extended from beneath a bandage covering my stomach that ran to the side, discharging a disgusting, yellow pus into a container beside the bed. I looked up and saw a kaleidoscope of fluorescent colors—red, blue, green, yellow, white, and turquoise—lighting up monitors on both sides of me. *Good God! I'm in the hospital.*

I saw Mom, who was deeply slouched in a chair to my left. She was always such a neat freak and immaculate in appearance. But there she was, temporarily transformed from a tall, slender, dark-eyed brunette who carried her beauty like actress Monica Bellucci, to . . . I don't know what. I almost didn't recognize her. She was asleep, looking terrible, more tired and rumpled than I'd ever seen her. Her hair was a mess, and a frown across her face cast deep wrinkles into her brow. Her mascara had streaked, probably from crying. I swear she looked more like my grandmother than the mother I knew. *Mom, I swear, I didn't mean that.*

Dad was scrunched in a chair next to her. He was wearing his usual casual uniform—Levis and a Princeton Tigers black hoodie sweatshirt. He stirred, maybe having felt me staring at him. At first, he seemed hypnotically dazed, staring back right through me, kinda like in a trance. Then suddenly, he came alive with an involuntary jerk of his head, as he noticed the slight movement of my lips when I worked up a whispered "Dad?"

He placed his hand under my head and lifted it slightly. "Hi, Luc. Let's lift your head a bit." He held a glass of ice water containing a glass straw. "Here, sip this, but very slowly."

I did as he said, maybe not slowly enough—and two immediate sensations hit me. The first, a welcome one, was like rain flooding the desert my mouth had become. But the other was a toxic venom when the water slammed into the pit of my stomach. I felt like puking and had to calm myself to keep it down. Even that small spasm caused terrible pain, way beyond bearable. I winced in agony. It brought tears to my eyes. Dad put my head back down on the pillow, and I closed my eyes, then opened them again as the pain partially subsided.

"Luc, you remember the Bellarmine game on Tuesday. Banning fouled you. He hit you hard in the stomach."

"What's today?"

"Friday."

"Friday?"

"You've been out for three days."

"Whoa, what happened?"

He repeated, "You remember Banning, the Bells' point guard, fouling you at the end of the game?"

"Yeah, what a *stronzo*.[11]"

"Hey, watch your language in front of your mother. Well, he must have hit you just right. Apparently, your appendix was already inflamed—you didn't feel any pain before the game, did you?"

Lying to my dad came easy for me, especially in situations like this. If I didn't, I'd have been a goner a long time ago. "No, I was fine."

"I thought so. What happened is your appendix ruptured and released toxic bacteria into your abdominal cavity, and it absorbed into your bloodstream, causing sepsis. By the time the ambulance got you to the hospital, you had a 103-degree fever and rising. They put you on an ice bed to bring your temperature down and then rushed you into surgery."

"Surgery?"

"Yes. They did their best to clean up your insides, but you're fighting peritonitis."

"What's that?"

"It's an aggressive bacterial infection, kind of like sepsis or blood poisoning. All these tubes and things you see, they're your army, shooting large volumes of strong antibiotics into you. Like I've always taught you, though, it's fine to take help when you need it, but it's on *you* to stay positive and fight this. Understand? You got to fight this damn thing."

Hoping to get closer to him, I barely got it out. "Like you always said, Dad, quitters are losers; fighters are winners."

"Yeah. I don't wanna get into it with you now because . . . well, you're down right now. But sometimes fighters are losers too. Like that three-pointer you took. It was like you went commando or something instead of following a direct order—the plan Coach drew up. You know, when I was your age . . ."

Gesu Cristo! I don't believe him. Forget it. I had to interrupt him. "Is Mom okay?"

---

[11] *Stronzo*—"Asshole."

"She'll be fine. Been here for three days. I had to go to the office, but she's stayed. Dozed off about an hour ago."

She must have heard us talking. Awakened as if someone had poured cold water on her, she leaped out of the chair. "Oh my God, honey, how do you feel?"

"I'm hurtin', Mom, but I'm sure I'll be fine in a few days." What could I say? Dad was staring at me like I was a whining, injured soldier.

She gently brushed my hair with her fingers. "I love you, baby. I'll check with the nurse about pain meds."

"Valentina!" My dad scolded my mom.

Even when I'm in the hospital in dire straits, he's gotta show me how a real man handles himself. Like I can't see right through him and his Special Forces motto: *De oppresso liber*,[12] which proba-bly really translates to "Don't ever be a wuss."

"I'm sure the doctors know what the hell they're doing here, Val. If they think Luc can't deal with the pain, they'll give him something. Right, son? You got this, right?"

Before I could answer, Mom made it clear that she wasn't hav-ing any part of it. "He's a boy, for God's sake—not one of your commandos!" She pushed past him out the door and to the nurses' station. He had a rule that he only took shit from superiors. Mom wasn't that, but he was smart enough to know not to get between a mama bear and her cub.

Dad said, "Luc, I'm sure everything's going to work out okay for you. But I've got to be honest. None of this would have hap-pened if you'd just followed the plan. Look, like I said, I'm not going to get worked up over it now. I mean, you're in the hospital. But while you're lying there and see what you've done to your mother and me, I want you to think about being selfless instead of Mr. Superstar with your long shot that risked the entire game and our chance to win the championship. What if you'd missed that three-pointer? What, then?"

Che diavolo! Another time. Just wait, old man, I thought as I felt every bit of energy leave my body. I dozed off. It was the only

---

[12] *De oppresso liber*—"To liberate the oppressed."

escape plan I had. But it turned out that it put me into a darker tunnel than I needed just to get away from him.

My fever started to skyrocket despite the antibiotics and the tube siphoning God knows what out of my gut. I'd slipped into unconsciousness due to the sepsis and the increasing level of blood poisoning. Opening a second front in the battle, the doctors put me on a temperature-controlled ice bed to break my fever, and increased the flow of antibiotics. But the sepsis attacking nearly every cell in my body with a vengeance was hell-bent on taking my life—and that it did, at least for a time when some kind of afterlife thing I never believed in, happened. Whether my father or anyone else believes me or not, I don't care. I'm as sure of it as I was that I'd make that three-pointer.

Suddenly I was awake and feeling good. No pain, no nothing. It was crazy, like I felt better than I could ever remember. I was happy and content just to *be*. It was some weird shit when I started to float and slowly go up toward the ceiling. I could see my body lying in the bed below, and two doctors and a bunch of nurses trying to revive me. They didn't panic—I was impressed. They reminded me of the kind of player you want taking the game-winning shot as the clock ticks down to zero. They did CPR. Then those electric-shock defibrillators. I watched, feeling content—maybe even a little bit entertained. Is that weird or what?

Mom and Dad watched through a glass partition, but not with contentment. Not for Mom. But for Dad? Hard to tell. She was crying, and he was doing his best to comfort her, trying to be the Rambo he's always been. I wanted to help, but I couldn't. That part felt helpless, but otherwise I felt no angst. Everything just seemed factual, unemotional, like that was the way things were supposed to be—*so, Luc, don't fight it*. It was funny, because when I thought about not fighting it, I laughed at what my dad would have said. I laughed hard, real hard. Shoot, I was glad I wasn't in my physical body. Otherwise, my stomach would have hurt like all hell.

As I kept going higher above the doctors and nurses, I couldn't help but notice an air-conditioning duct system sticking out about ten inches from the ceiling and running from one end of the room to another. There was a series of several duct openings, each covered with a screwed-in 5-by-12-inch steel louvered cover.

For some strange reason, what caught my eye was the one louver directly in front of my face, just a few inches away. Unlike the others securely attached by four screws, this one was hanging on by a single loose screw. The other screws had somehow fallen out, maybe from vibrations when the A/C was on. If that last screw fell out too, that steel cover would probably come crashing down on whoever was below. That could be serious, even deadly.

I tried to warn the doctors below. One of them was our family physician. I called out, "Hey, Dr. Farkas!" But it was useless. Not a sound came out of my mouth. As frustrating as that would have been under normal circumstances, I felt nothing. I'd done the best I could. I thought that was the way things were supposed to be. I kept rising higher.

The next thing I knew, I was passing through the ceiling, rising through the hospital until finally exiting the building into the cool night air. Palo Alto was lit up by orange streetlights that became fainter and then disappeared below me as I continued to rise. Suddenly I entered a massive tunnel, pitch-black at first, but I was moving slowly toward a distant bright-white light—which initially seemed like a pinpoint, but which increased in intensity and size as I got closer. And then I was no longer floating. I was walking toward the light.

It was so beautiful—the most beautiful thing I'd ever seen. I couldn't think of any words that would do justice to its magnificence. All I can say is that it was just a light. No, wait, it wasn't *just* a light. It gave off something, some kind of force—love—I don't know. I was overwhelmed by a profound sense of compassion, empathy, and caring. I felt stuff I didn't even know about—didn't even know existed.

I kept walking, and the light kept getting bigger. The tunnel was larger than I first thought, maybe 100 feet in diameter. I wanted to just sit down and stare at the light, to be with it forever, but something kept telling me to keep walking toward it. The pull increased as I got closer.

At first, it was strange when people of all kinds—men, women, and children of various colors, shapes, and sizes—were walking in the opposite direction, toward me, and then past me. I didn't recognize any of them, but they smiled at me. Their expressions were so warm and friendly. Even though they didn't say a thing, I felt welcome—like I belonged there with them. In those moments, it was like we were one big, loving family. They kept coming, silently smiling as they passed. This was both wild and warm at the same time. I loved it.

Just then, a tall, dark, handsome, neatly mustached middle-aged gentleman approached me. He was dressed all in white—white suit, white shirt, white tie, white shoes, and a white fedora. Unlike the others, he stopped to talk, though not verbally. We spoke to each other without saying a word. It was simply an exchange of thoughts. I don't know how else to describe it. But it wasn't weird or anything; it just felt natural.

"Hello, Luc. Nice to finally meet you. My name is Paulo."

"Do I know you?"

"Not really, but I know *you*. We never actually met. I passed on just a few months before you were born."

I looked at him more closely. There was something familiar about his face, like maybe I'd seen him in an old picture or somewhere. "Are you Nonno Paulo? Mom's dad, Paulo Catalano?"

"*Si, lo sono.*"[13]

"Nonno!" I moved closer to hug him, but he backed away.

"Look, Luc, we don't have much time. I'm here to tell you that you must go back. You still have too much to do."

"But I don't wanna go back. I wanna stay. I love it here, and I want to get to know you."

Mom had once told me that Nonno Paulo's father, my great-grandfather Francesco Catalano, had emigrated in the 1920s to New Jersey from Cammarata, Sicily, a not-so-well-known village located not far from the infamous town of Corleone. He initially worked as a laborer, but he eventually saved enough to start a small import-export business, bringing olives, olive oil, and Italian foods to New York, using his contacts in Sicily. Nonno Paulo inherited the business, grew it, and did well for his family.

---

[13] *Si, lo sono*—"Yes, I am."

We still had cousins in Cammarata. I had hoped to visit them someday . . . but now?

"Luc, you'll get your turn, but not just yet. Your mother and father need you—the world needs you. You'll understand what I'm saying soon enough. Please trust me."

The world doesn't need me, was my first reaction. I'm a kid with a killer jump shot from Palo Alto, California. That's it. It made no sense. What was he talking about? "I don't understand. Even if I wanted to, which I don't, how would I get back? I'm dead."

"Don't worry, that will be taken care of. And, Luc, I would be very appreciative if you would do me a small favor."

Still concerned about having to go back, I reluctantly agreed. "Sure, of course."

"Please be so kind and tell Valentina that I'm sorry. I was called suddenly and never had a chance to say goodbye. Tell her I'm sorry I was always working, traveling, and never made the time to show her how much I really loved her. Tell her I thought I would eventually have plenty of time for that, and it turned out to be the biggest mistake of my life. I wasn't a good Sicilian father. Tell her your grandmother and I love her and miss her, and that we're proud of what she's done with her life. Will you do that?"

"Nonno, are you kiddin' me? She'll say, '*Sei pazzo?*'[14] I can tell her, but she'll never believe me."

"Then tell her that for her seventh birthday, I was the one who found Freckles and placed her back in her dollhouse."

"What does that mean?"

"Just before your mom's seventh birthday, she lost her favorite doll, Freckles. She was so upset that she didn't even want the birthday party we'd planned. Nonna and I looked everywhere and couldn't find the doll. Then I happened to bring our car to the service station to gas it up and have it washed. As fate would have it, they found Freckles underneath the back seat. Not even your dad will know that story!"

I hesitated for a bit. "Yes, sir, I'll do that."

---

[14] *Sei pazzo?*—"Are you crazy?"

"*Mille grazie,*[15] Luc."

And that was it. I felt a deep sense of loss as I was spirited away, out through the tunnel and back into my body in the hospital bed. I didn't know how long I'd been gone, but I found out soon enough. I slowly opened my eyes and saw Mom and Dad. She was squeezing my hand. I thought I even saw concern and relief in Dad's eyes, but he was good at hiding that kind of stuff.

Mom choked back tears. "Thank God! Oh, Luc, we thought we'd lost you."

"Mom. You'll probably say I'm *molto pazzo,*[16] but I had the weirdest dream."

Dad jumped right in. "Get some rest, Luc."

"Listen to your father, Luc, please."

"Mom, I went down this huge tunnel of light, and you won't believe who I met. He said to tell you about—"

Dad interrupted again before I could finish. "He's hallucinating, Val."

"Luc, let's get you something to help you rest. This was a close call."

"Close call? I was doing well. I met your—"

"Oh, honey, you flatlined. You were gone."

"Flatlined? That doesn't make sense. How long?"

"Several minutes, but they brought you back. It almost didn't work. My God, we would have lost you. I don't know what we would do." She was still crying. "But enough of this. Please, Luc, get some rest." She kissed me on the forehead and held my hand for a moment longer before Dad, who was silent, tugged on her to go. He raised his hand as if to wave goodbye, and instead, changed it to a salute midstream.

Madra mia! Flatlined? Several minutes?!

---

[15] *Mille grazie!*—"A thousand thanks!"
[16] *Molto pazzo!*—"Very crazy!"

Chapter
Four

DISCLOSURE

I SPENT 12 MISERABLE DAYS IN THE HOSPITAL. For seven of those, my veins were continuously pumped with cefuroxime and metronidazole—whatever they are. During the first two days, I was in and out of consciousness with a high fever, but by the third, slowly, it started to break. Around the fourth day, the fever was gone, and my energy level began to pick up.

I almost immediately started wondering about flatlining and my tunnel experience or dream, or whatever it was. What might have happened if I'd had different doctors or a different hospital? Could I have died? I mean, like for good? Or would it still have worked out the way it did, including my "visit" with Nonno Paulo? After five days, my thoughts about him moved from curiosity to a hazy affection. I couldn't make sense of any of this.

Feeling much better, I began to think about the guys on the team and especially about Isabella. I'd had mixed feelings about her since kindergarten, and they pretty much stayed that way as we moved to middle school and now high school—except, now they were getting worse, if that's the right word. In my mind, I always thought of her as my best buddy, which only confused the hell out of me, because in my heart, I was jealous when any of the guys at school came on to her—not that she invited them, but it still bugged the hell outta me—a lot.

Bella had been a tomboy up until her early teens. And I tell you what, she was a lot tougher than most of the guys I knew. When we were in elementary school, if she fell flat on her face playing tag with the rest of us six-year-old boys, she would immediately get up without even a whimper, wipe the blood and snot from her nose on her sleeve or bare arm, and man-oh-man, she was right back in the game.

By about ten, she'd switched to all-girl team sports—soccer, softball, volleyball. In her early teens, her athletics made a graceful turn toward modern dance. Now at 16, she was tall and feminine, with golden-brown skin, long red hair, and striking green eyes—boy, those eyes were like piercing lasers when her temper flared. What a combo! Green eyes and red hair—really? Her family was from South America. Bella said her great-grandfather had red hair, which the family attributed to Danish Vikings who landed in South America during the 11th century. I guess the green eyes came the same way.

Even Bella's walk had changed—from a sturdy strut to a rhythmic sway—kinda like those tall, dark, shapely Carioca chicks I've seen in pictures parading along Ipanema Beach.

Bella's parents had fled Colombia to escape drug wars near the village where they lived, just outside of Bogota. They settled in Santa Clara Valley, California. Those were times when it was a hell of a lot easier for immigrants, especially of color, to enter the US and eventually get citizenship. Her dad got a job with Apple in one of their warehouses doing packing and shipping, and now, 17 years later, had made his way up to a managerial position. Her mom picked up housecleaning work where she could, and simultaneously attended night school to become a grade-school teacher. She did all that up until Bella was born two years later—prematurely and with a number of complications.

"Thank God for Apple's health insurance," Bella had told me when we were in fifth grade. "My dad never could have afforded all of that intensive care." Unlike the way I felt about *my* father, she was certain hers would have pulled out all the stops to save her. Also, unlike me, she's smart as hell. A consistent honor student, she tutors on the side for extra spending money. She's helped me, especially in biology, one of my least favorite subjects. Because of her, I now know that mitochondria are the famous "powerhouses of the cell," and stuff like that.

Mom had told me that Bella had called and asked if it'd be okay to come by, so I wasn't surprised when she pranced into my room announcing her arrival with her usual bravado: "Luc! How goes it? Gotcha you a present—Ben and Jerry's vanilla ice cream! Dude, I even brought a big spoon—actually, I brought two."

"Hey, what's up, Bella?"

"I can't believe, with all their great flavors, you always go for vanilla. That's messed up."

"It's not messed up. They make the best vanilla around."

"Just sayin', you could have Chunky Monkey or Cherry Garcia. All right, vanilla's your favorite, so you got it. Like your vanilla personality."

"Yeah, but not like your chocolate skin, señorita."

"Hey, don't be such a damn racist!"

"Don't be such a wiseass."

"Oh, poor Luc. Can't take a joke anymore. Maybe those chemicals they're pumping in your veins have gone to your brain."

"Keep it coming, Bella, while you can, 'cause when I'm outta here, it's gonna be vanilla payback!"

Bella smiled at me, shaking her head. She was probably thinking the same thing I was: *Why do we keep doing this childish teasing back and forth like we're tough and don't feel anything for each other?* Even my guy friends cut the crap after a while. Not us, though, at least not when we're nervous around each other. Nervous after so many years—would you believe it?

"Luc, you're a real butt pain, ya know? Don't know how I've put up with all your crap over the years, especially when you're sick. Dude, you're such a big baby! Big man on campus—I knew you when you were nothin'."

"Yeah, because you're somethin'."

"Bella regazza.[17] Admit it, you big jock."

"Yeah, Bella. *Che bella che sei!*[18] You got me on that. I admit it." We both shut up and smiled at each other. Oh, if those smiles could talk.

LATER THAT DAY, they started having me walk up and down the corridor. Dr. Farkas insisted it was the best way for me to prevent something he called *adhesions*—internal scar tissue attached to various internal organs and squishing them together. He said that could cause serious problems later on.

Madonna mia![19] Those walks were painful! With each step, I felt like the catch of the day getting gutted, until the pain dimmed the more I walked. Progress.

Around the seventh day, I began to sense something weird— not physically, but emotionally, or whatever, and it seemed to be getting stronger and scarier. Like, I knew when someone was about to enter my room, and who the person was. Before meals arrived, I knew what they were going to serve. When my cell phone rang, I knew who was calling without looking at my caller ID. It was freaking me out!

It was too "out there" for me, so I didn't want to mention it to anyone. They'd probably move me to the psychiatric ward. They'd think I'd lost it, and that the peritonitis had affected my brain. It was seven the next morning when I got the first clue as to what was going on, although I certainly didn't recognize it at the time.

I woke up feeling rested, but still in kind of a dream state. The nurses were beginning their usual daily routine, measuring my temperature and blood pressure, drawing blood for the lab, and doing a bunch of other procedures to see how I was doing. This time I got Nurse Flannigan, a puffed-up, blonde-haired, thirty-something lady. I'm lying there, got nothing else to do, so yeah, I looked her over and thought she was kinda hot. I mean, not my game, but still had something goin' for her. The top of her blue

---

[17] *Bella regazza*—"Beautiful girl."
[18] *Che bella che sei!*—"How beautiful you are!"
[19] *Madonna mia!*—"Oh, my mother! Oh, Mama!"

uniform was fine, but her pants were so tight they showed her panty line.

Now, this you gotta believe. One time Bella was wearing this cool tight skirt—I didn't notice, I guess, because we were supposed to be just friends—so I didn't see her that way. She asked if I could see her panty line. Since she asked, I looked, and told her, yeah, I could. She answered with something about needing to wear thong panties from then on. I shrugged. Yeah, whatever. I didn't give it any more thought until I saw Nurse Flannigan that morning. But I thought, *Probably not cool to give her that fashion tip.*

She gave me one of those cutesy nurse smiles. "Everything's lookin' better, Luc. By the way, Dr. Farkas won't be in. He had an emergency at El Camino Hospital in Mountain View, so one of his colleagues will be doing rounds."

"That's fine. No worries." While she recorded stuff on my chart, I closed my eyes to relax for a sec, still in kind of a dream state. Then I opened them. I was startled. "That's weird. Are you sure he's not coming in?"

"Absolutely. His service just called a few minutes ago."

"You're not going to believe this, but when my eyes are closed, I can see him. I just saw him pulling into the parking lot right here with his big, black Mercedes." Nurse Flannigan's eyebrows scrunched into a frown that seemed to say, "You kiddin' me? You're nuts!"

I closed my eyes for another sec. "I'm telling you, he's coming into the building. He's walking through the reception area right now."

"Really? Sorry, Mr. Houdini, not possible. He's at El Camino Hospital by now."

"*Minchia!* I'm not lying. This is like so weird." I closed my eyes again. "Dr. Farkas is wearing a pin-striped navy-blue suit and matching vest, with this—whoa, you'll think I'm crazy—he's wearing this bright rainbow-colored bow tie. People still wear bow ties? Anyway, he's just getting off the elevator on our floor."

The nurse was puzzled. "Luc, what's happening here? Let's get you out for some walking and clear your head."

At that moment, in walked Dr. Farkas wearing a pin-striped navy-blue suit and matching vest with that hideous rainbow whatever of a bow tie. In his usual upbeat style, he asked, "Luc, my friend, how are we feeling today?"

Nurse Flannigan looked stunned. With her mouth wide open, she alternated between staring at me and at Dr. Farkas.

"Nurse, are you okay?" the doctor asked.

"Yes, I . . . just . . . Luc? . . . Dr. Farkas, I . . . I . . . I thought you had an emergency at El Camino Hospital."

"I did, but Dr. Perlman is covering it for me. I wanted to check in on Luc."

Nurse Flannigan shook her head. "Must just be the end of a long night shift."

"Another long one, huh? Well, you're off at eight, right?"

"Yes, Doctor, less than an hour. I'm sorry, excuse me. I've got to close out my patient files for the next shift. Um, Luc's charts are . . . his vitals are normal. His CBC last night came back showing good improvement in his white blood count. Hydration levels are balancing."

"Well, that's all good news. What do you say, Luc?"

"Sounds great to me. Can't wait to get back on the court."

"I'm no Bill Belichick, but I think you'll need a few weeks of rest before you get anywhere close to a court."

"Belichick? That's football, Dr. Farkas!"

"Okay, fine, I'm no Steve Kerr. Same comment. You okay with that?" He smiled, waiting for my approval. I gave in with a grin.

"Doctor?"

"Yes, Nurse. Something else?"

"Have you seen any signs of hepatic encephalopathy?"

Dr. Farkas looked at her, then to me, and back at her. "No. You?"

"I'm not sure. Like I said, it's the end of a long night shift and all."

"Any of the other nurses have this concern?"

"No, not that I know of."

"Better to be safe. Run a full panel of liver-function tests. And be sure they do an ALP, an ALT, and a bilirubin."

"Yes, sir," she answered as she turned to leave, looking like she was on firmer footing in the medical world than the ethereal one. Three seconds and she was gone.

"What in the world is this hepatic *whatchamacallit*, or whatever she was talking about?" I asked.

"Not to worry, Luc. I really doubt it's an issue. Hepatic encephalopathy is serious and generally caused by a damaged liver. The primary symptoms are an altered state of consciousness and a usually severe personality change. You seem totally fine to me. The liver tests are strictly precautionary and likely will be completely normal."

"Well, that's good to hear."

"What do you say we take a look at that incision and see how it's coming along?" He peeled the gauze off my abdomen. As I lay there waiting for his verdict, I was reminded of my dream, or whatever it was. That loose air-conditioning vent on the ceiling in my room—was it for real? Should I say something just in case it was? What the hell.

"Doctor, a few days ago, I was staring up at the ceiling. I think I saw an air-conditioning vent cover held on by just one loose screw. I don't know, I can't see it from here, but I'm quite sure I saw it when I was coming back from one of my walks. You know it wouldn't be good if that vent cover fell off. Do you think you should mention it to someone?"

He glanced briefly at the ceiling and then shot me a puzzled expression. "What in the world are you talking about? How could you possibly have seen a screw in a vent 20 feet up there on the ceiling?" He laughed and continued. "Are you feeling any confusion, or an inability to concentrate, or even just difficulty thinking in general? Maybe those liver tests are not such a bad idea, after all."

"No, of course not. Are you thinking I might have that hepatic whatever you call it?"

"Not really. But sometimes a serious case of peritonitis, like you've had, can lead to hepatic encephalopathy. Big word, I know. That's why we're going to run some more tests just to rule it out.

But as I said, based on what I see and what you've told me, I don't think it's an issue. I'm not even sure why Nurse Flannigan brought it up."

I knew but wasn't about to say anything. "Yeah, okay. But maybe it wouldn't hurt to ask the maintenance folks to check it out. Would ya, please? I've been lying in this bed going stir crazy, worrying about lots of stupid things. Would ya just take this one off my mind?"

"They'll think we're both off our rockers, but if it puts your mind at ease, I'll mention it to the head nurse on my way out."

"Thanks."

'I'll tell her you're our . . . What is it your mother used to call you when you were a kid? "He's our hospital *passerotto*."[20] With that, he gave me a big smile.

"You nailed it. Sounds just like her. But, please, don't do me any favors."

"Right. Just keep doing those walks, at least three times a day."

"Gotcha."

And in a flash, he was gone, making his rounds.

THE DREAM, AS I'D COME TO CALL IT, WAS CONSTANTLY ON MY MIND. I had no idea what had happened to me—but maybe more disturbing—what would *continue* to happen. I'd probably end up on a funny farm if I let anything else slip out again. Besides, I thought it was just a onetime thing. *Once I'm home, everything will get back to normal, right?* It only took a few more hours to prove I was dead wrong.

Around midnight, I don't know why, I woke up, my eyes still closed. In my mind's eye, I saw my hospital room and everything around me in bright colors. Again, I started to float above my body. I kept my eyes closed to see what would happen. *Damn, I can't be dying*, was my first thought. Nonno Paulo had said not yet, and I believed him.

I floated down the hall past the nurses' station. An RN sat at her desk, one hand playing with the curls in her long blonde hair,

---

[20] *Passerotto*—"A sparrow learning to fly." When Luc was a young boy and Valentina brought him to the doctor, she sometimes referred to him as *mia passerotto*.

the other slowly paging through an issue of *People* magazine. I steered down the hallway and then to the floor below. I found by thinking about a direction, I would immediately head that way. I could also control my speed. Yeah, it was weird, but talk about a fun ride! At least it was at the time.

As I floated past Room 317, I sensed that something was wrong. Don't know why, I just did. So I went inside, and there on the floor was an elderly woman. She was shaking in pain and trying to get to the call button hanging just out of reach on the headboard of her bed.

Within seconds, I was out of there, up through the ceiling to the fourth floor, back in my room and into my body. I opened my eyes and pressed my call button. Nurse Flannigan was there in a heartbeat.

"What's up, buddy boy?"

"Look, never mind what you think of me. Hurry. There's an elderly woman on the third floor in Room 317. She fell out of bed and can't reach her call button."

She gave me the same strange look that she had on her last shift when I did what she called my "Houdini stuff" with Dr. Farkas. "And you know this how?"

"Please. I'm telling you, just do it. Call me crazy, run your tests on my brain, I don't care. Please, will ya? Please, help that lady!"

Nurse Flannigan sighed, and without saying a word, she turned and left, but not fast enough, as far as I was concerned. She didn't believe me. She just wanted to shut me up. But 20 minutes later, she was back in my room. Her eyes were as big as moons, and her mouth hung open in disbelief. After several seconds, her words finally spilled out. "Luc, not sure how you did that, but thank you."

"Is she all right?"

"She may have fractured her hip, which will heal, but it could have been much worse. She has a weak heart, so who knows what might have happened before the nurses found her."

I was relieved. "Thank God. Look, I know we've got this strange thing going on between us."

"You mean your Houdini stuff?"

"Who the hell is Houdini, anyway?"

"All right, how about your Jon Snow stuff."

"Oh, you mean Ghost, Jon Snow's albino direwolf?"

"Right, from the *Game of Thrones*."

"Got it. Yeah, okay, my Jon Snow stuff. Well, anyway, I'd really appreciate it if you could keep this between us. Not mention it to anyone. Please?"

"No, Luc. Dr. Farkas needs to know. Clearly there are some unusual neurological events occurring. I'm not going to call him now. It's not an emergency, but he definitely needs to know."

"Please. Come on, Nurse, be a good sport, huh?"

"I'm sorry. When he comes in tomorrow, he'll see it in your chart. I'll check to see if your liver-functioning test results came back from the lab. It might be that the bacterial buildup affected your brain and liver chemistry, and maybe that would help explain this. But I really don't know. I've never seen anything like this before. Only read about it in one of my nursing courses."

Sure enough, the next morning when Dr. Farkas checked in on me, he said, "The nurse logged her 'possible postsurgical cognitive changes,' but since your liver is functioning fine and there's no evidence of any resulting neurological damage, I'd say it's what we commonly see as temporary hallucinations or delirium. Nothing to worry about at this point. It will certainly clear up on its own when the inflammation in your body goes completely away."

But that wasn't the end of my hospital floating adventures, or Nurse Flannigan's concern about my "Jon Snow" powers, or whatever you wanna call them. Late one evening, a few days later, there was another incident involving Nurse Flannigan. It makes me laugh just to think about it.

I was entertaining myself, floating down the hall to the dark end where there were a few unoccupied rooms. As I passed Room 402, I heard moaning behind the door. I thought there might be someone in trouble. I couldn't really hear like normal when I was in what I later learned was an out-of-body experience (OBE), but

I had a kinda hearing-sense—and it was even stronger than my regular hearing.

I entered the room, and there was Nurse Flannigan on the bed making out with Dr. Kessler, one of the new interns. Things were heating up and just about to get interesting. Unfortunately—maybe fortunately—the equivalent of a cold shower was about to hit them. The head nurse was walking down the hall toward Room 402 calling Nurse Flannigan by name. "Kristin, are you in there?"

They jumped off the bed. Dr. Kessler ran into the bathroom and closed the door. Nurse Flannigan simultaneously straightened out her uniform and the bedsheets as the head nurse entered the room.

The nurse looked inquisitive, if not a bit perturbed, and asked, "What's up, Kristin?"

"Oh, I was just catching a quick couple of Zs. I didn't sleep well yesterday. This night shift is gnawing on me." Nurse Flannigan was clearly stressed, shifting her weight from one foot to the other, and her normally perfect bouffant hairdo was a mess. The head nurse noticed it but didn't know what to make of it.

Giving Nurse Flannigan a steely stare, she said in a soft monotone voice, "The patient in Room 409 needs his IV changed. Can you manage that?"

"No problem. I'm on it, stat."

The head nurse started to leave the room but then stopped. She turned and asked, "By the way, have you seen Dr. Kessler? His wife, Ruth, called. Said she couldn't get him to answer his pager, and it was important she speak with him. I know she's in her ninth month. Hope that's not the issue."

Nurse Flannigan nervously responded, "I have no idea where he is, but if I see him, I'll give him the message."

"Right." The head nurse left the room shaking her head.

The patient in 409 was me, so I zipped back and reentered my body. Sure enough, my IV alarm was blinking. It had to be refilled. As Nurse Flannigan entered my room, I couldn't resist having a little fun.

"So, Kristin, how's life, anyway?"

"How'd you know my first name? My name tag says K. Flan-nigan, and only the night head nurse calls me by my first name, and you've never even met her. Everyone calls me Flannigan."

"Oh, I guess it was just a lucky guess."

"Are you kidding me? Uh-huh, I see—a lucky guess. Interesting."

"By the way, have you seen Dr. Kessler? I hear his wife, Ruth, is trying to get ahold of him—and she's in her ninth month, ya know?"

She dropped the plastic package containing my IV, but as it hit the bed, I saved it from falling to the floor.

"Now careful there, Kristin, I'm sure this IV is quite expensive. You know, hospital prices, right?"

"Yeah, right. Why . . . why . . . why the interest in Dr. Kessler? And how'd you know his wife's name?"

"Oh, I don't know. I was curious why he likes to hang around Room 402 so much, especially in the late evenings. After all, it's not occupied."

She didn't say a word. She froze with surprise and suspicion. She quickly hooked up my IV and then headed for the door.

"Night, Luc, see you in the morning."

"Night, Kristin."

"Please don't call me that. I hate that name."

"Right. Sure, not a problem."

One last dirty look and then she was gone. Good thing she didn't see the smile on my face.

A few days later, Dr. Farkas asked me why Nurse Flannigan referred to me as the "Weird Wizard in Room 409."

FLIGHT OF FANCY

TWELVE DAYS IN THE HOSPITAL FELT LIKE AN ETERNITY. I was finally home, in my own room and in my own bed. Progress, right? I thought so. The doctor had said that if there was any temporary minor brain inflammation, common after some surgeries, it would take care of itself, so I figured after one day home without any floating-body events going on, all the stuff that had happened in the hospital was a thing of the past. Although it was kinda cool to be able to go on those floating safaris without being seen, it was good to be back to normal Luc Ponti.

Or so I thought—Day 2 showed me otherwise.

I WOKE UP AROUND 6:00 A.M. IN A SEMICONSCIOUS STATE, glad that most of the pain was gone, but I thought it was too early to get up. *Maybe I can go back to sleep*, I said to myself, as the rising sun peeked through the drapes. Except my mind started to race about lots of things— basketball, school, and especially about my "buddy," Bella.

As I thought about her, a strange feeling came over me. Then it happened. When I closed my eyes, those colorful visions reappeared, and I found myself floating out of my body, rising toward the ceiling. *Minchia!* I'd thought these floating things were gone.

What the hell, why not give it another shot. I'd gotten surprisingly good at navigating. As I found out in the hospital with the Flannigan affair, all I had to do was think of a specific direction and the speed I wanted to go, and there I went.

I flew straight up through the ceiling, through the roof, out of our house, down to El Camino Real, over to University Avenue, through central Palo Alto and toward East Palo Alto, where Bella lived. I gotta admit, it was an incredible feeling. At the time, I loved it so much that I started to tell myself I was glad this stuff wasn't gone. A dream? No way. It was weird, but it was real.

It was like being in a hot-air balloon about 500 feet up, except I could move much faster than a balloon and control my direction much better. The city looked strangely different and quite uninteresting from that height—just a bunch of rooftop air-conditioning units, black tar roofs, one after another.

Eventually, I crossed Bayshore Freeway, which as usual was bumper-to-bumper—even just past six in the morning—with horns honking and people stressed out trying to get to work or wherever. Yeah, it's a valley, but maybe they should change its name to Silicon Parking Lot. I made a right toward Bella's parents' small bungalow on Baines Street.

Floating up to the door, I was about to knock, but then realized that would do no good. They couldn't hear or see me, and it might scare the hell outta them. So I figured, why not—I started to pass right through the door and into the house. I stopped and backed up: *Am I nuts? What am I doing here?*

Suddenly I heard Bella's voice through the door. "Oh God, this is weird. Luc, is that you down there?"

Damn! How could she possibly know it's me? I wasn't even there. Not in the flesh.

"Luc?"

It was only much later that I learned that people in close relationships are so consciously connected, they can sense each other's presence in any form.

Then she called loudly down the hall, "Mom, where are you?"

"Isabella?"

"Mom, did you hear someone at the door?"

"Sweetheart, I don't have time for this. What is it you want? Is it important?"

"Nah, it's nothing. I must be dreaming."

I got the hell out of there and was back home in seconds. *I can't do shit like that, sneaking up on people, especially people I like. It's really messed up.*

AFTER FIVE DAYS AT HOME, I went back to school, but the doc had said no basketball for a few weeks. Still, it was great to see my teammates. That first week, I had a biology test—my least favorite subject—and didn't study for it. Yeah, I know, stupid, right? Especially after being out of school for so long. I sat at my desk in the rear of the classroom staring at the page, wondering if I could get a decent grade just by guessing at the multiple-choice answers. Time passed faster than I realized, and still not a single circle blackened in, when other faster and smarter kids started turning in their exams. Ms. Brothers, sitting at her desk, was just as quick. With the answer sheet directly in front of her, she raced through them with her red pencil.

I can't take a failing grade for this damn test. I closed my eyes and did one of my body floats. Back and forth between my desk and Ms. Brothers', in no time at all I completed the test. I wasn't the last kid left, which was a miracle all its own.

The next day I got my test back with a note from Ms. Brothers: "I don't know what they did to you in the hospital, but it sure helped your biological aptitude—a perfect score—*A* plus!"

Cool. I could do this and not get caught. But it wasn't long before I started feeling guilty. It wasn't like me to cheat on a test. If you wanna know the truth, I didn't like the whole idea, and not because my dear ol' dad would have done who knows what if he'd found out I'd cheated. I know a lot of guys who come up with all kinds of creative ways to cheat the system. It just never felt right to me.

Then almost overnight, I surprised myself even more, when to everyone's surprise, especially to me, I started getting straight *A*s, and not because I was cheating. It was amazing! Suddenly, I could speed-read, I had what seemed like a photographic memory, and I had an incredible comprehension of complex subjects. I liked that part of the new me. With that, I came to understand that my flat-lining dream wasn't a dream at all. I wasn't completely sure what it was, but I did know that it was real in some way.

I wished I had learned my lesson by then, but being a complete jerk, I really crossed the line one day at school with this cute girl named Carla who cussed me out after I told her the panties she was wearing were white with blue butterflies. For fun, I'd done one of my floating safaris into the girls' locker room during their PE class. Carla had no idea how I did it, but she was pissed. "Pervert! Asshole! Wait till Bella hears about your bullshit!"

She was right, of course. My first week back at school was a learning experience of its own. Lesson one—don't use my powers to cheat. Lesson two—don't use them to hit on girls. Lesson three was on its way.

Chapter Six

A BIRD IN THE HAND

I STARTED DOING SHORT, EASY RUNS IN THE NEIGHBORHOOD to get back in shape—Dad's decree. I had no choice.

On this particular day, as I entered the house, I heard someone crying the second I walked in. It sounded serious. I made a beeline for the kitchen. There was Mom; my 11-year-old sister, Laura; our next-door neighbor, Mrs. Bly; and her 9-year-old daughter, Becky, who was nearly out of control and beside herself. She was crying so hard, she could barely catch her breath.

Mom looked at me as I entered the kitchen. "Hi, honey, Theresa and Becky were just telling us about Becky's unfortunate problem."

Theresa added, "It's been a bad day. I feel terrible."

Mom had invited them over for cake and drinks, but cake and drinks were the farthest thing from Becky's mind. A skinny, somewhat hyperactive but nice kid, she was fine if you didn't have to spend too much time with her. She had a habit of whining about things that didn't go her way.

I asked, "Becky, what's wrong?"

"It's Rio," she pouted, then started crying again.

"Rio? Who's Rio?"

Laura offered, "Her parakeet, and he flew away today!"

"Oh, man, sorry to hear that."

Somewhat recovered, Becky sniffled out the details. "I came home from school, went to my room and closed the door so I could let Rio out of his cage so he could fly around my room. He loves it, and we have lots of fun playing games when he's flying. But my mom had opened the sliding glass door to the balcony to air out my room, and I didn't see it when I let Rio out of his cage. He flew outside and sat on the balcony railing. I tried to catch him, but he was scared and flew to the trees behind our house, and now he's gone forever, and I'll never see him again and he'll die alone." And with that, she started wailing again.

You've gotta know something about me, right up front—I'm a sucker for little kids in trouble. "Look, if you stop crying, maybe I can help you get Rio back. At least I can try."

"How? He's in all those trees. Or maybe he flew farther away. By now, maybe another bird or a cat ate him?"

"Do you have a picture of him?"

"Well, yeah. One where he's sitting on my shoulder."

"That's fine. Let's go over to your house, and you can show me his picture, his cage, his toys, and stuff, so I can get an idea of who he is. Then I'm gonna help you try to find him. Whaddaya say? You wanna give it a try?"

"Mom, can we?"

"Okay, sweetheart."

At least she stopped crying. Looking at Theresa, I checked to be sure. "Is it okay with you?

"Absolutely. I'm sorry, Luc. I feel so bad that I left that balcony door open. I wasn't thinking. But look, you just got home from the hospital. We don't want to impose on you."

"Nah, I'm fine, Mrs. Bly."

"You sure? God, the guilt a mother feels . . ."

As I was leaving, Mom whispered in my ear, "Luc, please don't get her hopes up too high."

"Yeah, right, Mom."

LAURA, BECKY, AND I SAT ON THE EDGE OF BECKY'S BED looking at Rio's things. I fiddled with a kind of shiny little mirror that had bells that must have rung every time he'd peck at his reflection or brushed against the toy. I sensed a connection between him and what I'd learned from Google were the OBEs I'd been having. I had no idea what the connection was or how to use it to find Rio, but at that moment that's all I had.

Laura, impatient as usual, asked, "Now what, Luc? What do we do?"

"Right now, I want both of you to sit quietly on the floor next to Rio's cage, and I'm gonna stay right here and lie down on Becky's bed, close my eyes, and meditate on where that little guy might be hiding. But please don't disturb me while I concentrate on finding him. It'll only take a few minutes. Is that okay with you guys?"

Becky was quick to respond. "I guess, if you think it'll help."

My sister wasn't so sure. "Really? You're just gonna lie there and think about where Rio is? Right!" she scoffed.

You know when I said I was a sucker for small kids? Yeah, well, I meant except for *my* kid sister. "Just be patient for a few secs, okay? Can you do that for me?"

Laura gave me a "You're weird" look. Then she went over and sat next to Becky near Rio's cage.

Lying down, I closed my eyes and took several deep breaths. The blackness in my mind's eye suddenly illuminated into bright colors. The grass lawn and toolshed in the Blys' backyard appeared. My focus moved to the tall evergreens and redwoods that formed a border between the Blys' yard and the property behind them. I couldn't see Rio, and for whatever reason, I knew with certainty he wasn't there.

Then my vision began to travel slowly out of the yard and down Los Robles to El Camino Real. Then over to Alma Street, across the railroad tracks, finally stopping at the entrance to Alexander Peers Park. Entering the park, I floated across the soccer field and past the playground, hovering, closing in on a short evergreen. Rio was in that tree. I just knew it.

I went to the evergreen and moved in between the branches. There! There in the middle, about six feet off the ground, sat a pulsating turquoise-and-blue bundle of feathers. Rio was resting in an abandoned bird's nest, edged up against the tree trunk, shaking with the fear and stress of not knowing where he was and what to do.

I came back into my body, and a moment later explained, "Girls, I think I know where Rio is. But we need to hurry. Quick."

They stood up immediately, their eyes wide open, and didn't say a word. Following me, we were out in a flash and running back to our house. I burst into the kitchen; the girls weren't far behind. Mom and Theresa, startled, stopped their conversation and looked at me.

"Mom, we have to move. Let's go."

"Luc, what are you talking about?"

"I know where Rio is, but we need to get there before he flies away."

"What? That doesn't make sense!"

"Mom, look, if the doctor had cleared me to drive, then I wouldn't be standing here. So I need you to please, please get up, get your keys, and let's go—*veloce, per favore!*[21] He's sitting in a tree in Peers Park. I need you to give us a ride—*adesso!*"[22]

I know she doesn't like me speaking Italian in front of guests, but she let that fly—didn't say a word.

Jokingly—I guess—she smiled and said, "What have you been smoking?"

"Mom! I'm not high. C'mon, let's go! I don't have time to explain."

With an amused look, she turned to Mrs. Bly. "Just you wait, Theresa, Becky will be a teenager in a few years too." They laughed and pushed their chairs away from the kitchen table. "All right, let's go."

No one said a word in the car until Becky popped off with, "Mom, Luc laid down in my bed and went to sleep, and then all

---

[21] *Veloce, per favore!*—"Quickly, please!"
[22] *Adesso!*—"Now!"

of a sudden he woke up and said, 'I know where Rio is, and let's go quick.'"

"That's nice, dear." Mrs. Bly's tone seemed like something between "What's this guy doing on my daughter's bed?" and "What's this guy doing getting my daughter's hopes up?"

Mom just looked at me kinda weird. She didn't say a word.

As she pulled into a parking space, I bolted from the door across the soccer field toward the playground. There stood the small evergreen tree I'd seen in my vision. The others were just coming across the field when I told them to wait there and to only send Becky forward. In a second, she was running toward me.

"Becky, please. You listening to me?"

She started crying.

"Not now. You've got to stop that. You hear me?"

"Mommy! Mommy!" Her crying morphed into a semi-meltdown.

"Seriously, you can't get excited like this. Stop it. Stop crying. You'll scare Rio away."

"Rio?" Just as quickly as her mood had escalated, it came right back down. She nervously tugged on the hem of her T-shirt as if negotiating with herself as to whether she should start crying again. "I don't think we're going to find Rio, and I'm really sad. But I really hope I'm wrong."

I took her by the hand, and we inched closer to the tree; then we began circling it. Because I was so much taller, I spotted his turquoise-and-blue-feathered shape before she did. I whispered, "You've got to stay very calm now. I see Rio."

"Oh my God, you do?"

"Yeah, he looks scared. When I tell you to, start talking to him in your normal voice the way you do when you two are in your room. Okay?"

She whispered, "Okay."

"Just don't make any loud noises or sudden moves."

"All right."

Still holding her hand, we slowly edged forward until she could see Rio. I heard a sniffle and then looked over to see tears welling up in her eyes. I sensed she was on the brink of exploding like usual, so I squeezed her hand and whispered, "Calm. Calm. Calm . . . " until the bomb was again defused.

"Oh my God, Luc—I see him!"

"Do not say another word. Here's what you're gonna do. I'll pick you up so you can reach inside the tree to get to Rio. As I do, start talking to him in a normal voice just like when you're in your room. Then slowly place your hands around him. Got it?"

She nodded at the same time she wiped tears from her eyes.

With that, even though Dr. Farkas had cautioned me not to lift anything over ten pounds for the next few weeks, I picked her up just below her knees and moved her so she could slide her arms between the branches to where Rio was perched, but still shaking like a leaf in the wind. Even at Becky's skinny 60 or so pounds, her weight was more than a strain on my stitches. I felt a pinch on my right side, and prayed they'd hold. "Okay, now, Becky. Just like in your room."

"Hi, Rio, I love you, and I've come to take you home."

He opened his wings, as if he might fly away. "Rio, I love you, so please come home because I need you." His wings collapsed to the sides of his body, recognizing Becky and her voice. "It's okay. I'm not mad at you, and it wasn't your fault, it was Mom's." He started preening himself as she slowly moved her arms toward the nest. Then, "Luc, I can't reach him."

"Minchia!"

"What does that mean, Luc?"

"Nothing, just keep your eyes on Rio."

I maneuvered myself sideways, taking the pressure mostly with my left hip, and lowered my grip to her shins. A beat, then another, and suddenly Becky let out a delightful laugh: "I got him! Thank you! Thank you! Thank you! I love you, Rio, and I love you, Luc!"

I set Becky down, with bird in hand. The others heard her laughing in uncontrollable excitement, and they came running toward us.

My little sister, for the first time in a long while, seemed in awe of her big brother. "Oh my God, Luc, you really found him! That's crazy. How'd you do it?"

Mrs. Bly knelt in front of her daughter. "Oh, Becky, you got your little guy back." Then she looked up at me. "I don't know how you did this, Luc, and I don't need to know, but thank you."

Mom, though, was not going along with all this without asking any questions. She looked baffled, and waited a few moments, a wait I knew all too well as she carefully chose her words: "Dear, is there something you need to tell me?"

"I don't know, Mom. Life happens."

She laughed. "The boy is now the wise man." Mom hugged me, though knowing her, her wheels were turning with "What did they do to my baby in the hospital?"

I wasn't about to get into my meeting Nonno Paulo in heaven or wherever that was, especially since I was still trying to figure it all out myself. But deep down, I knew the pieces were starting to come together.

Chapter
Seven

SUSPICIOUS MINDS

MOM AND I WERE IN THE CAR on our way to my first checkup with Dr. Farkas. Three weeks had passed without much news—physically, that is—so all I anticipated was the doc changing the bandage, checking the incision, and then removing the drain. However, I wasn't looking forward to even that routine.

We arrived five minutes early for my 9:00 A.M. appointment, but I wasn't called in until 9:30. Mom had given me a heads-up that the doc was a busy guy and very thorough with his patients, which is a good thing, unless you have anything important scheduled immediately afterward, because odds are you won't get there on time.

The examination room was quite small. Elevator music was playing, and there were paintings on the walls and several plants—it all worked to calm me down. I felt a little less stressed being there. An examination table sat in the center of the room, and a single double-arm office chair was next to it.

I'd never liked doctors—I mean, not personally, more philo-sophically. But Dr. Farkas was fine. I'd been coming to him off and on since I was a young kid. Now at 16, I was doing my best to become a star athlete. I remembered one sports commentator comparing Michael Jordan to a fine-tuned Ferrari. I liked that. I guess that was my aim in life. And in my book, Dr. Farkas was unquestionably a Ferrari.

According to the nurses at the hospital, Dr. Farkas was on a level of his own. He was on the faculty of Stanford Medical School and popular with the med students, plus incredibly smart. Apparently, he read stacks of medical journals each week, usually into the wee hours of the morning, to keep up with leading-edge breakthroughs. He must have read a lot of other subjects as well. No matter what topic I'd ever discussed with him, he had something interesting to say.

You couldn't tell that by looking at him. I mean, I was 6'7" and built like a baller, so it was a pretty easy guess I played sports. If I had to make a guess about *him*, I would have said a Las Vegas entertainer, diamond pinkie ring and all, and a great stage presence. His wavy salt-and-pepper hair, piercing blue eyes, fancy suits, monogrammed shirts, and on occasion, bizarre bow ties, said it all. I mean, like a bow tie is bizarre on its own. Who wears ones made from shimmering fabrics, bright colors, and loud patterns? It made it easy to see why doctors, nurses, and patients almost always turned their heads when he walked into a room.

That was certainly the case for me when he came into the examination room that day. In fact, just about every time I'd met him.

"Hi there, Luc, how are you feeling these days?"

"Okay, I guess. Much better. I'm anxious to get back on the court."

"All in good time. Have you been following LeBron this year? Lie down, please, and let's look at how you're healing."

"Of course. He's my hero—king of the three-pointers. I think he may pass Stephen Curry."

"LeBron is incredible, but I think it'll be tough to one-up Curry. He's got a knack for going into an altered state of consciousness before he shoots a three-pointer—super focused." He carefully removed the bandage and examined the incision.

"Yeah, they're both incredible players, but LeBron has a certain magic about him. It's hard to define."

"Luc, I'm going to remove this drain. You'll feel a pinch, but it will be over in a flash."

I nodded, wanting to get back to LeBron. "See, everything I read says he's likely to be considered the greatest basketball player and—"

"Don't move."

"Ouch! *Madonna mia*, you said a pinch, not a stab!"

"Sorry. I hear what you're saying. And I agree. We may one day talk about LeBron the way everyone speaks about Michael Jordan. They both brought great respect to their former teams— LeBron for Cleveland, Jordan for Chicago—"

"Dr. J with the Sixers and for basketball, in general—"

"Right, Larry Bird, Wilt Chamberlain, and the rest of those few superstars. Anyway, everything looks good here, but you're still on the bench for games. No-contact practice is fine. Understand?"

"Dad's gonna go nuts when he hears this."

"Yeah, I get that. My father pushed me to be a doctor. That made it harder, but it turned out okay. Just keep your eye on the ball—and work on your defense!"

"Thanks." I don't know if Dr. Farkas really knows much about basketball. But he sure talks a good game. I guess that's the entertainer in him.

He was nearly out the door as I started to get dressed when, with what looked like an afterthought—I'm sure it wasn't—he turned. "You remember that air-conditioning vent in the hospital ceiling you mentioned to me?"

"Sure."

"You were right. The maintenance people found it exactly as you said. If it had fallen and hit someone, that would have been a disaster. I'm sorry I doubted you." He took a step closer, looking at me with those sharp blue eyes of his. "Luc, what's going on? Open up. There seems to be something else going on here. I can help you more."

"I don't know, Dr. Farkas."

"Nah, I know you know. There was no way you could have seen that tiny loose screw, especially in your condition. What the hell's going on, my friend?"

Minchia! What am I gonna tell him? I hesitated. Dr. Farkas had been standing in front of me, but then moved to sit down in the armchair, crossing his right leg over his left, ready to listen. He wasn't going anywhere until I opened up about what had really happened. And so I did. I told him the whole story about my "flat-lining dream" in the hospital, meeting my grandfather, getting straight *A*s in school, floating around, finding Rio, all of it—well, not quite all. I left out my visit to Bella's place.

Looking at me with a pensive frown, he said, "You know, from what you've told me, I believe you may have had what's known as a near-death-experience—NDE, for short. It sometimes happens when a person experiences a flatline event as you did for several minutes, sometimes even longer."

Getting up from the chair, he put his hand on my shoulder. "It's nothing to be overly concerned about. What often happens is that when the patient comes back, in your case through defibrillation, they're stressed out by what they feel was a real experience but can't make sense of it, and so describe it as a weird dream where they were beckoned to cross a mystical river, or pulled toward a bright light, which fits with what happened to you. Almost without exception, most of them are reluctant to mention it because, of course, people may think they have something loose upstairs, if you know what I mean. But when they do finally open up about their NDE, they say the experience itself was magical and spiritually uplifting. They say they didn't want to leave and come back to the 'real world.' Am I making any sense?"

"Yeah, you sure are. I went on the internet and found the NDE thing. It's cool, but it's also freaky scary."

"In what way?"

"Well, like the whole idea that I was alive, then dead, and then alive again. It's like I'm now the walking dead or a zombie or something. So if I'm dead, or I guess I'm alive now, then when I'm dead again, it won't be a big deal. Or at least that's what I think will happen when it's my time."

"I've heard that's a common reaction with NDE patients." Dr. Farkas turned away, as if in deep thought, then looked back at me. His expression showed he had a lot of questions. "Look, this is not my area of expertise. Whatever I know about this is from reading a few science and medical journals.

"Unfortunately, the experience you and others have had is often distorted in the media. Too many quacks jump in and make up all these wild stories about NDEs to make a buck from gullible believers. But there are a lot more legitimate, qualified specialists these days who add a lot of credibility to the research on NDEs and what are often called out-of-body experiences, or OBEs. I can refer you to a friend of mine, Dr. Hampton Ross. He's a psychiatrist with a master's degree in physics. He has studied many NDE and OBE cases and may be able to help you."

I told the doc, "If I saw this Dr. Ross guy, my parents would find out. That's the last thing I want to do. Besides, all this floating-around stuff will probably go away on its own, so why worry my parents with this? I appreciate it, but I'll pass. I'll give it a little more time."

Dr. Farkas put his hand back on my shoulder. "I think it would help you, even if things go back to how they were. Can I at least give Dr. Ross your contact info and a little background about your case?"

I thought about his request. "Yeah, I guess so, if you want to tell him. But this is all private for everyone else, right? Patient privacy and all that. Like, I don't want my mom or dad in on it."

"Definitely, absolutely confidential. Just you, Dr. Ross, and me. That's it. Especially since you're not his patient, and he's not treating you. No one else needs to know. It's not a health issue."

"Fine, done deal."

Mom's first words when I came back out were filled with stress. "You were in there forever. What were you doing? Are you okay?"

"Like you said, he's thorough. And yeah, everything's fine. He took out the drain, and the incision is healing. All good." She bought it—can I sell, or what? But I sensed these powers wouldn't just go away on their own. No, just the opposite. They were growing in my brain, in my consciousness, or whatever you want to call it, and getting stronger. I could feel it. And I didn't know if I liked it or not. It was making my life more confusing.

AT DINNER THAT EVENING, all four of us were at the table for a change. With Mom and Dad's meetings and travels, it was more often Laura and me and just one of them. If it were Mom, she'd cook. She liked to cook, thought it was relaxing—said she needed a break from being in her head all day with psychology research and teaching. Dad, on the other hand, pretty much hated anything to do with domestic responsibilities. Paying the bills was his primary contribution to family life, which meant he ordered pizza, Chinese, sushi, or chicken—we were regulars with Pizzeria Delfina, Door-Dash, and Uber Eats.

Laura was in one of her moods. "You know, we haven't had dinner together in a month. I spend so much time at Astra's place when you guys are traveling, I was going to ask her if her parents would adopt me so I could be part of their family. Or maybe I should just pack a suitcase and go door-to-door looking for one."

Mom, who is basically a saint, patiently and apologetically consoled her. "I know, sweetheart. Dad's and my work schedules have been really hectic lately. We're going to have to do much better."

But Dad, a real *cullo saggio*,[23] added, "I agree, Val, you'll have to do better." Apparently, he missed her side-eye stare because he launched right in on me. "Luc, how'd your visit with Dr. Farkas go today?"

"Okay."

"Okay? What does that mean?"

"He checked the incision. He removed the drain from my stomach, which hurt like crazy. Overall, though, things are coming along."

"Did you get some local anesthetic and take painkillers afterward?"

---

[23] *Cullo saggio*—"Wiseass."

"No."

"Good. Because you got it easy. You have no idea about living with pain until you've been . . . on a battlefield."

I looked down at my dinner and thought, *Okay, what the hell brought that on? Let's not even go there. Whenever you start in on Operation Desert Storm, it goes off the rails—and I wind up getting run over by your fast-moving freight train.*

"I'm just trying to educate you about the realities of life."

"Carlo!" Mom was just about to take a bite, but immediately put her forked broccoli back on her plate. "There are some realities I hope he never has to face."

Dad hit back, true to someone who was "made into a man" by the Special Forces. "You're gonna make him into a mama's boy, Val. Ya know, too much *mother love* can become *smother love.*"

Oh no, he was winding up for his fastball, but Mom knew how to get him to step off the mound and check the runners on base. "Can we please change the subject? Okay?"

"Sure," he answered. "Did Farkas say you could start playing ball?"

"Yeah, he did, but no games yet, just practice for now."

Dad slammed his knife and fork on his plate. "First, you don't say 'yeah' to me. It's 'yes' or 'yes, sir.' Second, are you kidding me?"

"I don't make the rules. He gave me a note to give to Coach Ralston."

"Well, I tell you what, you give me that goddamn note. I'm gonna call Farkas in the morning."

"Carlo, he's a doctor. We need to listen to him," my mom said sternly.

"Oh, come on, Val. He's like all the other doctors. He doesn't want to get sued, so he overtests and overrests his patients. I'll let him know Luc needs to get back on the court. College scouts are looking at our boy. What are they going to think—that he can't handle pressure? He can't handle pain? Don't let 'em see you sitting on the bench. You learn to play injured, you hear me, Luc?"

Shit, I know they say women are from Venus and men are from Mars—but this guy must be from Pluto.

REVELATION

IT WAS NO SECRET—at least not to me—that Mom and Dad had been slowly drifting apart over the years. Laura was either oblivious or in unconscious denial. We never talked about it. I think if they hadn't worked and traveled on business as much as they did and instead had spent more time at home together, that might have been the end of their marriage.

The six-week executive sabbatical that Dad took at Tufts University in September 2017 gave me some hope. Distance seemed to be what they needed. When he returned home, I saw a real change that might have turned things around for our family. But soon enough, the growing positive link between them collapsed, and they started arguing again in the seemingly cramped cage Laura and I called home.

As for Mom, she's always been one of the kindest people I've ever met, despite some unusual quirks. Like, everything in the house had to be perfect. I mean, sparkly clean and corners squared away. Undershirts—even sheets—had to be ironed. Crumbs on the kitchen counter meant they had to be sponged off—immediately. Houseplants had to be pruned the moment a leaf wilted. Dad tolerated it, but his father, Nonno Marco, who'd lived with us for almost two years after my grandmother died, nearly went *pazzo*. I think that's why he went back to Jersey.

Okay, I can sort of understand those kinda things. But if Blanche, our cleaning lady, missed just one small spot, Mom wouldn't ask her to take care of it next time she cleaned. She'd dive right in and immediately do it herself. Also, although Mom had a busy schedule, when she did get to cook, it was always some kinda super gourmet delicacy. I mean, it was always tasty and all, but why spend so much time in the kitchen when Laura and I would be as happy as puppies with pizza Calabrese. Mom said she enjoyed cooking, but I think maybe she confused enjoyment with relief that her perfection monster could be nicely satisfied, at least in the kitchen.

The other thing was, she always dressed, as Dad liked to say, "to the nines." And that's every day of the week, even when she was hanging around the house. I'd never seen her in a pair of jeans. Dad was constantly on her about her Ferragamo shoes and Prada dresses costing a small fortune, but he didn't have room to talk, with his showy golf membership at Palo Alto Hills Country Club. As a world-class psychologist, Mom was probably well aware of her compulsive preoccupations. I guess she just had other priorities. And besides, they didn't really hurt anyone—except maybe her.

As for Dad, he was a real *caso pazzo*.[24] Mom had told me years before, right around the time I had my bone-aching growth spurt and started showing some great moves on the basketball court, that Dad had been happy, calm, and considerate before he went to Iraq. So I pretty much assumed it was the war that caused his intensity and anger. He was just so damn critical, especially of me. I couldn't even sneeze without him telling me I'd done it wrong. But I figured you don't watch your buddies getting maimed or killed, and the same with innocent civilians, especially women and children, and come back to your life at home the way things were before Iraq. Also, after seeing a movie called *Taking Chance*, based on a true story, I realized there's some kinda special connection

---

[24] *Caso pazzo*—"Crazy case."

among the soldiers who fought in Iraq that none of us back home could possibly understand or relate to.

Late one night, I was awakened when I heard my parents downstairs screaming at each other. Dad was yelling at Mom to get off his back about going to the VA for help. "What about *you*? You could use counseling yourself—and you're the psychologist in the house! You're a goddamn anxious, obsessive-compulsive head case. Because you feel you were never good enough for your mother and father? What? They never told you how great you were? Get over it! You beat them or they'll beat you, and right now they're winning. For Chrissake, Val, if you keep popping those goddamn Ativans, I'm gonna buy Pfizer stock." He could be a mean *bastardo*, but he was right—right about what he said, but, *minchia*, not the way he said it.

Mom's nerves were really getting the best of her since I'd come home from the hospital. I knew it would happen sooner or later. It was inevitable. I guess she had enough big things buggin' her; she just had to get some of them off her plate. I only wished it would have been later, because I wasn't ready.

But she couldn't let things go, especially when it was something important to her—like me. If she didn't deal with it right away, her anxiety would go through the roof, and she'd start with the Ativans. And right now, my strange behavior, like how I found Rio, was certainly crowding her already packed mind.

It was a warm, breezy Friday evening, and Mom had invited Bella over for dinner. We were sitting on the patio in our garden, and it was just the three of us. Dad was in New York on business, and Laura was at a sleepover at her friend Astra's house. Something was up with Mom. The dead giveaway was that she didn't do the cooking—instead, she hired Palo Alto Catering to unleash one of their over-the-top gourmet extravaganzas.

Talk about out-of-this-world dishes—like, I never heard of half of them. After a roasted fig salad with a goat cheese, prosciutto, and arugula appetizer and a chicken scallopini broccolini entrée, they served a chocolate-and-orange baked risotto dessert. While

I could have gone for my pizza Calabrese instead of the appetizer and main course, I had to admit the dessert was killer.

Afterward, we pushed our chairs away from the table and enjoyed the warm spring breeze that swept through the evening air, with Mom's beautiful garden plants and flowers swaying in what she poetically referred to as "nature's breath." Bella and I sipped on mint iced tea, and Mom had a double espresso.

"That was an amazing dinner, Dr. Ponti."

"I'm glad you liked it. They do excellent catering."

"Great chow, Mom. The appetizer and main course were good, for sure, but the dessert was to die for!"

"I agree." She took another sip of espresso and then set down her cup neatly on the saucer and stared at me. "Speaking of 'to die for,' there's something I haven't be able to let go of since the Rio deal in Alexander Peers park, and I wanted to discuss it with you."

Gesu Cristo, here it comes. "Yeah, what's that?" I tried to sound innocent, nonchalant, like I hadn't the faintest idea what she was talking about.

Mom continued. "Well, I was going to let it go, but Bella gave me a call and said she had similar concerns."

I felt myself rapidly getting pissed. "*Minchia*, Bella! *Che fai?*[25] Are you kiddin' me?"

"Luc, watch your mouth and speak English! Honestly, you don't have to mimic every profanity you learned from your grandfather. Bella was only thinking of you."

"Sorry, Mom. But why didn't she come to me first?"

Giving Bella my get-off-my-back stare, I said, "You gotta go to my mom?"

"I did go to you first. But it went right over your head. Like, it didn't register at all."

"What didn't register?"

Mom alternated looking between the two of us, probably wondering if she should jump in.

_____
[25] *Che fai?*—"What are you doing?"

Bella aimed straight for my ego. "Okay, I'll say it again. You've been acting like, not just strange, but really weird, ever since you came home from the hospital."

Although I had a good idea what she was talkin' about, I'd hoped that she hadn't noticed. Apparently, she had, but I went ahead and gave camouflage another shot. "What are you talking about?"

"I've told you a bunch of times over these last few weeks, but you don't seem to hear me. It's like you're in some kinda trance. Your head is somewhere else—somewhere way beyond the stuff that's normal between us. If that were all, I would have let it slide, thinking it's just part of your recovery. But there's other stuff that's freaking me out."

"Like what?"

"Like you know what someone's gonna say before they even say it, and you respond before they even finish. I'm surprised you're not doing it to me right now. Or maybe you are—I don't know with you anymore. Like, the other day when my mom was late picking me up at school and you said it was because of an accident on University Avenue at the 101 on-ramp. And sure enough, that's what Mom told me. Or when you told me not to worry when I thought I hadn't studied long enough for my calculus test last week because Mr. Rochester was going to get sick and would be out of school. And sure enough, he got sick. I'm not even gonna mention the whole bit with Carla's panties."

With Bella's last comment, Mom gave me a death stare and began to open her mouth to say something, but before she got the first vowel out, I jumped right in. "Look, I'm sorry. You're right. I have been a little out of it since I came home."

"I'm scared. I'm not sure you're the same Luc I've known my whole life."

I had to admit, "I'm not."

Bella and Mom shifted uncomfortably in their seats. I'd never seen Bella look that worried. Mom, on the other hand, seemed kind of amused. Maybe she was still rolling around Bella's comment about Carla's "panty thing" in her mind.

I continued to explain. "I knew I was doing the stuff you just mentioned, but I was hoping no one would notice. It's complicated, and I've been trying to figure it out. I just never realized how it would affect you, Bella, and you too, Mom, and maybe other people as well."

Mom pulled my attention back from my intent gaze down at the table. "Luc, do you know what a near-death experience is?"

"Yeah, I do now. Dr. Farkas told me about NDEs at my last appointment. That's why it took so long. Remember?"

"Really?"

"He noticed some funny stuff going on, and like you, he said that maybe I might have had an NDE after surgery. Look, I should have told you sooner, but I thought all this stuff would be gone by now. But it's not. I don't know what's happening to me. It's weird knowing what has happened or will happen—the only way I've been able to deal with it is to try to ignore it or avoid it by focusing totally on the present. But that takes a lot of work, and sometimes I forget and zone out, and I see the past or the future. I tried hard to stay focused tonight. I was so relaxed, so I did all right. I couldn't read your minds, at least. I couldn't tell what you were going to say, or what would be for dinner. I think that's all beginning to go away—really—this whole mind-reading thing seems to be almost gone—at least, mostly. That's what Dr. Farkas said would likely happen. All of it's supposed to go away."

Mom asked, "So you find yourself reading people's minds? That's unbelievable—and dangerous."

"Yeah, I agree. But here's the thing—I don't know if I'm reading their minds or seeing the future. It's gonna be a huge positive for my game. Right now, it's only practice, but I can tell you that during offense-defense practices, I know exactly what the opposing player's next immediate move is—probably before he does. That's why my game has immensely improved—at least at practice. We'll see what happens during a real game. But if I purposely tried to read someone's mind, at first I could easily do it, but for some reason, that capability is slipping away. I still can do it, but my head hurts like hell, and if I keep at it, I'm sure I'll wind up with a terrible migraine."

"Well, speaking just for Bella and me, that's good to know. We wouldn't want you prowling around our thoughts," Mom said.

"Yeah, I get it, Mom. I wouldn't do it any longer to anyone, especially to people I care about, if just to keep my sanity and my brain from exploding."

That was it. I couldn't hold it in anymore. I started pouring out everything that had happened since the hospital—everything except meeting Nonno Paulo. That was sensitive, and I didn't want to upset Mom. And nothing about floating to Bella's house. That was *in*sensitive, and I didn't want to upset her. She would have really been pissed. I told them everything else, though. Bella was shocked, but Mom was cool. I guess as an experienced psychologist, she already had a general understanding of NDEs and their aftereffects.

"Luc," Mom said, "these paranormal events, which no one has yet been able to explain in scientific terms, always go away after a short time."

Just sharing what I'd been going through helped, and I didn't want to act as if a dark cloud was following me around, but I felt like I couldn't keep up the charade. "Mom, I appreciate that, and maybe with reading people's minds and seeing the future, you're right, but I don't think that's what's going on with the other things that have happened to me. They're getting stronger. For example, I suddenly have a photographic memory. That's why I'm getting straight *A*s. Or, if I just try to chill and a place pops into my mind, no matter where it is—it could be halfway around the world—I'm right there. Or if I think of a specific animal, that's how I found Rio. Or a person, that's how I know that Dad is going to call you in a few seconds from New York."

"Oh, really?" Mom looked amused.

Just then, her cell phone rang. She grabbed the phone from her pocket, gazed at the caller ID, then at me and Bella. "Hi, Carlo. You okay?" She paused. "Good, can I call you back in a bit?" She put the phone back in her pocket.

What was amusing before was now deadly serious. "Luc, we need to get you some help and make you more comfortable with these changes and find out when they'll go away."

"Mom, you can't tell Dad. Please. He'll drive me nuts."

"More like he'd tell you to use the new you to read the defense so you can get open shots at the basket," Bella interjected.

"Dr. Farkas recommended some psychiatrist guy at the hospital, but I don't know. I mean a shrink. Really?" I said.

Mom jumped in. "And who's that?"

"Some doctor named Hampton Ross."

"I know who he is. I've gone to a few of his seminars. He's an authority on NDEs and paranormal phenomena. He could study you. Luc, if he's willing to see you, go for it."

"I'm not sure. I'm still thinking about it."

"What's to think about? You need to get some help. And you have nothing to lose but a little time."

I stammered. "There's . . . there's, more to the story. When I . . . I'm not sure I should talk about it now. It's nothing about you, Bella. It's just kind of personal for my mom."

"Of course. No problem. Dr. Ponti, thank you so much for dinner." Bella started to get up.

"Stay, please. You're practically family." Mom smiled at Bella. "Please don't worry about this. Luc, what is it you want to tell me?"

I hesitated again.

"C'mon. Out with it," she said.

"Okay. Here goes." I told her what had happened during my NDE—that I rose above my body, then the bit with the air-conditioning duct, and then that beautiful tunnel of light.

"Luc, that's amazing."

"Right, Mom, but there's something else."

She shifted a bit in her chair and sat up very straight. "Yes?"

"As I walked along that tunnel, there were a lot of other people I saw that I didn't know. They smiled at me as they passed by. But then I met someone I *did* know. Well, I didn't actually *know* him, not yet anyway, but he knew me."

"You're dragging this out. For goodness' sake, who was it?"

"Your father, Nonno Paulo."

Mom slowly scooted back in her chair. In deep thought, she grimaced, furrowed her brow, and stared out into the darkness. Her presence was falling away, and her anxiety was climbing higher. She began to do that thing she does with her hands when she gets nervous, rubbing them together like she's putting on hand cream or something.

Bella couldn't take the strain. "Dr. Ponti, really, I think I should leave."

"No, honey, it's fine. Please stay."

Trying to save them both from what was coming, I said, "Mom, please, we can do this another time."

"No, it's okay. How do you know it was him? My father died before you were born. You must be mistaken."

"He came right up to me and introduced himself as Paulo Catalano. I said, 'Nonno Paulo?' And he said yes, he was my grandfather. He told me I needed to go back and that I couldn't stay there with him in that big light thing we were in. He said it wasn't my time yet. He made me promise that I'd give you a message."

Mom got up from her chair and started pacing back and forth, waving her hands in the air. "My God, this can't be. Maybe you're . . . you're imagining this from something we talked about in the past?"

"No. He told me that he died suddenly and was always working so hard that he never gave you the love you deserved. He told me it was the biggest mistake of his life and to tell you he was sorry. He said he and your mom are both proud of what you've done with your life."

Bella just sat there, speechless, with tears in her eyes.

Mom went to say my name, but nothing came out. In anguish, she slowly sat back down in her chair. The tension in her body was intense, and she started shaking. I went over and knelt beside her. Gently, I pulled her into my arms. "Nonno said that if I were to mention something else to you, you'd know for sure that I'd really met him."

Mom was struggling. After several moments, through a choked-up whisper, her words finally came out. "And what's that?"

"Nonno Paulo said that he was the one who put your doll, Freckles, in your dollhouse for your seventh birthday. He said when he took his car to the service station to fill up the tank, the service attendant had offered to clean the car. When the man cleaned the interior, he found Freckles underneath the back seat."

"Oh my God."

Mom buried her face in my chest, sobbing. I wished I hadn't told her. "Mom, I'm so sorry."

"It's okay. It's okay. It's wonderful to hear this message from my mom and dad. Really. It's just you meeting your grandfather . . . it means so much to me, but it's a lot for me to handle now. It makes me wonder what's real in this world and what's not." Bella came to sit on her other side, and the three of us embraced, rocking gently. We were trying to make my mom feel better, but it also comforted Bella and me.

Buon Dio![26] *Quando finira questo?*[27]

[26] *Buon Dio!*—"Good God!"
[27] *Quando finira questo?*—"When will this end?"

69

ONE OF A KIND

SOMETIMES THOUGHT THAT MOM WAS A BUDDHIST MONK IN DISGUISE. She had a knack for distilling things down to the simplest language. Or so it seemed, because when I really thought about them, they often blew my mind. Like when I complained about something not going my way, her favorite saying was, "Everything happens for a reason."

If I pushed her, she'd complicate it so I wouldn't feel so dumb. "We live in a purposeful universe, so everything happens for a reason, as far as the cosmos is concerned. It's called 'cosmic balance.' It's a karmic response to something that's happened in the past, so everything stays in balance—we're all connected in some way." *Thanks, Mom.*

When my immediate response to something I didn't like was to push back in anger, she'd quickly advise me that I was fighting against the entire universe, which is why that approach never worked. Her advice was that accepting my current situation and disconnecting from the outcome would put me in the best position to change course to get what I wanted. *Whatever.*

I'd argue, "So I should accept what happens and just go with it?"

"No, you always have another chance and another choice, but you must follow the Buddhist three-point philosophy—first, have a clear intention for what you want. Second, put your attention on it. And third, do your best to detach from the outcome and let the cosmos handle the details. Although I admit that detachment is the tough part."

"Yeah, right, Mom. I'll remember that when I'm being double-teamed and shoot a jump shot off balance at the buzzer. I'll be sure to tell Coach that my airball was part of the cosmic plan. Oh, and Coach, by the way, don't worry, I was detached from the outcome." The truth is, I didn't understand Mom's mumbo jumbo, and at the time, I had the attention span of a gnat for that kind of deep stuff.

Her response was, "Not to worry. Someday you'll understand it and embrace it."

I rolled my eyes. "Can't wait." I admit it was sarcasm, but what was sincere was that I couldn't wait to get out of just going to practice and get back to real games, with or without Mom's cosmic philosophy. I'm sure it's clear by now: I'm obsessed with the sport. Obsession—I guess that's my genetic gift from Mom.

IT WAS A SATURDAY AFTERNOON, and I'd just finished my first basketball practice since the whole hospital-NDE thing. Coach Ralston had said I was playing better than ever—as if I'd never been out. He told me I'd developed a "great court sense to read the opposition's next play." But I sensed that my newfound ability to see the opposing player's next move was fading—at least I thought so at the time—and it was the one thing I didn't want to lose if things went back to normal. I knew it was an unfair advantage, but I couldn't help it. Hell, it was part of me, just like my size-16 Nike LeBron Soldier IXs. I wasn't about to tell Coach that I'd had out-of-body experiences, and could predict the future and read minds—he'd for sure send me for a psych evaluation.

My dad, on the other hand, would probably say something like, "You know, Dennis Rodman—alias the Worm, Psycho, Rodzilla, El Loco—wasn't any more whacked out than you, and he made it into the NBA Hall of Fame, so shut up and play to win on every possession of the ball, whatever it takes."

But he didn't know about my newfound powers, and I hoped he never would. He'd come to a couple of recent practices and noticed, as Coach did, that I was playing better than ever. You'd think he would've said something positive or patted me on the back with an "Attaboy" or something. But no—not dear ol' Dad.

The more I gave, the more he wanted. He'd always push me harder. When I did sprints the full length of the court faster than everyone else with my "long, beefy *Dago* legs," he told me to put on ankle weights and do the drill again. I did as he said—I had to. When I finished last, I felt that it gave him some satisfaction until Coach stepped in and made it clear it was *his* team, not Dad's— Boston Irish overruling a Jersey Italian.

I appreciated that about Coach, but he wasn't going to take control of my life away from my father. No, I was going to have to take it away from *him*. How, when, and on what terms, was still up in the air.

I WAS SITTING OUTSIDE IN OUR GARDEN IMMERSED ONLINE, checking out high school scouting reports. Before the accident, I'd broken into the top 25 of high school players in the nation, but now I'd slipped back to the 30s, behind a slew of kids from Georgia, Iowa, and Illinois. The phone ringing in the living room came just in time before I started ragging on myself to get back in gear. I walked inside to pick up the phone, wondering who the hell in this high-tech Silicon Valley still calls on a landline. We were supposed to have gotten rid of ours months ago.

"Hello."

"Hello, I'd like to speak with Luc Ponti. Is he available?"

"This is Luc."

"Hi, Luc. This is Dr. Hampton Ross at Stanford Hospital. Dr. Farkas gave me your name and number."

"Wow, I told him I wasn't interested. So, uh, hate to waste your time, but thanks for calling anyway, and—"

"Dr. Farkas told me you appear to have had an NDE, and he filled me in on some of your OBE experiences, during and after the event. Did he tell you that NDEs and OBEs are one of my prime areas of research?"

"Right, yeah. I think he mentioned that. But—"

"I lead a research team exploring the field of consciousness."

"Yeah, my mom knows of your work. She's also at Stanford."

"Oh, in what department?"

"She's a professor of psychology. Valentina Ponti."

"I see. I don't know many people over there. I feel like I live in the lab and don't get out to other departments as much as I should. Luc, I'm calling to see if you wouldn't mind chatting with me for just a short time so I can collect some information about your experiences and add it to our database."

"Like I told Dr. Farkas, I don't want to be fixed, so I think I'll pass." Truth was, I was a top recruit for a college scholarship, and that was more important than anything else. I didn't have time for any of this other *shifezza*.[28]

He pushed on. "This has nothing to do with fixing you. It's just collecting information, and it's anonymous. It won't take long, and you'd be helping a lot of people who've gone through what you did. I promise it will be quick—just one short meeting for maybe an hour at the most. I'd really appreciate it."

"I'm sure, but I've had all of the NDE stuff I wanna deal with. Even though it's been fun at times, the sooner I get back to normal, the better off I'll be. The psychic stuff, mind reading, and predicting the future . . . well, I think that's already going away. Not sure about the rest."

"I might be able to help you with that if you wanted."

"So says my mom. But I just want to wait it out."

"From what Dr. Farkas told me, waiting might not pan out."

"He told you it was getting stronger?"

"Not exactly. Come and see me. Let's talk about it."

I took a deep breath. "Oh, what the hell. One short meeting can't hurt. I can't miss basketball practice, though, so how about

---

[28] *Shifezza*—"Crap."

73

this Wednesday around five? But that's it, just this one talk. You write down my answers to your questions for your database, and then I'm done. I don't want to be one of your lab rats."

He laughed. "We don't do animal testing. See you Wednesday at five in my office in Jordan Hall. You know where that is?"

"Yup. Got it. See you then."

PRACTICE WENT LATE ON WEDNESDAY. I didn't even have time to shower before heading to Dr. Ross's office and getting that over with. I hopped on my bike and raced over to Jordan Hall. Yeah, that's right, I said my bike. I still hadn't been cleared by Dr. Farkas to start driving again. I guess he was worried I'd space out and have an OBE while driving . . . or whatever.

The door was open, and Dr. Ross was sitting behind his desk, typing away on his computer. He glanced up and offered a quick hello. "Hi, Luc. Sorry I'm running late. It'll be just a minute."

I thought, *What a strange-looking guy*—thick, wavy-blond hair; closely set intense deep blue eyes with oversized, fluffy eyebrows; a mouth full of large teeth; and a tall, thin body dressed in a three-piece business suit. His head seemed a bit too large for his lanky build. Peculiar but memorable. His office was quite the place. It overlooked a courtyard decorated with the Rodin sculptures that Mom loved—she said they're called the "Burghers of Calais." Stanford's got money for those kinds of extras.

"Just these last two sentences . . . and send. Done. The Central Intelligence Agency is not very patient with late reports, and they're a prime contractor for our research group."

"The CIA? You work for the CIA?"

"Yes, interesting work."

"What do they care about consciousness research?"

Dr. Ross thought for a few seconds. "I can't tell you much because it's classified. But parts of what they're interested in are in the public domain. Google it. They're interested in remote viewing as a means for safe distance-intelligence gathering. Basically, that means gifted people who can remote-view go into a kind of trance, and their consciousness then 'hears' and 'sees' things at vast distances—they could even be thousands of miles away from the target—and spy. It's James Bond without the Aston Martin."

I smiled. "No Bond girls either, I'm guessing."

Dr. Ross laughed as he reached across the desk to offer his hand. "So glad you could make it. Hey, anyone ever tell you that you look a lot like a young Michael Corleone in *The Godfather*? I guess that was Al Pacino in his younger days."

"Yeah. I hear it a lot—mostly from older folks. Never saw the movie. It was like a little before my time—like maybe 30 years." I thought for a few seconds. "Sorry, I didn't mean to imply you're old."

"It's okay, I *am* old. It's beyond implication. I see it in the mirror every day."

I liked him. Great sense of humor and obviously a smart guy, but he didn't take himself too seriously. I felt at ease. "What do you say we get started?"

"Sure. Let's do it." He stood up from his desk.

Whoa . . . I thought *I* was tall, but he had several more inches on me. As he grabbed some files out of a drawer, I asked, "Did you play basketball in school?"

"I did. I played for the University of Maryland. Still do some pickup games here when I can find the time. I hear you're the star player for Palo Alto High School and that scouts from around the country have their eyes on you."

"Something like that."

"A humble recruit. That's good. It keeps your mind sharp. Maybe at one of our pickup games, you can show us what a kid three times younger than we are has got."

"I think you're setting me up, Dr. Ross. I doubt I've got much that you haven't already run into the ground."

"You're too kind, Luc, but we're just old geezers having some fun!"

"Thanks for the offer. But not now. I'm kind of a busy guy and all."

"Call me if you change your mind." He handed me his business card. I looked at his card, then at him. He was serious about me playing ball with him and his friends.

Dr. Ross motioned to me. "C'mon, let's go into the conference room." I followed him into a room next to his office. He sat at one end of a long, oval mahogany table, surrounded by a dozen plush, coffee-colored, comfy chairs. I sat at the other end. After looking at his notes, he said, "I'd like to ask you a few questions, if you don't mind."

"Sure, go ahead."

He started with ones related to what Dr. Farkas and I had talked about. It seemed like he just wanted to confirm all the things I'd already told the doc. Finally, he said, "Luc, that device I set up on your right in the middle of the table measures the quality of your eyesight. I'd like you to go over and sit in front of it. Look into the double eyepiece and read the letters you see. Sometimes I'll block out one eyepiece so I can check each eye individually. I'll make some notes here. After you read each line, I'll change the screen to the next one. I'd like you to read until I tell you to stop. Okay?"

I got up and walked over to a large, black metal microscope with two eyepieces and several electronic attachments. I looked into the eyepieces and saw a string of small letters. I read them out loud as Dr. Ross took notes. I would finish one line of letters, and then using a remote control, he would change to a new one, mixing them between small ones and big ones. And then he tested each eye individually.

After a few minutes, he stopped and studied the results. "Okay, great, I see you have 20/15 vision, which is quite a bit better than 20/20 vision. Great for good basketball accuracy. Now I'd like you to go to the sofa over there by the window. Please lie down and close your eyes, or whatever it is you do to go into your trance where you can see things."

"Yeah, whatever."

Dr. Ross explained, "Usually a person needs to lie down and go into an altered state of consciousness, a kind of meditative state to begin distance viewing. It usually takes some time to connect with the intended target. But let's see what you can do."

I told him, "I don't have to do any of that stuff. I just close my eyes, and I see bright colors like a rainbow. And if I keep them closed, the colors arrange themselves into the scene or person or thing I focus on. Then I start flying to it at what I guess is faster-than-light speed because I'm there in an instant. So if I closed my eyes now and focused on the Golden State Warriors game, in a little bit, I would be at their game—well, my consciousness would be there."

"Really?" Dr. Ross looked somewhat shocked. "That's incredible. I've never heard of such a thing in all of my years of remote viewing and NDE research."

"Now I don't want you to think I send my spirit or whatever to events like the Warrior Games for a freebie. I always pay my way—a full-body thing, ya know."

"Right. I get you."

"What is it you want me to see?" I asked.

Dr. Ross placed a small, black metal box in the center of the table. "What do you see in front of me on the table?"

I closed my eyes for a few seconds. "I see the lid is open on a black box. At the bottom of the box, facing up, is an index card with some writing on it." Laughing, I read what was on the card. "I'll bet you're a better player than I am."

Chuckling, but clearly surprised and impressed, he said, "That's excellent. Now I want to see the range of your remote-viewing capability, so I'm going to put a different card in the box with much smaller type. See if you can read it." After making some notes, Dr. Ross replaced the first card with a different one. "Okay. Give it a go."

I laughed again. "You're a funny guy. It says: 'Luc would die a thousand deaths if he had to wear the same tight basketball shorts as Hampton and other players did in the '80s.'"

"That's amazing! Most people would need a magnifying glass to read something that small. Hold up for a minute—I'm going to my office to print another card." When he came back, he put the new card at the bottom of the box. "Okay. Please give this a try."

Same thing as before, except this time I burst out in hysterics: 'Coach K from Duke is on line one for you, Luc.' Mike Krzyzewski? Are you kidding me? Don't I wish!"

"Incredible! I would need a microscope to read that. Your mind's eye seems to be able to read anything, no matter what the size."

"I never thought about it. That's, like, so cool, isn't it?"

Dr. Ross was really excited. "Cool—are you kidding me? It's beyond cool or any other adjective you can come up with." He came over and sat on the edge of the table right next to me. "Luc, my friend, cool, epic, whatever, are an understatement. You've developed an amazing capability, and from what you tell me, it seems to be growing stronger. Who knows where your endpoint might be? I've been studying NDEs and OBEs for ten years and have never seen, read, or heard of anything like this."

He got up and started walking around the conference table and continued. "Down the road in Menlo Park at SRI International, during the '70s and '80s, two well-known physicists, Dr. Harold Puthoff and Russell Targ, studied hundreds of remote viewers from all over the world. Some were talented, but none came anywhere close to where you are today. Those studies were funded by government intelligence agencies, mostly the CIA, and focused on what they called 'psychic spying.' You can understand the value of not putting human operatives at risk in harm's way if they could gather the same information by remote viewing."

I thought this was weird. The CIA must be a strange group. Out of curiosity, I said, "Pretty weird stuff. Were they successful?"

"Yes and no. Yes, because they found that most people had the capacity to do some level of remote viewing, but no, because only a small number could be trained to get to a higher level of consciousness and view at any reasonable distance. But even with those who did, none came anywhere close to what you've demonstrated here today. Parts of the program have continued, but you don't have the security clearance for me to share that with you."

"That's all right. I'm not the spy type. Well, except for the Bond girls. Now that *would* be cool. But seriously, I was born to make a three-pointer at the sound of the buzzer. That's me, Luc Ponti, and that's my future."

"Luc, this is a five-pointer at the buzzer!"

"Five points? What are you getting at?"

"A three-pointer plus two foul shots for a flagrant foul. That's your five-point play. Three plus two! There have only been two five-point plays in all of NBA history: Dell Curry in 1995 and Kobe Bryant in 2003. Make history, Luc!"

"I already did. I had a five-point play in my last game against the Bells—the Dumb-Bells, I should say."

"That's high school, Luc. I'm talking about a first-round draft into the big leagues."

I didn't like his hard sell, and he must have seen it on my face.

"All right, Luc, glad you came by. Our hour's up, just like we agreed."

"Good to meet you, Dr. Ross." In my enthusiasm and anxiousness to leave, I stupidly added, "Hit me up if you need anything else."

He didn't hesitate. "Great! I'd love to do one more test. But we can't do it today. I'd have to schedule what's called a high-resolution functional magnetic resonance imaging scan, or an fMRI."

I didn't like this at all. "Look, I should have kept my mouth shut. I was just trying to be a nice guy. I mean, I said, 'Hit me up,' but you know I was just bullshitting."

"Kind of like when you say to a girl, 'I'll call you.'"

"Yeah, like that."

"But you never call."

"Right."

"But you still keep saying it even though you don't mean it."

"Well, if they really want it, then yeah, I'll call them."

"I really want this fMRI," he told me.

My immediate thought was: *Would this really be the end of it, or the start of something bigger, something that isn't for me?*

I could have peeked into his mind to see what he was really thinking, but I didn't want to do that. I didn't want the doubt and concern about where this was going, but shifting into all that clairvoyant shit meant giving up seeing what was happening in the present. I didn't like looking inside people's minds or into the future. It might seem like a gift, but I found it a big pain because people got pissed when I knew what they were gonna say before they said it. Besides, my head hurt like hell afterward. Nope—not doin' it. I decided to roll the dice and help a Maryland baller: "Okay, but that's it." This thing was growing much beyond what I intended. No more Mister Nice Guy.

MAGNETIC
PERSONALITY

I WAS ANXIOUS TO GET THIS WHOLE THING OVER WITH as I arrived at the MRI facility at Stanford Hospital. Sure, my new photographic memory, rapid learning skills, and ability to see stuff far away without being there—Dr. Ross called it remote viewing—was beyond cool. And although reading people's minds was becoming difficult—and painful—seeing the future wasn't my thing. But it was there in an emergency, if I needed it. And it certainly had improved my game.

But all these powers were making my life harder by raising everyone's expectations of me—my parents, teachers, Coach Ralston, the team. They were all probably thinking, *Wow, Luc has finally found his groove.* But the truth was, I'd be happy to go back to my old self. Sometimes good enough is just that—good enough. I'd even read in one of those self-help books that *perfect is often the enemy of good.* Whatever.

Now, there was one more log on the fire of pressure on me. Dr. Ross was waiting for me with anticipation. "Hi, Luc. Being straight with you, I'm still amazed by what you showed me you're capable of. I hope that what we do today will shed some light on what's happened to you and give you some answers. So thank you for your time today. I think it's going to be a win-win for both of us."

I nodded in agreement, not feeling much like talking.

Dr. Ross suggested, "Before we go in, let's grab a couple of chairs over here, and I'll tell you what we're doing today so you have a better understanding."

Again, I nodded. Didn't wanna show the least bit of enthusiasm. That's what got me here in the first place.

I guess he wanted to keep it private, because he tucked us way back in the corner. "You okay, Luc? How was practice?"

Small talk? Seriously? He wanted to make small talk? "Yeah, I'm fine, but can we get goin'? I gotta load of homework tonight."

"Sure, of course. Well, here's how this will work. Functional magnetic resonance imaging, or fMRI, works by seeing changes in the oxygen concentration in your blood and can detect its flow to various regions of your brain. Certain regions do certain things. When a region is more active, it uses up more oxygen, which means it needs more blood flow to bring more oxygen to it. That part of your brain lights up in a certain way. In some ways, it's a zero-sum game. A surge to one region means a zap to another. These surges and zaps show up as color-coded areas in the fMRI scan. By measuring them, we can map what parts of your brain are on and which are off for a particular mental activity."

I was really impatient to get out of there. "Mom said it's okay, so I'm good. Can we just get to it?"

"Sure, let's do that." We walked into the lab, where I saw a huge cylinder lying on its side. It had a small hole in its center and a narrow, retractable bed that extended from the hole. A lot of weird stuff with all kinds of electronics and monitors surrounded it.

I laid down on the sliding bed, which was then retracted into the tube—I thought of it as the mothership. It was a bit claustrophobic, but nothing to freak out over. Then, for just the slightest moment, I thought, *Hmm, Dr. Frankenstein.*

Dr. Ross's voice came through a small speaker within the tube. "Now Luc, I want you to focus on that small box I put at your feet.

Just like before, it has an index card with some writing on it. And just like before, please read what's on the card and stay focused on it for two minutes while we run the scans. Two things, though— please try not to move your mouth too much, just as little as necessary for me to understand what you're saying—and please don't move your head at all."

"Got it. Ready for blastoff." I closed my eyes, did my thing, and my mind's eye gazed into the box. "Okay, I have no idea what it means, but here it is—'magnetism sets your destiny.'"

"That's perfect, Luc! Now hold your focus on it for two minutes while I save these images."

That was it. Dr. Ross pulled me out of the mothership and invited me to wait if I wanted to see the results right away. I thought, *Che cazzo,*[29] and nodded in agreement.

About 15 minutes later, he came out into the waiting room, looking dumbfounded. He said, "I expected to see something different from the images we'd have for a normal brain. But, Luc, this blows apart my expectations. I didn't aim high enough. You're off the charts."

"Thanks, I guess, for confirming I don't have a normal brain. There are plenty of people who've been saying that about me long before this NDE thing. My dad is at the top of that list."

"I'm not sure you're getting this." Dr. Ross stood up. "C'mon, let's go where we have more privacy."

"There's no one else here." I opened my arms to indicate that the place was as empty as the Mojave. "I wanna go home. Can we just get it over with?"

"Not here, trust me."

Spies are everywhere—hiding in plain sight. I uttered an exasperated "Fine."

Without saying a word, Dr. Ross grabbed my arm, ushered me out of the hospital, and into the parking lot, where we sat in his car. I mean, was this CIA spy stuff, or what?

"Sorry, Luc, can't take any chances with these findings. First, I need you to understand that what I'm going to tell you is a

---

[29] *Che cazzo?*—"What the hell/f*ck?"

positive thing. But prescription drugs are as well—they can heal, but if used without guidance, they can kill. Look at opioids as an example."

"Well, that comparison is enough to scare the shit outta me. Pardon my French."

"No, nothing like that. As expected, your fMRI showed high activity in your cerebral cortex and thalamus. I was explaining before about the zero-sum game, which would normally mean those two areas get the ball in clutch plays, while the other areas have to sit it out on the bench. Know what I mean?"

"I like the basketball analogies. I get it." I gave him my first smile of the day.

"Your scan shows you don't have a zero-sum equation. You clear the bench. Everybody's in the game—your entire brain is lit up. It's as if every neuron is in open communication with all the other neurons in your brain. It's like a supercomputer—no, it's *beyond* a supercomputer!"

"Damn. Is that bad? Do I have brain damage because of my NDE?"

"On the contrary, your brain seems to be evolving into a much more advanced machine, if I may call it that. How it's doing that, I can't say at this point, but somehow it seems to be connected with your NDE. It's completely visible in your scan. Here, look at this. It's a scan of a so-called normal brain. Now look at yours. The other one is a scan of a mathematics professor here at Stanford while she was solving a complex differential equation."

Although I doubted that a mathematician, especially one at Stanford, could be thought of as having a "normal" brain, there it was in living color. There were a few isolated colored areas where her brain was actively working on solving the equation. The other areas weren't lit up at all. But the scans of my brain were lit up like a bright-red neon sign across the entire area of my skull. My brain looked like a large bright-red light bulb.

"Luc," Dr. Ross asked, "have you noticed any increased ability in your problem-solving capabilities at school?"

"As a matter of fact, I have. Even though I missed a lot of school with my surgery, I caught up quickly and have been getting straight *A*s in physics, math, and in fact, all my subjects, even biology, which is my least favorite. I can speed-read something once and recall it in total detail. It's like I have a photographic memory."

Dr. Ross explained why. "I think the reason is that there is now direct communication between the left and right hemispheres of your brain. In other words, you are actively and simultaneously combining your high-level analytical and intuitive skills to solve problems. Not only are all areas of your brain operating at super high levels, but you've also merged the power of your right and left brain so that they work simultaneously and synergistically.

"Your brain seems to be evolving at a much more advanced level than ever before known to science. It's abundantly clear that you're developing not just advanced cerebral powers, but I'd actually say, superpowers. Most of us must jump back and forth between the right- and left-brain hemispheres to solve problems. What we do is clunky; what you do is beautifully synergistic and is beyond powerful."

"So you're saying I'm a freak," I said wryly. I thought I'd beaten him to the basket, but Dr. Ross swatted the ball down.

"You don't think Kareem and Shaq are freaks of nature, do you? You've got a golden opportunity to go all out with it just like they did—and probably well beyond that. You can change the game with your new powers, Luc. You can change your life. Who knows, maybe you can even help change the world."

WE NEED YOU

MEMORIAL DAY WEEKEND WILL PROBABLY NEVER BE THE SAME for me after my meetings with Dr. Ross. I realized it was a special day of remembrance and recognition for all those who've given their lives in service to our country, but for me, it would always stand out as the weekend that changed my life in ways I never could have imagined—thanks to Dr. Ross.

I'D INVITED BELLA TO OUR PLACE FOR A SWIM AND FAMILY BARBECUE. We'd also invited her folks, but they couldn't make it. Her dad had to work overtime, something he was happy to jump at for the extra income, especially with the cost of living in the Bay Area continuing to climb. And Bella's mom was kind of old-fashioned—she didn't like partying while her husband made sacrifices for them. Their family was really tight in that way—nobody took anything or anyone for granted. Over the years, I'd seen the Morenos give up lots of things in that spirit. I can't count the number of times Bella had told me she dreamed of the day she would be a doctor and be able to help her parents financially.

The Morenos just had one car, which meant that Bella had a challenge if she wanted to drive somewhere. Still out of action with no wheels, per Dr. Farkas's orders, I decided to bike over to Bella's place so we could ride back together for the barbecue. On the way, I stopped at Yogurtland on University Avenue to cool off with a froyo.

I was sitting at one of their tables on the patio, along with some other customers, enjoying my Meyer Lemon special, when a tall guy came out of what seemed like nowhere.

"Hi, Luc," he said. His tone was soft-spoken, with a hint of a southern accent. He looked to be in his mid-40s, dressed in khaki pants, a short-sleeve blue polo shirt, and Nikes. He was lean, and tall—probably 6'4" to my 6'7".

"Do I know you?"

"No, you don't, but I'd like to get to know *you*. My name is Major John Dallant." He extended his hand. I hesitated, but the intensity of his brown eyes and the strained look on his face told me he'd probably already witnessed more than most of us would ever want to see in a lifetime—he was military. Out of respect—I learned that from my father—I extended my hand to his.

"Dr. Ross over at Stanford Hospital told me I should look you up."

"He did? He didn't say anything to me about you. Who do you work for, and why the interest in me?"

"I'm CIA, presently on loan to the NSA."

"*Minchia!*" I chucked what was practically my whole yogurt into the trash can next to me and stood up.

"You don't want to hear what I have to say?"

"No, I don't. I made it clear to Dr. Ross—one and done!"

"Your dad served."

"Which is exactly why I don't want anything to do with you and your organization. And how do you know about my dad? No, wait, I get it—you guys know everything!"

He stepped in closer. "Luc, please sit down and just listen for a minute."

I felt scared, but also kinda invincible. I sat back down. No harm in that—at least for a few minutes, anyway. "So, you're a spy."

"I prefer counterintelligence officer."

I was getting more nervous by the second and started to sweat. I looked around. We were in broad daylight. A mom with her two kids sat two tables away. A cute girl—probably in college, she looked too serious to be in high school—sat on a barstool to my right; and a couple of cyclists all geared up in their tight, black Lycra shorts and matching red, green, and yellow jerseys with 'Campagnolo' lettered across them, leaned against posts not more than a few feet away from us. Could he have picked a place any more normal? Guess not, when you want to disappear—hiding in plain sight and all that crap.

"Luc, let me tell you about some work that happened right here in your neighborhood." I worried that someone would listen in, but he didn't seem to mind. "A number of years ago, we began funding a program at the Stanford Research Institute, now called SRI International. It concerned things similar to what you've experienced. It's called remote viewing—namely, teaching people to attempt to see remote locations in their mind's eye in as much detail as possible, often at places that are thousands of miles away. In principle, it was meant to make our business easier and safer . . . and our clients safer as well."

"By clients, you mean . . . ?"

"You know who I mean."

He was right. I did. Americans, our allies, the rest of the free world.

Man, this dude was doing a sales job—flag, country, and apple pie. What he didn't understand was that my superpowers could be long gone—and soon. But maybe I was the one who didn't understand, because they hadn't gone away over the last two months and were getting stronger. Wishful thinking on my part? I cautioned myself: *Luc, stay calm.*

I said, "Dr. Ross mentioned a couple of names who used to work there but didn't say much more."

"That would have been Dr. Harold Puthoff and Russell Targ," he replied.

"Yeah, those are the guys."

"That was the very beginning of our research efforts. We had two parallel programs running, the one at SRI and an internal effort carried out elsewhere by CIA and NSA scientists. A lot of false conclusions were made about the SRI research, which caused Congress to shut it down in the early '90s. Some of that is on the internet through the Freedom of Information Act. But some of it isn't."

He'd gotten my interest. "Like?"

"I can't comment on that."

I persisted. "Like?" It came out louder than I'd intended it to.

"Take it slow and low, Luc." Calmly, the major turned his head and smiled at the mother with her two young children.

She glanced at him and mentioned, "It's Haley's birthday. She loves their banana-and-chocolate swirl."

"She's adorable. How old?"

"Today she's three. The baby is 14 months."

"Happy birthday, Haley!"

"Honey, tell the nice man thank you." The little girl curled up behind her mother. "She's shy."

"My ten-year-old was the same way when she was your daughter's age. Then the next thing you know, they're showing off their pirouettes to anyone who'll watch."

The two of them laughed. Then Dallant calmly turned back to me, and in a much sterner tone said, "Google some of those conspiracy-theory websites about remote viewing and the research at SRI. You'll learn about a part-time Christmas-tree salesman who found a top-secret US security facility hidden deep in the hills of West Virginia. Then there's the woman who remote-viewed an advanced Russian bomber that had crashed in the jungles of Zaire, which, because of her efforts, we got to before the Russians. Watch the movie *Red October* and you'll get another idea. What I'm saying is that conspiracy theories aren't always what they're cracked up to be."

I looked at him, puzzled.

He read my face. "Sometimes they're not conspiracies, but actually information hiding in plain sight. And sometimes they're not theories. They're important facts being kept secret by making them appear to be fake news."

"Well, that's progress, I guess. But probably not enough, since you guys closed down the research."

"At SRI, yes."

"I don't get it. Their stuff is on the internet, and they're done. That's what you said."

"Yes, that's what I said."

A few seconds of silence passed between us. Finally, I broke through. "It's what you *didn't* say."

"Dr. Ross says you may have other skills besides remote viewing that might be a good fit for our concerns."

The people who'd been sitting on the patio when we first started our conversation had left, and new ones had shown up. I lost myself in thought, then came back to reality, realizing that in addition to my remote-viewing capabilities, Dallant was talking about my ability to read minds and see into the future. But I really hated doing that kinda stuff. It drained me. And besides, even though my remote viewing appeared to be getting stronger, I could feel my psychic powers evaporating, slowly but surely—at least I thought so at the time, because it took increasingly greater focus and concentration to do it. And as for mind reading, forget it—much too painful for my head to deal with.

"You have a lot of marketable talents, Luc. You could be a real asset to our organization, and to your country."

"I'm not an asset, I'm a person." I leaned in and asked, "What do you want from me?"

He leaned in, too, so that our faces were only inches apart. So close that I could smell coffee on his breath and the fabric softener on his shirt. "I'd like to speak with your parents about a job opportunity with us."

"That's nuts. I've been working my whole life to play basketball. It's my passion and nearly my total focus in life. I'm a high school junior. College scouts are looking at me for next year after I graduate. I'm not throwing my dream away. No, man, not for anybody."

"Luc, you think I don't know that? I know about your 80 percent hit rate from three-point range. I know about your air balls from the corner and about your jumpers from the high post circling the rim before bouncing out. I know about you getting beat on crossovers because the offense has figured out that you move off your heels instead of your toes."

I looked at him in disbelief—then my disbelief hardened into disdain. They'd been digging into my life in great detail without even asking if I wanted in. I didn't! I'd already made that clear! *Dannata*[30] spies! Enough talk. I pushed away from the table and stood up. "This conversation is over! I'm late to meet a good friend."

"Oh, you mean Bella?"

Merda santa![31] *Spies, spies, spies—does he know what time I take my next piss? I don't wanna see this guy again. I'm outta here.* I walked away without even saying goodbye.

"See you soon, Luc."

He said it so casually, so confidently . . . but I took it as, "Luc, my boy, we'll get you one way or the other."

Chapter
Twelve

THE PARENT TRAP

"Hey, Luc, I'm thirsty. Can we stop someplace?" Bella asked.

Meeting Major Dallant had scared the hell outta me. I'd pushed myself into a dark corner, having hardly said a word to Bella as we biked back to my house. I squeezed out, "The Creamery?"

"Yeah, sure," she said.

I knew I needed someone to talk to but didn't want to get Bella mixed up in my mess. Sure, I'd told her and Mom at our dinner together about some of the crazy stuff that was happening to me. But that was then and this was now—the intensity was increasing, and things looked like they were going haywire. Then Dr. Ross and this *stronzo* Major John Dallant—I worried if there was any end in sight.

The Palo Alto Creamery was probably the only shop on the peninsula that still made 1950s-style milkshakes and malts. It looked like the place in that old TV show *Happy Days*. There was a long string of four-person booths with padded red-vinyl bench seats, a long counter surrounded by stools with circular, spinning, matching red-vinyl covered seats, and a 1946 Wurlitzer bubbler jukebox. Customers would pump in quarters to hear Elvis's "All Shook Up"; The Platters' "The Great Pretender"; Chuck Berry's

"Johnny B. Goode"; Connie Francis's "Where the Boys Are"—you name it from the '50s and '60s, they had it—and all on 45-rpm vinyl discs. I dug that music, or at least I could see how kids back then had dug it. It wasn't Twenty One Pilots, but it was simple, honest, and yes, definitely cool.

We took the very last booth in the back. I got a cherry Coke fresh from the soda fountain, with authentic syrup and old-fashioned seltzer water. Bella got a vanilla malt, so thick that the straw was almost useless. Our silence was just as thick until Bella pulled out the straw and opted for a spoon. "Yummy! Want some?"

"No, thanks." I anxiously tapped my fingers on the tabletop.

After a few more spoonfuls in silence, she said, "Luc, I've known you long enough to see when things are going from bad to worse. I'm beginning to lose sleep over this. I understand what you told your mom and me, and as much as I thought that had helped you by getting it off your chest, you seem like you're going downhill fast. What's happening to you? We've been friends long enough for me to know you worry too much. Maybe the problem isn't as big as your think." She sighed. "C'mon, stop playing Mr. Tough Guy. Look, you made an amazing recovery. Your playing on the court is better, your grades are higher. It's incredible. What's to worry about?"

I shrugged.

"Can't you tell me what's going on? Please. I wanna help."

I looked around the Creamery, hoping for something witty or lighthearted to say, anything that would take the heaviness off my mind, but I came up blank. *Should I or shouldn't I tell her about Dr. Ross? About that Dallant guy?*

Her patience was wearing thin. "Luc?"

"Okay, okay! Give me a sec, will ya?"

She gave up on her malt and pushed it aside. It wasn't even half-finished. Then she stared at me, with her hands folded neatly in front of her on the table. I saw those pretty green eyes of hers begin to well up. Bella's got three emotional settings: neutral, which I go along with; a temper, which I deal with; and sweetness, which I love and almost always give in to. She's figured out that the last two get my immediate attention.

I started to explain. "My body . . . is fine. My brain . . . not so fine. It's changing or evolving, or whatever the hell you wanna call it. Yes, I have what some would call superpowers, which can be a good thing. I can help people. But those powers can also be a huge challenge. I'm scared shitless. I didn't ask for this and don't want most of what I'm getting on all kinds of things. I want out, but it's overtaking me, like zombies or something, and every day there are more of them eating away at me. That's on the inside. On the outside, everyone expects more from me. I'm sick of their high expectations. I want my own life, my own future, not what other people want for me."

Bella reached out to hold my hands, both still fidgety. "I know you've been concerned about this, but who's putting all this pressure on you? I mean, other than your dad?"

"He *is* one of the biggest flesh-eating zombies, that's for sure!"

She laughed. She'd known about my dad's ways since I was six, when he taught me to catch a hard ball and drilled me on how to win at dodgeball against ten-year-olds.

"It started with that Dr. Ross guy who Dr. Farkas suggested I see. My mom said to go see him, too, remember?" Bella nodded. "He did some tests on me and was super amazed over how they turned out. I was supposed to be done after that, but he convinced me to do one more thing and take a specific brain-scan measurement in this huge tube."

Bella, who read medical books for a hobby in preparation for her dream of becoming a doctor, put out a line with bait: "You had a functional magnetic resonance imaging scan—an fMRI?"

"*Minchia*, how in the world did you know . . . ?" I looked at her, surprised, but then caught myself, realizing I shouldn't have been—not by her. "Yeah, right. That's what he called it."

"And?"

"He said that not only is my overall brainpower increasing, but also that the left and right hemispheres of my brain are constantly in direct communication. Dr. Ross said that raises my level of consciousness in a major way and lets me be highly intuitive and analytical at the same time. He's never seen or heard of this before. Also, it's like I've got a photographic memory now, which is why I've been getting straight As in biology and every other class."

Bella was shocked. "Biology? Oh, wow, *mi cachorro*,[32] you're acing biology?"

"Not bad, huh?"

"Yeah. Awesome! So it's not all bad. You know, maybe you can use your powers for good—world peace and all that jazz."

"Come on, Bella, cut it out, will ya? I just want to go back to being normal Luc Ponti. College and basketball are my thing. I wanna be the next John Stockton."

"But maybe you could help people as well."

She just wasn't getting it. "My sacrifices are for basketball. First as a recruit to a great college, and then to see if I've got enough game to make it to the pros."

"I get that. But that doesn't mean you can't help people too."

Honestly, she *really* didn't get it. But that wasn't her fault. It was mine, because I was holding back. I leaned in so she could hear my lowered voice. "What I haven't told you or anyone else is that Dr. Ross is a world-renowned expert on this stuff, and a lot of his research is funded by . . . by the CIA. They're into kind of psychic spying on our enemies. They call it remote viewing. Like *I* get it, whatever helps the country. But . . . uh . . . they want me in on it."

"The CIA?"

I tried to pull my hands away from her grip, but she wouldn't give.

"Wait a minute," she said. "Are you telling me that this Dr. Ross dude wants you to speak with the CIA about this, like to spy for them? Like on China? North Korea? Russia? Or whatever?"

"Yeah, I'm pissed because he already got in touch with the Agency . . . and guess what? Today, just about an hour ago on my way to your place, some guy named Major John Dallant—if that's his real name—came up to me at Yogurtland, introduced himself

---

[32] *Mi cachorro*—"My puppy." (Spanish; *cucciolo* in Italian)

as CIA, and tried to sell me on this. I mean, like hard sell. He wants a meeting with my parents and me."

"Oh my God, Luc. That's crazy."

"That *stronzo* knows all kinds of shit about me." I hesitated, not wanting to scare her, but then made the dive: "He even knows about *you*." A thought flashed through my mind—were they spying on us in the Creamery? Did they know what I was telling Bella? *Minchia*, this was really messed up. "Listen, you have to keep this CIA stuff to yourself. You're the only one who knows. I don't want Mom worrying about it. Dad can go to hell—he'd probably throw me in with them just to prove what a real man is: 'No son of mine is going to turn his back on God and country.'"

"Luc, are you out of your damn mind? You can't work this out by yourself. This is way beyond you, me, or anyone else we know. You gotta tell your parents."

I went quiet again. I just couldn't get her to understand. Pounding on me to get help from my parents was not the answer, but rather than argue with her, I tried to laugh it off. "Ponti, Luc Ponti, at your majesty's service."

Her look said more than a thousand words. She saw what I didn't want to: I was in trouble—big-time.

I told Bella I understood her concerns, but first I needed to give this whole thing some serious thought, and not overreact and make a huge mistake before I dealt with it. Fortunately, she went along with me—at least that's what it seemed like at the time.

MOM CALLED FROM UPSTAIRS, where she was putting on her perfect look, as usual. "Luc, Bella, can I ask for some help? Would you mind carrying some of the food on the kitchen table out to the garden, and please light the barbecue so it heats up?"

"No problem," I answered. We were sitting on the couch, flipping through photos from when we were in grammar school together. "God, Bella, you were funny-looking."

"Says the guy who looked like a really long broomstick with two Dumbo ears."

I nudged her, laughing, as we stood up to go to the kitchen: "Come on, evil bearer of my past."

She nudged me back. "Sire, I am but a torchbearer to keep you from embarrassing yourself."

A few minutes later, Dad joined us outside by the table where we'd placed the salads, chips, dips, and other goodies, waiting for the barbecue to take center stage. "Hi, kids, sorry I didn't get to fire up the grill. I just got off the phone. Out of the blue an old army buddy of mine called."

I hadn't recalled seeing Dad in such a cheerful mood for quite some time. It almost looked like it was a bit forced and he was trying to cover up for something.

"Who's your army buddy?" I asked him.

"Oh . . . Cap? We served together during Desert Storm. He and I became good friends, but I lost track of him after he was seriously injured in one of our missions and . . . I . . . he was shipped stateside."

Dad stopped for a minute. I could see that there was something heavy on his mind. He stared over the barbecue toward the tall redwoods that lined the fence in the back of our garden, his jaw clenched tight. He suddenly—probably out of sheer determination—snapped out of it and continued. "I had no idea Cap lived so close to us, in Modesto."

Dad seemed both happy and concerned that Cap was coming. I couldn't help wondering why.

He continued. "After Cap's recovery, he returned home to Rahway, New Jersey, where he worked as a guard at the East Jersey State Prison. He and his wife soon divorced. They had no children, so he moved back to his original roots here in California. He apparently took over his father's almond farm in Modesto after his dad died—but from what he said on the phone, he'd lost that as well. I completely lost track of him. I hope you guys don't mind, but Cap said he was on the peninsula visiting with a friend, so I asked them both to join us today."

I went over and sat at the table, being careful not to disturb Bella's good work, looked over at Dad, and responded, "No, not at all. As a captain, I guess he was your superior officer?"

"Oh no, he was my staff sergeant assigned to the platoon I led. His name is Charles Anthony Pendergrass, but we all called him Cap for obvious reasons."

"So who's his friend?"

"Apparently some air force major from the CIA, who's stationed at their headquarters in Langley, Virginia. He's visiting with Cap."

Figlio di puttana![33] *Che palle!* Air force major . . . CIA . . . ? Mom always said there are no coincidences in this universe. My blood went cold, and Bella and I shared an intense, worried glance. *Could it be? No. Can't be!* Dad caught it.

He looked at me quizzically. "Is there something wrong? I hope you kids don't mind my inviting them."

I tried not to stutter. "No. No. It's fine, Dad."

This should be an interesting barbecue.

---

[33] *Figlio di puttana*—"Son of a bitch."

GRILLED

TWILIGHT CAST DARK SHADOWS OVER OUR GARDEN, completely camouflaging everyone's faces. But Mom and the two men's laughter made for a bright entrance. I guessed the one in front with a cane was Dad's friend Cap. Sure enough, he and Dad hugged like two bears at play.

"Best NCO on the goddamn planet! Hot damn! How in the hell are you, Cap?"

"Just another day in paradise, Lieutenant!"

"I love it! That's my man! Still the same 'can-do' Cap." Dad stepped back a foot, with both arms extended and hands firmly grasping Cap's shoulders. "Man, you look great."

"Compared to the last time you saw me, Christ, I hope so."

I had no idea of the before picture, but the one after must have been a big change. I assumed Cap to be Dad's age or younger, but time had not been kind to him. Remnants of his physique showed through—a hint of squared shoulders had given way to a landslide. A commanding posture now extended to a fleshy belly that didn't seem to stop. He had a sparse tuft of hair that hinted at what used to be on his head.

I swear, I thought Dad was starting to tear up. I'd never seen him come anywhere close to showing this kind of emotion. Those kinda feelings just weren't in his operating manual. He swallowed hard. "Oh, hey, Cap, I lost my head . . . you met Valentina. This is my son, Luc. We also have an 11-year-old, Laura, but she's spending the day at her girlfriend's place."

I extended my right hand, not thinking about or paying attention to Cap's right hand, which was holding solidly onto his cane. He smiled and graciously crossed his left hand over for a left-right handshake. "It's an honor to meet you, sir."

"Sir? Lieutenant Ponti, don't tell me you got your son locked on to the military too." With a friendly smile, he said, "Call me Cap. Really nice to meet you, Luc."

"Cap, this is my . . ." I hesitated. For the first time, I wasn't sure how to introduce Bella. I landed on playing it safe: "My friend Isabella."

"Hello." She leaned in to give him a hug.

Cap went silent. He seemed genuinely touched by Bella's sincere gesture. A few heartbeats later, he cleared his throat. "Damn, you're a pretty young lady. You remind me of my wife, Marcie. She has striking green eyes just like you. Don't see 'em that often."

"I'm sorry she couldn't come. I would have loved to have met her." Bella's spirit can be amazingly charming.

"Oh, sorry, we're not together anymore. I say wife, but I guess I should have said my ex. At least that's what she calls me." He wobbled a bit on his cane as his friend extended his arms from the dark shadows cast by the overhanging ferns and evergreens, and steadied Cap. "Yeah, can't blame her, though. She sent out a full man and got back a bag of bones. Not a good trade-off, you know what I'm sayin', Lieutenant?"

Good ol' Dad, still the hard-ass. "Listen here, Cap, you still got the spirit of an eagle, so straighten up and fly right!"

"Copy that, *sir*," Cap responded, his volume going up several notches on "sir," just like he'd been ordered to do by the military.

As if on cue, Cap's friend came forward two steps out of the shadows and into the light. *Merda santa!* Right, Mom, no coincidences! I'd like to say I was surprised—but I wasn't, not by a long shot. I guess I was hoping against hope.

I muttered to myself, *Incredible*.

Bella nudged me so as not to look so obviously disturbed. I could see that she wasn't doing much better at recovering her composure. Without ever meeting the man before, she knew exactly who he was.

Cap again took the floor, which gave both of us some time to think. "Oh, what's wrong with me. This is my buddy from the East Coast, Major John Dallant."

I had to admit that Dallant's crisp air force blues, with a three-button coat and pins and ribbons on the lapels, a light-blue shirt notched up with a blue-patterned necktie, and a matching service cap, made him a striking figure. He looked important.

"Major." Dad extended a firm handshake. I could tell it was a military thing for him—the higher the rank, the tighter the grip. "And my son, Luc, and his friend Bella."

The major reached out to Bella. "Nice to meet you, Bella."

To which she responded with an Academy Award–worthy radiant smile, yet keeping her distance. "You too."

Then he turned to me. "Hi there, Luc." I stood there smiling despite my shock, and did my own best Oscar-winning performance by not looking the least bit surprised. I shook hands with this man and tried to figure out how he'd finagled his way into our home—and on the very first day we met! These CIA spy types are good—really good. It was scary.

The major turned to Dad. "Fine young man you have here, Lieutenant." Dad beamed. All the three-pointers I'd ever made in total couldn't match the pride he showed in that one compliment from Major Dallant. "Sure is a small world. I happened to run into Luc today at that place, what's it called? Oh yes, Yogurtland. I was waiting there to meet up with Cap."

Concerned, yet doing her best to keep things light, Bella chimed in, "Luc, you rascal, you didn't tell me you had yogurt before you came over. That's not fair."

With a real flair, the major added, "He got a froyo, so I think he owes you one."

"Yes, Luc. You owe me."

I smiled but didn't know what to say. The major had opened the vent and brought just the right stuff to the surface. "I was killing time waiting for Cap to show up, so Luc and I just kinda fell into conversation. Interesting young man. Say, Luc, let's catch up on our discussion later."

First, a deep gulp. Second, a look at my parents' faces. Third, awareness of Bella's tensed-up body. All I could muster was, "Yeah, right." The roulette wheel was spinning. I only hoped the damn ball stopped in the right place. God knows I needed all the help I could get. Was he gonna bring up all that shit with my parents? Should be a great evening.

I lost my bet at the roulette table, as Dad jumped in. "Wow! That *is* quite a coincidence." I half expected him to go into his bit about there not being any coincidences, just losers or winners who seize or miss opportunities. "But you two can catch up on all that later. Right now, I'm going to put some marinated sea bass and veggies on the grill. Dinner in 30. Hope you're hungry."

Although it was clear that Cap and Dad were like brothers, bonded in ways that I imagined only war could do, their hesitation and discomfort was also clear. The Iraq War was completely missing from the evening's conversation, which was probably a blessing. However, I overheard them mentioning several of the men in their unit a few times.

Dad's tour disturbed him. I knew that much because Mom said so, and I was usually on the receiving end of that disturbance. But that evening, I realized I was clueless about how bad it had been for him. He'd always refused to talk about it. Seeing Cap, crippled with physical and emotional battle wounds, gave me some insight into Dad's own crippling emotional wounds buried deep inside him. I tried hard to feel some understanding and compassion for him. Not easy to do.

Over cocktails, while waiting for dinner, Cap talked about taking over his family's almond-farm business after his father died, except it proved to be too demanding. "It shouldn't have been, but somehow the Iraqi sandpit blew up my body, my mind, and my spirit, and when I got back, it finished the job by blowing up my marriage and my business."

No one said a word—not even Dad. What could you say after that?

Now the bank owned Cap's father's farm, but he said he was fine now. He had lots of free time, and the VA apparently was taking good care of him. I wasn't so sure he was happy, though, not at all. He had a nearly constant frown across his face—even when he smiled—you know, the kind where the mouth is smiling, but the eyes and their surroundings are soaked in permanent stress.

Major Dallant, however, looked very much at ease—quiet, observant, and listening carefully—just like a spy, I guess. Bella and I did the same, though not with ease, especially during dinner. The conversation was mainly Cap catching up with what Dad was doing at the bank and learning about Mom's research at Stanford, and, of course—where I wanted to end up playing college ball.

After dinner, Mom suggested we go inside to the den for drinks. We did, and Dad fixed everyone a drink, as Mom brought out her favorite Swiss chocolates.

Although carrying what looked like permanent stress, Cap was visibly happy to be with us, and especially pleased to see Dad. He wholeheartedly expressed his gratitude. "Val, Lieutenant, that was a great dinner—thank you so much for inviting us! I really look forward to reciprocating at my humble place in Modesto. It's not much, but I've got a great barbecue in the backyard. And I can do ribs like you never tasted before—the secret's in the sauce. Got the recipe from Big Red." Cap immediately stopped talking and bowed his head.

Dad took over. "We lost Big Red in Desert Storm."

Major Dallant, presumably trying to help, jumped right in before Mom or Dad could respond to Cap. "Yes, Val, Lieutenant, everything was super. The sea bass was perfectly done, and those marinated veggies were out of this world. I'll have to get your recipe for my wife. I'm especially grateful that you invited me, a complete stranger, into your home this evening to meet you and join the party."

Dad responded, "Cap, Major, you're both welcome. It's especially great to know that Cap's a California neighbor. Looking forward to reestablishing our connection."

Mom smiled in agreement. "It was nice to have the opportunity to meet both of you."

But then the fuse finally was lit, as Dad took over. "So, Major, I know you can't talk about your work at the Agency, so tell me about your conversation with Luc earlier today at Yogurtland."

Major Dallant turned to me as if wanting to allow me to go first, but seeing that was a nonstarter, he pulled the trigger. He looked at Bella. "Bella, I don't know if you want to stay for this."

Mom and Dad seemed confused by his comment but didn't say a word.

Bella stood. "Oh, right, I better get going. It's late."

"You sure?" I asked, but truthfully, I wanted her to leave, and run as far away from this mess as she could. I really did. But what came out next was: "Please stay."

"I can't, Luc. I have a huge term paper due this coming week. My mom asked me to call her around this time. She'll be here to pick me up soon."

Mom smiled at Bella. "Come on, Bella. I'll walk you out and give you some food to bring home to your dad for when he returns from his night shift."

And there I was, quiet and transfixed in a semihypnotic state, pondering what kind of colossal tragedy was unfolding right in front of me.

Major Dallant asked Dad, "Lieutenant, do you mind if we wait for Val? I think she'd like to hear this."

"Not at all." Dad got up to refresh Cap's drink as well as his own. Major Dallant hadn't touched his. Dad finished just as Mom returned and joined us.

The major—I'm sure, unintentionally—squeezed off another spray of friendly fire. Looking at Dad and Mom, he said, "I'd planned to meet with you under different circumstances, but—"

"Hold on there, Major, am I missing something?" Dad set down his Scotch on the table. "What do you mean you had *planned* to meet with Val and me? I thought you just happened to be in town visiting with Cap."

Cap's crippled body struggled to lean forward in his chair. His perpetual frown seemed to pick up speed as it turned the corner and headed into deep distress mode. "Lieutenant, I'm really sorry. All is not as it seems. I had no idea. I hope you and Val will forgive me for not being up front about calling you today and coming over with John."

Dad raised his voice. "Cap! What the hell are you talking about?"

Mom was also confused, though like a gymnast on a balance beam hoping for a soft dismount, her dismay and her smile steadied perfectly as she interjected, "Major, what's going on here?"

Major Dallant sat back in his chair and lowered his pitch to his calm, assertive military tone of voice. "Cap, I'll take it from here. Val, Lieutenant, I work for the CIA, and I'm currently on loan to the NSA." Dad reached for his Scotch, then apparently thought better of it and pushed it away. "I met with Dr. Hampton Ross at Stanford Hospital about Luc's near-death experience and what appear to be his amazing new capabilities."

"Wait a minute." Dad was suddenly uneasy, but not as uncomfortable as I would have guessed. I soon found out why. But the next few minutes would change that. "So I guess you're referring to his game having improved a lot. Yeah, I think we've got a real shot at a call from the Pac-10 or the ACC, but what's all that got to do with national security?"

Mom's leap landed with a hard dismount. Her voice raised in pitch. "Why were you talking to my son's doctor without his or our permission?"

Major Dallant dodged both questions. "The CIA funds a large percentage of research in this field."

"Basketball? Are you kidding me?" For someone with a sharp mind, Dad was confused. But I guess it wasn't surprising, since he didn't have the info that Mom did.

"Hold on, Carlo. There's a lot you don't know." Mom stood up from her chair. Focusing on Cap and pointing her finger directly at him, she accused, "You come into our home disguised as a friend to help Major Dallant coerce or strong-arm our son?"

Dad was both shocked and pissed. He stood up. "Val, what are you talking about? Cap, what the hell's going on here?"

Cap's wide-open eyes revealed that he, too, was hearing the real story for the first time. He turned to Major Dallant. "John? What the hell is this? What are you saying?"

Before the major could say a word, Cap, who'd been looking at Dad, said, "Lieutenant, you've got to believe me. I had no idea about any of this. I got a call from John, and he told me he needed my help on a national-security matter. What would *you* do? So I said, sure, whatever you need. He told me you lived in Palo Alto, which I wished I'd known before, so we could have started up our friendship again years ago. He said he just wanted me to introduce him to you and Val. I figured the country wants me to make a phone call, I'll do it. But I swear to you, on the graves of all those men in the 7th Cav we lost in Operation Al-Fajr, I had no idea where this was going. I'm sorry, Carlo, Val. I'm so sorry." He closed his eyes, a casualty of betrayal. No one said a word, not even Mom.

Dad walked over and stood behind Cap's chair and put his hands on his friend's shoulders. "It's okay, man, it's okay. Look, we crawled through that godforsaken desert together, in and out of some of the worst of times. You never once let me or our unit down then. I know you're not now, either. It's okay, Cap."

"Thanks, Lieutenant. That means a lot to me. I appreciate it. I can't even begin to comprehend what you did for us, especially the guys we lost . . . you're the one who had to send each of them home to their families in a flag-draped box, their dog tags in an envelope . . . dear God, we lost some of our best." To which Cap immediately started reciting: "Pid, Mumbles, Bambi, Thromb, Coma, Animal, Merlin, Reaper, Boss, Hef, Skeeter, Big Red, Keebler, Boomer . . . I got a lot of time on my hands now . . . lots of time to think back. I can keep going if you like." Cap was now in an entirely different place.

"It's okay, Cap, it's okay." My father was massaging his shoulders. Cap leaned slightly forward and closed his eyes—feeling the pain and the power of war.

I'd never seen my dad this way. I thought maybe this was the man Mom had talked about. The one she thought she married. I wasn't sure how much more of this I could take.

Continuing his gentle massage, Dad said, "The best NCO on the planet." Straightening up, he returned to his chair, sat down, took a sip of his Johnny Walker Black, and turned to the major. "It's just us now. Leave Cap out of this."

Major Dallant nodded. He sat erect in his chair, tightened his lip, clenched his jaw, folded his hands on his lap, and began. "Lieutenant, I know that during your tour in Operation Desert Storm, you and your Special Forces team reported directly to the CIA, so I did some digging in our files and found that you and Cap were close friends."

"Brothers," Dad corrected him.

"Okay, brothers. So as it happens, he lived in Modesto. The rest you know."

"Bullshit. You didn't just happen to wander over to Yogurt-land and just happen to bump into my son. You knew we were having this party today. I know how your game is played."

Major Dallant was quick to respond. "Does it really matter?"

"Damn straight it matters."

I looked across at Mom and saw her trembling, rubbing her hands together, seconds away from popping an Ativan. As calmly as she could, looking intensely at Major Dallant, she said, "No more of this. I want you to leave."

In many ways I felt invisible. Here they were in this heated exchange over me, and yet nobody even looked my way—an innocent bystander caught up in the cross fire. I sat there and said nothing.

Major Dallant backed off. "I understand. Our business represents the highest ideals and also the lowest common denominator. Perhaps when you become aware of Luc's test results from Dr. Ross, you might reconsider." The major got up from his chair and stepped toward Cap, positioning himself to help the sergeant from his chair, readying him for both of them to obey Mom's demand that they leave immediately.

Mom looked to me. "Test results? What's he talking about?"

Figlio di puttano! "Mom, I didn't wanna worry you and Dad, so I didn't say anything. Besides, I thought this stuff would all go away, and those test results wouldn't matter."

Dad looked at me like he was focused down the sight of his sniper M-24, ready to pull the trigger. He was already pissed because he'd just found out about Dr. Ross in this heated exchange. And then he *did* pull the trigger.

"Tell me what the hell is going on, right now, Luc." I was startled—no, scared shitless—by Dad's demand. Not that I should have been. I mean, I've been spoken down to and cornered by him a million times. It's just that when I saw the way he treated Cap, for a moment I thought maybe he'd come back from the war, only this time like a normal person.

I froze, unable to find the right words."

"*Dannazione, mio figlio disubbidiente, adesso!*"[34]

My father had never yelled at me like this in Italian before. It wasn't his way. He was over the top. With that demand from my dad, Major Dallant found the words for me. "Dr. Ross found that unlike any other person the agency or the entire intelligence community has known of, the neurons in Luc's brain are collectively interwoven and in constant mutual communication. Not only is this unprecedented, but it has imparted in him paranormal abilities you might call superpowers."

"Oh my God, Luc." Mom started to cry.

"Mom, I told you, I didn't want to worry you and Dad. I was hoping this would all just go away by now, and that would be the end of it."

"Oh, Luc." She clasped her hands in front of her mouth, as if praying to heaven.

---

[34] *Dannazione, mio figlio disubbidiente, adesso!—*
"Dammit, my disobedient son, now!"

Dad, on the other hand, was a dragon breathing fire from hell. "Luc, are you out of your goddamn mind? Not telling us any of this? Going to that Dr. Ross guy?"

Shit! I should have listened to Bella and told them.

"I'm sorry. I should have said something. I guess I wasn't thinking straight."

"You weren't thinking at all, goddammit!" Then Dad turned his fire on the major: "What is it you want?"

Mom was several exits past her Ativan off-ramp. "Carlo, please, I don't want to hear any more from him. I want him to go."

Dad tried to pacify her. He lowered his voice several decibels. "I understand. I want to know what he has to say, and then he's gone." Mom relented, although she started rubbing her hands together even more rapidly than she normally did when stressed beyond her limit.

Major Dallant began: "Some years ago, the CIA funded a remote-viewing program right down the road from here at SRI in Menlo Park. Our interest then was in a safer, lower-cost means of gathering intelligence."

I turned toward the major. "You mean spying." Those were the first words I'd said to him the whole time he was in our home.

"Yes, spying, if you will. After a couple of decades, we closed that program and released some of the information to the public. I can't say much more than that. However, as I said, in all the work we've done, we've never seen anyone like Luc, and Dr. Ross believes there's more of it yet to come to your son."

Dad wasn't one to be at a loss for words, but this seemed to have stumped him. After a long pause, he questioned, "So, are you telling us that you'd like our 16-year-old boy to spy for the CIA?"

"In a manner of speaking, yes."

"In a manner of speaking, wrap it up, Major. You're on borrowed time."

"Right. What the Agency would like to do is employ Luc on a part-time basis to test the potential for his service to our national security. He could work directly from Palo Alto for, say, five hours a week. We would grant him top-secret security clearance and set him up close by in a secure office with our own state-of-the-art encrypted equipment that would enable us to communicate safely and securely. His primary mission would be to use his skills to remotely view intelligence targets abroad."

Dad wasn't my overbearing basketball coach any longer. He'd switched hats to be my commanding officer. "I'm all for Luc serving. I did and my father did. That's how he got his US citizenship. But if you put Luc in harm's way, and if he's successful and enemy intelligence agents found out, then what? You get your medal, and our family's Secret Squirrel gets his ass shot?"

"That wouldn't happen. We would quarantine his mission to one handler. That's how we run our quarantined operators. Luc would be just like one of them—one handler, no identifiers on output. My last point, and then we'll leave. We're prepared to offer Luc a contract as an independent consultant for a period of six months at $250,000, with a stipulation that if we offer an extension of that contract based on a favorable outcome, we'll pay all of his undergraduate college expenses for any university he enters."

Oh mio Dio![35] I couldn't control myself. "Seriously, 250K? That's a quarter of a million bucks, a financial windfall! Mom, Dad . . . hell yeah!" I nearly lost my head.

Buzz-killer Mom had a different idea. "Luc, forget it! It's too dangerous. You don't need that kind of money. *We* don't need that kind of money."

Major Dallant, trying to build his case, spoke directly to Mom. "Val, I understand your concern. I wish I were at liberty to disclose to you what your son's capabilities could mean to our country. Your husband went to Iraq in response to 9/11. He came home safe, but that doesn't mean we're safe as a nation. We're not. That's not classified information; just turn on the news and see nation-states and independent revolutionaries—terrorists—gunning for us. The potential contribution Luc could make is beyond your imagination. Please, think about it some more. We want to see what he can do. We *need* to see what he can do."

---

[35] *Oh mio Dio!*—"Oh my God!"

As Major Dallant and Cap were leaving, Mom just sat in her chair. She was staring at me, not saying a word. I didn't have to read her mind. I knew what she was thinking. She was afraid of losing me—and so was I.

Chapter
Fourteen

FAMILY MATTERS

SOME SAY THAT SLEEP IS A GREAT ESCAPE FROM STRESS—not for me. Lucky if I'd gotten three hours last night, and I felt like the walking dead. Heading downstairs for breakfast, I couldn't stop thinking about what had transpired. I understood Mom and Dad's concerns. I didn't want to spy for the CIA, and if I was good at it, risk having an enemy government gunning for me and maybe my family. But Major Dallant had offered two powerful reasons why I should consider it.

I was more than intrigued by the possibility of helping to prevent terrorist attacks. There had been so many lately. And men weren't the only targets. Women and children also suffered horrible fates. Whenever I saw that stuff in the news, I always skipped over it, recognizing that it was terrible, but what could *I* do about it? At least until now. What if there *was* something I could do? I was torn, thinking about it.

And then there was the money. Yeah, I get that Mom said we don't need that kind of money, and I'm sure we could afford me going to one of the top colleges, although it wouldn't be cheap, maybe $300,000 for four years.

Forget it. I wanted a full scholarship, so I could feel like I did it on my own while also helping my family. And I'm not thinking small—more like Duke, Princeton, or Harvard. I had few doubts I could get in now that I had these superpowers to help with my SAT scores, grade-point average, and my performance on the court. Probably a free ride for me would be an athletic scholarship, not academic—even though I had these powers, I couldn't make up for the grades I'd gotten during my first two years of high school. And if I didn't get a full ride, that $250,000 from the CIA would nearly cover my four years. I liked that backup strategy, even though it wasn't a big hit with Mom and Dad.

Just then, I heard a noise in the living room. I peeked around the corner. It was Dad, still dressed in the shorts and T-shirt he'd worn at yesterday's barbecue. A bottle of Scotch lay on its side on the coffee table in front of him. He was bent over, staring into an empty glass. Another one of his all-night binges. It happened every time he had a major life crisis. Drinking always hyped up his anger and temper. I hated it and didn't want to be anywhere near him when it happened.

I wasn't sure what to do, but I took a shot anyway. "Hi, Dad. Want me to make a pot of black coffee for us?"

"Morning, Luc." He didn't look up. "Yeah, that'd be nice."

"Right." He still didn't look up. But at least he wasn't blowing off steam.

In the kitchen I brewed the strongest Brazilian roast I could manage. I brought the pot and two mugs into the living room, sat down across from him, and we both sipped on our coffees. Neither of us said a word until I leaned over to pour his second cup.

He started in on me as he looked at me for the first time.

"Still in your pj's. You missed your morning run. Not good. You got to stay in shape, even out of season, if you want to play great basketball."

Really? Even at a time like this, that's all you can think about? "Yeah, I know. I know. But I just couldn't stop thinking about our discussion last night and Major Dallant's comments about me preventing terrorism. To tell you the truth, the whole idea bothers me a lot. Maybe I really could help, but me a 16-year-old kid working for the CIA? It's crazy. Just thinking about it gives me a headache. I'm really confused and don't know what we should do."

"Forget it. You're not going to spy for the CIA or anyone else. You've got a life of academics and sports ahead of you. And you've got to focus on that. Got it?"

Thanks for the encouragement and understanding. Now I feel great. "I know, but I'm torn between sitting back and watching those terrible things happen, seeing innocent people killed and knowing that just maybe I could have helped."

Dad got up from his chair, mug in hand, and started slowly pacing around the room. Even though he was arguing against me, I could see that what was bothering me—the whole terrorist thing—was probably getting to him too. He just didn't want to admit it or deal with it. I was thinking that maybe this meeting with Major Dallant had opened up some old wounds from Iraq, terrorist things he'd rather forget, or at least, bury deep inside.

He continued talking. "It just ain't gonna happen. Let the professionals do their job at the CIA. You want some foreign agent watching you and maybe our family, and ultimately making the decision to take you out if you threaten their plans? I have half a mind to tell Dallant and his CIA friends that I'll use my congressional contacts in Washington to deal with the CIA and tell them that if they don't leave you alone, I'll expose them for coercing a 16-year-old to spy for them and putting him and his family in harm's way with enemy governments."

"How does Mom feel about it? Did you guys discuss it last night?"

"No, we didn't. You saw her reaction to Dallant's ridiculous request. And she's right to feel that way. I don't want to bother her with this and create even more anxiety for her. She has enough in her life to deal with."

He may have been letting me have it, but I liked that he was concerned about Mom.

I relented. "I understand, I guess." But I really didn't understand. I just didn't want to push it any further. And then he opened up—just a little.

"Believe me, I've had experience in these matters—in Iraq, my unit reported directly to those bastards at the CIA. I'm telling you, you don't want any part of them or what they do."

What do you mean you had experience in these matters? I wanted to know exactly what he meant, but I knew if I asked him right then and there, it would have made things worse.

"What about all that money and a free ride for college? I got to admit, I wondered if we should consider going along with them just for six months to get the money."

"Not a chance. Don't be so naive. You really think the CIA would let you go after six months if you can do anywhere near what that Dr. Ross claims you can do? And by the way, I want to talk with you later about this whole Dr. Ross thing and whether he thinks this NDE thing is temporary. And what it is you can do with your so-called superpowers."

Shit, Dad, if you only knew.

We were both quiet for some time. I poured him a third cup. I could see a change coming over him, and it didn't look good. And then he uttered words I'd never heard from him before—ever.

He lowered his voice to nearly a whisper. "Look, Luc, I'm as sympathetic as you are about the terrorist challenge and other issues that Dallant raised. Believe me, my experience with those matters in the Middle East during Desert Storm was eye-opening and devastating. So terrible that I absolutely hate to even think about them. I can't. It's too painful, even now. They're a dark shadow in my life, and dwelling on them makes me sick. But I can tell you this: seeing innocent men, and especially women and children—Jesus, little children—slaughtered like animals, was beyond devastating. It burns my soul to this day. It's not the way we human beings were meant to exist with each other. I still have terrible nightmares about it. I haven't discussed any of it with any-one—not the VA, not even your mother."

"Why not? Maybe it would help."

Raising his voice, he snapped at me. "It's bad enough that one of us has been touched by these atrocities. I won't have it spilling over into our family." His eyes were filled with tears. He lowered his voice again. "I can understand that you want to help, but I can't let you risk your life to do this. And working for the CIA is a fool's game, believe me."

I'd never seen Dad like this. He'd done something I'd never witnessed before—spilling part of his guts out to me. I was grateful and frightened at the same time. I didn't say a word. Dad stopped cold and was quiet for several moments before regaining his composure. I sat there at the table staring blankly into my coffee cup. I didn't want him to know I clearly recognized the emotions he was feeling. Dad prides himself on being a tough guy. Honestly, I didn't know how to act at that moment.

"Luc, for your sake and our family's sake, you're not going to do this. Understand?"

"Yeah, I do."

"And I don't want any more discussion about it with anyone, especially your mother. She has enough to do with fighting the anxiety she deals with every day."

"I agree," was the comment from Mom. Her voice was clear as a bell, right behind us. I turned to see her standing in her white robe at the foot of the stairs.

"Hi, Mom. How long have you been standing there?"

"Long enough."

Although it may have been the end of the discussion for them, it wasn't for me. I was still torn between wanting to help the fight against terrorism and going back to being "normal" Luc Ponti—if he would ever return.

This was no longer only my issue. It was something bigger, much bigger. I was torn about what to do. I had to hang in there until the fog in my mind cleared and I could make the right decision—whatever that was.

BLACKMAIL

Like a magician, he materialized out of nowhere.

"Hey, Luc." Major Dallant came up behind me by complete surprise.

I jumped. "Shit! You scared the hell outta me. What do *you* want?" I pushed my backpack up on my shoulder—my treasure trove of books, lunch, phone, and whatever else I needed to get through the day at school—just in case.

"Easy, my friend. Everything's fine."

Looking at him, you'd think he was a stay-at-home dad. His pearly white teeth so perfect they were a dead giveaway—veneers. His dry-cleaned-too-many-times blue-plaid shirt was another— Burberry. This guy's a consumer junkie. He sure didn't look like CIA. *Oh, right, hiding in plain sight.*

"C'mon, stop sneaking up on me like that, and don't call me your friend. There's no way that'll ever happen. I've got to get to school. I don't have anything to say to you. My parents—"

"Don't worry about your parents. I'm taking care of them. I just want to know what your thinking is after our talk."

I didn't want to speak with him, and I wanted him outta my life. "I spoke with my dad. He's very adamant about this—my mom too. We're not interested."

"I spoke with your mom just after you left this morning."

Minchia! Figures. "So, then, stop bothering me. You got your answer."

"*An* answer, not *the* answer."

"What are you talkin' about?"

"Luc, we need you. This is way beyond your parents and 'good boy, naughty boy'—way past that. You know damn well the impact you can make to save lives. I saw it in your eyes at your home when we spoke."

I hit back. I got up in his face the way I deal with angry blowhards and bullshitters on the court. "Forget about it! I wouldn't do it without them knowing."

He decided to play hardball. "Look, Luc, you have your powers; we have ours. Here's the thing, short and sweet, without getting into all the nitty-gritty. Something terrible, something very unfortunate, happened when your dad and Cap served together during Operation Desert Storm. I'll save you the gory details. They're classified top secret at this time. But I can tell you this—if the media were to get their hands on that information, it would destroy your father's reputation and, for sure, his job and standing in the business community. We absolutely would not want that to happen any more than you would. That's why I'm coming directly to you."

Lecca mia cullo, bastardo![36] With increasing anger, I stared at him, but I didn't say a word. I was shocked and didn't know what to do or say. I thought, *Damn, maybe that's what's been eating Dad all these years. Good God, what had he done?* I didn't like what I was hearing. But finally, I came back at the major. "So, you tryin' to blackmail me?"

"We call it leveraging assets."

I seethed, and felt like bashing in those pretty veneers of his.

---

[36] *Lecca mia cullo, bastardo!*—"Kiss my ass, you bastard!"

He continued his sales job. "It's not like you're not getting anything out of this. It's a perfect and fair quid pro quo."

Before moving to Paly, my friend Billy'd had two years of Latin at St. Francis High School in Mountain View. He taught the guys on the team at least a half-dozen curse words, remarkably close to the Italian ones. I immediately came back with one of my favorites—*bovis stercus!*[37]

The major looked at me puzzled. I responded, "I'm a Latin scholar too!"

"Meaning?"

"Look it up!" Sure, Dad could be a real *stronzo*. I hated the way he treated me. Maybe he deserved this—but maybe there were reasons. Not that they would *excuse* him, but they might help *explain* him.

"Look," Dallant said, "I called it a quid pro quo. *Life* is a quid pro quo. You make choices. Hopefully, the rewards outweigh the pain. But at the end of the day, you're going to have a long list in each column. I don't know which column you'd put your dad in, but on the reward side, you'll be making a lot of money. The college of your choice that accepts your application will be totally free for four years. You'll be serving your country. You'll be saving lives. What else could you ask for?"

He'd hit all the right buttons. I'd wished that my father would disappear more times than I could remember. So why would I save him? Where's the quid pro quo in that? Why was I even hesitating? Those choices Dallant spoke about—yeah, whether he was a dick or not, he was right about them. So, what, I was supposed to be a bigger man than my dad? I was 16, and it was on me to look after him? Sure, I'd look out for Mom, and she'd be better off without him—at least the way he is now—wouldn't she?

"Let me think about this for a while."

Dallant shot back loud, sharp, and clear. "There is no 'a while.' We needed you yesterday."

Minchia. I felt like I was going to puke. I walked over and sat on the curb. Not even a second later, I could feel his presence. He'd

---

[37] *Bovis stercus!*—Bullshit! (Latin)

followed and was standing over me. A long silence—his choke chain tightening around my neck. There was no way out. . . .

"What do you want me to do?"

TWO DAYS LATER, LIKE A STEALTH DRONE, Dallant approached me after basketball practice as I walked down El Camino on my way home.

"Dude, I told you, *Gesu Cristo*, don't sneak up on me like that! It scares the hell outta me."

"I'm sorry. I didn't mean to startle you." He hesitated and then continued. "Look, if we're going to work together, I want us to be on good terms."

"That's not gonna happen. The only reason I'm doing this is because I have no choice."

"Luc, you always have a choice."

"Yeah, right. As a famous poet once said in different words and a different context, 'To destroy my father and family or to not destroy my father and family, that is the question.' Oh, let me guess, you were a test-tube baby, so you can't relate to the father-son thing."

He grinned. Or smirked. It was a look that seemed to say, "Luc, you can be a wiseass all you want, but I've got you by the balls."

"Major Dallant, let's get somethin' straight. I don't like you, or what you do. I understand you presenting this for the greater good, for love of country, but a lot of crazy shit is done in the name of love, especially love of country. Remember Hiroshima and Vietnam? Yeah, I hope I can do some good against what's out there—but you have to ask yourself if the end justifies the means."

Whether he really heard me wasn't clear. He made no comment. He just stared right through me with a poker face, like he was thinking about something he could never share with me. In those brief moments of silence, I thought of a family vacation we'd taken a few years earlier to Oregon's Crater Lake, the deepest lake in the US—1,949 feet. They called it "Deep Blue." It's perfectly clear and blue in color, with visibility far down into the water until it gets so deep that every last beam of light is finally absorbed by the water and all goes dark—light is the enemy of darkness. I felt that Major Dallant was like Crater Lake. He couldn't care less about anything not in his sights.

He finally broke the silence. "I've got something I want to show you. We've set you up with your own highly secure office suite in one of the towers at Palo Alto Square. Tenth floor, so a nice view, and it's only a 15-minute walk from school and from your home. Wanna take a look?"

"Very sure of yourself, aren't you?"

"What do you mean?"

"You just happen to have a fully outfitted secure office ready now, and it's just a few minutes from my school and home. And the tenth floor. Really? There aren't any vacancies in the towers, let alone on the best floor. There must be a waiting list for them a mile long."

"Something opened up."

"Something opened up?"

"Sure, you can find just about anything on Craigslist."

IN A HIGHLY COMPETITIVE REAL ESTATE MARKET, Towers One and Two in Palo Alto Square were among the city's most sought-after addresses. Palo Alto had strict height ordinances for buildings, and these two towers were at the max. Because neighboring cities up and down the peninsula had similar height ordinances, the towers' views commanded top dollar from a sea of ridiculously loaded venture capitalists and others more than willing to pay the price.

As I emerged from the special-access elevator, it was clear that the CIA had taken over the entire tenth floor. Why was it clear to me? Because I had to surrender my phone and go through a full-body scanner. Dallant too. In his world, everyone's a suspect.

After that, I followed close behind him until we reached a doorway.

"This is your office, Luc. Not bad, right?" Dallant said.

I didn't respond. Just gave him one of those who-gives-a-shit looks.

Looking out the floor-to-ceiling windows, I could see nearly all the way to San Francisco to the north and to San Jose to the south. To the east lay the San Francisco Bay, and to the west were the Santa Cruz Mountains.

Dallant was acting like a guy who'd gotten a babe up to his dorm room. "Some view, eh?"

Although I could only guess what a girl might say to a guy like him in that situation, I was fairly sure it would be something like, "No way you're getting lucky tonight." But I kept my sarcasm to myself and went with, "I've seen it before when I've hiked the mountain trails behind Stanford."

The office was large, with lots of natural light from the sur-rounding windows. It was mostly well decorated, with four cushiony armchairs facing each other in a circle at the center of the room, and a separate sitting area near the windows with a plush leather sofa and matching chairs. Not far from a cheesy-looking fake-wood desk and a high-back black-vinyl executive chair stood a large console on which sat a high-tech computer with a bunch of flashing multicolored lights. Even though I'd been born in Silicon Valley, compared to most of my friends, computers weren't my strong suit. I was happy with the Genius Bar at the Apple store in town telling me what to do. "You get that desk on Craigslist too?"

Dallant ignored that one. "The entire floor, walls, top to bot-tom, including the windows and the ceiling, are what we call a Sensitive Compartmented Information Facility, or SCIF, for short. That means no energy signals, high-powered lasers, high-powered microwaves, particle beams, or electromagnetic pulses can penetrate the facility. Physicists call it a Faraday cage. Excep-tions are those specialized signals authorized by the CIA and NSA directorates."

I'd wondered why the windows had a slight tinge of green, which, days later, I noticed you could only see from inside. On the outside, they looked like all the other windows in the building.

"You'll be going through brief training in accordance with the Director of Central Intelligence, Directive 1/14, affectionately known as DCID 1/14. We'll start by indoctrinating you on Person-nel Security Standards and Procedures Governing Eligibility for Access to Sensitive Compartmented Information. Let's go over a few other things. Here's a security card for the elevator to take you up here. Don't lose it. If you do, let me know immediately. We can remotely turn off its operability, rendering it useless."

He handed me the card. Next, he handed me a small booklet.

"What's this?" I asked.

"It's your passbook for a bank account in—"

"Dude, I'm good with mobile banking. I don't need this passbook." I held it out for him to take back.

"Sure, we'll set that up however you want. We'll make periodic electronic deposits for your payments. That'll be $250,000 at $41,666.67 per month over six months—no IRS, no nothing. Since those funds are tax-free, that's more like $300,000 coming to your account. The bank's offshore, so it's not like you have to drive through an ATM in the Seychelles to pull out a 20."

"A Jackson? Ha, I'm guessing you don't go out much."

"I'm married, and a 20 buys my four-year-old a couple of Beanie Boos. So, yeah, I'm good with a Jackson." He didn't wait for my apology, just changed the subject. "One thing we have some concern about is how you'll deal with certain foreign languages."

Trying to be a tad cooperative, I told him, "As my powers have evolved, I've found that I can translate foreign languages, even ones I've never studied. I've only tried German and French. In fact, if it weren't for my folks getting a note from my French teacher for unexcused absences, I wouldn't have to go to class anymore. They teach Mandarin at Paly. If you like, I could give it a shot and see what happens."

"That would be great. Let me know."

Major Dallant suddenly had one of those ear-to-ear smiles on his face. "C'mon, there's someone I'd like you to meet."

As we entered what looked like a conference room, I saw a tall woman with her back to us staring out the window. She had long jet-black hair, and was wearing a tight mauve-colored blouse and an equally tight lavender skirt. No panty lines showing—Bella would have approved.

"Excuse me, Tamara," Dallant said, "this is the young man Dr. Ross told you about."

She turned to face us. "Thanks, John."

Not that I was into older chicks, but if I were, I gotta say her getup finished off with black-suede stiletto heels made her look really hot.

She smiled as she walked toward me with all the finesse of a runway model. She extended her hand to greet me, and her grip was strong, mine not so much. But like all those games and our practices in the gym, I made defensive adjustments and tried to match her grip. But, forget it—she'd already blown past me for the dunk, and hung on the rim.

"So, you're Luc Ponti. I'm pleased to finally meet you. My name is Tamara Carlin, director of the CIA's Covert Intelligence Unit. Dr. Ross and Major Dallant have told me a lot of good things about you."

In basketball jive, I felt like she'd given me a head fake and I'd fallen for it, leaving her to take an open jump shot. I was burned on the first two possessions. "Hi. Uh, I didn't know . . . I mean, especially someone who looks like . . . Right, yeah, nice to meet you." I felt she could mop the floor with every minute of my 16 years of experience with girls. I kept staring at her, trying not to look in the wrong places, but . . . she was amazing! I didn't know lady spies could be so wow—except maybe that chick in the *Red Sparrow* movie—Jennifer Lawrence.

In a soft but no-nonsense voice, Tamara said, "C'mon over here, Luc. Let's sit down and talk." We walked over to the big table in the center of the room and sat—she and Dallant next to each other across the table from me. She started, "Did anyone ever tell you you're the spitting image of a young Michael Corleone in *The Godfather*?"

"I've heard it more times than I can count. Thank you."

"It's nice you appreciate who he was."

"Hard not to. He's a legend in our house—although, gotta say, I never saw the movie."

"That's too bad. It's a great film."

Her smile was refreshing while it lasted, which wasn't long. "Luc, I want to tell you that, together, we're going to be taking some huge steps in the way we gather intelligence. I want to be sure you clearly understand how we're going to run this operation."

"Like, don't you need to check me out or something before you tell me all this stuff? How do you know I'm not going to tell somebody? You know, like the KGB or something."

"That's cute. The KGB is dead. Still famous, but still dead. It fell with the collapse of the communist Soviet Union on December 25, 1991. Now, the Russians have what they call the SVR RF, but I get your point. The short answer is, we already did check you out, and you've been cleared for TS/SCI. Oh, I forgot, you're not familiar with our spook lingo yet. You've been cleared for Top Secret/Sensitive Compartmented Information with your access siloed on a need-to-know basis."

"And what about the second part?"

"The second part?"

"Yeah, that I'll keep this secret."

Dallant jumped in. "Luc, that's under the leveraging-assets discussion we had the other day. Remember?"

I sat there quietly. No need to say it out loud—my family and I are the risk assets that guarantee I'll do everything in my power to maintain secrecy. Our silence was as good as signatures on a contract. We had a deal.

Tamara added, "If it helps, I had a troubled relationship with my dad too."

"Why would that help?"

"So that you might understand leverages can be fickle, and in our business, we don't do fickle. What I'm saying is, we'll be watching you."

"Spies spying on spies. Great."

"It's called risk management. There's a risk with you, with John, with everyone."

"Even you?" I asked.

"Even me. We operate in a world of analyzing trade-offs and constantly adjusting acceptable levels of risk."

"Let me guess, I'm worth the trade-off."

"For the time being."

Tamara continued. "This office will be your base for all operations. You'll usually be working alone up here. Communications will be through this office, and you'll have a specially encrypted phone."

"This is really important," I said. "What kind of phone is it, 'cause I've got all my music saved on my iPhone. It better not be one of those skanky flip jobs."

She laughed. "It's a crypto-iPhone—created specifically by Apple, exclusively for the CIA and NSA—and we'll transfer your music and pictures for you." She got up and walked over to a safe implanted in the wall beside a desk. Her right handprint followed by a retina scan let her in. A moment later she was back at the table.

"Here. Take the phone. It's yours. You'll notice that it looks just like a regular iPhone—in fact, exactly like yours, color and all—we don't want anyone asking you questions. The difference is what's inside. It transmits through satellites, which means the planet is your Wi-Fi hotspot. If you lose it, you need to let us know immediately—there's a minute explosive charge in it that we'll detonate to destroy its contents."

"Swell, and I'll be carrying this in my pocket?"

"Not to worry. It's never discharged accidentally in the past."

"That's really comforting. All right—I guess."

"Next up . . . I'll personally be your handler."

That was hot. My smile started to spill out, but I quickly got it back in. Or so I thought.

Tamara stopped. She was more perceptive than I'd realized. "John, if I forget that we're working with a teenage boy with raging hormones, please be sure to remind me." Dallant laughed. Tamara went on. "Luc, instead of your handler, you can think of me as your case officer. I'll be your sole contact, both internally and externally, with other agencies. Your identity, the information you pass, the communication pattern, will all be absolutely shielded. In general, here's how things will work: You'll be assigned to do a remote viewing of a specific target. When you're finished, you'll write up a brief report and send it to me."

"What if I'm busy? What if I'm in school? Or on a date?"

A tiny bit of her laugh spilled out. "How many dates do you go on?"

"That's not the point. It's the principle."

"Okay." She smiled. "I'm your priority—always, no exceptions. So make up an excuse to leave whatever it is you're doing. The semester is almost over, so you'll be free for the summer. To be perfectly clear, you can never, and I mean never, disclose any of this to anyone else—not your parents, not your friends, no one. It could have serious consequences for us—and especially for you. Got it?" I hesitated for a few seconds and then nodded my head in agreement.

Okay, so maybe I was into older chicks and just didn't know it, especially women like her. Or maybe I wasn't, and she was some kind of special exception. I tried to switch from staring at her breasts to getting my head back in the game, like Coach Ralston always preached. But by the time I did, the clock had run out. We must have won, though, even with me spacing out, because she was all unicorns and rainbows when Dallant and I left. Later, I'd learn that "happy" in covert operations was a disguise with as much versatility as the color black in fashion.

Tamara walked Dallant and me to the elevator, and we said our goodbyes. She stepped back from the elevator door and said nothing, just stared at me with the slightest of smiles. The doors closed, but at the very last second, she winked at me, and she was gone. I know my stare was fixed on her—all over her. Shit, I hoped I wasn't drooling.

In the elevator, Dallant commented, "She's quite a lady."

"Right. I'll say." For once, I had to agree with him.

He added, "I'm not speaking just about her looks. She graduated at the top of her class at Harvard Law School; worked for five years all over the Middle East as a field agent; and speaks, reads, and writes more than eight languages, including Russian, Mandarin, Arabic, and Hebrew."

I was impressed—beauty and intelligence in the same package. "That's amazing."

"You bet. And by the way, she holds the record in our department for the best marksmanship with a service revolver. It saved her life several times in the Middle East."

You didn't have to be Sherlock Holmes to see that I was impressed.

BEGINNINGS

D<small>AD HAD HARPED ON ME MY WHOLE LIFE</small> that there'd be a time when I'd need to go from being a boy to a man, and it would probably be when I'd least expect it, so I shouldn't wait for fate to test me. He said I should make myself as ready as I could, as fast as I could.

My first memory of that kind of conversation, believe it or not, was when I was six years old. "Son," he'd said, "don't look for things to be easy. Use this time now while you're under my roof to learn that life is hard."

We were in the backyard, and Dad was teaching me how to repair sections of a wooden fence that was falling over. He had a step stool set up for me so that I stood eye level with the boards he'd positioned to reinforce the fence. His hammer drove steel nails into each plank with precision and efficiency, each stroke a bull's-eye.

Although this philosophy at that early age flew right over my head, like most young boys, I admired my father and wanted to be just like him, to hammer hard like he did. As I got older, though, I unfortunately saw that same trait in how he shored up parts of himself that were falling down. He boarded up his memories of Iraq, not with nails into wooden planks, but with rage into regret and back again into rage. He went through the same process over and over again, strike after strike, into what eventually became wooden relationships. God knows, he'd hammered me so hard, I felt like I was on the other side of that fence.

I thought of this during the three weeks of CIA training I went through—the seriousness of what I was involved in, the lives at stake, the consequences of me losing my focus and smashing my thumb with a virtual hammer. In that sense, I guess Dad was right. As much as I hated to admit it, he knew what he was talking about when he said that going from a boy to a man probably wouldn't be on my schedule.

Despite my new, enhanced learning capabilities, the month of May was a killer for me. In addition to studying for finals and attending off-season practices, I spent three weeks, five nights a week, locked in my room until the wee hours of the morning, viewing CIA encrypted podcasts and numerous encrypted Face-Time interviews with Major Dallant as he schooled me on the material necessary for me to finalize my security clearance. I was glad when it was over.

The day after I finished my CIA secrecy and security training, it was a Wednesday. I was up in my bedroom completing a paper for English lit on Kurt Vonnegut's *Slaughterhouse Five* when my phone lit up with a notification time stamped 9:33 P.M. Following the security procedures I'd just learned, I unlocked an encrypted message: "Office, now!" Encrypted and cryptic: Tamara needed me.

I put on my jacket, remembered that I owed Bella a text, so shot that out to her, then tried to quietly walk downstairs and out the front door. I saw Mom, her back to me, snuggled in one of the plush chairs in our living room, reading her students' papers. Just as I opened the front door, I heard her ask, "Where are you going so late on a school night? Don't you have finals coming up soon?"

The Agency had given me what they called a "light cover"—I was to be a normal kid in high school with a girlfriend I was thinking of breaking up with, so I needed time to sort things out with her, if they *could* be sorted out. Also, I'd allegedly gotten a summer internship at a "virtual" high-tech company called Amped. I went along with their drama.

"Oh, hi, Mom. Didn't see you. Thought I'd go for a walk over to the home of this girl, Jennifer, in my English lit class, and try to talk some stuff through. We've been having a bit of a tough time."

"Oh, is this a new one?"

"Kinda, well, not really. Anyway . . ."

"I've always liked Bella. She's been so good to you—for years."

"Yeah, right, but she's like my best friend." What I didn't say was that I had mixed feelings about Bella. On the one hand, she was so special to me. On the other, I kept thinking about us going our separate ways in another year when we went off to college—Bella on her long road through medical school—and me in basketball, maybe even eventually to the pros. I couldn't afford to be tied down to any one girl—at least that's what I thought at the time.

"I don't know. If I were you, I'd seriously consider Bella."

"Really? Then *you* should date her."

"Don't get smart with me, young man. I'll see you in the morning."

"G'night, Mom. Love you."

"Love you too—Mr. Wise Guy."

"Hmph."

AFTER-HOURS ACCESS TO TOWER ONE was through a side entrance. The swipe card to get in seemed so elementary, but the place was deserted, so maybe there wasn't much need for stricter security protocols. All those legendary hundred-hour workweeks by geniuses in tech start-ups didn't seem to apply to Tower One. I guessed that the property manager didn't need to take chances on those "ramen profitables"—that is, entrepreneurs making money and paying their bills, but with nothing much left for food other than cheap instant ramen noodles—even though they had investment angels waiting in line.

I took a rocket ride up in the elevator to the tenth floor and into my office. Then, through a series of security protocols: a blinking red light turned green, and there it was—my first assignment:

Luc,

Let's get started and see what you can produce for us. Your remote-viewing target is at GPS coordinates latitude 37.860429, longitude 112.521769. This in the vicinity of Taiyuan University of Technology Yingxi Campus in northern China. We believe there is an ICBM facility called Base 25 somewhere near there. Intel reports they've got DA-5A ICBMs with a range of 13,000 kilometers. Those would be in violation of the International Nuclear Non-Proliferation Treaty (NPT). See if you can get a sense of what's going on there. Let me know via protocols, and then I'll either call you, or alternatively, we can arrange a crypto-video conference.

Tamara

I reread her message a second time. Paced back and forth a few times, went to the bathroom and splashed cold water on my face, came back and ate some of the candy sitting on an end table beside the leather couch, downed a few cups of water from the water cooler in the hallway, then back into my office, with a deep inhale and an even deeper exhale, before finally sitting on the couch. Another inhale and exhale, then I laid down, stared at the GPS coordinates again, and closed my eyes.

About ten seconds later, my remote-viewing mind's eye kicked in, and I saw my "self" leaving my body and rapidly rising through the ceiling and high into the sky. In what seemed like an instant, I was over a large body of water—GPS coordinates latitude 38.082288, longitude 111.884557—the Fenhe Reservoir in Loufan, China. Where this ID information was coming from was a mystery to me. The only China-related stats I knew had to do with NBA Hall of Famer Yao Ming for his eight seasons with the Houston Rockets. Maybe Dr. Ross was right, after all, about my brain or mind or consciousness or whatever he said was evolving into something beyond a supercomputer.

I refocused on the original coordinates that Tamara had given me, and in seconds was hovering over Taiyuan University of Technology, Yingxi Campus. I flew around looking for Base 25, but had no luck, so I decided to expand my search. My intuition told me to go east: over Qianfeng N Road and Heping Road, then north to 37.865537 latitude, 112.507789 longitude, above 玉门河公园, Shanwai Fine Arts to my left and Washan Grilled Fish to my right, farther east to 37.879719, 112.493744, and due north, sharp to the west to Shanxi Hua Dunchunmi Fuel Tiaopei Center, north over 37.901961, 112.498638, farther north to 37.905195, 112.497788 . . . wait. Go back.

The GPS coordinates were obvious to me, the translation from Chinese to English was seamless, and an encyclopedic knowledge was mine for the asking—a photographic memory equivalent to a high-resolution camera that could take photos and store them in amazing detail for future recall. Nestled between the Dongshe and Huifeng Residential Districts, and just a short drive to the G2001 highway, was a drab-looking manufacturing plant. Latitude 37.901961, longitude 112.498638: 太原水泥製品廠, the Taiyuan Cement Factory. Tall, high-voltage electrical fences surrounded a nondescript perimeter on both sides of the barrier. Farther inside, though, concealed by huge sand piles, machinery, and a graveyard of scraps and rusting equipment, military personnel manned artillery posts, including surface-to-air missiles. And as I looked closer, hidden in camouflage, there were more posted on the factory rooftops.

I descended, self-conscious about my presence within the plant until I could reassure myself that no one could, in fact, see, hear, feel, or in any way sense that I was there—mostly this was only after I'd stood face-to-face with soldiers toting QBZ-95-1 assault rifles. I felt pulled toward a huge steel door. It must have been 75 feet wide and 50 feet high—like an entrance to an airplane hangar. I glided through it, registering it to be three-feet-thick solid steel.

On the other side of the door was a huge freight elevator. I floated down its shaft until I reached the bottom, some 1,500 feet below the surface. I'd learned in my recent security briefings that the Chinese are world renowned for their extensive tunneling throughout China, a safe harbor from a nuclear attack.

Exiting, I poured into an underground complex teeming with military personnel. An enormous missile silo dominated the expanse. Using my encyclopedic access, I identified the bunker as one designed by Qian Qihu, the same man responsible for the subterranean training grounds the Chinese used in their drills to initiate or retaliate from in the event of a catastrophic, hostile nuclear threat. I followed a set of railway tracks into a well-lit tunnel, about 50 feet in diameter, which opened into another cavern.

I stopped. There it was. Code-named the Great Wall, it was the next generation of China's DF-5B ICBM, carefully docked with electronic readouts continuously updating, like a pregnant woman counting the time between contractions when preparing herself to give birth. Scanning the adjacent staging area, I found the control room. Five Chinese soldiers, each as exacting as the digital screens they monitored, checked for conformities and anomalies within the weapon's system—the data spit out in real time second after second in a labyrinth of tests, evaluations, simulations, and contingencies. Behind them, on a raised platform, was a glass-encased booth—more like a fishbowl—from which the officer in charge could observe and command the control room. I pierced his aquarium and looked over his shoulder as he focused his attention on schematics of The Great Wall's construction.

I was a sponge soaking up everything I could see until the moment I sensed that it was time to leave. With that thought, I was back in the present moment in Palo Alto Square, Tower One, tenth floor. In my travels there and back, I discovered another feature about my remote viewing: If I told myself I was going to fly to China, I could do so at various speeds under my control and observe the journey in process. However, if I told myself to go immediately, I would be transported instantaneously. Hell, I'm faster than the speed of light! Now that's not just cool, it's epic.

Was I really faster than the speed of light? No—Einstein has never been proven wrong. But then again, his Special Theory of Relativity deals with light, which I knew from my physics course was electromagnetic energy. Maybe consciousness, spirit, or whatever it is that flies through space has its own relativity, its own energy, its own laws of physics, and can move instantaneously, much faster than light speed. Whatever. Anyway, violating Einstein's relativity or not, it was still epic.

My debrief for Tamara, including detailed digital art, just flowed out of me. It helped that I'd taken a computer graphics course during my sophomore year. It was like I was in the zone, like in our last game against Miramonte when I had a triple double: 28 points, 11 rebounds, 12 assists. I was on fire.

When I got home, Mom was still in the living room reading papers, as if she hadn't moved.

"Hon? That was quick. I thought you'd be out for a while."

I hadn't even checked the time. I glanced at my phone—10:22 P.M. I'd gone to China and back, had written my debrief, and sent it to Tamara in 49 minutes.

THE NEXT MORNING, I was awakened with a start at 4:30 A.M. My cryptographic phone was vibrating next to my bed. I thought Major Dallant had said that Tamara would only communicate via text messages on my cell phone. *And what in the world does she want at this early hour?*

Clearing my throat, I did my best to speak clearly. "Hi, Tamara."

"Hello, Luc. Sorry to call so early. I needed to speak with you for a few minutes before I go into an all-day meeting."

"I thought Major Dallant said mainly text messages by cell phone."

"Generally, that's correct, but your phone has been programmed with top-secret cryptography, and I wanted to speak with you directly and immediately. Today, I don't have time for text exchanges."

"Couldn't it wait a couple of hours? It's 4:30 in the morning here."

"Sorry about that."

"Listen, Tamara, before we start, I thought I was going to work on antiterrorist projects and help prevent terrorist attacks. What's with all this ICBM stuff?"

"I just want you to get your feet wet on this and see how things go before we dive into the more challenging antiterrorism projects. Once you get a sense of how things work, I think you'll feel more comfortable tackling the terrorism issues. Got it?"

"Yeah, right." What could I say? At the time, I had no idea of Tamara's real agenda.

She seemed quite excited. "I went through everything you sent me last evening, and it's unbelievable!"

"What do you mean?"

"Well, for starters, you may not have located Base 25, but you found something much more important. First off, the presence of that missile silo is in direct violation of the International Nuclear Non-Proliferation Treaty, the NPT. The UN will not be happy about that. You also identified the precise GPS location of the silo base to seven-decimal-places accuracy. Excellent! We had weak intel that there was a missile silo somewhere in that area, but no concrete proof. Now, thanks to you, we have it."

I was beginning to feel important. I looked forward to my antiterrorist work. "Did you understand my drawings? I did pretty well in my computer art-and-design course at school, so I think they should be accurate."

"They're perfectly clear. That's the reason I'm calling. That may be the biggest prize of all! I wanted to check in with you before my meeting. So, you're sure those drawings are accurate?"

"Yeah, they are. I discovered that I could take mental photos, which I can recall at any time, so when I wrote up my report at the office, I sketched to scale exactly what I saw."

"Fantastic. You're amazing!"

Whoa! That felt good! I guess I'm gaining in importance.

"If they're anywhere close to correct, China is not only in flagrant violation of the NPL, but your drawings indicate the presence of a missile powered by a nuclear engine, something China has been working on since the 1980s—everyone thought unsuccessfully. Nuclear engines essentially give the missile infinite range, but for a number of incredibly challenging technical and safety reasons, no one has ever made a workable system before."

"Isn't that what Putin was bragging about recently in the news—that Russia had succeeded in developing a nuclear-powered missile with a range of anywhere on the planet?" I asked.

"Yes, but most of our experts believe he was overstating his case. In fact, just recently, there was a fatal explosion in Siberia where the Russians were testing one of their nuclear-powered missiles. Our intelligence satellites picked up radiation dispersion for a radius of several miles. They're nowhere near a safe operating system. Also, of great importance, your drawings indicate that the Chinese missile is equipped with 20–24 MIRVs."

"What in the world is a MIRV?"

"That stands for multiple-independently-targetable-reentry-vehicle. They are miniature ballistic missiles contained within the primary warhead, each with payloads containing several nuclear warheads, and each capable of being aimed and programmed to hit one of a group of targets. Within 30 minutes of launch of the parent missile from that site, it could conceivably take out several major cities in Europe, Asia, or the US."

"Oh my God.

"Oh my God is right. I'm to discuss this material today with Anthony Stefano, director of the CIA. He'll probably give the information to the secretary of state, who will contact the United Nations to call a special meeting of the UN Security Council. The Chinese will be caught with their pants down, so to speak. You have no idea how important this information is."

I thought, *Who would have guessed that a 16-year-old from Palo Alto could do something that all the US intelligence resources were unable to do?* I was beginning to pat myself on the back—a little too hard—and then it really sank in. Important, sure. But if I were the Chinese, I'd be deeply concerned, and I'd want to know how the US had uncovered this information in such detailed accuracy—GPS coordinates to seven decimal places? I imagined that the Chinese would wonder if they had a traitor among them, or if the Americans had developed a much-improved "intelligence device." If they concluded the latter, that wouldn't be good news for me. *Minchia!* Maybe Dad was right.

Chapter
Seventeen

CAUGHT

TAMARA HADN'T CONTACTED ME FOR SEVERAL DAYS. I was relieved to have had some downtime. Okay, I'll admit it. My ego had totally soaked up our last discussion, given the way she'd praised me for providing detailed information after my remote viewing in China. She now had enough intelligence to corroborate prior intel. According to her, now the CIA could bring the matter to the attention of higher-ups, who would confront the UN National Security Council with this violation of the International Nuclear Non-Proliferation Treaty. Maybe, as Major Dallant had promised, I could finally move on to an antiterrorist project.

As I continued to stroke my ego, I was convinced I'd made two important discoveries for the United States. The first was that The Great Wall missile system was powered by a nuclear engine, something the Chinese had started working on in the 1980s, but was widely thought to have been hopelessly unsuccessful and thus abandoned. Reports of their discontinuing their nuclear-powered missile strategy were obviously dead wrong. With their efforts still alive and well, the fact that they'd successfully harnessed this form of power presented the terrifying threat of a missile with essentially infinite flight range. No place on Earth was safe.

My second discovery was that The Great Wall was equipped with 20 to 24 MIRVs, each programmable to accurately hit individual targets. As Tamara had explained, this meant that within 30 minutes of launch, one missile with its MIRVs could simultaneously take out several major cities in the US, Europe, Asia, or elsewhere else on the planet. I thought, *Not bad for my first flight—but good God, also very, very scary.*

Although it was great to have the downtime, I found myself increasingly thinking about Tamara. I had to admit that I was intrigued—out of my league, but still fascinated. She was a CIA agent, so the danger and intrigue inherent in her job were real turn-ons for me. Beautiful—no explanation needed. Brilliant—another plus. Accomplished and competitive—a big wow. Yes, she was quite a woman.

But then there was my regular "Clark Kent" life. Sure, Bella was also intriguing—in my league, but still intriguing, which was significant since I usually only wanted what I couldn't have. Talking to her about personal stuff was easy. She was smart and always had good input. And more than any other person in the world, except maybe Mom, she really cared about me.

But now, that would be near-impossible. I couldn't put her life at risk. I wouldn't do that to her. She was my best friend, practically my sister, I guess—which really messed with my head when my thoughts pointed in any direction more than that—and that was happening a little too much lately. But I wasn't gonna let that happen, especially now. We both had a lot of life in front of us, and no way was I gonna mess up hers—or mine, for that matter.

This break from Tamara gave me time to think and reconnect with Bella. I wanted to help her with any concerns she had about me, for both our sakes. It wouldn't be easy—she was so damn hardheaded, and I couldn't tell her everything. Once she got something in her mind that she was convinced was the right thing to do, there was no way in hell anyone could stop her. If I said too much to her, I was afraid she might do or say something we'd both regret.

EARLIER IN THE DAY, Bella had caught me in the back corner of the school cafeteria as I was finishing lunch at the jock table with some of the guys on the team. She asked if we could get together after basketball practice. I thought it might be a good opportunity to straighten things out with her.

We met in front of school, crossed El Camino, and started to walk through the park, which is part of the Stanford campus. It's not your usual kind of park—there were acres upon acres of land filled with what I've heard are various species of eucalyptus trees that date back to the late 19th century when Leland Stanford founded the university.

As we entered the park, I knew she had something heavy on her mind. Her fiery personality always made it a challenge for her to hold back on things that bothered her. We sat on the first park bench we came to, under the dense shade and the strong aroma of a giant eucalyptus. Sitting there was like being inside one of those inhalers used to clear your nasal passages.

On the way there, I must have been too distracted by my own concerns, because as she sat there gathering her thoughts, I only then realized how great she looked—high-heeled brown-leather boots, fitted white jeans, and a green silk blouse with a red floral print that made her green eyes and red hair more stunning than usual. But my admiring thoughts were short-lived.

"Luc, we've always been honest with each other, right?"

"Absolutely!"

"Well, I need to speak with you. It's been bothering the hell outta me. I spoke to my mom, and she said I should talk it out with you. Okay, so here goes." She took a breath, not too deep, but not too shallow either. "Why have you been ghosting me? I've waited for you after basketball practice—I know you've seen me there because I see you look and then look away. I've called your cell and left messages. Like, nothing comes back. Sorry, okay, a couple of times you've DM'd me something quick like 'Neat,' or you liked a few of my pics."

As usual when she was impassioned, her voice started to slowly rise in volume and pitch. "Then, when I pass you in the hall, you don't have time for me. Your mind is somewhere else. What's going on? I heard a rumor about you and Chelsea Carr. Is that it? Did I do something to piss you off?"

"Chelsea Carr? Seriously? No, nothing's going on with her, or with anyone else for that matter, or you'd know about it. As far as the other stuff, I've just been busy with a lot of things and maybe kinda distracted. I don't know what else to say. Homework, basketball. . . . Oh, did I tell you I got an internship?" I thought that might calm her down.

"No, you didn't tell me."

"It's neat. It's an online sports marketing company named Amped, and it's like a high-tech ad agency or event-planning thing with athletes."

"Wow, that's great. Do you get paid?"

"That'd be sweet, but no, just course credit."

"Still good, but a little extra money would be nice. I know *I* could use it."

She went silent and dropped her head, staring at the ground. "Hey, *bella regazza*, are you all right?"

"Yeah, just that—"

"Just what?" We sometimes played this cat-and-mouse thing. She'd look at me, and then I'd look away. I'd look at her, and *she'd* look away. It was like the stars had to be perfectly aligned for us to be looking each other in the eyes at the same time.

"Just thought I'd treat you to lunch next weekend or something. Maybe that would make things right with us."

"Oh, Bella, you don't have to do that."

"I know I don't have to. I *want* to. You've been my best friend, like forever. If there's something I can do to help you deal with the crazy stuff you're going through, well . . ."

"I'm good. Really. Don't worry."

"I'm scared about our friendship slipping away."

"Hey, come on, I really like you. We've always been there for each other. You're the only one I can completely trust. You know I've always been honest with you."

"Always honest with me? C'mon."

"I have."

"How about last Friday night?"

"What about it?"

"So, you remember I told you that last Friday was my parents' 20th wedding anniversary?"

"Yeah, right."

"Well, I saved up enough to take them to a movie and dessert at their favorite restaurant."

"That's great."

"We saw Pedro Almodóvar's film *All About My Mother*." She paused, waiting for me to jump in, but I missed the cue.

"He's one of their favorite Spanish filmmakers. They love to see his films whenever they're showing at any of the local arts theaters." Another pause, another missed cue.

"We went to the 8:00 P.M. show at CinéArts in Palo Alto Square." A third pause. This one caught my attention, but I didn't flinch.

"I'm guessing you guys liked it?"

"Very much. All hour and 41 minutes of it. Coincidentally— that is, if you believe in coincidences—when we came out of the theater . . . I mean, what are the odds, there was a text from you saying you were out with the guys."

"Yeah, that's pretty much how my weekends go. So?"

"Your text was at 9:34."

"Now you're checking up on me?"

"No, just questioning you saying that you're always honest with me."

"Ask Scotty. Ask Mike Zielinski."

"Your jock friends? Why? So they can get more ammunition for all the crap they say behind my back? Luc, I'm not the prettiest, the smartest, or the whateverist, but I'm not the dumbest either. Your buddies slice and dice girls' reputations like—"

"*I* don't!"

"Your silence does your talking for you!"

Like, right now when I don't have anything to say?

"Like your silence right now! I was getting ready to write you back. Instagram showed it was 9:45. Suddenly, my mom said, "Hey, isn't that Luc?" You'd just run across El Camino toward the towers. I yelled to you, but apparently you didn't hear me. I told my parents to go ahead to Tamarine's for dessert and I'd meet them there after I caught up with you. I was going to ask if you wanted to join us."

Her voice trailed off. I knew Bella well enough to know that her fire can burn for only so long before it becomes cinders. "At first, I thought you and your friends were just messing around, that they were chasing you, or you were chasing them. And then I saw you run around to the side of one of the Palo Alto towers, I think that's the one they call Tower One, and by the time I got around the corner, I saw a side door swinging closed. It was locked. I must have just missed you by seconds. So I went around to the front and looked through the glass.

"The lobby was deserted, except for, guess what? I saw you just about to enter one of the elevators. I was stunned and couldn't do a thing. In you went. I was scared. I couldn't figure out what you were doing there and why you'd lied to me about it. I was really pissed. When I got to Tamarine's, my parents could see I was upset. It was obvious it was about you, but all they said and ever say is to talk to you about it."

Is silence lying? I asked myself.

"So that's it?" she cried. "That's it?"

I'd heard it said that silence is complicity.

"Say something, goddammit!"

My silence stoked the cinders, and her flames leaped high again. "Luc Ponti, you're a bastard! Do you hear me? And I hate what you're becoming!" She stood up, started to walk away, then stopped for a second and turned.

"I'm sorry," I said weakly, but my apology felt like a garden hose against a forest fire.

She scorched me: "Don't be. I trusted you. That's on me."

SHOCK TO
THE SYSTEM

MONDAY WAS A SCHOOL HOLIDAY. After basketball practice and finishing my math and biology homework, I texted Bella and begged her to meet with me. I'd never realized how important her counsel—okay, I get it, *she*—was to me. She was so pissed and angry from our last discussion, she barely agreed to get together.

I was hoping I could somehow straighten things out and make her understand my concerns and my point of view. But how would I do that without telling her what I couldn't tell her? I didn't even try to answer that question. I just needed to be with her. I couldn't lose her.

I biked over to her house. Her mom made us a Spanish omelet and some Colombian waffles for lunch. For privacy and quiet time, we decided to go for a walk in the Ravenswood Open Space Preserve about a mile from Bella's home. We took our bikes to the beginning of the Bay Trail, just off Bay Road, locked them to a post, and started our walk. The trail is in the marshlands that form the beginning of San Francisco Bay. The hike is on flat land and not particularly beautiful, but it's populated with lots of birds of various species. But for today, the most important thing was that it was close to Bella's home.

As we walked the trail, Bella didn't say a word. I hadn't slept all weekend. I was like a zombie. I could barely think. I finally pumped up some steam.

"Hey, *bella donna,*[38] I know you're pissed because you saw me go into the tower at Palo Alto Square, and yes, I lied to you about it. But, believe me, there's a good reason for it. You've got to trust me. I don't want you to get hurt."

Bella is very smart and is better than anyone I know at connecting the dots. In my exhaustion, I wasn't thinking straight.

"Luc . . . be straight with me. Is that tower business somehow connected with all your CIA shit?"

I was stuck. I didn't know what to say. I hesitated for a long time. I wanted to say no, but that wouldn't be the end of it. That I knew, even in my state of exhaustion.

She wouldn't stop pushing. "Well?"

"*Minchia*, Bella! Yes, but I can't say another thing."

"Look, you know you can trust me to the grave. I've always been here for you, and I keep all that you tell me locked inside—no matter what, and I mean *no matter what!*"

To the grave, no matter what. . . . Oh, Bella please let it go!

But she didn't. Tamara better hope the Chinese never catch me and torture me. I caved. In a moment of weakness, maybe stupidity, I told her everything. It all came gushing out. I guess I wanted someone I could trust to speak with, to know what was happening in my crazy life. I told her about my meeting with Tamara and that the office in the Palo Alto Square tower was created by the CIA as my base of operations for them. I told her I was reluctantly working for them because they had something very serious on my dad that happened during his time in Iraq, and if they decided to make it public, it would destroy him and our family. And finally, I shared my remote viewing in China and what I'd found.

Bella was more than distressed. "Oh my God, Luc, that's insane—blackmailing you for your dad's situation in Iraq, illegal

---

[38] *Bella donna*—"Beautiful woman."

nuclear missiles in China, your own personal security—it's beyond insane. You've got to get help. Tell your parents, dammit! Tell them tonight!"

I nearly screamed at her. "No way—this is one of the reasons I didn't want to tell you—the other and most important reason is to protect you from the CIA. Who knows what the hell those *bastardi pazzi* would do to you if they found out what I just told you? Bella, you can't say a word to anyone! Do you understand? Promise me you won't! I may have already put your life and mine on the line. It could be worse! Do you know what would happen if my loose-cannon dad got in the middle of all this and tried to retaliate?"

"Look, I won't say a word, but you've got to. What you're doing is crazy and dangerous!"

She was shaking. I had to calm her down. "I'll think about what you've said. I know you're probably right. But right now, I don't want either of us to say anything to anyone. I need to think this through—can't make a rash decision. Is that clear?"

"Yeah, it's real clear, but I'm not going to let this go. I don't like what you're doing and what's happening to you—to us."

I wanted to move her away from this conversation. "We'll talk more about this, but not now. Just, please, give me some space."

She softened, just a little. "Okay, but please, let's not let this go too long and too far." She gathered her thoughts again and said, "There's one thing I've been thinking about, and maybe it'll help you understand what's happened to you and what you can do about it."

"What's that?"

"You probably know that my parents sometimes go to the Buddhist temple over on Louis Road. They're not Buddhists— still devout Catholics—but they like to attend some of the lectures there."

"Yeah, so?"

"When you talked to your mom and me at our dinner together, you mentioned that Dr. Ross said these powers you have likely come from a higher level of consciousness. Guess what? The speaker next week is a guy named Pham Tuan—Mom said he's a well-known Vietnamese Buddhist scholar and a monk—and he's giving a lecture on consciousness. Wanna go? My mom and dad know Reverend Daikan, who runs the temple. I'll bet they could get him to introduce you to the speaker. Maybe you could get an idea from another point of view about consciousness and its effects on what's happening to you. What do you think?"

"Look, I appreciate you wanna help, but at this point, I'm not gonna tell my parents, and I certainly don't want to speak with this Buddhist dude or Dr. Ross . . . or anyone. Okay? It's bad enough I unloaded on you." *Minchia!* Now I was getting pissed, and it wasn't even her fault. I knew she wanted to help. I just had to think. I needed some time to clear my mind.

I had just stupidly spilled my guts about the CIA. Now, in addition to my family's safety, I had to worry about Bella's as well—what was I thinking? I was beginning to be concerned she might tell my parents without asking me, thinking she was help-ing—except I knew that Bella was much more trustworthy on a promise than I was. She'd never broken one and had never lied to me—no matter what.

There was one good thing in the air, though. Tamara hadn't contacted me for several days, so maybe my work with the CIA was winding down, at least for the foreseeable future. Wish-ful thinking.

Bella softened her approach. "Okay, fine. I can understand why you don't wanna tell your parents. Maybe if you just spoke in strict confidence to Dr. Ross and Pham Tuan, you might learn something helpful and feel better about the way things are going. Maybe there *is* an end in sight."

Just then I looked at my watch. "Oh, shit! It's five o'clock already, and I promised Mom I'd be home for dinner. My dad will be back from his business trip, and she's planned a family dinner. We should head back. He'll be pissed as all hell if I'm late. You know what he's like. When he gets back from a business trip, it's like a command performance. Everyone has to look sharp and pre-tend we're thrilled that he's home."

As we approached the trail head, we saw two guys—tattooed, muscle-bound, upper-teens wise guys dressed in tight, ragged Levis and sleeveless white T-shirts—working on the locks to our bikes. They were stealing them! I raced over there. Bella followed, but she was quite some distance behind me.

I screamed at them. *"Figlio di puttana!* Hey! What the hell do you dipshits think you're doing with our bikes?" It wasn't the best thing to say to these two hulks, but I was angry and not in the best state of mind. East Palo Alto had had its share of crime over the years, usually radical-right gangs from neighboring Menlo Park and Redwood City fighting turf wars with the city's Latinx and African Americans. While East Palo Alto had worked hard to solve the problem, there were still criminal elements to be dealt with. I had two of them looking straight at me.

The bigger one of the two stared at me. "So what ya gonna do about it, big boy—or should I say, big *Dago?*

"Vaffancul, bastardi!"[39] They both gave a look that said, "What the hell does that mean?"

"Idioti!"

I took a deep breath. No way could I fight both these schmucks at the same time. "Look, man, I don't want any trouble with you guys. We need our bikes."

"Trouble? You better believe you don't want trouble with us. Now get the hell out of here, asshole." He threw both broken locks on the ground.

"We need to go. Give us the bikes already!"

"Well, go, dude, before you can't! Shit, man, you're asking for big trouble."

I was in over my head, not knowing what to do. There were two of them, maybe four, if you counted their monstrous biceps, and only one of little ol' me. At that moment, Bella caught up with us, and they started in on her.

The big guy called over to his friend. "Looky, here, Randy. We got us a cute little chiquita!" He grabbed her arm and moved to push the hair away from Bella's cheek.

---

[39] *Vaffancul, bastardi!*—F*ck you, you bastards!"

With that, I pushed him away. The Randy dude grabbed me from behind and held me as tight as vice grips around a chicken's neck. He must have done weights every day. He was like a taller version of Arnold Schwarzenegger. "Go on, Eric. I got him."

As Eric closed in on Bella, he crooned, "How about a little kiss, chiquita?" I was going bananas, and struggle as I might, I couldn't break loose from Randy's iron grip.

But Bella was no pushover. She pushed back and kicked the Eric dude hard in his left shin with her leather boot, which, unfortunately for him, had a pointed, decorative steel tip. He bent over and screamed in pain. Seconds later, as he limped and stood up, he began to raise his right arm to smack Bella across the face. "You little bitch!"

Figlio di puttana! I couldn't let that happen. I used every bit of strength I had to break free. In a fraction of a second, I freed my right arm, but he still held on tight as a vice around my chest and my left arm.

Then everything went to slo-mo. Raising my right arm, I clawed for Eric with the deepest anger I could recall. "Don't you dare touch her, you bastard!"

As his hand was swinging down to hit Bella's face, I felt a strong, warm feeling rapidly rise from the ground, into my feet and up through my body. It was instantly followed by a surge of bright blue-white light that appeared to spark from my fingertips like a bolt of lightning. It hit Eric directly in his chest. His body flew backward several feet, and he landed on his back as if he'd been hit by a Mack truck. Randy released me and ran to his buddy, who lay lifeless in a pile on the ground.

Bella stared at me in shock. Neither she nor I could speak. *What the hell had just happened?*

Randy knelt alongside Eric, shaking like a leaf in a strong wind, "Hey, man, what . . . what the hell did you do to Eric? Shit, man, you . . . you some kinda witch doctor?"

I raced over and knelt next to Eric as he lay on the ground, his eyes still open in a death stare. Randy and Bella were on his other side. I didn't know what to do. *How did this happen? Good God. Is he dead?*

Bella listened for his heart and felt for his pulse. "He's got no pulse, no heartbeat, and he's not breathing. Luc, we need to do something! We have to try CPR!"

I knew she was right, and even that might not help. *Did I just kill someone? But how?*

I froze for a second. Randy stood up and was screaming, "Murderer! Murderer! You killed him," as he backed away from Bella and me. We were still kneeling at Eric's side. Randy seemed to be afraid the same thing might happen to him. He stopped speaking, kept his distance, and watched frozen, in a kind of hypnotic state.

Bella was frantic. "Luc!"

"Okay." We started CPR as we'd learned it in health class during our sophomore year—chest compressions about two inches deep toward the heart at a rate of 100 times per minute with intermittent mouth-to-mouth resuscitation. I started by giving him about 20 strong compressions, and then as Bella was just inches away from his face, about to start mouth-to-mouth resuscitation—he coughed and began to stir, still unconscious. But now his eyes were closed.

He's alive. Thank God!

Bella checked his pulse and heartbeat. "He's alive, but barely. He needs a hospital. I've got my cell phone. I'll call 911. Stay with him in case he stops breathing again."

Bella called 911, and within ten minutes the ambulance was racing down Bay Road toward us. During that time, Randy went over and sat next to Eric and said nothing. Bella kept asking me what had happened. I told her I had no idea. Then she said something that pierced like an arrow through my heart. It got me thinking—and worrying. She asked if I thought this might be related to what happened to me in the hospital. And just then, the ambulance arrived.

One of the EMTs saw that Eric's shirt had a huge burn hole on his chest area. "What happened here, guys?"

Neither Bella nor I knew what to say. Before we could open our mouths, Randy stuttered his response: "Shit, man, that . . . that dude must be some kinda witch doctor! He threw an electric fire-ball, like a lightning bolt, at Eric—nearly killed him. Hell, maybe he *did* kill him. And then he brought him back to life with all of his mumbo-jumbo stuff. Shit, I don't know what happened."

Rolling his eyes and giving Randy an "Are you nuts?" look, the EMT muttered, "Yeah, right."

He put an oxygen mask on Eric's face and began to check his vital signs, lifting his T-shirt so he could use his stethoscope to check his heart. There, bright as day, were burn marks where the electric charge had hit Eric's chest. His chest had a five-inch circular burn, mostly black surrounded by a red circle. The three of us watched in dismay and anticipation.

"Well, I'll be damned." The EMT shook his head and gently moved the shirt higher to reveal the full extent of the burn marks. "It looks like he was electrocuted. Did he bump into any live wires?"

"No way, man." Randy shot me a furious look. "I told you this crazy dude shot a fireball at him!"

Before the EMT could respond, Eric began to shake and started to come out of what had looked like a death sentence. Dazed, he stared up at the four of us as we leaned over him. As soon as he realized he'd been out cold, he pushed away the oxygen mask.

In a slow, raspy voice, and looking directly at me, he whispered, "Man, what the hell did you do to me? You got one of those electric Taser guns, or whatever the hell you call them?"

Randy quickly concurred. "Yeah, that's it. He's got a Taser gun. Come on, man, let's see it."

"No, I don't have any weapons."

The technician interrupted. "Look, my friend, this was caused by something much more potent than a Taser. In any case, there's no time for discussion. We need to get you to the hospital, stat. Your vitals are very weak."

Eric was too out of it to argue. The EMT replaced the oxygen mask, and with the help of the ambulance driver, put Eric on a stretcher. Within seconds they were off to Stanford Hospital.

Randy and Bella both stared at me. He turned and slowly walked away, looking back occasionally to stare at me, maybe to be sure I wouldn't throw a fireball at *him*, or whatever the hell that thing had been.

Bella just picked up her bike and started to ride away. I caught up with her. We looked at each other occasionally as we rode. She was scared to death. So was I. Neither of us said a word all the way home. We didn't have the slightest idea what had happened. But I would soon find out.

When we arrived at Bella's home, she looked at me with great distress. Her eyes were welling up with tears.

"Look, Luc, I've told you several times this past week, you're my best friend—ever. But I'm frightened, and to be honest, I'm becoming afraid of you. I don't know who or what you are anymore. What just happened back there at the preserve with that Eric guy was way beyond normal. Some kinda high-energy electric bolt or something came out of your body and nearly killed him—and, what's more, it had no effect on you! I've never heard of such a thing. Whatever happened to you during your NDE in the hospital has changed you into I don't know what, and I'm scared, very scared—scared for me, scared for you, scared for us. Forget spying for the CIA—what kind of frightening thing will you do next?"

I told her, "I understand. I know I need help—someone's help. I can't explain this to Mom and Dad. They'd have me visit regular doctors at Stanford, and none of them would have the slightest idea what happened to me today. Look at what Dr. Ross did when I went to see him—he called in the CIA. What happened today is way beyond known human physiology. Maybe your Buddhist-monk scholar has the answer. I hope so. I'll meet with him, and maybe I can find out not only what's happened to me, but what I can do about it—if anything."

Bella replied, "I hope *someone* can help you. I want to help, but after what I saw today, I don't think there's anything I could do. I feel useless. And what's worse, as I said, I'm becoming increasingly afraid of you." She started to cry.

I hugged her, and she put her head on my chest. "Look, I deeply appreciate your thoughts and advice, but until I have a handle on what's going on in my body and my mind—maybe it's my consciousness—I'm gonna spend as much time this summer as it takes to find out what it is. So if I don't call for a while, please don't worry. I need to figure this thing out on my own terms. And when I do, you'll be the first to know. I'll go with you on Wednesday evening to meet this Buddhist dude, and then I'm on my own."

I'm sure she was banking on the monk being able to help, somehow, because all she said was, "All right."

"I've gotta go now." And with that, I gave her a kiss on the cheek and rode off on my bike.

I felt like a volcano ready to explode. I'd never felt so alone—or so lost.

TAKE TWO

"K<small>ILLING</small>" E<small>RIC AT</small> R<small>AVENSWOOD</small> P<small>RESERVE</small> was more than just a night-mare for me. I could barely sleep that evening. Things got even worse. I abruptly woke up at 4:30 A.M.—panicked and drenched in sweat. I'd had horrible dreams and couldn't go back to sleep. Now I understood how Mom must feel with her Ativan episodes.

Mental and physical exhaustion are terrible, especially when experienced at the same time. I found it impossible to go for my run, something that never happens unless I'm really sick. It was a good thing Dad had an early-morning meeting in San Francisco and had left at 5:30 A.M., otherwise he'd have been all over me for not being disciplined and committed to the game.

I sat on the edge of my bed in a daze, thinking about my messed-up life. Besides having basically killed someone yester-day—which is bad enough—it dawned on me that I'd told Bella, my lifelong best friend in this crazy, mixed-up world, to get lost while I solved my problems on my own. What was I thinking?

Summer vacation would start in less than a week. Sure, Bella had promised to go with me to the Buddhists' presentation, but that was tomorrow, and after that I was completely on my own.

Luc, she'd said, *I'm becoming increasingly afraid of you.* So maybe it was the right decision to go it alone. Should be a great summer.

I trudged through classes and did my best at practice. If it weren't for my ability to see what the opposing players would do before they did, Coach would have been all over me for playing poorly. My sense of the immediate future was fading—at least, I thought so—but thankfully in cases like this, slowly. Staying focused, I could still get a peek at what was to come.

On my way home from practice, my crypto-iPhone rang. It was Tamara. Swell.

"Luc, I'll be quick. I'm on my way to a meeting. The director has decided to wait for further supporting evidence before contacting the secretary of state and initiating the process to involve the UN Security Council for China's violation of the NPT."

I didn't know it then, but that was total bullshit.

"You mean to tell me that all of the data and info I sent you wasn't enough?"

"That's right. I just sent you instructions for another remote viewing to support our position at the council meeting. I want you to focus on getting detailed mental photos of the design drawings for the nuclear-powered engines used on those Chinese ICBMs."

And I thought I was done with ICBMs and on my way to an antiterrorist project.

"Yeah, right." I couldn't help bringing it up again. "But why all of this ICBM stuff? It's not that I don't think it's important, but I signed up to help you fight terrorism. When do we start *that* mission?"

"Look, you stumbled onto a critical potential threat to the US and our allies. Are you telling me you just want to leave it at that— 'all of this ICBM stuff'?"

Whoa! She was pissed. It was weird, but I was simultaneously frightened by her tone of voice and yet, could care less. I thought, *There must be something wrong with me. What the hell's going on in this new brain of mine?*

I relented. What else could I do? But I was beginning to think I was being sold a bill of goods. I just didn't know how big or what that bill of goods was.

"Okay, okay, I'm on it."

"I look forward to your report." She hung up.

What, no goodbye?

I went directly to the office, turned on the crypto-computer, entered my PIN code, and there it was.

Luc,

Proceed to the same GPS coordinates used in your last viewing. Return to the missile silo and the control room where you took your last mental photos. Get as many photos as you can of the details for their nuclear engine design. This is critical. As usual, your report is time-sensitive.

Tamara

I lay down on the sofa in the office, and in no time I was flying high over north-central China. I had the coordinates clear in my mind and could see the military installation at the Taiyuan Cement Factory just below me.

Landing casually inside the electrified fence, I came nose to nose with a machine-gun-toting guard. He was smoking a cigarette. I smiled at him. He unknowingly blew smoke into my face. Wow! It went right through me.

Moving through the huge elevator door, down the shaft, and into the silo at the end of the underground tunnel, I arrived in front of the control room. Only one technician was present this time, and he was glued to one of the computer screens on the other side of the room.

My first thought was, *Whoa, this dude looks too young for this. And he's a scarecrow . . . thin as a McDonald's single patty . . . without the bun . . . poor guy needs to eat something.* I christened him "Bones." He cleared his throat. His ears looked funny, but I dropped that thought quickly because people had teased me plenty when I was a kid about my ears being too big. He cleared his throat again, and then again and again. *Weird.*

Behind Bones I recognized a framed photograph of a crisp-saluting, laser-focused, high-ranking military officer. My cerebral encyclopedia identified him as General Li Zuocheng, chief of the Joint Staff Department of the Central Military Commission. His name had come up several times during my CIA security briefings.

Bones might have been funny-looking, but there was no question about his capabilities. Getting to where he was put him among the elite of the world's largest military force—the Chinese People's Liberation Army, or PLA. He was using a paper-filled binder as an armrest. I watched as he shook out his hand every so often. I guess carpal tunnel favors no specific nationality. He bent closer to the monitor. He was wearing glasses as thick as Coke bottles. As Bones did that, he pushed the binder away from him to his left onto a small, portable table on wheels. The table moved slightly behind him. I hovered closer to see what the binder was about.

It was labeled 外军动态. Wow! Slam-dunk and hang me on the rim! My mental translation told me it was the Second Department of the Joint Staff Headquarters' internal bimonthly report. It was stamped "Top Secret." I slowly opened the report, scanning and recording every single page into my memory, like documents fed through a rapid copy machine. I was careful not to make any noise.

While Bones concentrated on his monitor, I checked it out. He was reading new procedures to streamline communications between the PLA's five theater commands. From the little I read, apparently email spam favors no nationality either—I floated into the glass-enclosed booth on the other side of the room (the "aquarium") scavenging for morsels—in particular, more schematics of The Great Wall's construction and its engine design. I was willing to gulp down or bottom-feed on whatever krill I could find. I wanted to get this done ASAP so I didn't have to come back, and I could finally get to move on to antiterrorism.

What I saw was a huge gulp—large pullout drawers swarming with hard-copy files. I swam through them on the first pass with my mouth agape, scanning and recording every page. Then, I gorged on photographs, blueprints, renderings, and satellite images. There was one entire manual on the nuclear engine design alone, and it was mine for the taking. *Minchia*, this was going to be some helluva job to distill down into a concise report for Tamara.

Bones suddenly turned around and stared in my direction. What the hell? No—he couldn't possibly see or hear me. He kept clearing his throat, almost obsessively. It was annoying the hell outta me. I stopped, knowing I couldn't possibly be detectable. Maybe I'd made too much noise turning the pages. He walked into the aquarium, stood right next to me, and sliced his arms through the air as if trying to touch some invisible object. He moved around the room, his sweeping blades moving like a rapid windmill gliding right through my body. Deep groans alternated with even deeper throat clearings. He was swinging and grunting like a madman. I looked closer. *Shit!*

He couldn't have been more than 18 years old. I felt bad nicknaming this dude Bones. He wasn't just skinny, he was anorexic. And his ears weren't just funny-looking, they were what my mental encyclopedia registered as "low-settled with adherent earlobes." He cleared his throat time and again—it clearly was a major tic. My God, I finally realized what he was, as my encyclopedic knowledge began to spit out even more info. Damn, I gotta finish up and get the hell out of here!

Suddenly he started screaming. Not intelligible words but shrills! Cries! He jumped up and down like a madman, unable to contain his emotions, yet unable to verbalize them either.

I was closing in on trying to get mental pictures of the last few design pages. But he was driving me nuts. I backed up, shaking as if I had a limp that was becoming more pronounced and making it difficult to float in a straight line. Frantically, I kept scanning and recording—*mission critical, mission critical!*—trying to devour whatever krill were left.

Four Chinese soldiers ran in with their weapons drawn. Thunderous alarms shredded the quiet to pieces. Bones kept ranting and raving, jumping up and down, swirling in circles. His arms and legs kept circling like a chaotic whirlpool sucking him into a vortex in which he was the only visible victim.

Looking frantically at the guards, he yelled, "You got to help! An evil spirit took these documents out of the drawer and was turning the pages!"

Two of the guards started laughing, roaring uncontrollably and shouting, "Are you nuts, comrade? You must have drunk too much Baijiu at our team party last night, or you're losing your mind."

"No, dammit! I know what I saw. He's here. I can still feel him."

One of the laughing guards continued to make fun of him. "Wow, really, how does he feel? Do you like it?" His buddy put his machine gun on the table and was going apeshit, laughing so hard, he nearly fell over.

The other two guards, who were serious and not laughing or looking concerned, were dressed in different uniforms. In a few moments, it was clear why they weren't upset. They were speaking to each other, but not in Chinese. It was Korean. They had small photos of Kim Jong-un on their lapel security badges—they were North Korean. I thought, *That's strange. Are China and North Korea working together on nuclear-powered ICBMs?* Something was weird about this.

One of the laughing soldiers suddenly went dead serious and grabbed Bones by the shoulders, shaking him and yelling sternly, "Tell me again what you really saw!"

Bones exclaimed, "A ghost!" He opened one of the drawers and riffled through the files. "A ghost is here, and he's looking at our photographs, at our papers, at everything!" He yanked open the second drawer and then began ripping out its contents in an uncontrollable rage. Folders flew from his hands in a tornado, and the guards were trying to get ahold of him while the tornado tore through like a twister from Kansas. Kicking and slamming against them, Bones finally collapsed sobbing on the floor. He was physically spent.

The soldiers radioed to HQ, and moments later the alarms went silent. Seconds after that, a medical team arrived. One of the medics pulled out a vial. It was labeled 劳拉西泮. My translator-encyclopedia noted it as "Lorazepam, a benzodiazepine drug used to rapidly sedate the central nervous system." The medic fed the syringe and then regurgitated it into Bones's thigh. He went limp. They loaded him onto a stretcher and carried him away. Another young technician entered the control room and replaced him immediately.

"Crazy!" one of the soldiers scoffed as they all left the aquarium.

But I knew that wasn't true. Bones wasn't crazy. I'd figured it out moments before when we were face-to-face. He was autistic. And not just ordinary autistic, but an autistic savant with high-level intellectual and psychic abilities. My cerebral data told me that in the US, he would have been known as an Indigo Child, Rainbow Child, or a Starseed Child. In China he was known not as a child, but by his function: EHF—Exceptional Human Functions.

I kept searching and reading my mental references. In a declassified CIA report marked "Approved for Release 2000/08/11: CIA-RDP96-00792R000300420017-1," the agency asserted that the Chinese government, despite critics from within their scientific and military community, was exploring strategic applications of EHF. The report said the Chinese were at the forefront of tapping into this potential for military applications.

I also saw in my cerebral Wikipedia that the use of these EHF children had long ago been promoted by Qian Xuesen, one of China's most distinguished nuclear scientists and father of their ICBM missile design. By 1980, Qian had spearheaded China's successful launching of 12 satellites and the successful firing of an ICBM over 10,000 kilometers. His genius apparently had laid the groundwork for China's R&D program on intergalactic manned space missions.

Qian had been influential in the Chinese government and had likened the discovery of EHF children to other monumental advancements in the 20th century. He was quoted as saying, "This is reminiscent of the euphoria and excitement when the theories of relativity and quantum mechanics were introduced onto the stage of modern science."

What better poster boy could the Red Dragon ask for? In time, Qian convinced the Chinese Academy of Sciences to begin studying the relationship between EHF and *qi*, pronounced *chee*. They described *qi* as a psychic energy circulating through the body, like blood, and there were methods to increase its flow—the most common being through forms of *qigong*, meditation, deep-breathing *pranayama*, massage, and exercise. This kind of energy was not describable by the classical or quantum laws of physics. The Chinese speculated that it was the next step in physics. Done effectively, *qi* could raise incredible human powers—some might say paranormal ones. *Madonna mia!* This was sounding too familiar.

No, Bones wasn't *loco en la cabeza*.[40] He was high on *qi* and fully weaponized.

WITH THE MENTAL RECONNAISSANCE PHOTOS in cerebral storage, I flew back to the office. I had a huge "brainful" to deliver to Tamara. This time the entire process required less than an hour's time. I was getting increasingly efficient. Making drawings and writing my report also took less time, surprisingly.

I sent the material to Tamara and included a special request. "Please don't call tomorrow before 6:00 A.M. California time or after 8:00 A.M. Tomorrow's a school day. In fact, it's best for obvious reasons if you never call me at home." I really wanted to say, "Don't call at all."

I raced home for dinner. Mom wasn't happy. I was an hour later than usual.

She asked, "Long practice?"

Trying my best to act nonchalant and avoid a direct answer to her question, I said, "You know, Coach is working us like crazy. Says we'll have the best team ever for next season," which was actually a true statement.

---

[40] *Loco en la cabeza*—"Crazy in the head." (Spanish)

"Uh-huh, I see," she replied.

I wasn't sure she bought it, but at least she didn't pursue her line of questioning further.

After wolfing down dinner, I told Mom I needed to work on my term paper, so I headed upstairs to get started. At 10:30 P.M., my crypto-iPhone vibrated loudly. *Shit!* It was Tamara.

"Tamara, it's late to be calling here. And it's not a good idea to call me at home. My parents might wonder who would call at this late hour. Hey, isn't it 1:30 in the morning your time? Kind of late to be at the office, isn't it?"

Tamara was all business. "Some of us have to get our work done, before it gets us undone."

"Right . . . did you see my report?"

"I did, and that's why I'm calling. I read your material quickly, and I must say, it was another brilliant mission. You recovered complete design details of their nuclear-powered rocket engines, but equally important, those extra photos of their stealth guidance system are amazing. They appear to make it possible for their ICBMs to avoid detection and counter destruction measures by anti-ICBM missiles.

"And, by the way, catching those two North Korean soldiers at that site was immensely important too. And the continued commitment of the Chinese to EHF savants is also a big surprise. We knew about their interest in pursuing this, but certainly not their commitment. Congratulations! Well done!"

I didn't care if she got pissed again. "Does this mean we can finally move on to the antiterrorist work?"

Silence. She didn't like my question, took a deep breath, and finally responded, "We'll see. Soon—I promise. Okay."

"Right. Whatever."

"Luc, let me tell you, this may well clinch it. The Chinese are in significant breach of the NPT. I'm sure the Russians, Japanese, and a host of other Asian nations will not be happy to hear about this. I need to do some further work on how this all fits with intel we're getting on North Korea, and then I think we'll be in a position to recommend that the secretary of state take a summary of your two sightings to the UN Security Council. Great job! Thank you. This may take a couple of weeks or so. Hope you don't get out of practice. I'll keep you posted." And with that, she disconnected.

Gee, thanks, Tamara. I'll be sitting here on pins and needles waiting for your next call.

My intuition was cranking hard. Something was giving me what seemed like a warning. Something didn't compute. *Tamara, you're not being straight with me. I can feel it.* I wanted to pursue it further, but it was late and I was tired. I decided to let it go for now. Besides, a few weeks away from her might do me some good. I had no idea how much.

THE ERIC
CONNECTION

ERIC CONTINUED TO OCCUPY A BIG PIECE OF MY MIND as I slogged through my day. It affected nearly everything I did. I guess normal people don't easily get over killing someone. Was Bella right? Could that lightning thing be another result of my near-death experience? How else could it have happened? If so, what else was coming my way? Things weren't looking good.

Eric was still in the hospital. I called every day to check up on him, hoping to find out how he was doing. But I couldn't get a single nurse on his floor to tell me about his condition. Always the same response: "Family members only!" Because of Randy's ridiculous comments to the ambulance attendant, I had expected to be contacted by the hospital and possibly the police. The hospital likely wrote the incident off as an accidental electrocution, and with Randy's questionable background, he wasn't exactly the type to cozy up to the cops.

I had to see Eric, but frankly, I didn't really want to. After what I'd done, what would he think of me? How would he react? Would it just make things worse for him—and for me? Did he incur any permanent damage? Was he going to be okay—I mean, both mentally and physically? I had visions of our meeting breaking out into a brawl in his hospital room. I wanted to apologize for what had happened, even though I hadn't the faintest idea what it was or what it meant. As best I could, I pushed these fears out of my head and decided to go to the hospital anyway.

When I arrived at Eric's room, the door was closed. I shut my eyes and took a deep breath. I stood there for more than a minute. *I can't do this. I have to leave.* I'd lost my nerve. As I turned to go, a nurse pushed past me into the room. She had one of those electronic thermometers in her hand. As I froze in place, she rushed over to Eric and put it in his ear.

A few seconds later, she exclaimed triumphantly, "Completely normal, Eric—98.6."

He was awake, lost in thought, staring at the ceiling. He didn't notice me. I was still standing there like a statue as time whizzed by. *Shit, what should I do?*

"You've got a visitor, Eric. A very tall, dark, and handsome one at that. Looks a lot like a young, hot Michael Corleone." *Too late, you damned ditz!*

He turned his head slowly and saw me standing in the doorway. For some reason, it didn't faze him. Both of us looked at each other like stone statues. Not a word came out of our mouths. He turned his head back and continued gazing at the ceiling.

I barely got it out, almost a whisper. "Hi, Eric—thought I'd stop by and see how you're doin'."

He still didn't say a word—just continued staring into space.

"Well, I'll leave you two guys to chat," the nurse said. "Looks like it might be a short one." Smiling at me, she winked and whispered, "See you, Don Corleone." And she was gone.

I had to say something. "Eric, we . . . we never got a chance to be introduced. My name's Luc, Luc Ponti. I'm so sorry for what happened to you. You gotta believe me, man, I have no idea what went down at the preserve. This has never happened to me—ever. I'm still tryin' to figure it out." I didn't know what else to say.

Eric turned his head slowly and looked at me. "Well, I can tell you one thing, Mr. Don Corleone, whoever the hell that is, you did *something* to me, all right, something big, very big."

"Yeah, I know. I killed you—and nearly for good!"

"No, bro, I know you did. I'm not talkin' 'bout that."

"No? Then, what? What could be bigger than that?"

Eric was quiet. He'd turned back to his focus on the ceiling. It was like he was thinking but couldn't or wouldn't let the words come out of his mouth.

I couldn't stand it any longer. "Eric, what do you mean, 'very big'?"

When he turned his head again and looked at me, his expression was hugely different from when we'd first met. This wasn't the same tough punk I'd fought with at the preserve. Yeah, he was still built like a brick shithouse, but he'd mellowed—like, a lot. His jaw was tense, and his eyes were filled with tears and nearly popping out of his head. He was frightened. This hulk of a guy— frightened? *Minchia*, you gotta be kiddin' me.

"I can't explain it. You'll probably think I'm nuts. But after you hit me with that lightning bolt or whatever the hell it was and I was unconscious or dead or whatever, somethin' happened."

"Like what kinda somethin'?

He stared at me and reluctantly and slowly let it out. "I saw this incredibly beautiful bright light in a huge tunnel."

Before he could say another word, I raced over to the chair next to his bed and sat there face-to-face with him, just inches away. "Oh my God, Eric. No! You're kiddin'! Right?"

"No, I'm not."

I had to ask him. "Eric, did you rise out of your body and into the tunnel filled with that beautiful light?"

He sprang up instantly to a sitting position and nearly pulled out the IV pumping whatever through his veins. "Shit, Luc. How'd you know that?"

I hesitated for a few moments. It was clear to me that the two of us had gone through the same thing—an NDE.

"Because the same thing happened to me not too long ago after I 'temporarily died from a basketball injury,' right here in this same hospital."

"No shit, man, really?"

"No shit, really."

"Tell me about it, please."

With that, I told Eric briefly about my experience and that I thought that some of the things that happened to me afterward were because of what was called a near-death experience, or NDE, and that it sounded like the same thing had happened to him. He seemed relieved, appreciative, interested, and was clearly becoming more relaxed. He laid back down.

Eric told me that while he was in the tunnel of light, he met his father, who'd left his mom before he was born. He said his dad had died several years ago in a car crash. They'd apparently had a long conversation, and it was good for both of them, but it seemed like he didn't want to talk about the details. I didn't push it—I knew how it felt—even though I was desperate to know more. I thought it might help explain some of the things that had happened to me.

"Look, Eric, I'd really like to know about your discussion with your father. Maybe it would help me understand what's happened to me." He didn't say a word, so I explained in detail my journey through the tunnel, meeting Nonno Paulo, and promising to deliver his message to Mom.

Eric considered my request. I guess my openness helped. He told me what had happened. Apparently, before Eric was born, his father had connected with some mobsters from Mexico and the US, and they were smuggling heroin and cocaine into California from Colombia. He told Eric that although he'd been deeply in love with Eric's mom, he knew that where he was going with his life would be the worst thing for her and their soon-to-be-born son. He said there was no turning back for him, so he made the decision to leave her. It was difficult for him, but he knew it was the right thing to do.

Shortly after that, he was arrested by the police, and he went to trial and served eight years in San Quentin. When he got out, he wanted to contact Eric's mom and see their son, but he said he hesitated, which was a big mistake. As a former drug dealer, just out of prison, he couldn't get a job. Before he knew it, he was back in the heroin and cocaine business.

His life was basically lost, but he still dreamed and sometimes even talked about eventually going back to his family. He told Eric that the car crash that killed him had been no accident. Eventually, the drug lords in Colombia wanted him gone when they began to suspect that he'd changed his mind and wanted out of the drug trade to be with his family. They were convinced that if he went back to them, he'd be an unnecessary liability.

One foggy evening, north of San Francisco, running from a Colombian hitman, Eric's dad crashed his car into a tree and was killed instantly. The Colombians had tampered with his brakes. He lost control of the car racing around a curve. He said that his "hell" has been constantly wishing that he'd rejoined his wife and son after leaving prison.

"Wow, that's some story! Are you gonna tell your mom? Maybe that would help her."

"I don't know. I'm having enough of a problem understanding what the hell happened to *me*."

"I understand. But I think you should consider it. When I told my mom about her father, she freaked out at first and didn't believe me. But when it all sank in, it eventually was a big help to her."

I continued with a different subject of special interest to me. "By the way, have you noticed anything strange about yourself?"

"Whaddaya mean?"

"Well, after my NDE, I found that I could travel with my consciousness or mind, or whatever you want to call it, to distant places and see and hear things in detail. Maybe this whole lightning thing was also because of my NDE—kinda like a superpower."

After that, he thought for several moments. "I didn't want to say anything—I thought you'd probably think I was a nutcase. but maybe that explains it."

"Explains what?"

"Look." He raised his right hand, pointed it at the TV, and closed his eyes for a couple of seconds. The TV went on!

I was amazed, but maybe I shouldn't have been after what had happened to me. "Oh my God—wow, that's incredible!"

He pointed his finger again at the TV, and it instantly went off.

"Eric, this is too much!"

"Yeah, it may be a bit much, but like it's so out there! Right? I'm like a magician!"

"You may feel like a magician, but apparently, you have a superpower to turn electrical devices on and off. Have you tried closing your eyes and concentrating to see if you can do an OBE?"

"What the hell's an OBE?"

"It's an out-of-body experience, like your NDE, except you don't have to die to do it."

"Well, that's encouraging."

"You just close your eyes, and after several seconds, everything goes from black to living color, and if you want, you can rise out of your body just like you did in your NDE. Once you get the hang of it, you can steer your way in any direction, speed up, slow down, whatever. And believe it or not, if you want, you can go anywhere in an instant, like faster than the speed of light, dude! Try it!"

By this time, Eric was so excited that he sat up in bed again. I got up from the chair, he got outta bed, and he grabbed hold of the stand on wheels holding his IV. We walked over to the window, which looked down on a poinsettia garden below.

"I don't know," he said, "maybe tonight when everyone's asleep, I'll give it a shot. It sounds weird, but kinda neat! Wow! Just imagine what you could do with that power."

"I don't have to imagine. You're right. It can actually be fun, and sometimes it can even come in handy." I didn't say anything about my connection to the CIA.

"I'll give it a shot, then. Tonight."

"Look, Eric, we have some crazy things in common. Maybe we can talk about them. Maybe we can even be friends. When you get out of this place, please give me a call. Here's my number. I'd like to buy you lunch. That's the least I can do for killing you!"

We both laughed. I seemed to have made a connection. He was no longer the menacing dipshit I'd met at the preserve.

I had no idea how close we would really become.

INTO THE LIGHT

LIFE SUCKS. We'd broken up, even though there was really nothing to break up. I mean, we'd never been more than good friends, right? Well, not officially. We'd spent our summers together, it seemed like forever, but people change, I guess. They grow up—you know. Yeah, right . . . but when I thought about it, if I were truly honest, I missed Bella more than I wanted to admit—until I had no choice but to admit it. *Life really does suck!*

I sensed that my remote-viewing powers were on their way out and I'd get my life back. And then maybe everything, including my relationship with Bella, would be fine again. Then reality sank in—okay, *sensed* wasn't the right word—I *hoped* my powers were on their way out.

It felt like rising water was surrounding me on a small island, forcing me to what little high ground was left. There was Bella's fear and her distancing herself from me, Tamara and the CIA fiasco, Dad's hounding and whatever happened in Iraq. *Gesu Cristo!* Was all this stuff really meant to be? It was scary, so I didn't want to dwell on that possibility.

IT WAS WEDNESDAY EVENING, and Bella had planned to meet me at my house at seven o'clock to attend the Buddhist monk's lecture on consciousness—her last act of friendship before I went off on my own to find a solution to my problem. She insisted on biking over by herself. As usual, I wasn't happy about her riding through East Palo Alto, especially at night. But she's a dedicated supporter for her town. She often complained that the area had a bad rap for things that happened years ago. In 1992, it was the designated murder capital of the US, but it had long since recovered from that reputation. She claimed to know more nice folks in East Palo Alto than she'd ever met in snooty ol' Palo Alto. What could I say?

I waited outside, sitting on our front steps. As usual, she was on time. We hopped on our bikes and made off for the temple. On the way, neither of us said much. Our relationship had always been about as close as friendship gets—actually, closer. I could feel her concerns—and they hurt not only her but me as well. The thing with Eric at the preserve was still fresh in both our minds. How could we be so close, yet so far apart?

I wanted to tell her that I'd visited Eric in the hospital and what had happened to him, but I'd promised him that I wouldn't tell anyone about our discussion. I understood how he felt. He didn't want people to think he was a weirdo, or worse, on his way to the funny farm. Since Eric and I were in a much better place now, I wasn't gonna screw things up.

Bella and I parked our bikes at the back of the temple. It felt strange. I'd never been to a Buddhist place of worship. The exterior, with its Asian statues and a koi fishpond, looked to me like a Japanese shrine. We entered through the front door and made our way quietly up the center aisle to find a couple of seats. The place was packed. I guess the speaker was famous. Mom once said that in Palo Alto, there were lots of people who either claimed to be Buddhists, or at least identified with that philosophy.

We found two seats together left of the center aisle and a few rows back from the speaker's podium. The interior of the temple was quite bare and simple compared to the fancy churches and synagogues I'd been to for weddings and other celebrations. The walls were off-white yellow, interlaced with floor-to-ceiling, dark, natural wooden slats, spaced about every six feet or so. Similar large wooden beams crisscrossed the high peaked ceiling. It felt similar to what I imagined a Swiss chalet to be like. In addition to the center main aisle, there were two side aisles, each containing about 20 rows of benches.

Directly in front of where we were sitting, there was a raised platform with a lectern and a microphone for the speaker. And several feet behind that, centered on the back wall, stood an impressive ten-foot-tall bronze statue of the Buddha. There were two small, golden vase-like structures on either side of the statue. They were burning incense sticks, which I could smell as soon as we entered the temple. I kinda liked the aroma. I thought it made me feel a little bit better. Whatever.

A sense of peace seemed to fill the air. But I still found myself fidgeting and looking around to see what kind of people attended these events. They seemed like ordinary folks. I don't know what I expected—I'd probably seen too many movies where Buddhists were depicted as mild-mannered men and women with long robes, sandals, and shaved heads.

Finally, Reverend Daikan entered and stepped up to the lectern to introduce Pham Tuan. Now *he* was exactly what I'd expected—a smiling, mild-mannered Asian man with a shaved head, wearing a long brown robe with a white braided rope as a belt, and leather sandals. I couldn't guess his age—maybe somewhere between 45 and 60. He was thin and seemed to glide effortlessly across the floor with a sense of silent confidence. I guess that's what prayer and meditation do for you.

A gentle, soft-spoken man of few words, the reverend welcomed the audience and then told us about the speaker's background. He said that as a spiritual leader and peace activist, Pham Tuan was known throughout the world for his teachings and writings on consciousness, meditation, and global peace—he seemed like a pretty important guy. I wondered why he'd take the time to speak with me.

"Ladies and gentlemen, I give you Pham Tuan."

Pham Tuan made his entry to enthusiastic applause. He was much younger than I anticipated, maybe in his early 30s. A few inches more than six feet tall, he didn't have that frail look I kinda expected for a monk, like Reverend Daikan did. He was husky and had dark facial features, more like one of those rugged cowboy types. He, too, walked with an air of quiet confidence. Maybe it was a Buddhist thing? But he didn't glide like Reverend Daikan; there was a hint of a strut in his walk—a bit like one of those hip-hop singers. But just like Reverend Daikan, he had a shaved head and wore similar clothing.

As the applause subsided, he stepped up to the microphone, adjusted its height, and spoke his first few words. Unlike Reverend Daikan, Pham Tuan wasn't particularly soft-spoken—not at first. He spoke more like the ringmaster at a circus, loud and clear. And *madonna mia*, was he a big surprise. "Good evening, ladies and gentlemen. I'm happy to be with you tonight? You better believe it!"

I *didn't* believe it! Smiles and then uncontrolled laughter floated throughout the audience. He'd spoken those introductory words with the thickest Bronx accent I'd ever heard. Amazing—a Buddhist monk with a Bronx accent! How could that possibly be?

As the crowd calmed down, he spoke more softly and said, "I sense from your laughter—believe me, no offense taken, I've heard it many times before—that most of you have never heard me speak before. So as not to keep you wondering throughout my presentation, I want to share a bit of my backstory before I begin. As you can probably tell, I'm originally from the Bronx, having spent the first 13 years of my life in the Little Italy-Belmont section of that New York City borough. For additional proof, let me share one of my favorite Bronxian phrases with you."

He took a deep breath, folded his arms across his chest, slowly scanned the audience for a few seconds, then raised his right arm directly in front of his chest, pointed at the crowd, and said in a perfect wise-guy voice, "If you don't think I'm from the Bronx, you can *fugettaboutit!*"

The audience roared.

He went on to explain that he'd been born in the Bronx a number of years after his parents emigrated there after the Vietnam War. In Vietnam, they'd been college educated and had been recruited by the US military to work as intelligence gatherers. That's right—spies. They'd risked their lives for the US armed forces as they pretended to work as peasants on a farm close to Saigon. A deeply appreciative and concerned American colonel saw to it that they were rewarded with emigration to the States, and they were eventually granted citizenship.

In his early teens, Pham Tuan got into trouble with one of the gangs in his neighborhood. Concerned about their son's future, his parents scraped together enough money to send him to a monastery school in Nepal, where he studied under the guidance of a Vietnamese monk who was a family friend. He went there against his will, kicking and screaming.

While in Nepal, he became a climbing enthusiast. During one of his treks in the Himalayas, he had a serious incident, which was a life-changing event. As a result, he developed an interest in consciousness and the nature of the universe, so he decided to become a Buddhist monk and later went on to study theology, philosophy, and physics—all at the same time.

What he didn't tell the audience, and what I learned much later from Reverend Daikan, was that Pham Tuan went to Harvard on a World Bank scholarship and graduated summa cum laude.

This quirky, streetwise monk with the heavy Bronx accent appealed to me even before he started his presentation. I found it easy to relate to him. He was my kinda guy.

He spoke in simple, clear terms—no boring, fifty-cent words that some highly educated speakers often drop on an audience. He described the power of mindfulness, meditation, and consciousness, and why a mastery of them could have a positive impact on your life. He offered examples from his experiences and pointed out that there are levels of consciousness, and at high levels, it's possible to access increasingly powerful knowledge and capabilities—some considered to be in the realm of the paranormal. That really struck a chord with me.

Pham Tuan was charismatic, humble, and sincere, soft in his presentation, yet clear, direct, and believable. He also had a great sense of humor. There was something special about him. Although the ideas he spoke about seemed simple, to me they were profound. I could feel the energy of his connection with the audience, and especially with me.[15]

After the lecture and a long ovation, Pham Tuan graciously left the podium and retreated offstage through a side door. Bella and I worked our way through the crowd to Reverend Daikan.

He greeted us with a smile. "Hello, Bella. This must be Luc."

"Good evening, Reverend. Pleased to me you."

"And I, you, Luc. I've heard nothing but great things about you from Bella and her parents."

"Thank you, sir. The Morenos have been friends of our family since Bella and I started grade school together."

"And, Bella, how have you been?"

"Uh . . ." What could she say? "I'm fine, Reverend."

I'm sure he felt her hesitation loud and clear. He changed the subject.

"Well, I've arranged for Luc to meet with Pham Tuan. I'm sure you'll like him. He's a special person."

"I already do like him, and I'm sure he *is* special. I loved his presentation," I said.

"All right, then. Please follow me."

We entered a small room located immediately off the main room of the temple. The lights in the room were a dim orange color, and the floor was covered by a large, colorful Persian rug. It depicted a battle scene between ancient warriors on horses and elephants. Three of the walls had stained-glass windows, and there was essentially no furniture, just four chairs against one of the walls. They looked like they belonged to an IKEA kitchen set.

Almost on cue, Pham Tuan entered the room. Reverend Daikan made the introductions with a focus on me.

Pham Tuan smiled. "Luc, I'm pleased to make your acquaintance and to be here in your lovely city. Daikan-san has told me that you are quite a talented young man. I look forward to our discussion."

"Thank you, sir."

"Oh, please, no formality. Call me Thay, as my friends do." He pronounced it like the word *tie*.

Reverend Daikan explained, "*Thay* means 'teacher' in Vietnamese."

Up until that point, Bella had said nothing. I could feel her discomfort. She wanted out.

"And who is this lovely lady?"

Reverend Daikan explained, "Oh, this is Bella, Mr. and Mrs. Moreno's daughter. She and Luc have been friends forever."

Right, forever, I thought.

"Pleased to meet you, Bella. Will you be staying for our meeting?" Thay asked.

"Oh, it's my pleasure, sir—I mean, Thay. Oh, no, I promised my parents I'd meet them in Palo Alto for a quick dessert and drive home with them. I've got a term paper to work on."

He smiled. "Well, it was nice to meet you, Bella. I hope we see each other again. Perhaps you, Luc, and I could do dessert together sometime soon."

"That would be great."

With quick goodbyes to the three of us, Bella was gone. Reverend Daikan left as well. I was on my own. *Swell.*

Thay arranged two chairs in the middle of the room so that we could sit directly opposite each other. He signaled for me to sit in one of the chairs. Then he sat in the other.

He folded his hands in front of his chest and began with a brief silent prayer. I was nervous. I sat there not knowing what to expect, or how and when to begin.

Then he looked up from his prayer and asked, "Luc, how can I help you?"

Well, that's right to the point. What do I tell him? "I'm not sure where to start."

"Why not start at the beginning?"

I was hesitant, but after giving it some thought, I realized I had to open up to have any chance of getting his help.

I began by telling him about my struggles with peritonitis, my NDE, and the development of what appeared to be paranormal capabilities. I had to be honest, so I told him that these powers weren't going away, and, in fact, they seemed to be getting stronger with time.

He smiled and said nothing and actually seemed to be excited by what I was telling him. He looked like he was wondering why I had such an intense concern. Maybe it was because I didn't say a word about my involvement with the CIA. I couldn't disclose any top-secret information. Besides, it wasn't like I felt I had to tell him *everything*, like in one shot, you know.

When I finished, he said, "You've had an exciting and trying time over the last several months." He stopped, and with a piercing stare, said, "Look, my friend, I want to help you, but I sense you're holding something back, something connected with your newfound capabilities—and it's important. Am I correct?"

Minchia! Can this guy read minds, or what? I didn't know what to say. How could he possibly know I'd left something out? I didn't want to lie, especially to a monk. *Shit! What should I do?*

Thay noticed my discomfort.

"C'mon, relax, take all the time you need. You decide if you want to share this information or not. It's all right with me either way. It's just that the more I know, the more I can help you."

I was quiet. Thay showed no impatience. He simply smiled at me in his own nonthreatening way and seemed to enjoy just being present. I started to sweat.

Finally, I said, "You know, Thay, like, I'm not a religious person. But I understand from one of my basketball teammates that when Catholics go to confession, the priest keeps all the information he receives confidential, and under no circumstances would he tell it to others. I think even lawyers and the police respect that. Are you bound in a similar way?"

"Not really. But I can tell you this, if you share anything with me and ask me to keep it confidential, then so be it. That information will never leave my lips, under any circumstances. Anybody asks me about it, my response is simple: 'Fugettaboutit'!"

We both had a hardy laugh. I was feeling more comfortable with our discussion.

Thay's sincerity was enough to convince me that I could trust him. I told him about my work with the CIA, but not about the Eric fiasco. I was afraid that he'd think I was a nutcase and that would be the end of our discussion. I mean, come on—how could any normal human being create a bolt of lightning—and not get electrocuted? Let's get real. Maybe we could discuss it some other time, after we got to know each other a little better.

He looked at me and said, "Thank you for sharing what you've been through. Is that all?"

Madra mia! This dude can see inside my head! And he won't give up!

"Yeah, that's it." *Cavalo!*[41] *I'd just lied to a monk! I hope there's no such thing as hell!*

I was happy he accepted my response—at least I thought he did at the time.

Thay smiled and said, "Okay, now we begin."

There were several long moments when neither of us said a word. I finally began. "Can you see why I'm confused and concerned? I'm really scared—especially about this CIA stuff."

"Confusion is part of the natural order of things. As for your concerns, I understand—perhaps I can help."

"What should I do? There must be something."

He didn't seem to be worried. In fact, there was a flicker of excitement in his eyes, like we were about to take off on a thrilling adventure. He said, "Luc, you appear to have a special gift. Let me explain. I assume that you don't have much knowledge about Buddhist philosophy. Correct?"

"Yeah, that's right—actually, none."

"I also recognize from your earlier comments that you're not a religious person, so please know that what I'm about to share with

---

[41] *Cavalo!*—"Holy crap!"

you has nothing at all to do with religion. It is strictly a philosophy that was developed by wisdom seekers over several millennia,
starting more than 5,000 years ago. What may be of interest to
you is that certain key elements of this philosophy are now gaining a scientific basis and acceptance, primarily from the field of
quantum physics."

I said, "Okay," although it seemed kinda weird to me. I
thought, *How does Buddhist philosophy have anything to do with
quantum physics?*

"First, I would like to sense your level of consciousness. Please
allow me to hold both of your wrists." I placed them in his hands,
palms up. He put each of his thumbs on a specific spot on each
of my wrists. "Now close your eyes as I sense your spiritual pulse.
Take five deep breaths, hold each for five seconds, and then slowly
exhale, preferably with your lips pursed as if you were going to
whistle or blow up a balloon."

Although this all seemed strange to me, I did as he asked.
After a while, Thay released my wrists and put them lightly in
my lap. "Please keep your eyes closed. I want your mind's eye to
go deep inside to a place in the center of your chest to the right
of your heart. This is a place of inner quiet where you can experience a connection to what is called your higher self, your very
essence, your Personal Consciousness. I can assure you, it's the
real you—not your physical three-dimensional body. Your body is
nothing more than a package of well-known, ordinary chemicals
put together as an exquisite structure to carry out some amazing
functions—but only, as you will eventually see, for a short period
. . . called a lifetime."

I really wasn't getting all this spiritual jazz, but I liked Thay,
so I did my best to follow his instructions. I focused on every word
he said and followed them to the letter.[25]

Suddenly, I seemed to be floating in space, maybe outer space,
I don't know. I heard the most beautiful music I'd ever heard in
my life and felt the most intense happiness and joy. I didn't have
a body, just some kind of ghostly presence in space. There were

colors that were so amazing, I couldn't believe it. All of this I sensed—how can I say this—without any thought.

If afterward you'd asked me to hum the music, I couldn't do it. It wasn't normal music of any kind. If you'd asked me the names of the colors, I couldn't name them. They weren't any of the colors I'd ever seen or was familiar with. All I knew was that I sensed this beauty without a single thought and without a single label as to what it was. It was beauty beyond words. I would have been happy to stay there forever—wherever *there* was.

Just then I felt Thay gently touching my forehead.

"Luc, it's time to come back to your five-sense physical reality. Please take three deep belly breaths, slowly exhale, and then open your eyes when you feel comfortable doing so."

I felt like I was waking up from a dream. I opened my eyes and was overwhelmed by an intense feeling of peace and calm. I'd never felt like this before. The beauty I'd experienced was so incredible. I'm embarrassed to say that it brought tears to my eyes.

"How do you feel?"

"Amazing. I have no words to describe it. Was I meditating?"

"Indeed, you were, and very deeply, more deeply than I've ever seen before, even with experienced monks. The reason you can do this has to do with part of your so-called superpowers. Did you have any thoughts or sensations during your meditation?"

"I saw lots of beautiful colors, heard wonderful music, but no thoughts or physical sensations. After some time, I felt deep peace and tranquility. It was like my NDE experience. When I felt you touch my forehead and heard your voice, I was disappointed to leave where I was, wherever that was."

Thay said, "You were probably unaware of the passage of time, but for your first time meditating, you were able to block out all thoughts and bodily sensations and enter a deep meditation for more than 45 minutes. You—more accurately, your consciousness—was deep within what is called the 'gap,' or the absence of all thoughts and physical sensation."[35]

"You must be kidding! It didn't seem that long. It seemed like just a few minutes."

"That's because in the world of consciousness, there is no space or time. Time is a concept evolved by human beings to manage their five-sense reality. Meditation is similar to being in a dream state. It may seem long while you're dreaming, especially when you recall the details of the dream after you awaken, but it has occurred instantaneously."

"What do mean, *instantaneously*? I know from my physics class that Einstein proved long ago in his Theory of Relativity that information, signals, matter—actually, nothing—can travel faster than the speed of light."

"That's absolutely correct, but only for the five-sense physical world we live in, not for the spiritual world of consciousness. In that place, which is not a place, there is neither space nor time, and everything happens in an instant—it's hard to comprehend, but I can assure you, it's true."

"Wow! That's really weird! So, is my meditation experience important, and does it have something to do with what's happening to me?"

"It *is* important, and it has *everything* to do with what's happening to you. You have the rare ability to immediately lock into your spirit, what some call your fundamental core or essence—your soul, if you want to call it that—for extended periods of time. And in doing so, you can achieve high levels of consciousness. As a result, you have access to a broad range of knowledge—and as you recently discovered, special capabilities—well beyond those most of us could ever dream of."

I was having trouble comprehending the significance of what Thay was telling me, but it kinda made me feel special—certainly different. It would take quite some time, and much more of his counsel, before it hit home. But one thing was clear: it was the reason I suddenly went from a *B*-plus student to straight *A*s.

Thay paused briefly and then continued. "What appear to be paranormal powers are a result of your ability to access these high levels of consciousness. But I can honestly tell you that they're just the tip of the iceberg. You can do much more than you think, and access more information than you or anyone else, for that matter, ever thought possible. But first you must learn how to do this with absolute control of your powers. If you don't create this self-discipline, you may not only be pleasantly surprised by unexpected benefits, but equally important, become disheartened by problems you might inadvertently cause."

Thay could see the change in my expression as I thought about what he'd just said—*disheartened by problems you might inadvertently cause.* Good God, Eric, I'm so sorry. My head drooped, and I stared the floor.

"Luc, are you still with me?"

"Yeah, I am. Just thinking about what you said."

"It will require some time for me to clearly explain all the potential ramifications of your gifts, and how and when to access them with care and consideration. Only then can you use them properly and safely. Hopefully, our discussions will help you make an informed judgment as to how you want to proceed with your life."

I was excited and worried at the same time by what Thay had just told me. I was also impatient. I wanted a solution, and I wanted it then and there—before I made any more terrible mistakes like what I'd pulled on Eric. "That all sounds great, but how do we do that? I mean, how can you help me, and do it as soon as possible—like right now?"

"Patience, my friend, patience. Tomorrow I'll call my abbey and ask for a leave of absence. When I tell the abbot about you, I'm sure that he'll support my suggestion."

"Wow—that's fantastic! But why would he let you do that?"

"You will know soon enough. But I can tell you this—you've been endowed with powerful gifts, and from what I've studied over the years, this kind of thing has been seen only a few times over the past several millennia. But before I can explain the details of what you're experiencing, I need to give you some basic information so that you understand things in the right context. That may take a couple of sessions together. The rest is then up to you, if you like. In the meantime, be careful with these gifts. The best way is to avoid intense feelings of any kind—either extreme happiness *or* anger."

I again thought of what I'd done to Eric with my rage. *Incredibile.*[42]

Thay asked, "Are you up for discussions on what has happened to you and what you can do about it?"

I wasn't happy about having to deal with this whole business slowly and patiently, but it seemed like I had no choice if I wanted to work with Thay.

I told him, "I'm willing to take a shot at it, if you think it will help."

"It will definitely help. Let's meet again tomorrow at 9:00 A.M."

"Sounds good to me."

For some crazy reason, I sensed he was right. There just might be some light at the end of this long, dark tunnel.

[42] *Incredibile*—"Unbelievable."

THE MASTER

I ARRIVED AT THE TEMPLE AT 9:00 AM. Reverend Daikan was gardening near the fishpond. As I approached, he gave me a warm, welcoming smile.

The koi selfishly squeezed and pushed one another as they crowded near the rim of the pond, their heads bobbing above the water, mouths gaping open like suckling piglets squealing for Mama's milk. Seeing me, they charged forward, pushing and shoving for a prime position to be fed. We'd studied them in eighth-grade science class. I remember Ms. Sykora telling the class that for them, just about any food is filet mignon—shrimp, algae, worms, Cheerios, Lean Cuisine, Ritz Crackers—you name it, they'll eat it.

The reverend made this abundantly clear. "To say they're not discriminating eaters is an understatement. They'll eat anything that doesn't eat them first. And they don't seem to believe that rules are rules," he said as he pointed to the sign next to the pond: *Please Don't Feed the Fish!* "It means the kitchen is closed except when the temple's groundskeeper, yours truly, gives out one meal a day in winter and two during the warmer months."

I felt sorry for them. "What a way to live!"

"I don't know. They seem to enjoy the theater of it all. Anyway, come on in. Thay is waiting for you."

He led me to a room in the rear of the temple and opened the door.

"Please go in, Luc. I'm going to finish the gardening. See you later."

"Thanks, Reverend."

The room was a strange shape—hexagonal and minimally decorated, with a couple of large Persian rugs. It had tall, narrow, stained-glass windows on four of the walls. Centered on the fifth wall opposite the entryway stood a large red-stone statue of the Buddha, in front of which were three small brass containers with burning incense, one in front of the Buddha and one on each side. The aroma was pleasant but a little too sweet for me.

Thay sat in a lotus position on a large, purple silk pillow between the two windows on the east side of the room and to the right of the Buddha sculpture. The morning sun radiating through the stained-glass windows bathed him in multiple colors, giving him a kind of supernatural appearance. He had both hands on his smartphone and was focused on rapidly texting with his thumbs—or so I thought.

He didn't look up as he acknowledged my entry. "Luc, come on over. I'm almost done here."

"Sorry, I didn't mean to interrupt your texting."

He looked up and stopped what he was doing. "What texting?"

When I got closer to him, I understood his response. I freaked out! He was playing *Super Mario Bros.*" I couldn't believe it.

"Wow! You play video games?"

He set his phone down on the floor next to the pillow he was sitting on. "Only those that improve my focus and concentration."

Amazing—a well-connected 21st-century monk!

"Namaste, Luc, and welcome, my friend."

"Good morning. What does *namaste* mean? I've heard it many times before."

"A loose translation is 'the spirit within me honors and bows to the spirit within you.' It's a way for someone to acknowledge that the true reality in all of us is not material but spiritual. True reality, as we will discuss later, is your infinite, eternal, Personal Consciousness, which is connected to all other consciousness throughout the universe."

"That's quite a translation for a single word. And as for its meaning, whoa, it's beyond comprehension."

Thay said, "We will get to the meaning soon enough. As for the translation, that's usually the case with Sanskrit. A single word can have many meanings, and when translated into English, it often requires an entire sentence or more to provide the right context."

"Hmm . . . interesting." I immediately thought, *That wasn't the right response*. Dad once told me that's what he says when someone takes him to dinner, and he doesn't want to offend the person when commenting on the bland taste of the wine they ordered.

"Please sit on the large pillow in front of me. Make yourself comfortable."

Earlier that morning, having finished my five-mile run with 15 minutes of stretches, my legs felt quite limber. I managed a lotus position quite easily.

Thay continued. "What I'm about to tell you may sound like theology or religion, but again, I have to emphasize that it's neither. It's certainly spiritual in the sense that it has everything to do with spirit, meaning nonmaterial things, but little to do with the three-dimensional world we perceive with our five senses, and nothing to do with any religion."

I smiled. "That's good. The last thing I need is an old-fashioned Sunday-school lesson."

He laughed and straightened his pillow. "I'm going to share concepts with you from the emerging field of spiritual physics. It's a science that seeks to uncover answers to important questions posed over the ages by scientists and philosophers— questions such as: *What is consciousness? Who am I? Why am I here in this universe? What is my purpose? Where did the universe come from? What happens to my consciousness after I die?*

"These might be considered aspects of what some physicists call the Theory of Everything, or the TOE. As you will eventually see, all of this is related in some way to what you experienced during and after your near-death experience. Does that make sense to you?"

I thought for a second. I'd read *The Elegant Universe* by Brian Greene, in which he talked about the TOE, but this seemed a step beyond that. It was over my head, but I was willing to see where it might lead. I loosened my lotus position and sat back slightly, supported by my arms outstretched on the floor behind me, and responded to Thay's question. "Not really. Those are big questions. Let's give it a shot, though. If I'm lucky, maybe something will sink in."

"These are not only big questions; they are *the* questions. But, trust me, with your intelligence and the information you have access to through your high level of consciousness, you'll soon understand the answers. I ask that you be patient. It will take only a short time to overcome some of the subconscious preconceptions you may have developed over the years. Some of them may not be useful for you and your future. We need to erase them so that you can proceed in the best possible way to realize your life purpose."

He smiled and went on. "We all have these *pre*conceptions and, in some cases, they're *mis*conceptions. It's part of the path of our human thought and evolutionary development. As we move through life, we tend to take on beliefs and values from those people with whom we spend the most time. Swiss psychiatrist Carl Jung called this the Collective Unconscious. Don't misunderstand, some of these preconceptions are useful, but some may not serve your purpose anymore."[45]

I told Thay, "I'm not aware of any preconceptions or misconceptions, but hey, if they're there and I don't need them, or if they're standing in my way, let's get rid of them. You're not going to hypnotize me, are you?"

"No, not in the way you're likely thinking. You'll do that on your own."

"I'll hypnotize myself?" Thay just nodded. I could already see that this was going to be a complicated lesson. But, hell, I wanted to do my best and make it a perfect swoosh of a three-pointer.

"Okay, then, we'll start at the beginning, although as you'll quickly see, there was no beginning and there will be no end."

Just as I thought—complicated. I was baffled by Thay's comment. He saw my look of confusion. I had no idea what he was talking about, but that didn't stop him.

"Patience. You'll understand soon enough."

Patience, right, but I couldn't see how it was going to help me with Bella, the CIA, my father, and especially, these damn superpowers.

Thay began. "Our physical universe as we know it through our five senses is the reflection of something much greater than the universe itself, something well beyond our three-dimensional world. Spiritual physicists call it by several names: the Universal or Infinite Mind, the Unified Field, or as we Buddhists do, Cosmic Consciousness. The name is irrelevant. But what *is* relevant is that it is infinite and eternal. It always was and always will be. It occupies every point of the physical universe and extends beyond that into what can be called Infinite Nothingness, a place that is not really a place, where nothing exists but Cosmic Consciousness. Einstein would say, 'No space, no time, no energy, no matter—absolutely nothing.'"

I sat there with my mouth slightly agape, thinking, *Thay, I hope you're right about my intelligence, and I sure as hell hope it kicks in soon. I haven't the foggiest idea what you just said.*

"However, in the words of quantum physicists," he continued, "we can say that in this nonplace there exists an energy field of infinite possibilities, which under the right circumstances, any one of which can be coaxed into our three-dimensional, five-sense reality and create those things we seek in life. The fundamental question you will soon learn the answer to is just how do you nudge the possibility you want into your life?"

This is really, really, weird—a place that's not a place yet it contains a humongous number of possibilities—and I can just grab the one I want and change my life. Really?

Thay could see I wasn't buying this, but he kept going. He was on a roll. "All things—absolutely everything—come from this nonplace, and eventually return to it in the form of consciousness. Those with a religious orientation might prefer to call it God, but it's certainly not God in the sense taught by organized religion. And, in fact, it should not be considered an aspect of any religion."

I was trying to be patient, hoping this stuff would eventually gel into a picture that made sense to me. "You previously mentioned this new science, spiritual physics. What does it say about our purpose and the purpose of the universe, anyway?" I asked.

I must have posed the right question at the right time. Thay's eyes lit up, and he enthusiastically charged ahead. "The purpose of all physical things in our universe, including you, is to enable Cosmic Consciousness—God, if you want to call It that—to be continuously and intimately aware of Its presence. I say 'Its' even though Cosmic Consciousness or God, if you will, is genderless—not he, she, or it. Spiritual physicists would say It's an energy field, but not energy in the classical or quantum physics sense, but a spiritual energy. And as for the pronoun, we need to invent a fourth one that represents an intimate combination of the other three.

"There's still a lot to do to understand the nature of this kind of energy, how It works, how best to access It, and how to use It. But progress is being made by capable scientists who understand that this is our future. The most important point for you to understand is that your role—actually, the role of everyone and everything in the universe—is to make God intimately aware of Itself."[5s]

I said, "Hold on! Look, I'm not a religious person, but even *I* know that most religions preach that God is an all-knowing supreme being. Why would He, I mean, It, need help from me or anyone or anything to know It exists?"

"Cosmic Consciousness—God—is all-knowing and definitely supreme. And yes, It knows It exists. It doesn't need you and the rest of the material universe to know this, or to know about the existence and intricacies of the universe. It's got that down pat. It needs you for awareness, just as you need your five senses for awareness. You need your eyes to appreciate the magnificence and beauty of the mountains and the sea, or a Caravaggio painting or a rainbow. Your genius and power are in your mind and Personal Consciousness. Your five senses bring awareness to your genius. Without your sight, you would be no less of a genius; and without the physicality of the universe, God or Cosmic Consciousness would be no less knowing or supreme.

"I'm sorry for bringing the word *God* into our discussion. What I'm presenting to you is not related to any religion. It's a science and philosophy that can explain the workings of the cosmos. I simply want to put it in a context that you already know. But it's true, it *is* an oversimplification."

My eyes glazed over. I was losing focus. Thay saw my confusion. Not being a religious person or a philosopher or a scientist, this was foreign stuff to me. I tried my best to be considerate with my comments. "That's a lot for me to comprehend."

"I know it can sound confusing, especially the first time you hear it. But the picture will soon come together when we discuss your personal experiences. You'll need this background information to appreciate and understand your paranormal powers, but more important, how to use them safely."

"Okay . . . I guess." My response was as iffy as his was firm. He just kept pushing ahead. My head was spinning. I decided to do my best to stay focused, hoping that what he was telling me would help me manage my life.[65]

Although at that moment I wasn't getting all the spiritual physics stuff, I somehow felt it was important, probably because this cool monk from the Bronx was very smart and obviously believed deeply in what he was telling me. And, most important, he was trying to help me out of the mess I was in.

"Collective Consciousness is consciousness associated with the overlap of the consciousness among all species. In fact, every single piece of material matter in the universe, right down to the atoms and subatomic particles that form all matter, has some level of consciousness."[7s]

"This stuff may be interesting to scientists or philosophers or whoever, but why me?" I asked.

"Because it's the reason we can mentally communicate with others, and in its most highly developed state, it is what enables remote viewing and other superpowers. The more highly developed this form of consciousness is in an individual, the more success he or she will have in managing these powers. Your strong ability in remote viewing, your cerebral translator and encyclopedia and much more, are all directly connected to your ability to quickly access super high levels of consciousness, and therefore, the knowledge and wisdom of the cosmos."

"Okay, I think I'm beginning to understand.[8s] But isn't consciousness really just our mind?"

"No. It's true that consciousness operates *through* the mind, that aspect of our brain that perceives, thinks, reasons, and evaluates. And just as we live at the level of the body, we also live at the level of the mind. The mind, in fact, is pure potential energy, and physics tells us that we can convert potential energy into kinetic energy. So, you see, we can change our physical world simply by changing our thoughts and beliefs. That's why we say that *you are what you believe.*"[43, 9s]

"If that's true, it's an amazing power. Are you telling me that I create my life by my consciousness and my mind, and if I choose to, I can create the physical world I desire by changing my thoughts and expectations?" I was incredulous.

"That's exactly what I'm saying, although there are two rules that you must follow to be successful, and I mentioned them previously. First, what you want to bring into your life must not hurt anyone, and second, in some way it should make the world a better place—even a little bit. This is not for good-hearted or benevolent reasons. These two rules are necessary to keep the universe evolving its totality of consciousness, Unity Consciousness, to increasingly higher levels. That's the Cosmic Purpose—the sole purpose of the

[43] Bruce H. Lipton, *The Biology of Belief*, Elite Books, Santa Rosa, California, 2005.

universe—in a nutshell, and we human beings are the tools to help make it happen. What an incredible role we play!"

"I'll say."

"So, you see, your mind is a kind of control valve between the infinite knowledge of Cosmic Consciousness—some might call it the mind of God—and your Personal Consciousness. Based on past programming by others in your life journey, your mind decides how much information from Cosmic Consciousness comes through to your awareness. If your mind didn't provide this kind of control, the immense amount of information you would have access to in your five-sense world would be overwhelming for your human experience.[10s]

"There is also a clear and definitive answer to what philosophers and scientists call the *Hard Problem*, which goes back to my comment about the mind—namely, does the mind create consciousness, or does consciousness create the mind? Spiritual physics maintains that consciousness creates the mind."

Apparently, I had the wrong idea about the mind. "I always thought that our mind was responsible for our consciousness."

"Yes," Thay explained, "most neurologists thought so for decades. However, more and more scientists, especially those skilled in quantum physics, are finding that consciousness creates the mind and not the converse."

My legs began to cramp. I got up from my pillow and started to walk and stretch. "Why are scientists changing their position on this?" I asked.

"You have the answer from your own NDE."

I sat down on my pillow, my arms wrapped around my bent legs, my chin resting on my knees. "I don't understand."

"Think about what happened to you. Biological science has shown us that during an NDE, when your heart stopped beating, seconds later, your brain and mind shut down completely. There were no measurable brain waves. You were physically dead. Yet you had a vivid and clear experience of floating above, observing your dead body, seeing a defective air-conditioning vent, traveling through walls, reaching the tunnel, and encountering the Great Light.

"You also brought back specific and accurate information from your deceased grandfather to be shared with your mom. This would have all been completely impossible if your consciousness had shut down when your brain and your mind shut down. There are literally hundreds of thousands of well-documented accounts of persons who have gone through an NDE, then accurately described things that he or she observed while they were dead."

"Now that part makes sense to me."[11s]

"Great! I'm sure you've studied biology and the evolution of species. I can tell you that in addition to physical evolution as described by Darwin—survival of the fittest and natural selection to create more perfectly designed physical species—consciousness throughout the universe is also evolving toward what is necessary for the effective functioning of physically advanced species. This is all connected with what we can call the Meaning and Purpose of Life."

"I'm not sure I get that."

"You will. For now, let's say it in simple terms—the *Meaning of Life* is to find the special gift or gifts you came into this world with—everyone has at least one—and the *Purpose of Life* is to share your gifts with others and make the world a better place. Namely, you should be manifesting into this world things that make it a better place for others, and improve your life as well. That, my friend, increases the level of Universal Consciousness, sometimes called Unity Consciousness."

"That helps."

Thay increasingly spoke more slowly and took more pauses. I sensed that he knew I had a hard time keeping up with him, but he pushed on anyway. I was beginning to feel more confident that I would eventually get what he was talking about.[12s] But I was running out of focused energy.

"My head's spinning. I mean, how could we possibly know this about the universe and about ourselves?"

"Good question. Spiritual physics says we do this by accessing the Universal Mind, namely, Cosmic Consciousness, which is infinite and all-knowing."

"Yeah, but how can we do that?"

Thay smiled, leaned closer to me, and opened his eyes wide. "Now, I'm going to tell you an ancient secret. Promise not to give it away?"

He was kidding, of course, but I couldn't help but smile back, which started to relieve my tension, anxiety, and diminishing concentration.

He whispered with the skill and animation of a Broadway actor. "Spiritual physics maintains that there is a record of every action, thought, word, intention, emotion, and event that *has* ever occurred or *will* ever occur in the universe, and that information is encoded in Cosmic Consciousness. The ancient wisdom seekers of the East called it the *Akashic Record. Akasha* is a Sanskrit word that means "the fifth element"—namely, beyond the primary four elements of alchemy—Air, Fire, Water, and Earth. Loosely speaking, the Akashic Record can be considered the Mind of Cosmic Consciousness, or some might say, as Einstein once did, the mind of God."[44]

"If that's true, how could we access that infinite information?" I asked.

"Through very deep meditation—the deeper the meditation, the higher the level of consciousness, and the greater access to the infinite knowledge in the Akashic Record. This is how certain spiritual people have been able to read the thoughts of others, predict the future, and know what we think to be unknowable and do what we believe is undoable. One of the most astonishing points is that in such states of higher consciousness, it's possible to do what in our five-sense world appears to be time travel."

"Wow, if that doesn't sound like science fiction, I don't know what does!"

---

[44] What Einstein said was, "I want to know the mind of God. Everything else is just details."

"Luc, my legs are also beginning to lose circulation—a vestige of an old climbing injury. Let's get up and walk slowly around the room. Okay with you?"

"Sure."

We left our cushions and strolled across the room. From what I'd read in ancient history, it reminded me of Socrates lecturing one of his students as they walked around the Greek Lyceum—engaging in what was later known as the Socratic Method.

Thay responded to my earlier comment. "You're right. Most would think it smacks of science fiction. But for certain gifted people—and you appear to be one of them—it's possible for their deep conscious awareness to travel backward or forward in time to retrieve information from the Akashic Record. That's why, under certain circumstances, you've been able to know what others are going to say or do before they say or do it. It's why your basketball game has significantly improved. You know what the opposing player is going to do even before *he* does.

"In the language of spiritual physics, we would say that all information about events, past and future, is recorded in the cosmos at a higher-dimensional level of vibration—again, what our Buddhist ancestors called the Akashic Record. Today, some scientists refer to it as the Akashic Field.[13s]

"I can assure you that all of these paranormal effects can be accessed by a person who is gifted with this ability or has learned to shift his or her consciousness to higher levels and thereby access the Akashic Record. This capability accounts for many experiences and events that occur in near-death situations, or immediately following biological death. This includes out-of-body experiences, or OBEs, like you had in your NDE and afterward. What's quite amazing is that even people who were born blind have reportedly seen vividly, accurately, and in color during an OBE or NDE."[14s]

I said, "This is all amazing stuff. But what does it have to do with my NDE experience and the powers that seem to be overtaking my mind?"

"Everything. We will discuss that in our next meeting. You've had enough for one day."

"You can say that again."

I left Thay that morning not knowing whether I should look forward to our next meeting with a sense of excitement or apprehension. But one thing I *did* get out of our discussion is that my NDE somehow increased my capability to achieve high levels of consciousness, which enabled me to access information from a great distance and see possible futures that I could choose from. I guessed that if I learned how to direct my powers, I could tap into the immense intelligence and wisdom in the Akashic Record. Now that would be exciting—I think.

Chapter
Twenty-Three

ENLIGHTENMENT

THAY AND I PLANNED TO MEET ON SUNDAY AFTERNOON AT 2:30. Since our last meeting, I'd thought nearly nonstop about what he was teaching me. Like my NDE, but this time in my mind's eye, a light went on and started to glow brighter with time. Thay was right—I was finally getting it. His ideas started to make sense, and things were falling into place. Hopefully, with a little more time, it would *all* make sense.

I'd gotten a call from Eric, who was finally home from the hospital. As promised, I invited him to lunch at the Palo Alto Creamery before my meeting with Thay.

I arrived there just before noon. Even though only the first two booths were taken, I sat down at the last booth in the back of the restaurant. I liked that one for quiet, private conversations. A few minutes later, Eric arrived. I waved to him. As he walked toward the booth, I saw a person who was completely different from the one I'd fought with and "killed" at the preserve.

For one thing, his Mohawk was gone. He was growing back what looked like the beginnings of thick, wavy-blond hair. And gone was the tight, sleeveless T-shirt showing off his large muscles and colorful tattoos. He wore a blue-and-white-striped long-sleeve shirt over his jeans, and a pair of black-and-white Vans sneakers. Eric had lost his wise-guy, I'll-punch-your-face-in strut. He seemed like a normal person. Meeting his father in his NDE must have changed everything. What a difference in such a short time![45]

"Hi, Eric. Glad you could make it. I've been thinking a lot about our discussion in the hospital. Are you okay, now—I mean, kinda back to normal?"

"Normal? Hell, what's that?"

"Yeah, right." As he sat down across from me, I fumbled with my menu and just had to ask. I was so curious. "You know, when Bella and I met you at the preserve, you were—if you don't mind me being honest—a real wise guy and an obvious troublemaker. What's changed?"

Eric explained. "I think you probably can guess the answer to that, but let me give you a few things to think about. Before my NDE, my life was the shits. I had no family except my mom, and she worked six days a week to pay the bills and was a real Prozac case, depressed most of the time. Having just quit school, I couldn't find a decent job.

"I finally had to admit the truth. I hated growing up without a father. There was no one who could relate to what I was going through at school and in the neighborhood. When I was 12, I got mixed up with the wrong guys—you met one of them at the Ravenswood Preserve—they became my family.

"After my NDE and my discussion with my father, everything changed. I took your advice and told my mom what happened. At first she thought I was hallucinating and wanted me to see a shrink. But when I told her some of the things my father had said, she knew I must have seen him. There was no way I could know half of those things. She cried for two days, but then she, too, began to change. She's off antidepressants, and I've never seen her look so good. She's even got a date next week—as far as I know,

---

[45] Based on studies of thousands of near-death experiences, this is a common aftereffect. It is estimated that about 5 percent of the global population, nearly 300 million people, have experienced some kind of NDE or OBE.

her first since my father left. Yeah, I can tell ya, our lives have changed—and it feels pretty damn good."

"Wow, Eric, that's great! I understand, and I'm happy for you and your mom."

Perfect timing—the waitress came to our booth with a couple of menus and some ice water and then walked away. Eric opened his menu and asked, "So what's good here?"

I told him, "They've got great burgers, super fries, and their milkshakes are the best around. Most everything on their menu is good—depends on your taste."

"So what are you gonna have?"

"I think I'll get a cheeseburger, fries, and a vanilla malt."

"Sounds good to me. Let's double it."

The waitress came back over and took our order. She smiled, seeming pleased to multiply everything by two.

Just then I looked up and, *merda santa,* was I freaked out? Thay walked through the door.

I thought, *Cavalo!* But then I caught myself. *Think fast—okay, no choice.*

"Eric, a friend of mine just walked in. I had no idea he'd be here today. Do you mind if I invite him to join us? You'll like him. He's different, but trust me, he's a really neat guy."

"No problem. That's fine with me. Ask him."

I reluctantly waved to Thay, and he waved back. He padded over to our booth. Eric turned around and saw him walking over to us.

"Your friend is a monk? A neat guy—really?"

"It's a long story. I'll fill you in some other time. Trust me, you'll like him."

"Sure. I guess."

I introduced Eric to Thay. Just like everyone who met the monk for the first time, Eric was amused by his accent. He smiled and stared at Thay but didn't say a thing. He didn't have to. Thay was very perceptive, and no stranger to this kind of initial reaction. He smiled back.

"Thay, would you like to join us for lunch?" I asked.

"Super! Beats eating alone. I'm not used to it. I usually eat in a large dining hall with about 50 other monks." He cracked a smile. "It's a really spiritual—but boring—experience every mealtime."

The three of us laughed as Thay slid in next to me. The waitress came over almost immediately and took his order. Thay ordered a goat-cheese omelet and green tea. Surprisingly, a dynamic conversation soon ensued among the three of us, especially between Thay and Eric. He was impressed with Thay's background, especially growing up in the Bronx and then in the Himalayas. Eric asked Thay if he would take him climbing someday. Thay loved the idea.

He asked Eric about his background and interests, which he didn't hesitate to answer openly and honestly. He didn't seem to mind Thay's curiosity about his personal life at all. The two of them got on like old friends. I was happy for Eric.

Although I was pleased about the way things were going, I felt guilty that I hadn't said anything to Thay in our previous discussions about what I'd done to Eric. It's the only thing I'd held back from him. I had to get this off my chest, but obviously not in front of Eric.

The three of us got along so well that we decided to meet again. I could sense from our conversation that Eric would benefit from discussing with Thay what had happened to him at the preserve, his NDE, and what occurred afterward with his father. But first, I had to come clean about what I'd done to Eric and why I hadn't told Thay.

Thay had borrowed Reverend Daikan's car. Leaving the Creamery, the two of us walked a couple blocks to the public parking lot to drive together to the temple. As we approached the car, we saw two wise guys sitting on the fence in the back of the lot sharing a cigarette, which turned out to be a joint. They weren't from Palo Alto. They looked like part of the crowd that Eric had previously hung with—same uniform—ragged Levis and white, sleeveless T-shirts. These hulks looked more menacing than Eric and Randy did at the preserve. They jumped off the fence and strutted over to us as we were ready to get into the car.

"Well, looky what we got here, Brian. If it ain't the big *Dago-Wop* who put Eric in the hospital. The prick couldn't take him in a fair fight, so he shot him with one of those electric guns. And he's got a monk with him." Laughing, he said, "You on your way to church to ask for forgiveness for what you did to poor Eric?"

I guess they hadn't heard what had really happened to Eric, so based on Randy's input, they'd concluded I'd shot him with a Taser. I wanted to be careful with these two muscle-bound thugs, especially because Thay was with me. I didn't want anything to happen to him.

"Hey, *Dago*, got your electric pistol with you?" one of the guys asked.

"No. I never had one. Look, man, we don't want any trouble, all right?"

"Hey, Brian, he left his gun home. Ain't they just a pair of weirdo freaks? What a couple of funny-looking dudes. And the tall *Dago* dude doesn't want any trouble. Well, ain't that just sweet of him?"

Thay didn't say a word. He just stared at them—without a single iota of fear—at least as far as I could tell.

The Brian punk responded sarcastically, "Oh, Kenny, please don't hurt the tall pasta-gobbler and his sidekick monkey. We should put a leash on the monkey and make him dance for us. Good idea. Get that rope outta the trunk. Let's hook this monkey up." Brian went over to the car next to ours and opened the trunk to get the rope.

Thay stepped in front of me and faced the Kenny thug. He turned his head and whispered, "Not to worry. I got this."

What in the world was he thinking? He's a head shorter than I am—and a monk!

Standing behind Thay, I could see the Kenny punk clear as day over his head. Thay calmly advised him, "Look, we have an appointment and don't want to be late, so we'll be on our way, okay?"

Kenny, a good two inches taller than Thay, and using his left hand, grabbed Thay's robe under his neck and stared into his face with a fierce smirk. I thought he was going to pick him up in the air and throw him, except Thay was 6'3" and solid muscle. He'd be a heavy throw even for *this* guy.

I wasn't gonna let this happen. "Why you *bastard, vaffanculo*! I tried to get past Thay, but he reached back with one arm, and with strength like tempered steel, held me back.

Thay calmly and slowly said, "Look, my friend, I suggest you take your hands off me. You're being rude, and I don't like rude."

"Hey, Brian, the monkey says I'm being rude, and he don't like rude. Don't you just feel sorry for him?"

Thay stood there in Kenny's chokehold, his face turning red as a beet, but still calm as he stared into Kenny's face. I tried to go around him again to help, but he pushed me back with his right arm.

Kenny laughed, let go of his chokehold on Thay, took a puff from the joint hanging from his right hand, and blew the drug-laced smoke directly into Thay's face. Like a speeding freight train, Thay did some kind of a martial-arts maneuver, so quickly that within seconds Kenny was flat on his back on the ground and nearly unconscious, his eyes rolling back while he tried desperately to catch his breath. Brian stepped forward toward Thay and raised his right arm to hit him.

Thay caught his arm in midair, stopping it cold as if it were caught in a vice. Thay calmly but firmly advised him, "I wouldn't do that, young man, or you'll join your friend on the ground, and it won't be a good ending for you—worse than for him, that I can promise you." Thay released his arm. Brian got the message, loud and clear.

I stood there in awe, trying to figure out what had just happened.

Brian helped Kenny to his feet, and the two of them limped off down the street, Brian looking back just once to give us a middle-finger salute.

"Wow, Thay, where in the world did you learn to fight like that?"

"I don't believe in fighting, just self-defense. I studied martial arts at the monastery in Nepal to develop my focus and concentration."

It was only later that I learned from Reverend Daikan that Thay held a ninth-degree black belt in tae kwon do—the highest level possible.

ON THE DRIVE TO THE TEMPLE, I couldn't stop praising Thay. I was so amazed by what he'd just done. I knew he was no ordinary monk, but this went way beyond that. What else could this guy do?

I was more and more motivated to learn whatever he could teach me. During the ten-minute ride to the temple, our conversation was mostly about his life in Nepal and how what he initially thought was a terrible move turned out to be life-changing and one of the most important things that had ever happened to him. That comment echoed over and over in my mind. Could it be . . . ?

We arrived at 2:30 P.M., just in time to start our discussion. Thay parked in the driveway alongside the temple. We entered and stood for a few moments in the entryway. He looked me in the eyes and said, "You know, the three of us had a great lunch together. Yet I had a sense that you were hesitant to invite me to join you guys, and during our discussion, I felt there was something bothering you. Am I off base?"

He was right, of course, and it had been troubling me ever since our last meeting together. I'd spent the last few days going back and forth about whether or not to tell him.

I caved. Keeping it from him was driving me crazy. "Yeah, you're right. There *is* something bothering me, but I'm not sure how to explain it to you."

"Don't worry about how or where to start. Just say what's on your mind, and especially what's in your heart. You need to release what's troubling you. It'll help. It doesn't have to be perfect. You're not in English class, so fugettaboutit! Okay?"

We laughed. I loved Thay's Bronx accent and his wise-guy imitations. Never got tired of it. He knew how to break the ice. "You're right. What's bothering me is that I didn't tell you everything in our last meeting. There's one terrible thing that happened when I was hiking with Bella a couple of weeks ago. It was creepy, and I have no idea how or why it happened—"

Thay interrupted me. "Hold on a sec. I tell you what. Let's get out of the entryway and off our feet. Let's go into the big room and sit there quietly." Which is exactly what we did.

We sat on large pillows opposite each other, and I explained in detail what had occurred at the Ravenswood Open Space Preserve. Thay didn't flinch or express the slightest surprise.

When I was done, he said, "That's amazing, and I think I can explain it to you, and I *will* before you leave today. But first, building on our last discussion, I need to touch on a couple of other points, which is the main reason we're meeting today. I want to explain what's happening to you in the larger context, and try to guide you in your thinking so that you can understand it and hopefully accept it."

Understanding is fine, but I wasn't so sure about the "accept it" part. That didn't sound good to me. But I put my trust in Thay and agreed to proceed.

He closed his eyes, folded his hands in front of his chest, and was quiet. He mumbled something in another language—Sanskrit, I guessed. Then he opened his eyes and reached over and put his palms on my ears, embracing my head.

"Close your eyes and inhale and exhale deeply and slowly until you feel light-headed. This is what the Wisdom Seekers called *prana-yama*. It will open your heart and your soul."

I did as he instructed until I felt a heady feeling—it was kinda like drugs without the drugs—and then I went back to normal breathing.

"Now, I will lead you in a special meditation so that you can quiet any concerns you may have at this moment. I want you to repeat this mantra three times in your mind: *Om, Vardhanam Namah.* In Sanskrit it means, 'I nourish the universe, and the universe nourishes me.'"

I did as he instructed. Thay removed his hands from my head.

"As we did once before in meditation, I want you to go inside to that place in the center of your chest, immediately to the right of your heart. Remove all thoughts. And should any begin to creep into your consciousness, silently repeat the mantra, *Om, Vardhanam Namah.*"

I followed his instructions, and the next thing I knew, he touched my forehead.

"It's time to release the mantra. Take three deep breaths and exhale each one slowly, and when you feel ready, open your eyes."

Again, I did as he instructed, and as I opened my eyes, I saw Thay smiling. "How do you feel?"

"I feel much better—incredibly rested. Thank you."

"Don't thank me. It's you who have the power to do what you've just done."

I told him, "I had the most amazing experience during my meditation, very much like the last time you helped me meditate—incredible colors and music and a complete sense of joy. From all I saw and heard, I guess I was under for quite a long time. Sorry about that. But I was in such a magical place. I didn't want to leave. I can't wait to tell you about it."

Thay smiled. "You may find this hard to believe, but I let you meditate for only five minutes."

"Really? I don't understand. How can that be?"

"When you're in such a deep meditative state as you are so very capable of, you're walking in the world of pure consciousness, where, as I mentioned during our last meeting, there is no time or space, or as physicists like to say, no space-time. Anything and everything can and does happen instantly. Tell me about your experience."

"It was like my NDE all over again," I told him. "I saw myself sitting here with you as my body rose smoothly to the ceiling above and then through the building high into the sky. I again entered a huge, dark tunnel, and as I drifted farther down the tunnel, a light began to shine, brighter and brighter as I moved toward it. It was brighter than anything I've ever seen—brighter than ten suns—and it seemed to communicate with me, not by voice, but by thought. The brightness didn't hurt my eyes. I knew clearly the thoughts it was sending me."

"What did it tell you?" Thay asked.

"It said, 'Luc, relax into your destiny, and accept it as an intimate part of your future. You are a chosen one. You have powers that can make a big difference and change the world for the better. It will not be an easy journey for you to use those powers, surrounded by others whom you love and who love you. They could never completely comprehend what or who you are, but that is how it must be. Eventually, you will not be alone. You will have *The Two*, and they will help you. The universe has conspired to make this happen—and therefore, it *will* happen. It is written perfectly and clearly in the Cosmic Plan.'"

Thay shifted forward on his pillow and placed his outstretched arms on my shoulders as he stared into my eyes. "How did that make you feel?"

"Honestly? I was frightened and excited at the same time. I knew at that moment that there was a special purpose I had to pursue, and it was greater than I am, and probably greater than I can understand, at least for now—but hopefully not greater than I can handle. I desperately wanted to know what it was. And I wanted to know who *The Two* are who will help me. I asked the Light, and It said, 'Fear not, Luc. You will know in the fullness of time. There are some things that must happen first. That is the way it must and will be.' Whatever that means."

"Anything else?"

"Yes, probably the most important thing of all—the Light told me that when I go back, I should seek the guidance and counsel of the *Spiritual One*, and that I know who that is . . . it's you, Thay. The Light wants me to be your student."

"I understand, and I am at your disposal and would be honored to serve you in any way I can to help for as long as you want and need me."

I told him, "I don't understand. I'm concerned, even scared. But it seems like I'm being called by a higher power, maybe even pulled, to do something big, something important. I'm not sure what it is, or if I could do it, or even if I want to."

"Luc, allow me to provide a perspective that will be both clarifying and perhaps a bit frightening."

"Clarifying, I like. I don't know how much more frightening I can take."

"I understand. First, you should know that your NDE was the means that Cosmic Consciousness—what you have called a higher power—used to 'wake you up' and let you see that you've been chosen as a special person with special powers for a special mission."

"How's that?"

Thay went on to explain that throughout history, just as there have been nearly instantaneous jumps—at least on a geological scale—in the physical evolution of species, there have also been several of these jumps in the evolution of consciousness.

The big difference is that while jumps in physical evolution happened via a rapid escalation of Darwin's "survival of the fittest and natural selection," jumps in consciousness evolution required the presence and help of a specially gifted person, sometimes even an Avatar, here on Earth.[15s]

"Do we know who any of those people were?" I asked.

"Yes, some. For example, Moses, Abraham, the Buddha, Rumi, Confucius, Jesus, Mary Magdalene, Mohammed, Joan of Arc, Teresa of Avila, and Bernadette Soubirous, to name a few of these wise ones. Some, though not all of them, were Avatars—that is, physical entities who were intimately enmeshed with Cosmic Consciousness—or as some might say, the Divine in a human body. The Buddha and Jesus, and possibly a few others, were examples of such Avatars."

I looked at Thay in disbelief. I saw this as fantasy and hard to believe. "With all due respect, you've got to be kidding me. I don't see myself in a class with any of those folks, I mean, an Avatar, really? And second, many of them were responsible for starting a religion, and I am way far away from that."

"To your first point," Thay said patiently, "none of these highly conscious souls saw themselves in the company of those great ones who lived before them. It's true that certain prophets tried to convince Jesus that he was the son of God and had a special path to follow. He, at first, repelled this assertion. In fact, he often said, 'God and the Kingdom of Heaven are within you,' meaning that he didn't see himself as special, and that all people already had the presence of God within them.

"And yes, the Buddha was born a prince into an aristocratic family, which he rejected and left to find out who he really was. He did not find aristocracy a special position compared to others. Both men were humble, unassuming, ordinary people. But they were gifted with special powers, as you are. Perhaps not the same ones, but those necessary to accomplish their mission.

"To your second point, none of them who today are held up with piety and devotion as the founder of a specific religion had any intention of starting and growing an organized sect, cult, or faith. Those religions were created by men who sought power and control over the masses, long after these highly conscious individuals were gone from the face of the earth. For example, it's well established that Christianity was formally founded during the reign of Constantine the Great, more than 300 years after the death of Christ."[16s]

I asked, "What about all those people who followed Jesus while he was alive?"

"In many important ways, they were no different from those who followed philosophers like Plato, Socrates, Pythagoras, and Descartes. They were interested in Jesus's philosophy of life. It helped them find hope and a means to cope during troubled times. And most important, it helped them find out who they really were."

"All of that's news to me," I said, "and I'll bet modern-day Christians wouldn't be happy hearing it—but they probably wouldn't give a hoot or a second thought anyway."

"You're probably right. What do you say we change the subject for now? You'll need some time to think about what I've just told you. How about we go back to your question about what you did to Eric? Interested?"

"Heck, yeah! Now you're talking." I reviewed exactly what had happened that day at the preserve.

Thay explained, "So here's what happened when there was the appearance of what you've described as a fireball of lightning striking Eric and his subsequent electrocution. You created an event known as electrokinesis, the ability of a person with an extremely high level of altered consciousness to generate and control the path of lightning or electricity without ever touching it. It is a rare phenomenon, but it has been documented throughout history on various occasions. It's considered by modern science to be folklore and completely impossible based on the known laws of classical and quantum physics."

I added my two cents. "I would agree, if I hadn't seen it with my own eyes."

"I understand. And if you draw on the existing laws of physics, it's impossible to explain the generation of such powerful energy by a human being and its release without that person being electrocuted."

"So, then, what did I do to Eric?"

"What you did in a moment of high anxiety and anger—an expression of your unconditional caring and loving concern for Bella—was to use your high level of consciousness energy—a force not recognized by conventional physics, only by spiritual physics—to generate separate yet very close to your body a microscopic, invisible black hole, quite similar to the much larger astronomical ones in deep space studied by astrophysicists. You created it from what is known in quantum physics as the zero-point energy of the universe. We can discuss the physics, if you wish, some other time. What I *can* say at this time is that physicists would like to find a means to tap into the zero-point energy field, as it would offer an infinite level of free energy to the planet. So far, all efforts to do so have failed. But you, because of your ability to access high levels of consciousness, can do this."

"Whoa! That's incomprehensible to me. Are you telling me I have access to those kinds of capabilities?"

"Yes, you do, and you must learn to use them wisely, discreetly, and safely."

"But why wasn't I also electrocuted by the lightning bolt since it came from my hand?"

"Because you never touched the microscopic black hole, but you were able to create it from zero-point energy in a space immediately adjacent to the surface of your hand and direct it at Eric with a powerful consciousness force field that you clearly have the capability to generate, especially under stress. As that minuscule black hole flew toward Eric, it swallowed the atmosphere existing in its path, and ionized the oxygen and nitrogen components of air to much higher energy levels, similar to putting an electrical discharge through a gas such as neon, as is done to make neon signs, but at much higher energy levels.

"As the atoms of the excited ionized nitrogen and oxygen degenerated or fell back to what is called their ground or normal state, they emitted high-energy photons—that is, light particles in the form of the high-voltage electrical discharge you experienced. When it hit Eric, it electrocuted him. He was lucky that you created a small black hole. Otherwise, he might no longer be with us. He would have been fried to a crisp."

"Oh my God! I did that?"

"Yes, you did. And you likely have other powers that you're unaware of, so you must be careful. I'll do my best to help you to identify them, to understand them, and to teach you how and when to use them."

This was scary stuff. "As I hear more about what happened to me and what I'm capable of, I'm concerned about what I could do. It would be much easier for me and safer for others to be plain old Luc Ponti again."

"That's unlikely to happen," Thay said. "You may or may not be an Avatar. We'll eventually find out. But like the others I mentioned, you were likely put here on Earth at this time for a special mission. Perhaps it can contribute to saving humanity from itself and the atrocities it's creating at an ever-increasing rate. Look, I'm not trying to puff this up greater than it truly is, but you may be a key part of the further evolution of consciousness here on Earth."

"That's mind-boggling—me, a 16-year-old student at Palo Alto High School, who mostly enjoys his friends and playing basketball—helping to save the world? You gotta be kidding me!"

"No, I'm not, Luc. You really have no choice but to follow your mission. You have powers way beyond most, if not everyone, on the planet. Both humanity and the planet *need* your help, and they need it now. All are connected. As we Buddhists say, 'One is One, One is Many, Many is Many, and Many is One.'"

This was too much for me to process. I was in shock. *What do I tell Mom and Dad? Do I even tell them at all? How do I live my life? What will my future be?* I lay down on the floor, put my head on my pillow, and stared up at the ceiling. There, engraved in beautiful gold leaf, was a picture of a snake in a circle, biting its tail. Thay saw me staring at this unusual symbol.

"Do you know what that is?" he asked.

"Not really, although I've seen it before."

"It's the Ouroboros, an ancient Egyptian sign of introspection, something constantly re-creating itself. It symbolizes the infinite cycle of the universe's endless creation, followed by its eventual destruction, then re-creation. It's the eternal cycle of life, death, and rebirth. It's this process that makes everything increasingly better, both physically and in consciousness."

"I wonder what part of the cycle we're in at this point in time." I closed my eyes.

"I don't know, but you have the power to eventually find out."

"Thay, let's call it quits for today—okay? I need to rest and think about my life."

"That's a good idea, my friend. But before we leave today, I want to share a parting thought with you. Is that okay?"

"Sure, I value your thoughts. I just don't know how much will stick in this discombobulated mind of mine."

"I understand."

I sat up and looked at Thay.

He told me, "Luc, you are clearly a chosen one and have been given a great gift for a special and challenging mission. There's nothing we human beings seek more than to have a sense of purpose that makes a difference, one that makes this a better world. The bigger and better the difference, the greater the sense of purpose, passion, and fulfillment associated with that mission.

"I suggest that you not let all this concern you too much. Don't think of yourself as a spiritual mystic, as were the Avatars of old. I can assure you that you can live a life filled with joy, health, compassion, friends, and whatever else you choose—even basketball. But equally important, you can create such a life for those around you. Why not accept this opportunity and celebrate the truth of your magnificent existence? Embrace your potential to be, do, and have whatever you can dream of for yourself and for humanity, who desperately need your help."

Thay continued. "Think of these words before you run away from this incredible life purpose. As we used to say in the Bronx, 'Buddy, if you play your cards right, you can have it all.' But equally important—you will be in a position to give so much to so many."

I nodded, and bowed to this great man, offering my thanks.

With those words, as exhausted and weary as I was, it was the first time in my 16 years that I asked for guidance from something Thay said was part of me—Cosmic Consciousness—so help me God.

TO RUSSIA WITH LOVE

I T HAD BEEN MORE THAN A WEEK since my last meeting with Thay. My brain was still running in circles over what he'd told me. It was both exciting and frightening at the same time. Everyone, even Coach, knew that I was distracted by something. I wouldn't admit it. What could I say?

I felt overwhelmed by Thay's teachings. Some of it didn't seem to fit. Me, a possible Avatar? No way. The ability to enter high levels of consciousness that turned on a bunch of superpowers and a life purpose to help humanity? Really? It was a lot for me to grasp and swallow—and accept.

Sure, it might seem like this was all good stuff, but I couldn't absorb it all at the time. I needed time to think—to see how all the pieces might fit into my life. How would I follow my dream of majoring in engineering at a great school, playing college ball, and maybe even going pro—and at the same time help save the world? I hadn't the foggiest idea how that could happen. My life was breaking bad.

If it weren't for my respect and admiration for Thay, I could easily have convinced myself that these messages would never sink in, or maybe his conclusions weren't correct. I don't know.

It was so weird. On the one hand, I sensed they were important for my future. On the other, I found them difficult to accept and understand. *Minchia*, did my head hurt! Yeah, I needed time to think, or maybe, *not* to think. But I also needed a break from all the heavy stuff—some kind of simple but enjoyable distraction. I came up with just the right thing.

Look, I'm a Sicilian and therefore a foodie at heart, so I went home and decided to cook one of those simple meals Mom had taught me over the years. She didn't like me eating junk food when she and Dad were traveling. They were both gone on business, and as usual when they're not here, Laura was spending the night at Astra's place. I could finally veg out alone and relax.

Sicilian it would be—penne pasta mixed with small cubes of sautéed chicken breast, smothered with pink sauce and Parmesan cheese. It was simple. I cut a salted chicken breast into bite-size cubes and sautéed them in virgin olive oil, chopped onions, diced garlic, and a touch of oregano. I warmed up my favorite quick-and-easy, out-of-the-bottle basil-tomato sauce and stirred in some Philadelphia cream cheese until the right pink color appeared. Finally, I drained the al dente–cooked pasta in a colander, poured it into a bowl, mixed in the sautéed chicken, smothered the chicken and pasta with pink sauce, and topped it off with loads of grated Parmesan cheese and a few pieces of fresh basil. Done in 20 minutes. *Mamma mia—toute e perfectto!*[46]

Unlike many of the guys on the team, I don't drink much. I don't like the way it makes me feel in the morning—especially before a long run. But, hey, I wanted to follow Thay's advice and celebrate my new powers instead of worrying about my future. Dad had an open bottle of Barolo sitting on the kitchen counter. I snatched half a glassful. He wouldn't miss it. Yes—a perfect meal!

Dinner was great. I ate in the living room watching an episode of *Riverdale* on Netflix. Afterward, I took a long, hot shower and decided to go to bed early, getting up in the morning earlier than usual for a longer-than-usual run—a great stress reducer, and it helps clear my mind.

---

[46] *Mamma mia—toute e perfectto!*—"Mama, everything's perfect!"

I was in the bathroom listening to Twenty One Pilots and had just finished brushing my teeth when I heard my cell phone vibrating on my desk. I turned off Spotify. It had to be *her*.

Sure enough, it was Tamara. It had been ten days since we'd last spoken. I hesitated and was tempted not to answer, but that would have only put off the inevitable to the next day, or maybe the middle of the night. I decided to get it over with. Lying down on my bed in shorts and an undershirt, I kicked off my slippers and pushed the "Accept" button on my phone.

"Hello."

"Hi there, Luc. Sorry for the delay in getting back to you. How've you been?"

"Fine. I was hoping you'd forgotten about me."

"You know I would never do that. I *love* working with you."

"Right. Like I have a choice."

"You always have a choice. It's just a matter of the outcome you choose."

"Right, from the ultraselect choices you give me."

"Choices you're being handsomely rewarded for."

"Fine. What do you want?"

"Oh, come on! I haven't bothered you for ten days. We've been busy here following up on that great intel you collected. It's been incredibly helpful. You'll likely never know how much!"

"Thanks. I'm sure I won't, and that's fine with me." I just wasn't in the mood for her bullshit.

"Also, we didn't want to raise suspicions with the Chinese that we have a much more effective intelligence source. Don't want them digging around."

"That's so kind of you to think about my welfare—or was it yours?"

"Don't be so bitter. Look at all the money you're making. In several weeks, you'll have enough for a free college education. That's not all that bad, is it?"

God, why is she always sweet-talking me?

Recalling Dad's warning, I said, "Like you're gonna let me go in a few weeks, right?"

She changed her tone—all business. "Supply and demand, Luc. We'll see what the market says then. Don't go overestimating your worth. Assets can crash, you know."

"Fine, I get it. Whaddaya want?"

Several beats and the real Tamara was back with her deep, no-nonsense voice, going right to the matter at hand. "Look, something's come up, and it's of the highest priority. Your remote viewing would be perfect for this."

It wasn't worth bickering with her further; she always wins. "What's that?"

"Remember during our last call I told you we wanted to see what the North Korean connection was about? Well, we've just learned from one of our assets in Beijing that China's President Xi Jinping and North Korea's Kim Jong-un will meet in a top-secret, high-level summit in Pyongyang in several weeks."

"So that's a big deal?"

"It is. It appears there's a more extensive relationship developing between China and North Korea than we'd thought. Our source says the purpose of the meeting, among others, is to smack Mr. Kim's knuckles for North Korea's recent show of might by test-launching ballistic missiles. You may have seen in the news that one was directed into the Yellow Sea. Another flew directly over South Korean airspace into the East China Sea, and a third was directed through Japan's airspace. This is serious. We've had two meetings with the president. He plans to personally address the UN Security Council."

I said, "I guess it is serious if the president wants to address the council." Since I'd begun working with the CIA, I'd started following the U.S.-North Korea thing on TV and in the newspapers. "Why would China collaborate closely with North Korea? I thought Kim was a wild card. And besides, some of the North's launches have been duds, right?"

"Some appear to have been duds, but we have good reason to believe that was a smokescreen to mislead the world as to how advanced they are in the development of their nuclear arsenal. We recently got high-resolution satellite images of their

Punggye-ri nuclear test site at Mount Mantapsan in the south of North Hamgyog Province, where they do their nuclear testing in huge underground tunnels. It appears that at least two of their recent tests involved a booster strategy. That's a warhead design in which thermonuclear material—namely, hydrogen bomb fusion fuel, is added to a fission atomic bomb to increase its energy output. Hydrogen bombs, which are based on atomic fusion— welding atoms together—are orders of magnitude more powerful than atomic bombs, bombs based on fission—breaking atoms apart."

"Thanks for the science lesson. We covered that stuff long ago in physics class."

Tamara continued, but her tone clearly said, "Piss off, wiseass!"

"They also appear to be layered bombs, where they use alternating layers of thermonuclear fusion fuel and uranium fission fuel packed in a specific shape, around the spherical core of an atomic bomb. This significantly increases the power output and is only a step away from a pure thermonuclear fusion hydrogen bomb, which would be a thousand times more powerful than the bomb we dropped on Hiroshima. This strategy together with what you found during your previous viewings—MIRVs, nuclear-powered engines, and advanced ICBM stealth technology—would be big trouble for us and our allies. We're deeply concerned."

As I focused on the actual substance of what she was telling me, I realized how serious it really did sound. Good God! Why can't the CIA deal with this? Trying to stay calm, I asked, "So why the big concern with the China-North Korea thing?"

She replied, "Because we believe that China is collaborating with North Korea to set up a nuclear strategic pact that will put the West and our friends in Asia at a significant risk and disadvantage."

I asked, "Why would China collaborate with the fat madman of North Korea? He's known to murder those who don't agree with him—even family like his uncle and his brother—and he's about as big a liar as they come. From what I've read recently in the news, even China has been known to disrespect him as a leader."

"Luc, you are by far the youngest person in the history of US intelligence to have top-secret clearance at the highest need-to-know level. It feels strange, but I will gladly share our current thoughts on this matter."

"Feel free not to. I'm totally fine with that."

"Not at all; I want to fill you in. It may increase your motivation for what I'm asking you to do, and it certainly will help when you remote-view their upcoming summit meeting. Here's the key point. All is not exactly as it seems with respect to North Korea. You're right, Xi is not enamored with Kim. He sees him as a dangerous man. His flippant, caustic, rhetoric toward the West, and those ballistic missile flights over Japan and South Korea, are examples of his volatile character. He's a liability. Xi could care less if he were gone tomorrow."

"You know that for a fact?"

"My dear boy, we deal only in facts."

"Fine." Still concerned, I asked again, "So, then, what's your thinking?"

"We believe there are good reasons for this cooperation. In developing their nuclear arsenal, North Korea has made more progress than most nations know. They've bought and stolen their way close to the forefront of ICBM technology. Today, they could easily launch a devastating nuclear attack on Seoul and Tokyo, killing millions of people and destroying those cities. It's only a matter of time, a short time, before they can accurately reach Los Angeles or San Francisco."

Now that's really getting close to home. I sat up in bed and massaged the muscles tightening in the back of my neck. "That's creepy."

"It is, and it gets worse. If they were to attack Seoul, South Korea is ready to instantly retaliate with an all-out nuclear attack on the North. Since China is allied with North Korea, and the US with South Korea, this could possibly bring China and the US to the brink of a global nuclear war, not unlike what happened during the Cuban Missile Crisis face-off in 1962 between Premier Khrushchev of the former Soviet Union, and President Kennedy in the US."

I stood up and started walking around my room. With some degree of doubt, I asked, "Could that really happen?"

Tamara's voice was getting louder and more high pitched. "Absolutely, it could, and I can assure you that China wants to avoid it at all costs. They have an envious eye on the technology know-how in South Korea. It would be invaluable to advance China's plan for the development of their country to a global front-runner. For this reason, they'd love to replace the US as the protectorate of the South and access this technology peacefully."

I found myself walking rapidly in circles. Now I was really interested. "So how do you think they'll proceed?"

Tamara replied, "We think Xi will propose that the US put a freeze on its military activity in the Korean Peninsula in exchange for suspending the North Korean's long-range ICBM and testing. That would safeguard the US and Europe. However, North Korea would still have an effective means to destroy Seoul and Tokyo."

"That doesn't sound like much of a deal for the rest of Asia."

"It's not. But we have solid intel that Xi has an immediate, top-secret second step in mind to which, as you'll see for obvious reasons, North Korea is not privy."

"What do you mean?"

"Xi is smart. He doesn't want China to be put in a future position where they have a choice between a humiliating deference to the US or all-out global nuclear war. That's a no-win for everyone. So he asks himself, how do we avoid that outcome down the road and become closer to South Korea?"

"Is that even possible?" I asked.

"It may be, but it depends on several difficult decisions within the US political leadership and Congress. Our assets tell us there is highly reliable intel to suggest that the first step in China's strategy would be to get Kim on board and comfortable with China by convincing the US to cease military activity on the Korean Peninsula. North Korea, in exchange for a stronger alliance with China, would stop development of ICBMs.

"In a complex, yet clever, next step, China would immediately depose and eliminate Kim and his inner circle and foster a friendly reunification of North and South Korea, the way it was before the Korean War and the buildup of the American presence. In this instance, the 'big brother' overseeing the newly united Korea would be China and not the US."

"That would be a major change. Would the US even consider it?" I asked.

"It would be a huge change, and we might consider it under the right conditions. In that scenario, Mr. Xi would be proposing that China and the US work together to create a new structure for East Asian nuclear security. The presence of the US in South Korea, which costs us a huge sum every year, is a historical accident.

"It came about in 1950 when the North attacked the South. We stepped in to help the South and avoid the spread of communism within Asia. You may not be aware of this, but the 1950s were the height of Senator Joseph McCarthy's anticommunist congressional hearings. The US was nearly paralyzed by its fear of communism. Movie stars, academics, and many high-ranking businesspeople—regardless of their personal loyalty to our country—were blacklisted right and left if they even had a friend or family member who belonged to the Communist Party.

"We think that China believes that if it removes the Kim regime, disassembles North Korea's nuclear arsenal, and reunifies the peninsula under a new non-Communist government in Seoul that would be friendly to both China and the US, that we would remove our military presence on the peninsula and end our active military alliance with South Korea. We know that several senior US political figures would consider this strategy risky and a non-starter, but under the right circumstances and international commitments, they could be convinced it's a winner. It's a scenario we want the president to consider."

I said, "I find that hard to believe. It's a lot to swallow. Do you really think that China will depose and eliminate Kim and his regime?"

"We think so."

You think so? I thought you only dealt with facts.

Something she left out didn't feel right. I decided to mention it to Tamara. "Suppose this strategy was not to happen, and because of it, North Korea attacked Seoul, and China and the US were to come within moments of nuclear blows. We studied the Cuban Missile Crisis last year in our American History class. Don't you think Xi would back down just like Khrushchev did when he put the Soviet Union in the same spot with the US?"

Tamara responded, "Most people believe that Khrushchev backed down. He didn't. At the 11th hour, he and Kennedy had a phone conversation, and as a result, they *both* backed down. Neither wanted a global nuclear war. Russia removed its missiles from Cuba, and unbeknownst to most people, the US agreed to quietly remove all of its missiles from Turkey—something we told the Soviets we would never do. Turkey has had it in for us ever since.

"Xi is clever. He wants to avoid a no-win devastating situation, and at the same time get oversight over both North and South Korea as one reunited country. Under the right conditions, this could be beneficial to the US as well as to the world. And we would finally get rid of the diabolical Kim legacy. The emphasis here is 'under the right circumstances'; otherwise, it's a nonstarter."

"It sounds scary to me, very scary. Now I can understand why those antinuke folks are always picketing at the airport."

"You're right," Tamara agreed, "but it's our best line of defense. We need to gather intelligence at the Chinese-North Korean summit and present it to the UN Security Council. If we provide the right information, it's likely the council will put international sanctions on both China and North Korea, unless, as we plan in a top-secret meeting, the US and China agree to the circumstances I just outlined."

"What if China and the US can't come to an agreement?" I asked.

"If China doesn't agree to this proposal, there will be international support for the US to broaden its nuclear defense arsenal by placing advanced missile systems in the Czech and Slovak Republics, something that's been on hold after President Obama's meeting with President Putin several years ago."

My mind was moving rapidly into deeper analysis. I wondered for the briefest of moments, *When Thay told me I had been chosen for a mission of higher purpose, could this be part of it? Could I possibly make a difference in a high-level, international threat like this? I mean, like helping to save the Western world?*

As I delved deeper, something else was bothering me. Why hadn't Tamara mentioned it? *Che diavolo,* I decided to put it out there. "I was just wondering. Speaking of Putin, you never mentioned the other big player—Russia. Do you really think he's just going to stand by and watch the show?"

Tamara shot back angrily, "Why should we consider Russia? They're irrelevant in this situation."

"Really? What about Putin's comments last week in the news concerning Russia's new nondetectable, super-duper ICBMs? And then I found the real thing in one of China's missile silos. You even sent me back to get design details for you. Is there a connection here? Like, is the CIA concerned about how Russia will react to all this?"

"Look, Luc, it's true. You're a covert spy and an exceptionally good one. And you're smart. But you don't have the right information and experience concerning relevant international politics. But you know what? Forget about Russia, and let's just get this done. All right?"

Whoa—I must've hit a sore spot. Something doesn't sound right in her voice.

I didn't want to stir the pot any more than I already had. "What do you want me to do?" I asked her.

"We need to know what transpires at that summit meeting. Your detailed intel is critical to our country's safety and strategic defense system. Over the next several days, I'll send to your computer at the office in Palo Alto Square as much detailed information as I can gather from our sources in Asia. You'll need it for our discussion before you remote-view the Pyongyang conference. Are you with me on this?"

I couldn't put my finger on it, but after she let me have it, I knew something wasn't right. She was hiding something. I just didn't know what it was, having been jolted and distracted by her cutting comments. I decided to do something I'd promised myself I would never do again. For some reason, it was fading anyway. I could still do it if I pushed hard enough on my concentration—but it was very painful and made my head feel like it would explode.

I took a deep breath and focused as hard as I could on Tamara's comments, tuning in to her thoughts for just a few moments. It only took a few seconds. *Oh, shit! Why am I doing this? The pain is excruciating!*

But there it was. I could hear her thoughts: *Why is this jerk asking these goddamn questions? He can't possibly know what's going on. He's one big pain in the ass. If he thinks he's irreplaceable, he'd better think again.*

My head was pounding like a hammer hitting a blacksmith's anvil. I caught myself moaning in pain.

"Luc! Are you there? What's that sound? Are you okay? Are you with me on this?"

Thank God, she woke me from my misery. I could barely speak. "I guess so."

"Look, my friend, there's no guessing on this. Dammit, are you with me?"

"Yeah, okay, okay. I'm with you." *Not really, you witch—not until I find out what the hell you're up to!* My head was still throbbing. I desperately needed a couple of ibuprofens.

Tamara caught herself and recovered. "Good."

She hung up without saying goodbye. Obviously pissed.

I felt something drip out of my ear onto my T-shirt. I looked down. It was blood.

GOTCHA!

AFTER MY CONVERSATION WITH TAMARA, I couldn't sleep—I wasn't sure if it was the intense pain from my headache or my deep suspicions about her motives. From now on, purposeful mind reading was an absolute no-no. I was asking for a permanent migraine or worse.

Although my head was a complete wreck, I couldn't get over Tamara's comments and thoughts. "Russia's irrelevant"—right. I'm *a jerk and a pain in the ass. If he thinks he's irreplaceable, he'd better think again.* Her second point was probably correct, but I was still pissed, and my brain was moving into high gear trying to figure out what her game was.

Although I'd been hesitant to use these damn powers of mine, it suddenly occurred to me, *Why not use them to find out what the hell she's up to? Wouldn't that be for the greater good?*

I prepared to do a deep meditation the way Thay had taught me. I created a clear intention and put my focused intention on it: *What is Tamara up to, and what should I do about it?* Then I detached from the outcome and trusted that the cosmos or whatever would work out the details and give me the answers I needed.

Five hours later—at 4:00 A.M.—I came out of the meditation. It had been an incredible experience. Although I hadn't slept much, I was more alert and energetic than I could recall. Things began to gel in a way that felt right. I must have dipped deep into the Akashic Record. *Thay, I think it's all starting to come together.* Deciding to sleep until 7:30, I fell asleep instantly and awoke at 7:30 on the nose, well rested as if I'd slept for nine hours.

Lying there in bed, I knew exactly what to do about Tamara. Yes, I was going to break a law, which was probably punishable by lots of years in a Leavenworth prison cell. But what the hell? I'd probably already broken several by disclosing what I did to Bella and to Thay. I decided to do a remote viewing of Tamara's operation in Washington.

It was just after 10:30 A.M., DC time. She should be in full swing at CIA headquarters in Langley, Virginia. Within moments of retrieving their GPS coordinates: 38° 57' 6.47" N and 77° 08' 47.71" W, I was out-of-body flying at breakneck speed across the US.

I entered CIA headquarters, located in as stark a building as I'd ever seen—nothing but hallways lined with high-security doors and lots of cameras everywhere. Then I directed myself to Tamara's office. She's wasn't there. Her office looked much like the decor of the building—simple, clinical, and boring. The desk and everything else in the room were totally bare, not a piece of paper anywhere, not even in the trash can.

I sat down at her desk in front of her computer. It was like the one I used in the Palo Alto office—flashing colored lights, a phone-fax system, a digital camera, and a large video screen. Of course, it required a password. *Not to worry,* I thought, *I'll just tap into the Akashic Record.*

I stared at the screen, closed my eyes, and thought, *Tamara Carlin's password.* In a few moments, it popped into my head. I opened my eyes and typed the word ARMAGEDDON. *Shit, Tamara, I hope your password isn't a sign of what's to come.*

Great! I was in. But the big challenge was how to find anything in her humongous database, especially when I didn't know what I was looking for. I went to the "Find" function and entered the word *president*. Hundreds of files appeared. Then I entered: *President's North Korean strategy*. I was in luck. Ten files. It took only seconds to find what I was looking for—an email from CIA director Anthony Stefano to Tamara, subject: President's Proposed North Korean Strategy. It was dated three days ago. I read it and took a mental photo.

Tamara:

Here's a summary of the strategy I received from the secretary of state and which the president proposes to use in his approach to North Korea. He has already had two top-secret discussions in Beijing with Xi Jinping. Let's discuss this immediately.

TOP SECRET

Proposed US Strategy to Address the North Korean Crisis

United States and China

- The president meets with President Xi Jinping to develop a mutually acceptable strategy—see below.

- The president meets at a summit to be held in Beijing with Kim Jong-un involving all three countries' top personnel. The meeting is hosted and facilitated by Xi Jinping.

- The US proposes to immediately cease all military training operations in South Korea, and gradually over 12 months pull out all troops and military assets from that country.

- The US and China would remove all sanctions on North Korea and, after 12 months, if the intended peace meets the milestones mutually agreed to, both countries would support North Korea joining the global markets, free of economic constraints and sanctions.

- China would become the new protectorate of both North and South Korea.

- The two countries would reunite to form one Korea. A joint U.S.-China team would oversee the political elections and transition process.

- Protecting the interests of the South until the newly formed country is politically and economically stabile, the US would install three mobile ICBM installations in Japan, which would be removed after three years of peace within the new, united Korea.

- Once the US, China, and North Korea have an agreement, they would bring Russia into the discussions. There will certainly be some concessions to the Russians. A statement of our intention not to arm the Czech and Slovak Republics with nuclear weapons should have significant leverage.

North Korea

- North Korea would immediately discontinue all ICBM developments.

- North Korea would immediately begin dismantling its existing ICBM installations, a task to be overseen

by a joint China-US team and completed within
24 months.

This didn't sound like what Tamara had told me, especially with respect to North Korea. I needed to find out what the hell she was up to.

I floated over to Director Stefano's office, which was on the seventh floor. There was a meeting going on inside. I entered and saw the director and Tamara in a heated discussion. It felt weird to be in their presence without them seeing me.

Director Stefano was a husky, slightly balding guy with jet-black hair combed straight back and dark-brown eyes—from their size, it looked like he was wearing contacts. He was dressed in a black, three-piece pin-striped suit, a white shirt, and a bright-yellow tie—with one of those white silky-type handkerchiefs stuffed in his top-left suit pocket. He either had a tan or naturally dark skin or both.

The director was seated behind a huge desk, his eyebrows scrunched in what looked like disbelief. He was impatiently grasping the armrests on his oversize black-leather chair like he was getting ready to eject or coming in for a turbulent landing.

Tamara was pacing rapidly back and forth in front of him like an injured cat. "Anthony, I'm still concerned that the president's strategy will backfire. I don't believe for a moment that the Chinese and North Koreans will buy it. And the Russians—forget it. Not a chance."

The director stood up from his chair and quickly moved front and center of the desk. "Look, you've been here long enough to know that's not your call. We need to do our part to help the president get this done. It's too important for global security, not just for the US."

"I agree, but how can we pull this off successfully? Do you really believe that China will be able to unite North and South Korea in a way that serves both them and the US on an equitable basis?"

The director said, "Well, we all know China is a powerful force, but I'm confident they can be dealt with in a way that keeps everyone satisfied. I need you to be with me on this. I'll help the president and his chief of staff line up the right power brokers in Congress. Timing is of the essence. We need to get this before Congress in the right way and lose no momentum before the president has his next meeting with China."

If facial expressions could only speak. Tamara looked both defeated and pissed. She lowered her voice. "What do you want me to do?"

Boy, have I heard that tone before. Man, this is so sweet! You deserved it—a con artist in sexy clothing.

"I want you to use your assets and get as much high-level intel as possible on that upcoming summit meeting. We need to know if the president's strategy will be generally acceptable to both the North Koreans and the Chinese. That intel will be critical to how we package our strategy and presentation. I'll worry about how to deal with the Russians."

"Will you fill me in?" she asked.

"You just worry about your end, and I'll do mine. Let's get this done!"

It was clear to me that Tamara didn't like anything she heard from Director Stefano—but why? She also seemed concerned about what he would do about Russia, even though she'd told me they were "irrelevant."

She finally conceded. "Fine, Anthony, I'm on it." She turned and headed for the door.

The director, now smiling, asked, "Hey, by the way, don't you have a promising new asset in California who might be able to help with this?"

Tamara turned very slightly toward the director. He couldn't see her twisted face. "I'll give it some thought. Not sure yet."

As she left the director's office, she was fuming. I focused, and tuned in to her thoughts, although the effort made my migraine start to come on again. Not surprising, her thoughts were about me.

My California asset—he's a smart-ass kid, all right, too smart for his own damn good. He suspects all is not as I've told him. And his pesky, redheaded girlfriend who keeps nagging him about his paranormal powers doesn't make things any easier for me. They'd both better fall in line. As powerful an asset as he is, he, too, is expendable—and as for her, no issue there.

And I was worried about the Chinese? She knows I told Bella what I'm up to with the CIA. Not good. And why hasn't she confronted me? What the hell is she planning?

I had to get into action quickly. After what I'd done for Tamara and what I knew, my life, Bella's, and probably Dad's, depended on it.

While scouting Tamara's office, I'd seen her coat and purse hanging on the back of her door. I knew they couldn't possibly contain anything confidential or incriminating. I was right. But her purse did contain her driver's license and her home address. I memorized it for future reference.

While I was in Tamara's computer, I'd seen her daily calendar, which is how I knew she would be in the director's office. She was scheduled to be in meetings at work for most of the day. I decided to pay her home a visit. I was digging myself deeper into more shit than I'd planned to, but it was too late to turn back.

AFTER RETRIEVING THE GPS COORDINATES FOR TAMARA'S HOME, I floated directly there. I was impressed by all the monuments I passed on the way. DC is quite a city—don't know if I'd like to live there—home to too many acronyms: CIA, NSA, EPA, ugh—but far worse than that are the hundreds of doublespeak politicians.

In no time, I was in front of Tamara's home. She lived in a large super neat condo located in the Foxhall section of the city. It looked like it might be one of the most expensive areas around—huge homes and condos, plush gardens with tree-lined streets and fancy streetlights. The neighborhood reminded me of a tour I once did in Beverly Hills—*Homes of the Rich and Famous.*

I entered and found my way to a large office, beautifully decorated with oriental rugs and amazing paintings and sculptures, probably originals. Even if she were renting the place, how in the world could she afford it on a government salary? Dad always said that government jobs offered great security but didn't pay well. The extra money had to be coming from somewhere else.

I spent a couple of hours in her home, mostly in her office. The two most interesting things were her computer and a large wall safe, hidden behind a picture in the office closet. It took me a while to figure out her password. Accessing the Akashic Record for information can be challenging at times, especially under stress, but that wasn't the problem this time. This computer, like the one in her office, was cryptographically protected.

When I closed my eyes and focused on the password, I kept seeing a word in my mind's eye that wasn't familiar to me. I misspelled it several times, but finally got it right: DOSTOYEVSKY. If I'd read something by this Russian author, it might have given me an idea what I was about to discover.

It blew my mind. There were numerous encrypted conversations and memos between Tamara and someone in the Kremlin with the code name *Seagull.* There were also numerous exchanges between Tamara and the ambassador at the Russian Embassy in DC. I was glad that during my prior remote viewings for Tamara, I'd discovered that my mind could instantly translate essentially any language. My internal-language computer was able to unscramble them, although it took some time.

It suddenly hit me like a ton of bricks right between the eyes. *Holy shit!* From what I read, almost all of which was in Russian, either I was naive, or Tamara was a double agent working for the Russians.

I thought back to our last conversation. That's why she didn't want me to do any remote viewing of the Russians. To quote the lady, "They're irrelevant."

It was looking like she wanted the information I gathered on the Chinese and North Koreans for Russia. In the recent news announcements, maybe Putin was overstating the Russian nuclear technology—Tamara would know. If so, it was probably the only truthful comment to come out of her mouth.

She'd been playing me. I had to figure out what she was doing for the Russians. I needed to work my way through the information I'd gathered and put the pieces together. It would take some time, but the payoff could be big for Dad, Bella, and hopefully, for me.

I needed additional information, and I knew just how to get it. If the results came out the way I imagined, they were going to make some people very unhappy. But in the end, it just might help the greater good.

It was all starting to come together, and even though I was still anxious and foggy on the details, I liked what I saw. I wasn't completely ready for what I had to do, but I would get there fast.

DELIVERANCE

AFTER MY "VISIT" WITH DIRECTOR STEFANO AND TAMARA, it was clear—Tamara was a Russian double agent working against the US. If successful, she would not only jeopardize the security of this country, but the entire free world—and *Gesu Cristo*, I was helping her! I was probably the only one besides the Russians who knew her game. And there was no way I was going to let her win.

To say I was scared shitless was an understatement. After hearing her argument with the director, it was obvious he didn't know, and as for Major Dallant, although he was much more than a pain in the ass, I had my doubts that he was mixed up in this. But eventually I'd have to be certain.

There was no other choice for me. I'd begun to fill in the blanks and connect the dots to a plan I hoped would release my family and me from Tamara's conniving grip and catch her before she did irreversible damage to the US—and to the world. I knew what I needed to do. But first I had to know what had happened in Iraq—the secret she held over my head, blackmailing me to work for her. What had Dad done that was so terrible that she could ruin his life forever? Whatever it was, it was like a crank slowly tightening a vice grip around my head.

If I could find out what had happened, along with what I'd just learned about Tamara, I was convinced I could get Dad, my family, and me out of this mess. So, Iraq was the next blank to fill in.

I thought about comments that Dad had made the morning after the barbecue, when I'd found him with an empty bottle of Scotch, all torn up. The booze must have temporarily warped his self-control. He'd begun to do something he'd never done before—speak about his time in Iraq. Yeah, it was brief, but just the way he spit out his comments meant there was much more behind his words than he was saying.

Over the years, I'd overheard arguments between Mom and him about this thing—whatever it was—that caused him to wake up in the middle of the night in a cold sweat. As usual, Mom always started out with patience and understanding. But his nightmares turned into hers when he started to scream at her and refused to go to the VA for help.

When his intensity and aggressiveness became unbearable, she usually ended up shouting back at him, something like, "Someone, Carlo, please! If not to me, goddammit, go talk to someone! Please get some help! You won't listen to me."

He finally did go to the VA, but after a few visits, he told Mom it was a waste of time, and his problems were something he would have to deal with on his own terms.

I knew there was no way I could get the information I needed from him. Cautioned by Thay, I'd promised I would never use my powers on family or close friends. But it suddenly occurred to me that maybe I could use them to get what I needed another way—yes, Bella, for the greater good. In this case, for our *family's* greater good.

I wasn't poking around in people's thoughts anymore. That was physically painful and just not the right thing to do. But I was getting increasingly good at connecting to the Akashic Record for information. Here was a chance to use this gift for a worthy purpose.

In Dad's study, I'd seen a dated photo of him and Cap in uniform, taken in Iraq. Before going into a deep meditation and connecting with the Akashic Record, I concentrated on the two of them during the period they were in Iraq. In my meditation, I saw them during some pretty ugly fighting. It was terrible—extremely hard to watch. But a few visions kept popping up in my mind's eye, over and over again—a bridge, a little girl, and a building, kind of a hospital. I had no idea what to make of them.

Going online, I dug into sites about Desert Storm to see if there was anything that would help. After reading tons of material describing events during Dad's stay, it still wasn't clear to me what the visions meant. One thing was for sure, though: They didn't feel right. In fact, they made me feel awful. When I came out of one of my meditation sessions, I was usually nauseated. I knew I had to pursue this, and there was only one person who could help.

I called Cap at his home in Modesto and asked if I could visit him. "Absolutely," he said, "but why would you come without your folks? You lookin' to learn something about almond farming?"

When I said I wanted to discuss his time with Dad in Iraq, the tone of his voice changed instantly. His immediate response was, "Not a chance. It would be a total waste of time." I didn't like what he said and the way he said it. Somehow I knew he could help. I decided to go anyway.

By car, Modesto's only an hour and a half inland, directly east of Palo Alto, but not having a vehicle meant that I had to take the four-hour Modesto Area Express (MAE) bus ride. Amazing! Why they call it an express seemed weird to me. But apparently, it was an important means of public transportation for migrant workers.

Sitting next to a young man on the bus, I learned from him that many farmworkers who lived in Modesto got unskilled jobs in Silicon Valley during their off-seasons to supplement their annual incomes. Some took the MAE every day to and from work, a nine-hour round trip for an eight-hour job that paid minimum wage—at best. Incredible. Whoever said migrants weren't motivated to be self-sufficient wasn't looking at reality.

All I did during the long ride to Modesto was meditate on what I'd learned so far about Dad, Cap, and my reading. I wanted to connect this information with what was in the Akashic Record, which could complete the picture for me.

I'd caught the 6:00 A.M. bus on Middlefield Road in Palo Alto and arrived in Modesto just after ten o'clock. The Spanish tile roof and peach-colored stucco island at the Modesto Downtown Transit Center, surrounded by a gray patch of cement lanes that ferried buses in and out, seemed pretty, yet humble. I guess that was fitting for a town whose Spanish name literally meant "modest."

It was an easy 30-minute walk that skirted the edge of Moose Park on Encina Avenue down to a small, white-stucco ranch house, well kept, but in keeping with the community's namesake, quite modest. Groves of some kind were nearby, but they were too far away or the fruit was too small to make out what was growing. *Probably almonds*, I thought, since that was about all Modesto was famous for—oh, right, and the birthplace of *Star Wars* director George Lucas.

After hesitating several seconds, I moved slowly up the walkway and climbed three steps to the porch. I hesitated at the front door, but then finally reached out and rang the bell.

I heard it ring inside the house, followed by heavy footsteps as someone made their way to the door. It opened, and there he stood in baggy jeans held up by red suspenders and a brown-leather belt with a large brass buckle engraved with a bucking bronco. He wore a dirty, tight, white T-shirt with a couple of small stretch holes near his left sleeve. Cap's bulging belly was set solidly on top of that bucking bronco. "Luc, I thought I told you not to come."

"Right. And I told you I wanted to discuss Dad's and your time together in Iraq."

"Don't you get it? Under no circumstances would I do that!"

Cap was unaware of my ability to use the Akashic Record to pry into his past at a level that I'm sure would have frightened the hell out of him. I'd learned something during my meditation on the MAE ride to Modesto and was hoping it would push him into telling me the details of what happened to Dad in Iraq.

As I looked deep into his dark-blue eyes, I saw something. Thay had told me more than once that the eyes are the gateway lenses to a person's soul. I saw enough pain in Cap's consciousness to encourage him to open up. I was convinced it would be good for everyone, including him.

"Cap, I know something terrible involving you and Dad happened in Iraq, and you both suffer because of it. He still has horrible nightmares. I'll bet you do too. I think there's something you can tell me that would help him, and eventually you, as well."

"Luc, you're not thinking straight. There's no way you could or should know anything about what we went through over there. And there's no way you or anyone else could ever help. Look, I know you mean well and wanna help. But you can't. You'll just stir up a hornet's nest and make things worse for everyone, including you. That's water under the bridge. So, please, let it go. I think you'd better head back to Palo Alto. I've got work to do. I'm leaving in a few minutes to do some errands. I'll drive you to the bus station on my way."

It was time to drop the bombshell—something that had finally become very clear to me during my meditation on my bus ride. "Speaking of water under the bridge, Cap—what happened in Baghdad on February 20, 1991, west of Al-Ahrar Bridge?"

Cap's face twisted in panic. He was stunned as if I'd hit him with a club. He couldn't utter a word. He fell back slightly and steadied himself with the door frame. After several deep breaths, he spoke slowly in a near whisper: "How in the hell could you possibly know about that? Did your dad say something?"

"No, he didn't. But it doesn't matter. I know. What *does* matter is that something happened that day on or near that bridge. And that something has been haunting Dad, and I'm guessing, you, as well. I wanna help both of you. Please give me a chance. I need to know what it was."

Cap took several deep breaths. Finally, he looked me straight in the eyes and said softly, "Come on in." I had no idea why he caved. All that mattered to me was that he did. Maybe he just couldn't live anymore with a secret that had haunted him every day since his discharge from Iraq. Maybe he just needed someone to talk to. Or maybe he felt I just might be able to help. I prayed he was right.

The entry into Cap's home was directly into the living room. Still in a state of shock, he stopped and looked around, dazed, as if he'd never been there before. Without saying a word, he sat down on a large, worn-out, dark-brown, felt-upholstered chair. I sat opposite him on a matching sofa. A scratched-up oak coffee table topped with several empty beer cans separated us.

Cap bent forward and put his face in his hands, elbows on his knees. I didn't say a word. I was praying that whatever he'd say next would be good for both Dad and for him. I sat there thinking, *Damn, I hope I'm doin' the right thing. I don't wanna hurt him or Dad.*

Finally, he picked up his head and sat back in his chair. There were tears in his eyes. He spoke slowly in a low, halting voice. "Luc, what I'm about to tell you, I've tried every day since Desert Storm to forget. Some days when the sun was bright, I'd have a few beers and my mind would be on hold, that kinda worked. But on most days, forget it, the details keep flashing, sometimes nonstop, in my mind. It's been a nightmare, and I'm sure it's mentally crippled me for life. I hope you're right and it'll at least help your dad. He's a prince and he deserves it."

I sat there patiently and didn't say a word. Cap rubbed his eyes, cleared his throat a few times, and then continued. "You're probably not aware that during your dad's ROTC stint at Princeton, he demonstrated rifle marksmanship that had never been seen before by his military profs. He won several sharpshooter medals and was urged by those guys and some bigwigs from Washington to become a professional sniper for the marines or the army. He refused. Not surprising, knowing Carlo. Instead, he signed up and trained with the Special Forces and became a platoon leader, which is where I met him. Our outfit reported to—of all things—the CIA."

"I know. After quite a bit of Scotch one night, Dad told me that much."

"Anyway," Cap went on, "during the afternoon of the date you mentioned, the lieutenant and I were caught in a skirmish in Baghdad. We'd been separated from the rest of our platoon by a series of enemy cross fires. We made our way under heavy machine-gun fire to Al-Ahrar Bridge. Near the bridge entry, we came across a wounded officer from the infantry, a Major Phillip Dunstan. He was conscious but not very alert. He'd been shot in his right leg and was bleeding heavily. Dunstan was dazed and without his weapon—he lost it crawling rapidly to the safety of cover at the bridge. We put a tourniquet on his leg to stop the bleeding so that the three of us could crawl across the bridge to the other side, which we felt would be safer."

"You and Dad must have carried him. It was a miracle you didn't get shot crossing the bridge," I pointed out.

"Yes, we did carry him, and yes, it was a miracle, but that miracle didn't last long. After crossing, we found ourselves again in enemy cross fire. Somehow, don't ask me how, we managed to get Dunstan safely into a building, which was occupied by more than a dozen Iraqi separatists. Unfortunately, they were low on firepower and ammo. They were doing their best to treat several injured American soldiers and some of their own guys, while simultaneously holding off Saddam's troops in a building directly opposite them. Those guys were essentially in a makeshift hospital under siege.

"Your dad and I decided we had to escape and bring back reinforcements to help these poor bastards and the soldiers they were treating. It wouldn't be easy. Major Dunstan could barely walk, but at least the bleeding had stopped, and he was now more alert."

This was much more than I'd bargained for. All I could think was, *God, this better have a good ending.* But I knew from what Dad and Cap had been going through since then that it wouldn't.

Cap explained, "Your dad made his way to the roof of the building, and I moved to a point under heavy brush cover, on the ground on the right side and halfway between the two buildings. By continually changing our positions, we were going to try to convince Saddam's troops that there were more armed soldiers than they thought. If that worked to stall them, one of us would make haste to a half mile west of us, where a rifle platoon of marines was entrenched in a small village under US control."

Then Cap laid out the most horrifying part of what happened—the real reason he and Dad didn't sleep nights. "Within minutes before we could change our position, a little girl, no more than five years old, stepped out of the building that held Saddam's troops. Both sides stopped firing." Cap stopped briefly to take a deep breath. "I won't forget her face as long as I live. She was wearing a tattered pink dress, white sneakers, and a yellow Snoopy backpack." He started to cry. He bit his lip and did his best to regain some composure and continue.

I was so choked up by then that I couldn't move or say a word—afraid of what Cap would say next.

He finally went on. "With some help from the Iraqi separatists, Major Dunstan was doing better, so he'd taken over command. As he cautiously peeked out the window with binoculars, he warned your dad that the little girl might be carrying a bomb in her backpack, and that with his position on the roof and being an excellent sharpshooter, he should be prepared to take her out, if he called for it.

"Luc, your dad and I couldn't believe the terrifying situation we'd gotten ourselves into—and I'm not just talking about Saddam's men, those lousy bastards! Oh God, that little girl."

I was desperately afraid of what was coming next. All I could get out was a stuttered, "I . . . I understand, Cap."

"Dunstan asked if we were carrying any MFA—mercury fulminate ammunition. It's a high-tech ammo that was developed for the Special Forces and used to explode C4 bombs, since normal bullets often go right through C4 explosives without detonation. The Iraqis always had their suicide bombers use C4. It was easy for them to get. We told him we each had one MFA round. He ordered both of us to load up, just in case the little girl was carrying a bomb and had to be taken out."

I could see it was getting more and more difficult for Cap to speak—and for me to listen.

"She kept looking back at the building she came out of, listening to someone speaking to her in Arabic, and then inching her way slowly toward our building. She was about 15 feet away when Major Dunstan made the call: 'Ponti, take her out—straight through the chest so you get that backpack.'

"Your dad pleaded, 'Sir, she's a young kid, and look, that backpack isn't fully packed—nothing like a bomb. It's too small and almost empty.'

"'Goddamn it, Ponti, take her out! Take her out *now*! That's an order,' was Dunstan's urgent command.

"From the tone in your dad's voice, I'm sure he wished he were anywhere else in the world but Baghdad. He reluctantly acknowledged the order: 'Roger that.' From that response, you can be sure he had his finger on his rifle's trigger, his eye in the scope, and was about to squeeze it very slowly, as sharpshooters are trained to do to achieve maximum accuracy. We were both sure there was no bomb in that backpack.

"What happened next took less than a couple of seconds, if that. Hearing Dunstan's order on my communicator and using my position at right angles to Carlo's location on the roof, I immediately took a shot with my MFA shell aimed directly at the backpack, not the girl, to show that there was no bomb. I was able to do it before your dad had a chance to pull the trigger on his weapon. Tragically, there *was* a bomb in the backpack. Her beautiful little body was gone—vaporized by the intensity of the blast."

Cap took a breather to stop from crying. My stomach was in knots. I didn't say a word.

Then, "The explosion also blew off part of the face of the building holding the American casualties and knocked Carlo backward from his position on the roof. He gashed his head on a brick wall and was knocked unconscious. I got shrapnel in my right leg and chest. The severity of the explosion either killed or severely injured all of Saddam's troops who were sneaking around the side opposite me to overtake our building. I managed to make my way back to the building.

"Climbing to the roof, I found your dad unconscious and bleeding profusely. As I'd thought, he never had a chance to fire his rifle—his MFA round was still in the chamber. As I lay next to him, I immediately fired it into the air. I knew if he or Major Dunstan found his rifle unfired and containing the MFA round, he would face a court marshal and a dishonorable discharge for disobeying a life-saving order from a superior officer. So all these years, your Dad thought he'd obeyed Major Dunstan's order and fired at the girl, but he never had a chance to fire his weapon. I'm sure he was about to, but I beat him to it before he could get his shot off. For obvious reasons, I couldn't tell him or anyone else what had happened."

I was deeply relieved for Dad, but so sorry for Cap—what he'd had to endure all these years!

Cap said, "I tried to wake Carlo up, but I soon passed out myself from a heavy loss of blood. Fortunately, those marine reinforcements arrived almost immediately. They demolished the remaining Iraqi troops and freed the injured Americans and separatists.

"They found Carlo and me, both unconscious on the roof. I was treated, flown to Germany for surgery, and then back to the States and discharged because of my injuries. Your dad was also eventually discharged. He received a medal of commendation for saving all those lives. He would have gotten it anyway. I just beat him to the target. Like Carlo, I really didn't think that poor little girl carried a bomb. That's why I only hit her backpack. I've died with her every day since then."

After telling me this, Cap put his head in his hands and cried uncontrollably for several minutes—and so did I. There was nothing more for either of us to say.

Cap's account of what had happened that afternoon in Baghdad was frightening and unexpected, but exactly what I needed. I thanked him and got up from the sofa. It was time to leave. I gave him a big, long hug. He called a taxi for me so I could make it home in time for dinner.

We both walked out to the porch and sat on the top step waiting for the taxi. We didn't talk about anything important, but I could see that Cap seemed to breathe a bit better than when I'd first appeared on his doorstep. At least, I thought . . . I guessed . . . I hoped so.

The taxi arrived and Cap walked me to the curb. As it drove off, we looked at each other, both relieved and concerned at the same time. This thing wasn't over.

It had been one of the most painful hours in my life—worse than my peritonitis and surgery. I had to think carefully about what to do with the information Cap had shared with me. How would I approach Dad? He would be at dinner that evening. I had no idea what to do, but I had a four-hour bus ride in front of me to figure it out.

CRISIS

MOM HAD MADE ONE OF HER ITALIAN SPECIALTIES FOR DAD because he'd promised to be home by six. Siciliana melanzane Parmigiana, otherwise known as Sicilian eggplant parmesan, is one of his all-time favorites. He became addicted to it some years ago when they vacationed in Southern Italy. Mom had gotten a special recipe from an elderly Italian woman who cooked at the B and B where they stayed in Taormina, Sicily.

Dad was in an unusually happy mood—I had no idea why. What I *did* know was that I dreaded being the one to tear it down. And it had to be done that evening. With his crazy travel schedule, my keeping what I'd learned from Cap for an extended period just wasn't something I could live with.

Mom noticed that something was on my mind. "You're exceptionally quiet tonight. Is the melanzane okay for you?"

"Toute e perfectto, Mamma!"

"Thanks, Luc, you're a sweetheart. But, honey, please, you know we only speak English in this house."

"Oh, come on, Mom, where's your Italian spirit?"

"Don't misunderstand me, I'm proud of my Italian roots. But if you had to deal with the kind of prejudice Dad and I faced, he, growing up in Newark, and I in San Francisco, you'd understand why we've tried our best to Americanize our family. I wouldn't want you to have to deal with it as well."

Ha—tell that to Coach Ralston—"beefy Dago legs."

"Luc, you listen to your mom. She knows what she's talking about."

"Right. Look, I'm fine. It's just been a long day."

As Dad devoured his melanzane like a lion who'd just caught a zebra, he looked over at me. "I'll say. You were up and gone before I left for work this morning."

"You know I like to run and get an early start when possible."

He just chuckled. "It sure was an early start. I had a breakfast meeting in the city and left at 6:00 A.M., and you were long gone by then."

"Well, you know what they say, 'The early bird catches the worm!'"

Mom looked at me quizzically and smiled. "Well, aren't you the philosopher this evening."

"Thanks, Mom. But to change the subject, any chance I could grab you and Dad after dinner. I wanna share some important thoughts with you guys."

As usual, Dad didn't give her a chance to respond. "Sure, let's do it," he said.

God, if he only knew what was coming.

After dessert, Dad suggested, "How about we meet in the den after I help Mom with the dishes? She deserves help after that incredible meal."

"Well, thank you, Carlo."

Wow! He never offers to help with the dishes . . . and a heartfelt compliment for Mom's cooking. What's he smoking? Her dinner must have really gotten to him. Damn, was he in a good mood or what? I wasn't sure I could go through with what I wanted to say. But it was too late to pull out now; the ball was already in play. Both of my feet were nervously tapping the floor. I was having a difficult time just sitting still. I couldn't wait anymore.

"Look, I hate to be pushy, but can the dishes wait until after we have our discussion? I'll even be glad to do them."

Again, Dad jumped right in before Mom could say a word. "Well, that's a first! Offer accepted. I'll grab my Barolo. Let's go to the den."

I guess you can take the man out of the military, but . . .

Mom gave him a strange look as if wondering whether she should appreciate or resent his rapid responses before she could respond. She graciously added, "Well, thank you, Carlo."

So, without saying much more, the three of us marched off to the den and sat facing each other, Mom and Dad on the sofa, with me opposite them on the large, puffy armchair.

Mom was the inquisitive one: "So what's so important that it couldn't wait for another 30 minutes?"

Damn, this isn't going to be easy. I leaned forward toward them, tapping my finger on the coffee table between us. "Mom, Dad, what I'm gonna to tell you will be painful for the three of us, but I think that it has to be said. I hope it will start a healing process for the whole family."

Mom's concern was visible on her contorted face. "Good Lord, you sound like a psychotherapist! What in your life could possibly be that serious?"

Dad was in his military mode: "If you have a serious problem, let's have it. We'll deal with it."

"Dad, it's not about me—it's . . . um . . . it's about you."

"Me?"

They looked at each other in dismay and then back at me.

"I got to thinking about your comments the morning after our barbecue concerning your experience in Iraq. You didn't say much specific stuff, but I could see there was a lot of pain behind what you did say."

Dad's entire demeanor was changing rapidly—from happy-go-lucky over dinner, to attentive and focused when we sat in the den, to what now began to look like the angry gorilla he could easily become.

"Luc, it's none of your goddamn business. And even if you're right, it's nothing I want to speak about. I've told you before and I'll say it again. I don't want to bring any of my wartime experiences into our family."

"I know, I know. But there are some important details you're not aware of. If you were, I think they might set you free from your nightmares."

"You don't know a damn thing about them. And if you did, you couldn't possibly help anyway. What the hell's wrong with you? You're talking nonsense. As for my time in Iraq, there's no way you could know any of the details."

"Look, I decided to see what my powers could do to help you and our family. I spent time after our last discussion focusing on you, Cap, and your time together in Iraq. I kept feeling that something happened, something you were completely unaware of, and if you just knew the truth, it might help—maybe finally set you free.

"I also felt that Cap knew something he never shared with you or anyone, for that matter—not to protect himself, but to protect you. I couldn't figure out what it was. So I called him, and after that call, I knew I was right. He refused to speak to me about his time with you in Iraq."

"Great! Not surprised—that's Cap for you. He's my man."

"So I took the bus to Modesto and paid him a visit anyway."

Mom was shocked. "Oh my God, Luc—no, you didn't!"

"I did, and I'm glad I did. And in a moment, you'll see why."

Dad went ballistic. "You did what? Jesus Christ, Luc! How could you? How could you put your damn nose in my private business, and especially my time in the military?"

Trying to calm him down, I said, "Please let me explain. I decided to try to use my new powers to help you and our family. So on my four-hour ride to Modesto, I had lots of time to meditate on this issue. At first, I saw nothing. But then, something kept playing over again in my head. I held my breath and then I said it—Baghdad, February 20, 1991, west of Al-Ahrar Bridge."

Dad froze for several seconds—almost in paralysis—his face distorted not unlike Cap's when I mentioned the bridge. He lowered his voice, still in shock, and said, "My God, no! That's not possible. How could you possibly know about—"

"But I do, Dad. And when I confronted Cap with this, he had the same reaction. That eventually started him on an hour-long replay of what really happened that afternoon, something you're not aware of. It was painful for him and for me, and I think it will be for you and Mom too. But you gotta know what really happened—the truth. I'm convinced it will help you, and probably eventually do the same for Cap—and our family."

"No, I don't want to hear about any of it! I don't care what you found out, or how you got it with all that goddamn psychic shit of yours. Damn it, Luc! Let it go, for Christ's sake."

"Please, Dad, trust me. I really care about you. And I think this will eventually set you free."

Mom was in shock. She started her anxiety thing—rubbing her hands together, faster and faster. But she probably sensed from the look on my face and from the tears in my eyes that I honestly knew something important and believed it would help. "Carlo, I don't want to see you suffer any more than you already have, but I think there's something we need to hear from Luc, and if he feels it will help you, help us, we should at least listen to what he has to say. Please, let's trust his judgment . . . please."

Dad didn't say a word. He just kept staring blankly down at the floor. So I began by relating the events of that afternoon as my parents listened with increasingly intense and nervous attention. Dad's brow was tense, and he was squeezing his hands so tight, he had white knuckles. I could almost see his bones.

I started slowly and told them everything I learned from Cap. Dad just stared alternately between the floor and into space. God, he was a wreck, squeezing his hands together tighter and tighter. I thought the veins in his arms would burst any second and spout blood like an oil strike from a Texas gusher.

Tears were streaming down his face. He couldn't stop them. Could this be my father? Mom moved closer to him on the sofa and put her arm around his shoulder. She, too, was crying.

Dad couldn't take it. He cried out, "Luc, no more. I don't . . . I don't want to hear the rest."

"Dad, please trust me. You have no idea where this is going. It will help, I know it will."

Mom did her best to speak between tears. "Carlo, please, honey."

He didn't say another word.

When I finished, he and Mom were beyond wrecked. Neither could say a word. I did my best to share my thoughts. "I guess you'll never know if you would have shot that little girl, so stop torturing yourself. And now it doesn't matter anyway. Both you and Cap didn't believe she had a bomb in her backpack. Cap solved the issue in a way you could never have done from your position on the roof. You would have had to shoot directly through that little girl's body to hit the backpack. And what if it didn't have a bomb in it? What if it were empty, as it appeared to both you and Cap? As you aimed your rifle at her, I'm sure you had the same thought in constant replay. But because of him, you didn't have to pull the trigger, even if you intended to.

"He saved the day, maybe not for him, but for you and for those men in that building. And he's had to live with the consequences all these years. So you can rest now, knowing that you did not kill that little girl. But I guess you'll want to do everything you can to help Cap. He never intended to tell you. It would have opened a can of worms for all concerned and especially for you. If I hadn't confronted him with what I knew, he would still be suffering and holding it inside."

Something had happened that I'd never experienced in my entire life with my family. It was frightening and joyous at the same time. Dad was crying, almost beyond control. The three of us were. Mom put her arms around him. She now understood that inside, he was truly the man she'd married, and she knew what he'd been going through all these years since Desert Storm, all in the interest of protecting his family.

"Carlo, honey," she told him, "I love you."

We hugged as a threesome for more time than I can recall. We'd never done that before. I felt so bad for Dad, but that hug felt so good. I didn't want it to stop—ever.

Sometime later, when the three of us had regained some sense of composure, Dad pulled his cell phone from his pocket, wiped the tears from his face, and dialed a number. In halting speech, he closed our discussion for the evening.

"Cap . . . I . . . I'm so . . . my God, Cap—thank you . . . hey, buddy, I've got a medal here in my desk drawer waiting just for you. Jesus, I love you, Cap."

TRAGEDY

YES, THERE WAS LIGHT AT THE END OF THIS DARK TUNNEL. It might've been dim at first, but it was there, and it was getting brighter. It was Friday evening, nearly a week since my heart-wrenching discussion with Mom and Dad. But I could already see a change in them, and it felt so good. Sure, it was small, but it was growing, and it was a start. A huge weight had been lifted from their shoulders—and mine.

Dad had just returned from a business trip to Toronto. After dinner, he watched TV with Laura and me—and never said a word about basketball, my grades, college, or my future. We watched *Mission Impossible 5*—for the second time—with a large bowl of Laura's homemade, overbuttered, super-salted popcorn. For the first time in months I could breathe easily—and damn, it was awesome.

I hadn't heard a word from Tamara. She'd said she would contact me in a few days with the Beijing Summit intel. It had been nearly a week. *God, or whoever, just keep it up, please.* With any luck, maybe she'd decided I was too much of a pain in the ass and would never get back to me. Was this crazy situation with Tamara and the CIA going to work out after all? Wishful thinking.

I WAS HAVING AN EARLY BREAKFAST and feeling such a sense of relief that I finally decided to play a pickup game with Dr. Ross and his local athlete friends. I knew from discussions with him that most of those guys had played collegiate ball, and then, like Dad, went to grad school with no intention of going pro. Dr. Ross had called me several times and asked me to play. I'd always declined. He was surprised when I called him and asked to play in the next game.

Dad was coming downstairs and caught me just as I was about to leave. "You're up early for a Saturday."

"Yeah, well, I did my run early today and decided to play a pickup game with Dr. Ross and his friends."

"Really? Did he play college ball?"

"Yeah, played for Maryland, and boy, is he tall. He makes me feel like a midget."

"He must be tall. You guys have fun."

After a couple of beats, Dad asked, "Say, can I have just a few minutes of your time before you leave?"

It was great to see him in such a good mood. In the past, he never would have asked for a few minutes of my time. He would have demanded them. "Sure. Why don't I join you for a quick cup of java?"

He smiled. "That'd be great."

We sat down at the kitchen table across from each other. He cleared his throat as I poured us each a cup.

"Look, I don't want to make a big thing of this," he began, "but I think it's important, and I need to share it with you."

Oh no—here we go again—now what did I do? "Gee, did I do something wrong?"

"No, no, nothing like that. It's just that . . . well . . . I've been unfairly tough on you over the years. It wasn't you. It was me. I was angry as hell at *me*. But I want you to know I'm gonna work hard to change that. I agree, you should live your own life. Sure, I like giving you input and guidance—it's my job as a parent—but I believe when it comes down to it, you'll make the right choices. And if you don't—so what? You'll learn. That's what life's about, anyway. It's not about being perfect every step of the way. I'm sorry if I put a huge dent in your personal enjoyment. I'd like to do better for you, and I promise, I will."

I was blown away. A little choked up, I swallowed and slowly replied, "You'll never know how much I appreciate that, Dad."

"I'll bet. I can only imagine. I also wanna tell you how grateful I am for what you did for me and Cap—for our family. You started a healing process for two people who would have gone to their graves with stress they didn't know how to deal with. We are both deeply grateful for that."

He grabbed my arm across the table. "Son, I'm proud of you and I love you. I always have and I always will—no matter what."

Now I was really choking up. It was the first time I'd ever felt so close to him. It was incredible.

"I love you too, Dad. I really do. And I do appreciate your advice."

I bowed my head and swallowed deeply, trying to regain my composure. Neither of us said anything for a few seconds.

He cleared his throat again and changed the subject before we both started bawling. "Well, I guess you'd better get going. Don't want to keep those college stars waiting."

"Oh, I don't know about that. I'm about to get my butt kicked, I'm sure."

"You never know."

Things were really looking up—I thought.

I HEADED HOME AFTER THE GAME. I'd surprised Dr. Ross, and myself for that matter, with my performance. Two former Stanford players and I played three games against Dr. Ross and two former Rutgers players. We beat them two out of three games. Dr. Ross pulled me aside and commented that I must have had an unfair advantage because of my superpowers. I tried to convince him they were on their way out. He didn't believe me. I could feel it. But I felt great. I was still on a super high from my discussion with Dad.

When I got home, I called Bella immediately to tell her that I had some great news. This might be just the thing to get us back on the same path together. After a shower and a change of clothes, I met her at the Creamery for lunch. We sat in our usual booth at the back. We ordered cheeseburgers, fries, and a vanilla malt with two straws. She kept pushing me to share the news, but I insisted that we wait until lunch arrived. I don't know why. I was as impatient as she was to put it out there. I guess I needed some time to figure out how to say it. After all, it was some pretty heavy stuff.

Lunch came, but I wasn't hungry. I was too excited to tell Bella about my meeting with Cap and with Mom and Dad. Now that I had proof that Tamara didn't have anything on him, I decided to tell Bella everything, including the work I was doing for the CIA, how I'd been blackmailed, and of course, what appeared to be unfolding as a happy ending.

"Okay, I'm ready," she said. "What's the great news? Did you hear from Princeton?"

"No. Not yet. It's something else, something much better."

"How could anything be much better?"

"You'll see. Look, I'll start at the beginning. Please don't faint or say anything before I finish."

"Come on, tell me. I can't wait anymore."

And I did, from the beginning until everything that had happened that morning. Every other sentence, Bella was like, "Oh my God! No way!"

When I finished, it was her turn. "Why didn't you tell me all this when you were suffering through it? I would have been there for you."

"Remember, I told you I'd solve these issues on my own, and you'd be the first to know when I had something that looked promising. Well, this is it, and if all goes as planned, the old Luc will be back with his old life. I didn't want to tell you anything until I felt it would be safe. I didn't want to put your life at risk. Who knows what those crazies at the CIA would have done if they'd found out that I'd told you everything I was doing for them?"

"Thanks for your concern. I feel so bad that I wasn't more understanding," Bella said softly.

"Don't! Look at the bright side. It's now behind us, and I'm so happy that I can't sit still. I feel like I'm gonna burst!"

"I'm so happy for you and your family. Your dad must be ecstatic to know you're no longer owned by the CIA, and they can't touch him."

"Yeah, he was like through the roof after I told him about my discussion with Cap. I've never seen him like this. But I didn't tell him about Tamara's scheme and the CIA. And I don't plan to. It wouldn't do any good now, and it would really piss him off. Who knows what he might do? And I sure as hell don't wanna push him backward. He's in such a great space right now. So I beg you not to *ever* mention a word to anyone. Please, Isabella."

"Whoa! It must be important. You just called me Isabella. All kidding aside, I understand. My lips are sealed. Anyway, who cares, now? It really doesn't matter anymore."

"Thank you."

"When do you intend to confront Tamara so you can break free from her?"

"Soon, but I have a couple things I need to do first."

Bella looked a bit puzzled. "A couple things? What now, Mr. Mysterious?"

"I'll fill you in, promise, after I square away my own thinking. There's so much happening in my mind right now—I mean, good stuff."

"Okay, Luc Ponti, I trust you. But I'm gonna hold you to that promise. By the way, have you seen any decrease in your powers?"

"Not really. If anything—and I hate to even think about it—they might be increasing. For the longest time, I thought the mind reading was fading, but it's not. It just changed in some way. I can still read people's minds if I want to, but doing it on purpose gives me a super headache. And as for seeing into the future, I can see even farther now." I closed my eyes, took a deep breath, then opened them and looked at my watch. "Like in ten minutes, Jimmy and Billy are gonna barge in here and ask me to go to some crazy car show with them."

"Come on, Luc."

"Really. I'm not kidding."

Bella smiled. She was convinced I was joking. "So what are you going to do about your powers? Maybe see Dr. Ross for help?"

"Nope, I don't think so. After our game today, he asked me what was happening. I told him not much. That it seemed like my powers were on their way out."

"What did he say?"

"He looked at me strangely and said, 'Really?' I don't think he believed me. To tell you the truth, I don't know what to do. It still concerns me, but after what's just happened, not nearly as much as before. Besides, as far as reading people's minds and seeing into the future, I now have all that under control. It no longer happens unless I want it to by doing a mini meditation. That's what I did a few minutes ago to know that Jimmy and Billy are on their way here. And as for reading minds—no way! Who likes migraines?"

Bella thought for a few seconds. "Can I make a suggestion?"

"Sure."

"Why not continue to work with Thay? He likes you, you like him, and I'm sure he'd love to continue to be your guiding light, guru, or whatever. Besides, he's such a neat guy. I really like him."

"I like him too. But I don't know . . . maybe. I'll give it some thought."

"Since we haven't seen each other lately, I've had lots of time to think about what you're going through. If those powers don't go away, I think you should consider how you could use them to help people who really need help—you know, like you did for your dad and Cap. Maybe that's your real thing—working for the greater good and helping others who really need it."

"Maybe. That also occurred to me after I saw what these powers did for Dad and Cap. I've pretty much stopped worrying about if and when they will go away. My only concern is to see how all of this can be worked in with college and the rest of my life. And before thinking that through, I wanna be sure Tamara and the CIA are long gone."

Just then, Jimmy and Billy walked in. Bella and I stared at each other. The wise guy in me had to say it. I looked at my watch. "See what I mean? Right on time."

Bella's eyes popped open. She just laughed. "Yeah, right."

Jimmy came over, and before we could say a word, he let out with, "Hi, Bella, Luc. Luc, we saw your bike outside. Come with us to the Stanford Mall. There's an exhibition of the latest electric cars. There are even several fuel-cell cars. Should be great! Come on. Let's go!"

Bella just smiled.

"I don't know, guys. I promised Bella I'd ride back with her to her place."

"Come on. You're the one who's always preaching about the environmental value of electric cars. Remember your comments last week in physics class about how fuel-cell cars can solve the lithium-battery recycle problem. Here's your chance to see one of those buggers up close. Come on."

"You guys go on without me. I'll go tomorrow."

Billy responded, "No way. The exhibit closes tonight."

Bella, always the considerate one, said, "Go on. I'll bike home on my own."

I felt bad, but I really wanted to see the cars. "Are you sure?"

"I'm sure."

"Thanks. Okay, guys, let's go. I'll get the check on the way out."

"Oh, and Luc . . . ," Bella said.

"Yeah?"

"Really think about my suggestion for your future."

What's she talking about? Oh, yeah, the greater good.

"Right. Thanks."

THE EXHIBITION WAS AMAZING, but I was terribly distracted. For some reason, I couldn't focus. Something heavy was troubling me. I kept pushing it away, but it kept snapping back at me. I felt terrible, almost ill. I didn't know why—I did when I got home.

I walked in, and Mom and Dad were sitting in the living room. Her eyes were red. She'd been crying. Dad's face was as sad as I'd ever seen it.

I stood there and asked, "Mom, Dad, what's wrong? Is Laura okay?"

Mom got up and came over to me. "Laura's fine. We tried calling you on your cell phone, but there was no answer."

"Sorry, Mom, I forgot it at home."

Dad stood up and took over. He came over and put his hand on my right shoulder. "There's been a terrible accident. Bella was hit earlier today while riding her bike. It was a hit-and-run driver."

"Oh my God! Is she okay? How serious are her . . . injuries?"

Dad grabbed my arms tightly. "She's in a coma, and the outlook is not good."

I broke free from him and walked over to the sofa. I fell on it in a ball of anguish and pain. I thought my entire body was about to blow apart. With my face in both hands, I cried, "No, no, no—not Bella. Please, God, not Bella. You can't let her die!" I was beside myself. No one could help. I cried like a baby.

AFTER SOME TIME, I PULLED MYSELF TOGETHER. I had to see her. Mom and Dad drove me to the hospital, where we met a distressed Mr. and Mrs. Moreno in the waiting area down the hall from Bella's room in the ICU. The doctors wouldn't let anyone else in to see her.

It wasn't long before my devastation turned to anger. I lashed out at God. *How could you do this to my Bella? She's such a good person. Why not me? What are you doing to us? One big wound heals, and you open an even bigger one. I'm not sure there's anything left for me in this goddamned life, and yes, I mean "goddamned."*

The doctors convinced me to go home. They simply wouldn't let me see her. Bella's condition, while critical, wasn't getting any worse—but I guess the worst it could get would be the end. They'd stabilized her, and although she was in a coma, they said I could probably see her in the morning.

I got home and went up to my room. Exhausted, I laid down on my bed and fell fast asleep, clothes and all.

DAD WAS SITTING IN THE CHAIR NEXT TO MY BED when I woke up the next morning.

"Good morning. We didn't want to wake you after what you'd been through. Is there anything I can do?"

"I don't think so. I wanna take a shower and head over to the hospital. I got to get into the ICU to see Bella."

"I understand. But first, I'd like to share a thought with you. While the challenges I went through in Iraq weren't the same as what you're facing now, I can empathize with your pain. I spent too many years in anguish and suffering. It took love and compassion from family and friends, especially Mom, you, and Laura. But then Cap's revelation pulled me out of that deep, dark hole. I want you to know that Mom and I are here for you.

"Another thing, and you sure know my thoughts about doctors, but I don't simply accept their views about Bella. She's an amazing girl with a big heart and incredible mental and physical strength. We all need to stay positive that she'll pull through this."

"Thanks, Dad. I appreciate your thoughts, and I will try to stay positive."

And that's how my day ended and a new one began, from a hallelujah high to a near-deadly low.

THE GREATER GOOD

Mrs. Moreno called last evening. The news wasn't good. Because of the serious head injury Bella had suffered, the doctors didn't expect her to make it, and if she did pull though, they said that she'd probably lose much of her memory and communication abilities. I slipped deeper into that black hole of depression. I had to see her, to be with her.

I got to the hospital around 8:00 A.M. A harried nurse, who seemed to be in charge of the ICU, said I could visit briefly with Bella at nine. I waited that long hour torturing myself with all kinds of terrible what ifs.

I finally got to see her. She was lying there, flat on her back, eyes closed and her right arm in a full cast. She was so pale that her tan complexion was almost colorless. Several machines monitored her vital signs, the most frightening one, a ventilator attached to her mouth, pulsating rhythmically every few seconds with an unbearable clunk-and-squish sound. But it was helping her breathe. She looked like she was being kept sort of alive.

My world was crashing down on me. I scooted a chair up to the left side of her bed, pulled her arm out from under the covers, gently laid it next to her side, and held her cold, lifeless hand. I was hoping that maybe she could hear me and my words would do some good.

"Bella, you gotta pull through this. I know you can do it. Your family and your friends need you. I need you. I mean like I *really* need you." I felt a hurricane force building up inside me, already a fast-moving category 2. I had visions of it growing to a full-blown Katrina-like category 5 and sweeping me away to who knows where. I didn't care. But then the nurse came in. My visit was over.

When lightning strikes, you never know where or when. And that's what I was supposed to believe about Bella having been a victim of a hit-and-run. It bothered me a lot, especially when I saw Mrs. Moreno at the hospital, and she said the police had no leads whatsoever on who the driver was, and they told her husband it was highly unlikely they would catch the perpetrator. She said the cops said it was a sign of the times, or some shit like that.

I couldn't accept that. I *wouldn't* accept it. After leaving the hospital, I went to the East Palo Alto police station on Demeter Street to speak to the person in charge of Bella's case. I sat there for about 30 minutes, twiddling my thumbs before a tall, good-looking, well-built Detective Ryan James came out to reception.

"You Luc Ponti?"

I stood up. "Yes, sir."

"What can I do for you?"

"I'm a good friend of Isabella Moreno. I heard it's highly unlikely you'll find the driver who hit her. Is that right?"

"Essentially, yes."

"And why's that?"

"Look, I appreciate your concern for your friend, and I can understand you're not happy with my answer, but people are people. Let me give you a few hard facts about the reality of this case. Are you any kind of a numbers man, Luc?"

"A little bit."

"In the entire Bay Area, about 6 percent of these hit-and-run cases get solved. In Oakland, it's only about 2 percent. Even in the monster that LA is, with its 9,000-person police force, only 8 percent of hit-and-run cases get solved. I have ten cases on my docket—most of them murders, attempted murder, rape, or grand larceny. And I have only two officers working part-time on all of them. What happened to your friend is a tough crime to crack when you don't have good evidence or any witnesses."

"Or a motive," I added.

"Most of the time, nobody sets out to commit a hit-and-run. It usually happens inadvertently—a drunk driver or they're not paying attention—and well, people are people. They get scared and they run. We're not giving up. I'm not saying we're giving up. I'm just saying the same thing I told her dad."

"Detective, I don't mean to be pushy, but if you had more evidence, would you follow up?"

"Absolutely. I don't think that's gonna happen, but definitely, if we got some tips, we'd follow them."

"Okay, good. Can you tell me the exact place it happened and anything else? Maybe I can ask around. Ya never know."

"Sure, why not." He motioned to me to follow him to his office in the back. When we got there, he flipped through a small notebook that was lying on his desk.

"Here you go," he told me. "It happened two blocks from her home at about 2:30 P.M. on Thursday near the eastbound corner of East Bayshore Road and Clarke Avenue. We searched the area and found nothing except one small triangular piece of glass that we're fairly sure came from a headlight. The lab has already checked it for DNA, but they found nothing. It could've been just stray glass lying in the street. We don't have a good concrete reason to tie it to the crime scene."

I wanted to push more, but I didn't. I had a different plan. I thanked Detective James and left. Jack Farrell Park was just across the road from the police station. I found a nice out-of-the-way spot under a tree, laid down in the grass, and did my OBE thing. In seconds, my spirit was floating into the precinct, past reception and into the evidence room. There were floor-to-ceiling shelves, each of them jam-packed with all kinds of stuff sealed in ziplock bags, some of it totally creepy, like a pair of yellowed false teeth and what looked like part of a human leg bone.

Stashed in a corner sat an old, green, four-drawer metal filing cabinet. Something told me to go there and look in the third drawer under the letter "M." The files were sort of alphabetized, and then . . . bingo! I found the case file labeled Moreno, Isabella. There was nothing in it but a few scribbled notes, pretty much saying the same thing the detective had told me, and there was a small plastic bag with the triangular piece of glass in it that Detective James had mentioned. I grabbed it.

Getting into the evidence room had been easy, and getting out would have been easy too, since no one could have seen me. I was invisible. But the plastic bag I was holding, that was something else. Anyone in reception would see the bag floating past them in midair. That could be heart-attack material.

The hallway from the evidence room was clear, but speaking of heart attacks, an elderly lady and, of course, the receptionist, were out front. So I waited and I waited. The thing about remote viewing was that you come out with what you go in with, nothing more, not like *Star Trek*, where Scotty can beam up all sorts of stuff.

After what seemed like a lifetime, the receptionist led the old lady down the hallway, past the evidence room, through a door at the end of the hall and into an office area. Quickly, I zoomed down the hall into reception and out the open front door to the park and back into my body, with the plastic bag in hand.

I rode my bike to the intersection where Bella had been hit. Just as Detective James had mentioned, there wasn't much to see evidence-wise—a real bummer, which meant that the triangular piece of glass needed to give me a hit just like Rio the parakeet's toys helped me find *him*. I sat down on the curb, laid back on the grass behind me, closed my eyes, and squeezed gently on the small evidence bag with the glass inside.

Within seconds, I was doing an OBE north onto the 101 freeway, which ran parallel to East Bayshore Road where Bella was hit. In less than a mile, I was floating in front of the Four Seasons Hotel at the U.S. 101 on-ramp between Palo Alto and East Palo Alto. I was drawn to the hotel's parking area. Something was there;

I needed to check it out. I rapidly floated back to the intersection where Bella was hit and reentered my body.

After riding my bike back to the hotel, I began snooping around the parking garage, trying not to be too obvious. There didn't seem to be much out of the ordinary. But after walking around the various areas, I noticed a black Ford Mustang, license plate 3SAM173. I made a mental note of the plate. Its right-front bumper and right-front fender were both dented, and there was a glass chip missing from the right headlight. The hole appeared to be the same triangular shape and size as the glass chip in the evidence bag.

I took the elevator to the hotel reception area. Sitting in a chair at the far side of the lobby with my back to the reservation desk, I pretended to be playing with my phone. The good thing about these upscale hotels is that they bank on big spenders, not on volume, which meant the place was kinda dead. So I closed my eyes and slipped into remote-viewing mode. Floating to the reservation counter, I saw two stand-alone check-in desks. I waited for one of the attendants to step away from her computer. A minute or two later, the one on the left went into the back room with a bunch of papers, so I moved in.

I scrolled through the guest list on her computer, but then had to stop when she came back for some information. When she was done, I went back to looking for anyone who might have checked in with a Mustang in the parking garage. The attendant came back again. This second time, she had a surprised look on her face. She'd left the computer on a specific page showing hotel events booked for the week, but now the screen showed the guest list. "Whatever," she said to herself, and returned to the back room with her paperwork.

Scrolling, scrolling . . . trying to match up with 3SAM173 . . . maybe—no license plate number listed, but I found a 2016 black Ford Mustang registered to a Mr. John Smith in Room 317—John Smith! *Minchia! Are you kidding me, bro? How original.* My spirit moved quickly to his room, past the Do Not Disturb sign on the door, as if that was going to stop me, and entered his room. His stuff was there, but he wasn't. Good, that made it easier, so I searched the place.

In a trash can under the desk, I noticed a bunch of McDonald's food wrappers—a gourmet eater, obviously—and an expired membership card to a Manhattan gym. He must have stupidly thrown it there. His real name appeared to be Isaac Prostor.

Then to his laptop on the table. An easy hack and I was in. Username: Anonymous. Recent Documents: empty. Emails: scrolled down through lots of spam except he hadn't marked it as spam: FREE AMATEUR WEBCAMS and NUDE PICS!!! and HOT TEEN GIRL TIRED OF BOYS WANTS REAL MEN. Then to his web browser and more of the same.

Then to his computer trash. That was easy. It was empty except for one file. The file extension was labeled "aes." I double-clicked on it and "Access Denied" popped up, but a firewall was no match for me. Something about the sender felt, I dunno, familiar. But the message? Gone. Those encrypted messages were generally programmed to auto-delete within five minutes after being opened. Must have been a glitch. The message got wiped, all right, but not the sender's name—*Seagull. Merda santa!*

Seagull was the code name of the person communicating with Tamara in several encrypted messages I'd found at her home. They'd been sent to her from an operative in Moscow.

I returned to my body in reception, went back to the garage, got on my bike, and raced back to the police station. After returning to my favorite spot in the park, I did an OBE and carefully reentered the police station. I had to be careful, because I had the plastic bag in my hand. When the receptionist left the room, I moved like a stealth bomber to the evidence room and returned the glass chip. After reuniting with my body, I crossed the street and went into the station and asked for Detective James.

This time, I waited only five minutes.

"Hi, Detective James. I think I found your guy."

He looked at me like I was nuts. "Yeah, right, and my name is Dick Tracy. Are you kidding me? Look! Don't come around here wasting my time. As I told you earlier today, I've already got too much on my plate."

"No, I'm not kidding. His name is Isaac Prostor, and he's staying in Room 317 at the Four Seasons Hotel just down the road. He drives a black Ford Mustang, California license plate 3SAM173. The car had a dented right-front fender and bumper, and one of the headlights had a triangular piece of glass missing. It's the same size and shape as the glass you have in your evidence bag."

In my haste—*cavalo*! What did I just say? Looking at me skeptically, Detective James asked, "How could you possibly know the exact size of the glass chip? You never saw it."

Doing my best to recover, I said, "Actually, I don't. But the car I saw looked like it had hit something, and one headlight was missing a small triangular-shaped piece of glass, just as you described this morning, so I put one and one together. And by the way, the car's a rental."

Detective James started pacing back and forth in front of me. I think he was getting pissed. "Luc, you gotta be mistaken. How could you or anyone else, for that matter, possibly have done all this in a few hours, if ever? You must be wrong. Now please let me get back to work." He turned around abruptly and headed down the hall to his office.

Before he left the reception area, I suggested loudly, "Would it be possible to plug the license-plate number into your computer system and see what comes up?"

He stopped and turned back to me. "Yeah, but it would be a waste of my time. I doubt it will be anything important."

I pleaded, "Come on, Detective. Please give it a shot."

He looked at me sympathetically and said, "Ponti, you look like a good kid, but you sure are one big pain in the ass. Okay, to humor you and because I believe you're sincerely trying to help, I'll do it. But don't expect much. And after that, I don't wanna see your face around here again. Understood?"

"Understood. Thank you, sir."

He went back to his office. I waited in the reception area. Ten minutes later he came back out. I stood up quickly. He looked mystified. "Luc, can you tell me how you went from my office this morning to the crime scene to the Four Seasons Hotel and identified that black Mustang?"

"I can, and I promise I will, but it'll take quite a bit of time. But for now, please just trust me. And not to be a pain in your ass, but did you find anything helpful when you searched the plate?"

He smiled. "Man, I can't wait to find out how you did this. Yes, your finding is *most* interesting. The Mustang was in fact rented to a guy named Isaac Prostor from New York City. What's also interesting, from what I can see in our database, is that he's a Russian immigrant who spent most of the past ten years in jail, mainly for grand larceny. Prostor allegedly has connections with the Russian Mafia in New York. I'm sending someone to the Four Seasons right now with a warrant to take evidence from his car and his hotel room. I'll call you and the Moreno family if we find anything of interest."

As I left the station, Detective James still looked flabbergasted—but then again, so was I.

THREE DAYS WENT BY BEFORE I HEARD FROM DETECTIVE JAMES. I'd been waiting anxiously for his call. He finally phoned me just as I was going out to shoot some hoops with Billy and Jimmy, my therapy for dealing with Bella's challenges in the hospital.

"Hi, Luc, it's Detective James. I have no idea how you did it, and it doesn't matter right now. Miracles are fine in my book if they work the right way. We found skin and hair samples on the Mustang's bumper and fender. They're a perfect match to Bella's DNA. Prostor is in custody and has been charged with hit-and-run vehicular manslaughter. Because of his prior record, he'll likely go away for a long time."

I didn't want to disclose my connection with the CIA, but I wanted to know if they'd found the message from Seagull in his computer. "Did you find anything else of interest, and also, was he drunk when he hit Bella and then left the scene of the accident?"

"Nothing else showed up. We have enough information to convict him. Whether he was drinking, we can't tell, but it doesn't matter at this point."

"I was wondering—who does he work for?"

"It's funny you should ask. He said hitting Isabella Moreno was an accident, and he fled the scene because he's a private consultant with top-secret security clearance, working undercover for a high-level government official. He told me he'll be out of jail in no time."

"I sure as hell hope that's not the case."

"I sincerely doubt it. He's a typical mobster wise guy—all mouth and bullshit."

"In any case, I'm so glad you called. You've made my day."

"No, Luc, you made mine." He laughed. "If I could, I'd hire you. I'll bet you could get those ten cases off my docket in no time flat, and we'd both take a vacation—at my expense!"

"I don't know about that, but I was glad to help."

"Which reminds me—don't forget your promise to tell me how you did this."

"I will if you promise not to mention my involvement to anyone."

"Provided you didn't break any laws, I can do that. . . . But you know, you appear to have a special ability. We've worked with psychic types before, but never with results like this. I can tell you, this crazy world could use your kind of help. You should give it some thought. You could make a huge difference."

Where have I heard that before?

PROMISES

I MISSED BELLA MORE THAN I COULD HAVE IMAGINED. There was so much I needed to say that I'd never gotten the chance to express. Erase that. I'd had *lots* of chances. I just hadn't taken them.

I skipped an all-day Saturday preseason practice that Coach had planned for the team. Even though he was wild as a tiger when it came to practices, I knew that things being what they were, he'd understand.

Instead, I went to the hospital to see how Bella was doing. She was out of intensive care, so that was good. On my way to her room, I saw her mom pacing in the waiting area. She gave me a big hug and started to cry. I could only imagine what it was like to have this happen to her only child. An only child not by choice. Her first, Alejandro, had died some years before from multiple sclerosis. That's what motivated Bella to want to become a doctor. Her dream was plain and simple, at least as dreams go—to help her folks financially and find a cure for MS—in that order.

I suggested to Mrs. Moreno that she go outside for a bit to get away from the hospital, with its depressing energy, and be with her husband. She nodded in agreement, trying to dredge up a smile of appreciation, and giving me a quick hug with noticeable confusion about how to be—angry, sad, hopeful, hopeless?

"You're right, Luc. Oh, my Santiago. He works even harder when he's suffering. It's his way to manage his stress."

When I entered Bella's room, I was overwhelmed with my *own* confusion about how to be. I lightly touched her left hand, then nervously let go—I don't know why—and gently began to stroke her forehead. The monitors said she was still with us.

"Hi, Bella, I know you're in there—somewhere. I don't know if you can hear me. I guess the chickenshit part of me hopes you can't. But I have a few things that I wanna tell you, that I *gotta* tell you.

"I'm so sorry. Like, I've never been so sorry for anything in my whole life. I'm sorry this happened to you. It's my fault. I shouldn't have gone to that damn car show with the guys. I should've ridden home with you. *Buon Dio, mia bella regazza,*[47] maybe none of this would have ever happened.

"I'm also sorry for the fights I caused between us. They were all my fault. I know it now—and if I'm honest with myself, I knew it then. My life was moving so fast. I was distracted by things that I should have recognized were much less important than our relationship—I couldn't keep up. I messed up big-time losing you. Maybe you don't know how really special you are to me. I mean, yeah, you probably don't, because I never said anything, and what I did say was, well, you know . . .

"Oh, Bella, I'm confused. With all that's happened between us, you probably think I'm just your best friend. Well, I am, for sure, I'm that. But, it's like . . . it's like there's more than that. Really. *Minchia*, I don't know what the hell I'm mumbling about here. I can't even think straight.

"Yeah, I admit there are those wannabe girls who hang around with me and the guys on the team. But they're just that—girls who wanna look like they're attached to someone they think is important—anyone—on the varsity team. The guys call them 'thirsties.' For them, that's the be all and end all in their life. And I guess my

---

[47] *Buon Dio, mia bella regazza*—"Good God, my beautiful girl."

ego liked it. And I really mean 'it,' not them. I guess I got good at it—and bad at *you. Minchia, che idiota!*[48]

"I admit, I don't know much about this kinda stuff. But I do know that my heart feels weird—I mean, nice weird—every time I see you. And I guess I kinda believe it's because you've always been like my best friend. But I know that's bullshit.

"Maybe . . . it would've been easier if you were like those thirsties. What am I saying? *Minchia!* Thank God you're not. So I guess I should grow up and show you how much I really appreciate you. Well, *bella regazza,* I finally got a wake-up call—in the worst way—you in a coma in the hospital. *Gesu Cristo* . . . Bella, what the hell am I gonna do now?"

I took a deep breath and reached for her hand again. "Okay, here goes. I wanna tell you somethin' that has really been driving me nuts for the past couple of years. Try as I might, I couldn't let it go. I thought maybe someday we would. . . you know . . . get closer. At least that's what I think I was hoping for.

"But then I'd think about where you and I are in our lives and where we're goin'. You wanting to be a doctor after a gazillion years of college at God knows where, and me wanting to play college basketball at God knows where, and then maybe going pro. So it was like, why take a really hard fall later? It would only hurt both of us much more. So it was just like, step off the cliff now. Well, I did, and I wish I hadn't. I hit bottom, and man it hurts like hell. I can't stand it.

"Bella, maybe it's crazy, but I don't know what I'd do without you in my life. I'd be lost. I don't think I could do this kind of thing again—with anyone. I'd be measuring everyone against you, and none of 'em could ever measure up. Please don't take this the wrong way. But sometimes I want to run away from you as far as I can. Why?

"Because I hate myself for loving you. *Minchia!* I said it . . . okay, I love you. I had to wait until you were in a coma. I mean, you are definitely my best friend—and I love you too. Is that possible? Can you love your best friend? Wow, do I need help!

---

[48] *Minchia, che idiota!*—"Shit [or damn], what an idiot!"

"So, yeah, I hate that this happened so soon. I hate that we both didn't go out more with other people to understand what's special between us. And I really hate that every time I was with one of those 'thirsties,' I was thinking only of you. And then I gave them even more time to try to stop thinking about you—what a mistake. I did it because I was thinking *about* you, and not thinking *of* you. *Bella mia*, I know I sound all messed up. Sorry. I'm sorry for everything that went wrong with us." I started to let go of her hand and went back to gliding my hand in circles across her forehead.

Just then, I could swear, Bella squeezed my hand. At first, I thought I was mistaken. Maybe I squeezed hers. But then her arm twitched. I scrambled for the call button. A voice came from the other side: "Hello, can I help you?"

Before I could answer, Bella was coughing into the ventilator anchored in her mouth and deep into her throat. By then, all I could get out was, "Nurse! Help!"

The monitors went crazy with their own alerts as nurses ran in. They were shouting all kinds of medical-speak, and one of them tried to push me out of the room. I refused. Seconds later, a doctor rushed in. They worked quickly to remove the ventilator from Bella's mouth.

She was coughing, at first in heaves, hardly catching her breath before the next wave, and she kept at it until continued attempts at clearing her windpipe at last allowed her to breathe on her own. I was excited, happy, and scared, all at the same time. Her eyes opened. She looked frightened.

By then, the doctor and three nurses were in the room. The doctor told her, "Bella, I'm Dr. Schiff, and you're in Stanford Hospital."

Bella looked around the room, her gaze scanning the doctor's face, and then the nurses', and then mine. She held it there, with a slight smile, confused, and within a few blinks, her eyes fluttered until they were still, and she fell into a deep sleep.

MRS. MORENO WAS LEANING OVER BELLA'S BED, their heads touching each other gently like worker bees on a flower. She was speaking softly to her daughter. With what little Spanish I knew, I picked up enough of her words: *"Humildemente ahora me alcanceis de la Majestad Divina la gracia que al presente os pido"*[49]—her favorite prayer, *Our Lady of Grace: "Oración a la Milagrosa"*[50]—the only prayer I had any familiarity with, in both English and Spanish. It was part of my dark memories from visits to the Morenos' home when Alejandro was in his final stages of letting go. I waited in the doorway as she finished: *"Solo a lo que sera honra y gloria de Dios, y salvacion de mi alma. Amen."*[51] She looked up. "Luc."

"Hi, Mrs. Moreno. How is she?"

"Better. There's still slight swelling in her brain, but at least she's out of the coma, and so far, it seems positive. They said the swelling is going down surprisingly fast. The doctors don't understand why. They've never seen it before in someone with such a swollen brain, recovering from a severe coma. They're going to do more MRIs and some other special tests to see if they can figure out what's happening. But it all seems good. I guess after that, it will be physical therapy, speech therapy, and . . ."

While this was all incredibly positive, I couldn't help but look at this woman and think, *Remarkable.* "And how about you, Mrs. Moreno? How are *you* doing?"

"Doing much better now that Bella is on her way back."

She sent a long, compassionate look to both Bella and me. As devout as she was, years earlier she'd lost Bella to SBNR—Spiritual But Not Religious—just like me and some of my friends. And though I wasn't religious and couldn't speak like a Catholic to Mrs. Moreno, I sure as hell was fluent in speaking loneliness.

"You know, Mrs. Moreno, I'm learning about relaxing into your destiny and accepting it as your future. I must tell you, you *are* making a difference. You've made a big difference in Bella's life, and in mine, just by bringing her into this world. It's not easy to make a difference, especially if others you love and who love

---

[49] *Humbly, from thy Divine Majesty, may I receive the grace I now ask of you.*
[50] *Prayer for a miracle.*
[51] *For the honor and glory of God, and the salvation of my soul. Amen.*

you back don't understand you, or maybe, just *can't* understand you. I guess they're not there yet, but that's the way it is."

"Such a wise young man you are, Luc." She took a deep breath. "Will you be here for a while? I don't want to leave Bella alone, and I think I'll take your advice and step out for a little while . . . go wash my face, try to reach Santiago and tell him how our daughter is doing, and maybe go for a short walk in the beautiful gardens outside."

"That's a great idea. Don't worry, I'll be right here until you return. Take all the time you need. I'm not going anywhere."

She nodded and slipped by me, stopping for a moment before clearing the doorway as if she'd forgotten to say something, to add something to what she'd already said, but then on second thought, she was gone.

I stepped toward Bella's bedside, and a deep pit opened up inside me. She hadn't been conscious since she'd come out of the coma. I started to rub her forehead, as I'd done yesterday when she opened her eyes for the first time. I said many of the same things again, hoping it would help, praying that something would happen.

"Oh, Bella, I want you to come back, to be your old self again." I closed my eyes in deep meditation. Suddenly, my hand and her forehead were getting warm. I saw a rapid movie in my mind's eye, all the fun things we'd done growing up together—climbing Mt. Whitney in the driving rain and almost falling off a cliff together, skipping school in fifth grade on a boiling-hot day in May to swim at Rinconada pool, each of us winning a gold medal in the eighth-grade Junior Olympics, and many more adventures together.

I was awakened from my meditation by Bella's cast-covered arm pushing to her left, over her chest, and repeatedly touching me. I opened my eyes. Hers were already open. She cracked a smile but said nothing. I pushed the call button. "Nurse, get in here right now!" The commotion began again, and within seconds, two nurses and a doctor were racing into the room. They were all over Bella, asking her questions but getting no response.

After finally settling down, Bella looked around the room, her gaze skipping over the doctor and the nurses before landing on me. She stopped, gave me a smile—this time a big one—and in a low, raspy whisper, said, "Hi, Luc. How are you? What's happening? Where am I?"

My heart jumped into my throat. "Oh, Bella."

One of the nurses echoed what the doctor was probably thinking: "Oh my God!"

The doctor took over and was more than stern in his demand for me to leave the room. He came over to me and said, "Luc, you either leave the room quietly this time, or I will have to call security."

"Fine. Bella, I'll be right outside your room, and as soon as they're finished in here, I'll be back, okay?"

"Okay, Luc."

I WAITED MORE THAN AN HOUR while the doctors took Bella's vital signs, or whatever they were doing in her room. For me, it seemed like an eternity. All I could do was pace up and down the hall. I kept wondering if she'd heard anything I said while she was out of it.

After everyone left her room, I overheard the doctor in the hall speaking on his cell phone to Mrs. Moreno. "We have no idea how it happened, but she seems completely recovered. We'll do a series of neurological and MRI tests and several detailed blood panels to be sure, and see if we can understand what happened. All we know right now is that Luc Ponti said he was sitting at her bedside speaking to her and massaging her forehead while she was in a deep sleep, and several minutes later, she awoke, spontaneously."

I, too, wondered what had happened. The only other time I'd seen something like this was when I electrocuted Eric, and while massaging his heart, he suddenly came back. I'd heard about healers. Was this what had happened? Was it another power I had? I let that thought go. There were more important things to think about right now.

The doctor had asked me to wait another 30 minutes before I went in to see Bella. He said she needed time to mentally adjust to being out of the coma. When he spoke to Mrs. Moreno, she'd gone to pick up Mr. Moreno at work, so they were on their way to the hospital. I looked at my watch, and after exactly 30 minutes, I went back into her room. I sat at her bedside and gently asked, "Hi, how are you feeling?"

In a scratchy voice, Bella whispered, "I've got a bit of a head-ache, and my throat is sore from that tube, but the pain seems to be going away—and fast—which is great."

"Did you hear anything I said while you were in the coma?"

"I can't remember. Was it important?"

"Oh, I was just chatting about lots of things to keep you company. We can talk about it some other time. Do you remember what happened to you on your bike?"

"All I remember was, as I turned my head, I saw a black car bearing down on me from behind. I moved toward the sidewalk to avoid being hit, but it seemed to follow me, and then—nothing."

"Well, I can tell you that it was more than nothing." I filled Bella in on what had happened, and that Isaac Prostor was in custody and would be arraigned today on attempted-murder charges. She was shocked, but relieved to hear he'd been captured.

I could feel that there was something she wanted to tell me, but she was holding back. I asked her, "Is there more to this that's bothering you? You seem different in a quiet kind of way. I guess I shouldn't be surprised after what you've been through. But you know how connected we are."

"Yeah, right. Well, actually, there is something—something really crazy," she said.

"Really? Like what?"

She spoke slowly and reluctantly and said that after the car hit her, she, too, had experienced an NDE like mine. In the tunnel of light, she met her great-grandfather, who'd been a shaman in the jungles of Colombia. During her meeting with him, he gave her special knowledge, and a method to create a trance that would enable her to venture into the future. He told her never to use it unless it was necessary to help someone.

"That's amazing! Are you gonna give it a shot to see if it works?"

"I don't think that's a good idea based on what my grand-father told me. He said it could backfire if not done properly and for the right reasons."

"I guess you're right, then."

"Say, could you help me sit up in this bed? It's not easy with this broken arm, and my butt is sore as hell from lying in one position for so long."

"Sure—butt assistance coming up!"

"Just watch where you put your hands. You're still a smart-ass, but I gotta admit, I love it!"

"Thanks—gotta stay in practice."

"Luc, there *is* something else. I discovered it accidentally after the doctors left my room and before you returned."

"What do you mean?"

"I wanted my cell phone to call my mom, but it was over there on the table, and I felt too weak to get out of bed to get it."

"And?"

"I'll show you. Here, put my phone on the table on the other side of the room."

I did as she asked. With that, she raised her good arm and pointed it at the cell phone, and it suddenly flew rapidly through space across the room and landed in her hand.

"Wow! You're like a giant magnet! That's incredible! How'd you do that?"

"I don't know—just by thinking, and it's not just small things. You see the TV over there on the table?" She pointed her finger at it, and it quickly and easily slid across the table, stopping just before the edge when she put her arm down.

It was so incredible that I had to tell her about Eric—that the three of us had gone through NDEs and had come back with unusual powers. What were the odds? Then I recalled what the Great White Light had told me: "Eventually, you will not be alone. There will be *The Two*, who will help you." When I had asked the Light who they would be, the response was, "You will know in the fullness of time." Could *this* be the fullness of time? I wasn't sure. I decided to think about it before saying anything to Eric and Bella. Besides, she needed time to recover, with several weeks of physical therapy to get her arm and other body muscles back in shape. She had her work cut out for her.

I told Bella, "You know, as I look at what you can do, it seems as if you've acquired a power that's like a gravitational force that can be attractive or repulsive, depending on your thoughts and directions—what *Star Trek*'s Mr. Spock called *telekinesis*. Do you have any idea how powerful that is? I mean, you moved your phone and the TV. Do you think you could move bigger things, like a car?"

"I don't know. I haven't tried anything else, just what I showed you."

"Well, you'll have plenty of time for that when you get out of here. You know, there's something I suggested to Eric. When you feel up to it and no one's around, close your eyes and relax in a kinda mindful state, and see if you can do an OBE. He found he could do it just like me. It would be amazing if you could as well."

"I don't know. I feel a bit frightened about what's already happening. I don't think I'm ready for that."

"Eric said the same thing at first. But trust me, you'll get over that fear quickly."

Bella abruptly stopped talking, her eyes glued to the TV, which was still sitting at the edge of the table where she'd moved it with her gravitational or whatever force. It was on, but the volume had been turned down. "Luc, didn't you say the name of the guy who hit me was Isaac Prostor?"

"Yeah, why?"

She pointed to the TV. "Look at the scrawl running across the bottom of the screen."

And there it was: "There's been a drive-by shooting outside Police Headquarters in East Palo Alto. The victim's name is Isaac Prostor. He was being transferred to Palo Alto Municipal Court for arraignment on charges of attempted vehicular murder when he was shot as he walked with deputies to the transfer van."

We both looked at each other, perplexed, but not saying a word. I muttered quietly to myself. *Damn, Tamara—you don't leave anything to chance, do you?*

I had to get on with my plan. Once she found out that Bella had survived, her life would still be in danger.

No loose ends, huh, Tamara? Or was it Seagull?

OMG!

AFTER MY VISIT WITH BELLA, I just had to reconnect with Thay. Bella was right. I needed his help more than I realized, and I hadn't seen him for a while. How would the things he'd taught me work out for my future—I mean, the future I dreamed about? But Bella's rapid, yet unexplained, complete recovery gave me hope that things would eventually be fine. I also wanted to tell him what had happened to Bella and how she miraculously—oh, that's right, no such thing as a miracle—recovered.

I COULD HAVE CALLED THAY, but I wanted to see him in person for this discussion. Leaving the hospital, I made my way to the temple. I knocked at the door, which was locked. No answer. Going next door, I rang the bell at the small cottage where Reverend Daikan lived.

In no time at all, the door opened slowly. Reverend Daikan bowed and greeted me. "Namaste, Luc. So nice to see you. Please come in."

"Namaste, Reverend."

I entered a large sitting room sparsely decorated with a few simple chairs, several colorful pillows, and a small altar holding an emerald statue of the Buddha and a burning scented candle—frankincense, I was quite sure. Much to Mom's dismay, I used to burn the stuff in my room when doing my homework. Bella had told me it reduced stress and increased your focus and had other health benefits as well.

"Luc, please sit. We haven't had the opportunity to speak since Bella's accident. I want to express my concern for both of you. How are you managing? How's Bella doing?"

We sat down across from each other. "Good news—a miracle! She's out of her coma and making a speedy recovery. No one can explain how this could have happened—and so quickly. Even the doctors are amazed."

"That's wonderful." He hesitated for a few seconds. "Luc, I'm sure Thay must have told you, there's no such thing as a miracle. With our limited knowledge of the spiritual laws of the cosmos, it's just our inability to explain how certain physical things happen."

"Yeah, right. Thay did tell me that. Maybe so. But I'll take it, miracle or no miracle."

Reverend Daikan smiled. "I'm so happy for everyone, especially for Bella, you, and the Moreno family."

"Thanks. Oh, right, the Morenos are in seventh heaven. Mrs. Moreno can't stop with her *Gracias a Dios!* I'm so happy for them, for Bella and for me. But the reason I'm here is that I need to see Thay. Is he around today?"

The reverend lost his smile. "Oh, goodness, you don't know. Two weeks ago, Thay was called back to his monastery in Southern California by his abbot. I wasn't here. I was visiting friends in Canada, so we didn't speak before he left. He *did* leave me some notes, one of which said he tried to reach you several times on your cell phone but was unable to. Not surprising with all that's been going on in your life these past weeks. He asked me to express his sincere farewell and good wishes and to give you a letter. I've been so busy since I came back from Canada, I didn't take the opportunity to call you about it. I haven't even spoken with Thay yet. He's probably quite busy as well."

Damn, this couldn't be, not when I needed him most. My energy level fell to the floor. I had to reconnect with Thay and somehow get him back to Palo Alto.

Reverend Daikan got up and walked to a small desk on the other side of the room, picked up an envelope, and gave it to me. I thanked him, said goodbye, and biked over to the park on El Camino Real next to the University. I sat on a bench and read Thay's letter:

Dear Luc:

I regret that I have not been able to reach you before leaving Palo Alto. My guess is that you were busy and focused on something important.

Having not heard from you for several weeks, I was thinking that perhaps you're managing quite well and not in need of further counsel. I certainly hope that's the case because the abbot insisted that I immediately return to the monastery.

I had asked for a permanent transfer to Palo Alto so that we could further our friendship and I could continue to offer you my counsel. But he wouldn't consider it for two reasons.

First, the monastery is short of help, particularly in the fields of Eastern philosophy and the hard-core sciences, my fields of training. You wouldn't believe how these two areas intersect and how important they are for many projects we do both inside and outside of the monastery.

The second and main reason is that two representatives from our monastery have been invited to attend the first International Meeting of the World Interfaith Forum. It will be held at the Taglyan Complex in Los Angeles. The entire meeting is being funded by an anonymous donor, and the subject is timely—"The Role of Religion in Addressing Global Terrorism." There will be more than 300 internationally recognized attendees—high-level political and military figures and representatives from nearly every religion, including Buddhism, Christianity, Confucianism, Hinduism, Islam, Judaism, Shinto, Sikhism, Taoism, and Zoroastrianism.

Because of our abbot's international reputation, we have been asked to give the opening plenary lecture, and he has designated me as the presenter. So, you see, my plate is quite full.

I will miss being with you, my friend, but hope to visit in a few months to reconnect our friendship. In the meantime, I wish you, Bella, and your families the best of health, happiness, and fulfillment.

Namaste,
Thay

All I could think was *Oh my God—no!* Thay obviously had not heard what had happened to Bella. I shouldn't have stayed away so long. I was too focused on myself and my own issues. And now he was gone. I was more than bummed out. He was my great hope, my friend, and now he was out of the picture? Incredible. One step forward, two steps back.

THE NEXT COUPLE OF WEEKS WERE CHALLENGING. Bella had gotten out of the hospital, which was great, but she was busy going through physical therapy for her arm and several badly stretched muscles and tendons. School had started, and I really missed being with her. Also, I'd gotten a call from Secret Enemy Number One, who said that her Beijing contact was having success in acquiring important intel that I'd need for the upcoming China-North Korean summit. Lovely—I couldn't wait.

I finally realized how much I needed Thay and his guidance. I didn't know what to do. That began to change on Saturday evening.

We'd beaten Bellarmine again in a preseason game, and the guys were going out to celebrate. I begged off, even though I'd been the high scorer. I decided to work on my history term paper and try to get most of it out of the way. I'm not a big fan of history, but for obvious reasons, the title I was assigned interested me—"The Age of Terrorism."

As I studied the subject over the past week, one of my conclusions was that terrorism was a direct product of the male psyche and energy, which had existed since the beginning of civilization. And the two forces that drove its growth were the wealth and power of the upper class. This created a huge gap between the "haves" and the "have nots," until things got so bad for the have nots that they had nothing more to lose. So they resorted to revolution and terrorism.

The big issue for our current world situation was that weapons of mass destruction now existed and were readily obtainable by just about anyone. A simple bomb made from a bag of ammonium nitrate farm fertilizer mixed in with a barrel of ordinary fuel oil could take down a large building. I'd read in some of the material I reviewed that this is exactly what happened in Oklahoma City in 1995 when homegrown terrorists Timothy McVeigh and Terry Nichols destroyed a government building, killing nearly 170 people and injuring many more. What an insane world we live in!

My thoughts went to Thay. Distracted for several moments from my term paper, I laid on my bed and reminisced about our times together. I couldn't get him off my mind. Closing my eyes to rest for what seemed like only a few seconds, my multicolored vision kicked in. I suddenly saw a large building—I didn't have to guess its identity. The sign on the front of it said it all—Taglyan Complex. That's strange. It's the same place where Thay would address the World Interfaith Forum in two days. My ability to see the future had kicked in. I guess there was no headache, since I wasn't purposely trying to do this. I was about to awaken myself from what I thought was just an ordinary vivid dream of the near future when I saw two men on the roof of the adjacent building, St. John Armenian Church.

They'd placed a large board as a bridge extending from the church roof to the roof of the Taglyan Complex. *That's weird.* They were transporting packages onto the roof of the complex. I thought that maybe they were doing roof repairs. I continued to observe them. After several minutes, all the packages had been attached to various structures on the roof. The packages had a strange shape—they were metal hemispheres. The bottom of each hemisphere was a shiny metal sheet that they'd placed facedown toward the roof. The top of the hemisphere globe had a green blinking light facing upward. The men made their way back to the church's roof and used a rope to lower themselves to the ground. They sure weren't doing roof repairs.

Within minutes they were gone in a white van. Seconds later, the flashing green lights turned red. Instantly, a huge fireball explosion skyrocketed upward. When the heavy black smoke cleared, the entire Taglyan building was gone. I awoke in a cold sweat.

I knew from my work with Thay that this was the most probable future outcome. But he also taught me that there are numerous *possible* future outcomes, and if you didn't like the most probable one, you could manifest a more desired one if you had enough relevant information to act upon it. He said it was the basis for free will. I had to talk to Thay—immediately.

I called his cell phone, but it kept going into voice mail. I was about to give up and call the Los Angeles Police Department, when on my last try, I finally got through.

No hello, no greeting. I jumped right in. "Thay, you've got to listen carefully. I just had a vivid dream of the near future, and in it, I saw two men placing explosive devices on the roof of the Taglyan Complex. They drove off in a van, and within seconds there was a huge explosion that flattened the building. I'm convinced this is a planned terrorist attack on your meeting. You've got to contact the police."

He was quiet for several seconds.

"Thay, did you hear me?"

"Yes, I did. I was thinking. But first I want to express my sorrow for what happened to Bella. I only found out yesterday. Reverend Daikan sent me a text message, which seemed to suggest she would recover. I was going to call you."

"Thank you. Right, Bella's gonna be fine. By some miracle, she's recovering, and very quickly. But did you hear what I just told you?"

"Yes. But by now you know there's no such thing as a miracle."

"Yeah, yeah, I know. But dammit, Thay! What should we do?"

"Relax, Luc. I'm thinking about how best to deal with this. I know you have powerful foresight, but this is not something that's easily transmitted to the LAPD, especially based on input from a 16-year-old high school student, no matter how clever or insightful he is. Did you notice the vehicle these men came in?"

"Yeah, I saw the vehicle as they were leaving, just shortly before the explosion."

"Luc, this is important. Please take deep *pranayama* breaths like we've done in the past to relax and calm your mind. It's not important whether you need to take 5 or 50. You need to first quiet your mind. Then I want you to close your eyes and think carefully. Go into your mindful meditative state the way I taught you. I want you to describe the vehicle."

Impatient as I was, I calmed down and did as Thay instructed. "Yes, I can see it. It's a white van, looks like a Ford, and it's parked alongside the complex on La Mirada Avenue. There's a gated parking lot there. They must have climbed the fence and made their way to the building next to the complex: St. John Armenian

Church. They climbed to the roof at the rear of the church and then made their way to the roof of the Taglyan Complex. They attached the bombs to various structures on the roof. I assume they intend to trigger them either with a timer or remotely. God, Thay, it'll be horrible."

"Luc, please stay calm. Keep your eyes closed, and relax and stay focused. Are there markings on the van?"

"I can't see it clearly. There are trees next to the truck. It all happened so quickly. I never thought to move my mind's eye to the truck. But I can tell you that as they drove away, I saw the word *plumbing* on the side of the van."

Thay remained calm and direct. "Slowly, Luc—any other writing on the truck?"

Finally: "Yes. There it is—Best Plumbing."

"You did fine. Don't do a thing or say a word to anyone. I will handle it from here."

"Yeah, but your meeting's tomorrow. You gotta act soon. Like now!"

"Please don't worry. I'll take care of it. I'll speak with you tomorrow evening after the meeting. And by the way, concerning Bella, I'm so happy to hear she will fully recover. But again, my dear friend, as you should know by now, there is no such thing as a miracle. So I want to put a thought in your mind—a big thought."

"What's that?"

"Both Eric and Bella have made a complete recovery from what were critical injuries—injuries that almost certainly should have resulted in their deaths. That's why you keep referring to their miraculous recoveries."

"It seems reasonable to me."

"Luc, these were not miracles. They were the result of being in the presence and touch of a person of extremely high consciousness—an Avatar. I'm sure you remember those words of the Great Light—'There will be *The Two* to help you.'"

I didn't say a word for a few beats. "Thay, you must be mistaken."

"I'm not, and I've suspected as much for some time now, and if you're honest with yourself, you probably have as well. The forces of the universe have conspired to put these pieces together."

I couldn't respond. I was overwhelmed by his comments. I knew he was right.

"Don't overthink what I've just told you, and don't worry about the conference. I know exactly what to do. Everything will be fine. We can speak tomorrow evening. Goodbye, Luc."

I was dumbfounded. All I could say was "Goodbye."

I didn't sleep that night. I tried not to think about this Avatar business. I wondered how a Buddhist monk like Thay would handle such a complicated and dangerous problem as a planned terrorist attack. But somehow when he told me not to worry and that he'd take care of it, I knew that he would. He was no ordinary Buddhist monk.

THE NEXT MORNING, I WENT DOWN TO BREAKFAST after hardly sleeping all night. Mom had been up before all of us. Since our crisis-cleansing meeting some weeks ago, both Mom and Dad were in a much better place. She'd made us a huge stack of buttermilk waffles and crispy bacon—usually one of my favorite meals. Ironically, it was exactly what I'd had for breakfast the day my appendix exploded into peritonitis, but I wasn't really hungry. I had faith in Thay, but I was still worried about him and the conference.

Mom had left early to catch a plane for a meeting in Chicago. She does some kinda alchemy to the waffle batter—she adds a small amount of baking powder. Apparently, the baking powder, which I'd learned in chemistry class is a mixture of sodium bicarbonate and tartaric acid, reacts in the waffle iron, giving off carbon dioxide bubbles, which make the waffles puffy and light. They're the best I've ever tasted. But that morning, I didn't think I could eat a thing.

I was sitting there worrying about Thay's conference and praying all would go well, whatever he had planned, when Dad came down to breakfast.

"Morning. Looks like you're eyeing Mom's waffles and bacon."

"I appreciate her taking the time to make them before she left, but I'm not hungry this morning."

"Well, that's a first! I thought they were your favorite."

"They are. I guess I must have eaten too much pasta for dinner last night."

"I didn't think that was even possible," Dad said with a grin as he performed his usual morning ritual—flipping on the TV in the kitchen to catch the *Bloomberg Financial Report* before he left for work.

I muttered, "I think I'll just grab a cup of coffee and get something later at the school cafeteria."

I'm not even sure Dad heard me. He was so focused on the TV, taking in the stock quotes and the financial discussions. Suddenly, the commentator said, "Breaking news. Barbara Westmore is on the scene."

> Well, Dean, police, acting on an anonymous tip, captured two men with a white van full of electronic equipment and high-powered explosives. As you can see from our video, the van, posing as one belonging to Best Plumbing Supply—a nonexistent enterprise—is parked adjacent to the Taglyan Complex. It appears that the target was the complex, which today is hosting the first International Meeting of the World Interfaith Forum. Ironically, the subject of the forum is religion's role in addressing global terrorism. The conference has been delayed, but only by an hour or so, as police and the FBI double-check for any additional bombs.

My heart skipped several beats. *He pulled it off! Thank God— or someone!*

Dad just looked at me. "Incredible. It's fortunate that somebody tipped off the police. There were so many high-level political, technical, peacekeeping, and religious folks attending that conference. If those bombs had gone off, it would have been a huge tragedy."

I said, "You're right, but I don't get it. Why would Muslim terrorists do this, especially to many of their own people, who would have been in the building when the bomb went off?"

"What makes you think the terrorists were Muslims?"

"Well, from recent events, I'm sure that . . ." But I never had a chance to finish my sentence.

The commentator continued. "Here's Barbara Westmore again."

> Dean, I overheard members of the police and the FBI discussing the alleged perpetrators. They apparently are both white males in their mid-30s and belong to a small radical-right group based outside of Austin, Texas. The police will not disclose the name of the group until the FBI has an opportunity to investigate further. Back to you, Dean.

I turned to Dad and confessed, "Guess you were right. I must be brainwashed by the past—one of my subconscious preconceptions, I guess."

"One of your subconscious whats? Oh, forget it. I was doing my best to be objective about the whole thing—which, as you will recall, has not been one of my natural states of being. But, more important, you look like you're breathing a huge sigh of relief."

"I am," I told him. "A friend of mine, a Buddhist monk I met through Bella and whose lecture I attended several weeks ago, is at that conference. I'm so glad the police caught those guys. If those religious leaders can get their act together and kinda go in the same direction, maybe there'll be hope for the rest of us."

"I agree."

"You know what, I'm hungry after all. Pass the waffles and bacon. I think I'll have a couple, maybe more."

AND THAT WAS IT. Thay had saved the day, and even though he wouldn't be my teacher, I was happy I hadn't lost a friend. I hadn't felt that grateful since Bella had opened her eyes in the hospital. What a feeling! As Thay had taught me, it's impossible to experience gratitude and not feel a strong sense of happiness and fulfillment. So true.

That evening I was getting ready to shower when my cell phone rang. "Hi, this is Luc."

"Hi, Luc, it's Thay."

"Thay, thank you for whatever or however you did what you did. I'm so relieved. I tried to call you today, but I couldn't get through."

"Sorry about that. I was busy after the conference helping to tie up some loose ends for the abbot concerning this near-tragedy. But listen, there's something I want to share with you about how I was able to thwart the efforts of the terrorists. I ask that you keep it to yourself."

"Absolutely. What's that?"

"It wasn't an anonymous tip, as disclosed in the news. I discussed the problem with the abbot. Believe it or not, he has a friend, a former monk from our abbey, who left the order years ago. He joined the LAPD and eventually became a detective. We notified him with the details, and he took care of the rest."

"Amazing! That's fantastic!"

"Listen, Luc, there's something else I must share with you."

"What's that?"

"The abbot asked to see me this evening. He was moved by what you did and how you saved the forum and the lives of the attendees. He, like I, is convinced that you and I working as a team would have a strong possibility of making an important difference. He's releasing me from the monastery to work with you. I'll arrive next week as a transfer to Reverend Daikan's temple. I did agree to make myself available from time to time as a consultant to the abbey. Isn't that exciting?"

"Exciting? Are you kidding me? Fugettaboutit, it's fantastic!"

We both had a good laugh at my attempted accent. "Close, Luc. With a little more practice, you'll be a true Bronxian."

"Thanks."

"I'll see you next Monday. Should be fun."

"I'm sure. We've got lots of work to do—I've got a number of challenges in front of me."

BELLA—TAKE TWO

I WOKE UP SUNDAY MORNING THINKING, *Damn, this must be how LeBron felt after game six of the 2016 NBA Championships when he won it for the Cavaliers—41 points, 8 rebounds, 11 assists, 4 steals, and 3 blocks—beyond unbelievable.*

After my conversation with Thay, I was well on my way to straightening out my life. I couldn't believe what we'd worked out together.

Bella was doing great. They'd taken the cast off her arm and put her on a more comfortable temporary cast just for sleeping at night, and she was down to the last of her physical therapy sessions. Her therapists and doctors were astounded by not only how rapidly she'd initially recovered from the coma, but also how quickly the healing process in her body was continuing to proceed. Although at first a mystery to me as well, with increased guidance from Thay, it was clear that neither Eric's nor Bella's recoveries were miracles—no such thing. Spiritual physics explained quite clearly what I'd done.

Eric and I were becoming good buddies as well. We'd taken a couple of hikes at Edgewood Park Natural Preserve, not far from where he lived in Redwood City. He'd made a complete 180 and

was nothing like the guy I'd electrocuted at the Ravenswood Preserve. Life was good, except for that dark shadow of the CIA. It was
no small thing, but it was increasingly clear that I had to get that
monkey off my back.

I'd spent time with Bella and Eric separately, and as unbelievable as it seemed—at least to me—all three of us had paranormal
powers, with no sign they were going away. Like so many times
before, and especially after speaking with Thay, I thought, *Could
this be an omen based on what I "heard" from the Great White Light?
Was there a message here—the possibility for the three of us to work
as a team and do some good together? Are these* The Two, *and was it
finally the "fullness of time"?*

I was sure this must be it. I couldn't think of two better part-
ners. But would they even want to help with the plan that was
coming together in my mind? Sure, we would have to deal with
Tamara, but maybe there was something even bigger than that to
consider.

Eric and Bella had followed my suggestion when each of them
was in the hospital and found they could easily do an OBE. In fact,
like me, they were beginning to enjoy the experience. After some
practice, Bella had become quite the expert at using her gravitational force field, even with larger objects. But up to how big? She
had no idea what the limit might be. After several OBE pranks
with the doctors and nurses in the hospital, Eric finally got serious and mastered his electromagnetic skills. Like me, he found
he could also do electrokinesis, although we both needed more
instruction from Thay on how to use it safely—no more inadver-
tent electrocutions.

I arranged for the three of us to meet at the Creamery.
Although Eric was apprehensive about meeting Bella for the first
time since the fiasco at Ravenswood Preserve, he was hoping to
make amends. I couldn't say the feeling was mutual. I'd told Bella
that he was a completely different guy, but that hadn't sunk in yet.
She had to see for herself.

Bella sat close to me, with Eric across from both of us. He broke
the ice. "Bella, I never had a chance to apologize for what happened

at Ravenswood. I don't know what the hell I was thinking. Like, I was really messed up at that time. I hope you can forgive me for it, although I'm sure you'll never forget it. I know *I* won't."

Still hesitant, but beginning to see the changes in Eric—in the way he dressed, in the way he looked and walked, in the way he spoke, and given his obviously newfound integrity, she put an olive branch out: "Look, I'll try to understand, but you gotta give me some time. The Eric I remember scared the hell out of me."

"No doubt. He scared the hell out of me too—and thinking back to that day, he still does."

Bella smiled. "I see from what Luc told me that you seem like a completely different person—a much *better* person."

"I hope so. After my NDE in the hospital, my OBE adventures, and acquiring these powers, I see the world in a totally different way."

"That I can easily relate to."

I jumped in. "Look, guys, that's why I asked us to meet. I have a humongous mother of a problem, and that's Tamara Carlin. And, Bella, to your way of thinking, I see this as a project for the greater good."

"So, I guess Eric knows?"

"About the CIA, yeah. I've already broken so many laws to get this far, I thought why not tell him, especially since I'm gonna need help from both of you. I see possibilities in the long run for the three of us to work as a team. But first I was hoping you'd help me with Tamara and Major Dallant to get out of the shitty mess my family and I are in. I'll just lay it out there. Like me, you both have superpowers, and you've both said that you'd like to use them to do some good. Well, here's a chance to do that . . . for the three of us *together* to do that."

Eric looked intrigued. "Sounds like an adventure. What've you got in mind?"

"I did an OBE and distant viewing and went to Tamara's home . . . and I found something." I carefully looked around the restaurant, double-checking to make sure no one else was looking or listening. I leaned in and whispered, "She's a double agent working for the Russians and has been using me to get highly classified information from the Chinese and the North Koreans to pass on to Russia. I'm not sure yet how deep she is into this, but I intend to get more info and fit the pieces together. So I'm asking for your help with those pieces—what, where, when, and how."

I was straight with them about my request, but only hinted at another reason I wanted to meet with them—as a team, we could be unbeatable in dealing with all kinds of problems that fit in with Bella's idea of contributing to the greater good. To give them a better sense of the kind of good I was talking about, I told them what had happened at the Taglyan Complex in LA and how Thay and I had pulled it off. The story had been all over the news for several days, and everyone was still talking about it.

Bella exclaimed, "Oh my God, that was you and Thay?"

"Yeah, but you can't ever tell a soul."

"My lips are sealed," she promised.

Eric jumped in: "Absolutely! Damn, that's amazing!"

Although they were stunned by the news, there was no time to wait for them to catch up. And besides, I wanted to secure them as a team for the long haul. "And I gotta tell you something else."

Eric looked at Bella and me and said, "Whoa—I think we might've had enough for one day. Don't you, Bella?"

"Totally."

"No, guys. Listen to this. Some weeks ago, when working with Thay during a deep meditation, I saw a beautiful light in a tunnel—just like the one the three of us saw during our NDEs. It 'spoke' to me. It said I wouldn't be alone with my superpowers. It said I'd meet a couple of people called *The Two*, who would help me. It's gotta be you guys. This could be just the beginning for us—I mean, for the three of us as a team."

"Wow, you're full of surprises." Bella's smile revealed that she was all in.

"Oh, great tall one, lead the way," added Eric.

"Perfect. Let's start with what I'm planning for Tamara once I get more information. But I can tell you this—it'll involve catching her red-handed as a traitor, and in a way where we won't have much backup. It'll probably just be us."

As I was finishing my sentence, a couple sat down in the booth next to us. They were almost unnoticeable. Alarm bells went off for me—*hiding in plain sight*? Were my instincts right, or was I being paranoid? Either way, I didn't want to risk it.

"Let's bail, and finish up outside," I told Bella and Eric. We agreed to meet the next day for a hike in the hills behind Stanford—there's a path that goes around the dish, a huge radio telescope. Bella and I had walked it many times. Not many people went there, and it was quiet.

Eric replied, "Never been there, but I'm sure I can find it." Injecting some of his wise-guy humor, he said, "I'm on foot, though. My mother grounded me from driving, I think until I'm 30, but anyway I got no wheels."

I asked him, "Can you take the bus down El Camino from Redwood City to my house and get there at about ten tomorrow morning? I have an extra bike. You can keep it. Consider it a gift for what happened at the preserve."

"After what happened there, I should be giving *you* a gift."

"Ah, let it go. We're good. Okay, Bella and I will meet you at my place at 10:00 A.M., and the three of us can bike over to the trailhead together."

"I'll be there," Eric said.

"Oh, one last thing to put in the back of your mind. Think a little more specifically about how the three of us could work together after high school. Like, what if we formed an official team? We could stay in touch when we went off to college or whatever. We could meet when one of us found a critical situation that would benefit from our efforts together and our skills. Bella and I will likely end up at a college on the East Coast, so that makes it somewhat easier for us to link up. Maybe we could think of a way to hook up with you, Eric, if you're still in California—"

He immediately interrupted. "Look, it's too early to say anything, but I'm working on something, and if it goes the way I hope it will, I'll share it with you in a couple of weeks. It would make the three of us working together after you guys graduate Paly a whole lot easier.

Bella chimed in, "Oh my God, that would be amazing!"

"I agree. That would be super. Can't wait to hear what you have in mind."

Bella came back with an idea—a hilarious one—or at least I thought so at the time. "Guys, we gotta have a team name."

I wanted to laugh but thought better of it. Besides, I didn't want to discourage her. "I don't know. But if you've got one, let's hear it."

After about five seconds, a spark caught hold for her. "Got it—the "SPI Team," for Super Paranormal Intelligence Team. You know, like the Central *Intelligence* Agency."

I couldn't help but laugh. "God, you're a real drama queen. At least we got one good idea from the CIA."

"Come on, guys, don't you wanna make this fun?"

Eric, in between his own laughter, backed her up. "Sounds cool to me!"

Little did we know that Bella was just getting started. "We also need names. Eric, you could be *Electer* because of your electromagnetic skills. I could be *Gravitas* because of my knack with gravity. And you, Luc . . . let's see . . . got it! You'll be *Emperius*, our 'imperial' leader. Now tell me those aren't great names!"

Eric and I were about to split a gut from laughing. I thought Bella's naming thing was a bit weird, but I liked the fact that she was committed to helping, and most important, that she wanted to get on with dealing with Tamara.

"I'm not sure about the direction this is going," I told them, "but if it will keep you happy and focused, it's fine with me. Electer, you okay with Gravitas's suggestion?"

"Yeah, I'm good with it, oh great Emperius."

I said, "We better end this discussion before Bella comes up with a secret handshake."

Bella couldn't help herself. "Now why didn't I think of that?"

And such was the first day of the newly formed SPI Team.

We'd been standing and talking outside the Creamery. As we were about to go our separate ways, a loud black-and-silver Harley turned off Alma Street onto Hamilton and motored slowly toward us. The driver's muscular build made it clear he was a guy. He was dressed in black leather, and the dark visor on his black helmet was opened just an inch or two at eye level. As he cruised by, in a smooth, even motion, he pulled a large pistol with a silencer and a laser sight from his saddlebag.

Eric was in a position where he immediately saw the laser's red dot targeted on Bella, creeping up her leg toward her heart. Without a thought, he lifted his arm and shot an electromagnetic pulse at the Harley. Since he wasn't quite proficient yet with his electrokinesis powers, he didn't want to aim directly at the guy, afraid he might kill him. The motorcycle jerked to a stop, almost knocking the rider off the bike, and certainly surprising him.

Shaken but not stirred and still determined to complete his mission, the assassin jumped off the bike and started walking toward us, his gun still aimed directly at Bella. In a flash, she shot a gravity pulse at his arm. It threw him in the air, jolting the gun from his hand and careening it into the bushes along the roadside.

The guy's intense scream and the twisted position of his body on the pavement said that something was probably broken. Still, he managed to drag himself back to his bike and saddle up, but unfortunately for him, in the throes of pain, he drove into the path of an oncoming cement truck. He was thrown more than 20 yards and landed in a nondescript heap of flesh and bones. The three of us were in shock. We looked at each other and didn't say a word.

A crowd had gathered. A few were screaming for help. A couple of people ran to him, but even a Boy Scout with a CPR merit badge would have realized that this carnage and the huge pool of blood meant the guy was gone, gone, gone. It was also clear that the onlookers had no idea that we'd launched silent and invisible electrokinesis and gravity-pulse forces at the guy. *Best to keep it that way,* I thought, and the three of us were out of there before the police arrived.

Good God, we were just teenagers going up against these bad guys. But as crazy as it may have seemed and even with the odds against us, I was starting to see that if we used our powers in the right way, we could gain a huge advantage. We had a lot going for us. Sure, we had our new powers and special insights—but we'd also found a purpose, maybe part of our life purpose—fired up by our passion to do the right thing. And giving our powers over to the CIA for them to decide on how, when, and where to use them wasn't gonna happen anymore.

Tamara, you conniving, heartless witch. First my father and then Bella—twice! No loose ends, right? We're coming for you!

PUTTING IT TOGETHER

I DESPERATELY NEEDED MORE SPECIFICS before I, okay, sorry—before the *SPI Team*—could finalize our plan. *What* exactly was Tamara going to do with the information I got for her, *when* and *where*? The only way I knew how to get those answers was another OBE to her home and hope that I could find what we needed.

I LEFT PALO ALTO AT 6:00 A.M. CALIFORNIA TIME and arrived at Tamara's home essentially instantly, at 9:00 A.M. DC time, while she was at CIA headquarters. During my last visit when I'd hacked into her work computer, I'd taken a mind photograph of her schedule for the next few weeks. Hopefully, there wouldn't be any changes, or I might be in deep shit—like, very deep.

Arriving at her home, I moved immediately to her office and again went through her desk, computer, and the other places I'd searched the first time. I didn't find much more the second time around.

But there was that safe in her office closet. It was tucked away in a hidden compartment behind a framed photo of Tamara with her Harvard graduating class. Last time, overwhelmed by what I'd found in her computer and running out of time, I didn't bother with the safe. I had to scan lots of documents and email them to my own computer and clean up and delete any trace of my cyber activities. This time, though, I had to get into that safe—but how?

The only ammunition I had was what Thay had taught me about how to access the Akashic Record—a record of every thought, word, deed, event, emotion, and intention that had ever occurred in the past, as well as those in the present and future. He told me that this information is encoded in an infinite, eternal, nonphysical, alternate dimension called an "ethereal plane." Boiled down, to me this meant that the combination to that safe was definitely in the Akashic Record, and I had to get it. I'd done it before—why not again?

I entered the closet, removed the photo, sat on the floor in a lotus position, and sank into as deep a meditative state as I could manage. After several minutes, I stood up with my eyes closed and my right hand set lightly on the safe's combination dial. *I can do this. What's the combination to this safe?* Nothing. I tried again: *What's the combination to Tamara Carlin's safe?* I was about to give up when I suddenly felt warmth building up in my hand. I froze until it got to the point where it was steady and almost uncomfortable.

Then, turning the dial slowly to the right, I began to feel a pulsing sensation in my hand. It increased as I continued to turn the dial slowly to the right, with the heat in my hand moving rapidly up my arm to my shoulder. I stopped turning the dial the instant the pulsing stopped. Was this the first number? I prayed it was.

I moved the dial to the left, the heat in my arm rapidly moved back to my hand, and the pulsing started again. I followed this procedure again toward the right and then twice more, alternating directions until I felt a distinct click in my fingers, and the heat immediately and completely disappeared.

I opened my eyes, took a deep breath, and pulled down on the door handle. Nothing. *Damn!* I froze, but then took another breath and this time pushed the handle up. Success! The door opened. *Thay, you're amazing. And so is the Akashic Record. I'm sure it won't be the last time I'll need its wisdom.*

Going through the documents in the safe, I found one from the Chinese Embassy by the commander-in-chief of the People's Liberation Army to the newly elected president of South Korea. It was in Chinese. Not a problem—I could read any language with my internal translator.

It was pretty much what Tamara had disclosed to me previously—except for one important difference. The president of South Korea was actively cooperating with China in its plan to reunite the two Korean nations in exchange for China's assurance that he would become president of the newly united Korea. *Wouldn't the US president and the UN Security Council love to know about that?!*

There was also a lengthy memo from Moscow by the mysterious Seagull operative to Tamara, acknowledging and agreeing to her plan to wait until September 18, when a top-secret, yearlong security and safety study of all US nuclear installations would be completed, along with a list of all the new ICBM launch codes.

On that date, she was to proceed to the Russian Embassy in DC, bringing with her all of the missile design data, a copy of the Chinese-South Korean plan, the new US ICBM launch codes, as well as a number of other top-secret American military documents. I guess I could have deciphered them all right then and there, but I was getting nervous knowing I still had to straighten things up to look exactly the way they were when I'd arrived and get the hell outta there.

Just as I was about to close the safe, I spotted another memo in the back of the safe from Seagull to Tamara. It said that well before US officials became aware of what had happened, she would be safely transported to Moscow the next morning, on September 19, by private jet.

The memo said that detailed plans were in place to provide her with a new identity and a new residence in a highly desirable location—not specified in the memo. There was also a brief mention that they'd procured the Russian plastic surgeon she'd previously met with and requested. Boy, this was beginning to sound like a James Bond flick.

An important postscript at the bottom of the memo said that the Russian Federal Security Service (the Federalnaya Sluzhba Bezopasnosti), also known as the FSB, had good intel that the CIA director had increasing concerns that there was a mole in their ranks and had put together a secret high-level task force. The CIA was currently conducting an intense internal search and planning extensive polygraph testing of all its employees, starting at the highest level. They were moving in on Tamara.

I had to do two things immediately. First, I had to find out if Major Dallant was part of this conspiracy, or if, in fact, he was completely unaware that Tamara was a double agent. And second, I had to make a copy of the incriminating Chinese and Russian documents and get them to him if he *was* one of the good guys. If he wasn't, the SPI Team, the US, and the world were screwed.

With no other realistic option, I decided to roll the dice and take a chance. I scanned the documents, emailed them to my home computer, and then erased all traces of my cyber actions on Tamara's computer.

After returning the documents to the safe, I floated to CIA headquarters and to Major Dallant's office. From Tamara's calendar schedule, I knew he was in meetings most of the day with her and Director Stefano. As expected, Major Dallant wasn't in his office. After going through his emails, I was convinced that he had no idea Tamara was a double agent. With a sigh of relief, I immediately traveled back to my body in Palo Alto.

It was clear that the SPI Team needed Major Dallant's help to bring down Tamara. He was the only one who could erase all the CIA links to Bella, my father, and me in exchange for the intel I'd gathered on Tamara, Russia, China, North and South Korea, and their intentions in the Korean peninsula. I decided that the only way to do so was in person.

From the cash I'd accumulated through CIA payouts, I bought a round-trip ticket to Washington. It was a red-eye flight. I told Mom I'd be staying at Jimmy's for the night to tutor him for our upcoming physics final. There was no other way to deal with this critical situation.

WHEN I SPOKE WITH MAJOR DALLANT by phone and requested a meeting, and asked him not to mention anything to Tamara, he sounded perplexed but reluctantly agreed. We planned to meet at the McLean Family Restaurant, in McLean, Virginia, a kind of down-home place a short ride from CIA headquarters.

In some ways, it reminded me of the Creamery in Palo Alto, a step back into the '50s. There were several groupings of booths, each separated from one another in small, partially partitioned rooms. Each table was covered with a red-and-white, checkered vinyl tablecloth. A single plastic rose in a small vase was sitting on each table accompanied by the usual salt-and-pepper shakers.

I got there early and chose a booth in a small area in the back of the restaurant, away from the other folks. When Major Dallant arrived, we didn't exchange many pleasantries. It was all business.

"Luc, what's so important that you had to fly all the way from California to meet me and insisted on excluding Tamara?"

How the hell could I tell him what I'd found? I wasn't 100 percent sure he wasn't involved with Tamara. Nervous as hell, I looked down and took a sip of ice water. Saved! The waitress arrived. The major ordered black coffee and a cheese Danish. I did the same even though I knew I wouldn't touch it.

"Luc, what is it? Did you blow your cover? Is it your father? What?" he asked.

There was no more stalling. "Look, I . . . I hope . . . I hope to hell you're the right guy to come to."

"Fine. I hope so too. What's on your mind?"

I pulled a package out of my backpack. "I'm gonna give you this. Please don't ask me how I got the contents—at least not right now. We can talk about that some other time. For now, as you'll see, they show without question that Tamara is a double agent working for the Russians. I sure as hell hope *you're* not." Was I really expecting him to admit it if he was?

Major Dallant immediately stiffened, and his face went to the only frown I'd ever seen on him. Even he, the cool cucumber that he was, was somewhat taken aback. "That's quite a charge on your part against Tamara. I'm not going to push you right now for the source of these documents, but you can count on it that I will."

"I understand. But please, just trust me for now, okay?"

"Yeah, right. You understand that I'll have to study these documents to understand what you're talking about. Many of them will need to be translated." And then with a crack in his sternness, he threw in as if it were a humorous afterthought, "Just to ease your mind, I don't work for the Russians, or any other country, for that matter. Essentially all my professional life, I've been gainfully employed by the US government. Why are you bringing this information to me? Why didn't you mail it to the director?"

"Because I want something from you in exchange. And you're the only one who can give it to me."

"What's that?"

"My dad, Bella, and I need to completely cut all ties to the CIA. And the way I see it, with what I've just given you, you're the only one in a position to make that happen."

"Let's see what these documents say, and then we'll talk."

I continued. "You'll see two sets of documents in the package. The first is an exchange between Tamara and some Russian agent in Moscow code named Seagull. He seems to be the one running the show and directing her to get certain information from the Chinese and the North and South Koreans—and, as you'll hear in a moment, also from the US."

Major Dallant had recovered his solemn stare. I was amazed by how relaxed he appeared in light of what I'd just told him. I guess that's part of CIA training. But the next thing I told him *did* shake him out of his tree, and gone was his calm demeanor.

I continued. "The second thing you'll find is a directive from Seagull for Tamara to wait for a CIA study on new ICBM launch codes that's supposed to be completed this week. And then, on September 18, she is to bring a copy of that study and all of the information in this envelope to the Russian Embassy, where she'll be given asylum. Somewhere hidden, she also has stacks of top-secret information I copied during my remote viewing in China."

Major Dallant's expression froze into a frown. He didn't say a word for several seconds. A small bead of sweat ran down his forehead and stopped cold at his left eyebrow. "How could you, or anyone, for that matter, possibly know about that study?"

"I don't know. I'm just reporting what I read in these documents. I have no idea how they got the information. But maybe this will help—in the envelope there's a memo from Seagull to Tamara saying that there's some kinda high-level sweep currently being carried out at the CIA to uncover a mole."

Now, the major was even more tense. More beads of sweat were running down his forehead, and they weren't small anymore. He began to crack his knuckles under the table. I've got excellent hearing. I know what that sounds like. I hoped his response was because of the importance of what I'd uncovered, and the fear that the mole, Tamara, might have compromised our entire ICBM strategic initiative and our international security system. The worst-case situation, though, was that Major Dallant was Tamara's accomplice. *Shit! Now* that *would be the end of me, and everything I hold special in this world. Gesu Cristo, Luc, don't even think that way!*

Major Dallant never quite regained his normal, unreadable spy expression. That worried the hell out of me.

"Luc, I'll get back to you within two days." He looked me straight in the eyes and said, "Not a word of this to anyone. Do you clearly understand me? And don't misjudge me, Luc Ponti, that's not an order, it's a threat."

I was *shaken and stirred* but didn't say a word. He put a twenty-dollar bill on the table, got up, and walked immediately to the entrance and disappeared out the door.

I asked the cashier to call a taxi to take me to the airport so I wouldn't miss my flight home. I sat on a bench outside the restaurant waiting for my ride, basking in the Virginia sunshine. I thought, *How could it be such a beautiful day in light of what's happening in this crazy world?*

IT WAS SEPTEMBER 14, only four days until Tamara had planned to run off to the Russian Embassy and then to Moscow with all that top-secret information, eventually getting a new identity from the Russians and settling in as a rich, retired double agent on some island paradise, or who knows where—maybe close by—in plain sight.

It had been a long two days when I received a text message from Major Dallant on my cryptophone. It read:

> Luc—now all is clear to me and how and where you got the information. I understand your concerns. Regretfully, you're right on target. Everything is now under my complete control. Will not involve other agents to deal with this. Proceeding along the lines you requested. You'll get your quid pro quo. Not to worry. Back to you immediately after September 18.

Everything is now under my control . . . not to worry. What does that mean? I thought otherwise. I called a meeting with the SPI Team. We had work to do.

Chapter
Thirty-Four

THE EXECUTION

O N OUR HIKE, I LAID OUT EVERYTHING IN DETAIL for Bella and Eric—Tamara's Russian connection, my thoughts on how to get out from under her thumb, and my meeting in DC with Major Dallant, even though he'd warned—no, threatened—me not to say a word to anyone. I couldn't live with that, though, since my plan called for help from the SPI Team, and they needed to know the whole picture of what was going to happen. Besides—prison cell or not—I was already used to breaking the rules with the CIA.

Eric and Bella were freaked out by what I told them. Bella wondered if Major Dallant was leading me on and was working with Tamara. I discussed several private emails between him and Tamara, after which they, too, failed to see any connection. They were glad to hear he wasn't a double agent as well. I told them that he said not to worry, that he had everything under control. Their reaction was the same as mine: "Yeah, right! Like we're gonna sit here on our hands and wait for a call."

Major Dallant said that in order to avoid exposure of Bella, my family, and me within the CIA, he had a plan that wouldn't involve other agents—only him. We had no choice but to assume he'd come through with his promise. There was no other possible option for us. But nothing could stop us from providing backup, which was now the most important part of our plan. We had to go to DC and be there when Tamara attempted to enter the Russian Embassy.

Bella and Eric were on board and eager to help, especially since Tamara had brought so much hell into all of our lives. I withdrew cash from my Wells Fargo account and bought three round-trip tickets to DC. Unfortunately, they were for the red-eye outbound flight again—a nonstop leaving SFO around midnight. It wasn't because earlier flights were all booked solid, but because we needed to give our parents believable excuses for not coming home that night—studying into the night for finals at a friend's home was like catnip for them. If all worked according to plan, with the three-hour time difference, we'd be back the next day in time for our afternoon classes, at least physically. But whether our minds would be there was anyone's guess.

We rented a nondescript gray van at Dulles Airport using Eric's California driver's license. It had been forged to show his age as 22—one of many souvenirs from his past delinquencies. His photo showed a beard and a Mohawk haircut—the real deal back then. Now he'd begun to move to his newly conservative self.

The guy at the Enterprise rental counter asked if Eric was really the person in the photo. Wise guy Eric responded, "Nope, I'm better-looking." We were lucky to get the van, but we still had to pay their underage fee. As we found out from the Enterprise guy, in the US, the minimum age for renting a car is 25, although most agencies will rent to people between 21 and 25 for a stiff extra fee. We were plain lucky that Eric had chosen 22 for his forgery. The guy looked at Eric and sarcastically quipped, "But then again, you probably know all that, right?"

Eric didn't lose a beat. "Right, absolutely!"

It was 10:15 A.M. in DC by the time we settled into the van. We drove off, heading for Tamara's home, but Eric had another priority first. "Hey, guys, I need to make a pit stop. Keep your eyes open for a Dunkin' Donuts. I can hold out, but I need some breakfast before we go into action."

I couldn't believe it. "Are you kiddin' me?"

"No, I couldn't eat that junk they served on the plane. I need some energy."

Bella questioned that. "You couldn't eat the junk on the plane, but you can handle those doughnuts?"

"Absolutely! Have you ever tasted their freshly made glazed doughnut? It's so delicious and incredibly light, I can eat five of 'em for breakfast."

Bella and I just shook our heads and smiled.

We finally came across a Dunkin' Donuts—actually, two more before we arrived at Tamara's place. That part of DC looked like a fast-food playground. True to his word, Eric ate five glazed, washed down with a Pepsi. I hoped he wouldn't have a huge sugar high that would interfere with what we had to do.

When we arrived at Tamara's place, her car was in the driveway, meaning that she was still home. Great, we were still on target. Even more telling was the large truck parked in front while movers hustled in and out, packing up her place. We were well prepared with binoculars and the Nikon digital camera I got as a present the previous Christmas. It had a telescopic lens, which made it great for close-up photos. It really felt like we were the ultrasecret SPI Team, but that might have been from watching too many episodes of *Homeland* on Showtime.

We weren't there 15 minutes when a neighbor walking her dog stopped in front of the van as her pet did his thing. She kept staring at Eric and me in the front seat. It wasn't a friendly stare either—more like, "What are you lowlifes doing in my neighborhood?" When the dog was done, she pulled a plastic bag and cardboard scooper from her coat pocket and picked up his doggy do, gave us one last serious look, and was on her way. That incident might have ended badly, except she more than likely thought we were with the moving company.

About an hour later, we finally got our sights on Tamara. She was dressed in a fitted black-and-white pin-striped pants suit, a white ruffled blouse, and black Christian Louboutin stiletto heels.

How did I know the brand? Easy, they have distinctive red soles, and Mom wears them all the time.

Tamara's hair was up in a large bun held in place by a silver jeweled comb. Since she was on a government salary, I at first assumed the stones were cubic zirconia, then thought again. Who knew how much she was getting from the Russians? She was striking, as usual, but so is a black widow.

She appeared to be giving last-minute instructions to the moving guys. After several minutes, she jumped into her silver Mercedes and was on the move.

Following at a more-than-safe distance—after all, she was a trained operative—it became clear that she was heading to CIA headquarters, probably to get whatever she was taking to the Russians. We backed off, waited several minutes, and then drove quickly to the CIA facility.

We parked some distance from the main entrance so we wouldn't raise suspicions with the guards at the gate or have our presence registered on any of the security cameras. But that wasn't a done deal at such a highly secure place. If we were unlucky, it could be a matter of minutes before we were detected and were hauled in for interrogation.

The layout and position were such that by using the telescopic lens on my camera and the dinky binoculars that Eric had brought along, we could see every car entering or leaving the main entrance to the headquarters.

After an hour of constant jitters, we finally saw Tamara's Mercedes leaving the parking garage. We knew exactly where she was going. Rather than tailing her and risking being made, we sped ahead before she'd even cleared the guard station and raced to the Russian Embassy on Wisconsin Avenue. We parked at a distance, awaiting her arrival, but more important, for Major Dallant's arrival. If he were the chess-master he said he was, he'd take out the queen before she got inside the embassy.

Minchia! It suddenly occurred to me from having studied the local map that the Russian Consulate was a separate building on Tunlaw Road NW, directly behind the Russian Embassy.

Research I'd done on the embassy mentioned something about an underground tunnel connecting it with the consulate. I worried, *What if that's where she's going and* not *to the embassy? Shit, what should we do?*

"Eric, you and Bella take the van and head to the consulate. Keep your cell phones close by, and let me know the second you lay eyes on Tamara's car. I'll keep watch from that side street over there, Edmunds NW. I'll call you if I see her arrive on this end."

I was nervous as hell letting those two go off on their own. Apparently, they were, too, because they must have called me five times to check if there was any sign of her.

On the sixth call, Eric's voice sounded fearless. "Luc, I got eyes on Tamara. She parked way up the block and is just sitting there. Wait. Hold on. She's getting out. She's carrying her purse and a black briefcase."

"Hang tight until I get there. Be there in less than a minute." I ran as fast as my *long, beefy Dago legs* would take me.

I was there in a flash and holed up behind a cement retainer wall so that Tamara couldn't see me. I signaled to Eric, who was sitting in the driver's seat. He acknowledged my presence with a thumbs-up and waited.

What happened next was like a slo-mo dream—or I should say, nightmare. Tamara walked casually toward the consulate entrance, and as if on cue, a shiny black Caddy Escalade slowly came around the corner and parked on the opposite side of the street, facing Tamara as she approached. Because of the curvature of the street, I doubt she could see it.

As she got closer, the Escalade driver's door opened very slowly. Holding my breath, I waited to see who would step out. *C'mon, c'mon, what's taking you so long?* A man's foot slowly emerged and stepped cautiously onto the pavement. Major Dallant. Alone. Crisp. Locked in place. He stood there until Tamara was about ten yards from the gate to the consulate, and then the show began as he walked toward her.

"Hi there, Tamara. Catch you at a bad time?"

As Dad used to say about these kinda women, "She's been around the block more than once." I guessed that meant there wasn't much she hadn't seen before. Having worked with her, I had no doubt that she was stronger than steel—no, stronger than Kevlar.

Without even flinching, she responded instantly with a smile. "Hi, John. That all depends."

"On what?" he asked.

Her smile broadened to almost a giggle. "On whether you trust me."

"Trust? That's what my wife used to say when I wanted to stop our four-year-old son from jumping sky high on his bed—'Honey, you got to trust him. He'll do fine.'"

"Well, kids just want to have fun. Maybe you should've listened to her."

"Oh, I did. Then one day he jumped a little too wildly and took a dive off the bed and cracked his head open. Had to have ten stiches."

They both were standing very still, staring at each other. "Is that what's gonna happen to you today, Tamara—you lookin' to get your head cracked open?"

She had the briefcase in her right hand and her purse in the other. She slowly lowered both to the ground, and with her arms, pushed her open trench coat back and placed her hands on her hips, just standing there looking like a cover model on a Neiman Marcus catalog. Still smiling, she casually said, "Oh no, just got my hair done yesterday. And besides, I'm exhausted from all the late-night meetings we've had this week."

"I see."

"Now, John, I have an important meeting here and don't have time to chat, so we can catch up later at the office. Whaddaya say?" At first slowly, but then with increasing speed and precision, she moved her right hand from her hip toward her back, and before Major Dallant could stop her, she produced a small handgun, simultaneously dropping to the ground on her chest like a paramilitary marksman, firing a single shot squarely into

Major Dallant's chest directly at his heart. As he fell, he fired the revolver that *he'd* whipped out—but a fraction of a second too late. He missed. He lay on the ground not moving. Good God!

Bella, Eric, and I rushed over to him. Tamara turned toward us and took aim at Bella—one of her loose ends. No way take three was gonna happen. Two attempts on her life were enough. Within a nanosecond, Eric, now skilled in controlling the intensity of his electrokinesis power, shot a low-energy electric pulse at Tamara that was meant to paralyze, but not kill, her. She let out a single high-pitched scream and fell unconscious to the ground, her gun scattering away to a full stop underneath my boot.

The three of us checked on Major Dallant. Our mouths dropped open—no blood? He was just coming out of it, then looked up at us and whispered, "Christ." He grabbed his chest and told us, "I'm sweating like a hog in this Kevlar vest—I think I cracked a rib— but, damn, they do come in handy. Where's Tamara?"

She was coming to as well and getting to her feet, but was disoriented and wobbling like a drunk trying desperately to over- come the effects of a fifth of vodka.

Bella shot a weak graviton pulse at her and knocked her back down. Major Dallant was back in action. With gun in hand, low- ered at his side, he walked toward Tamara. She, in turn, reached with her right hand for a sidearm holstered to her right ankle just beneath her slacks. A woman of iron, she willed herself to stand, left her purse on the ground, but picked up the briefcase with her left hand and steadied herself as best she could.

She staggered toward the gate of the consulate and pushed the visitor button. The gate slowly began to open. The security guards in the gatehouse had witnessed the entire thing. They were watch- ing intently, clearly expecting her, but were doing nothing to help her or interfere with what was happening outside Russian territory on US soil.

Major Dallant, probably hoping that she'd surrender, said, "Now, Tamara, as a lawyer, I know you're aware of the US code on treason."[52]

She stopped for a moment, well aware that all her good options were gone.

One foot on US soil and one in protected Russian territory, she answered, "John . . . I'm sure you wouldn't shoot your boss in the back."

"That all depends."

"On what?"

He smiled. "On whether you trust me."

"Of course I do."

In an instant, gathering all the strength left in her pathetic, injured body, she spun around, dropped to one knee, and aimed directly at the major. Before she could squeeze the trigger, he got off a single shot. It was all that was needed. It hit her squarely in the forehead just above the bridge of her nose.

Tamara fell over, collapsing on US territory, inches from Russian asylum. There she lay, blood trickling across her face, her beautiful hair now in complete disarray, her clothes tattered like she'd been dragged by her Christian Louboutin stiletto heels from one end of the block to the other.

Although Tamara had been my nemesis, I closed my eyes and swallowed deeply. I couldn't help but feel a deep sense of sorrow for how this had ended.

Major Dallant, who, like us, was momentarily stunned by what he'd had to do, suddenly came back to his normal sense of the way things should be. "What the hell are you kids doing here? Luc, I thought I told you not to discuss our meeting with anyone."

"We thought—"

"Never mind what you thought. Look, you guys saved my life, and for that I'll be forever grateful. But . . . get the hell out of here—now! Quickly! In a couple of minutes, this place will be

---

[52] US Code 2381—"Whoever owing allegiance to the US, levies war against them or addresses to their enemies, giving aid and comfort within the US, or elsewhere, is guilty of treason and shall suffer death or severe punishment to be determined by a federal court of law."

crawling with CIA and FBI agents, and the police. If you want the outcome you asked for, you'd better be gone ASAP. I'll get back to you. Now go!"

We had to trust him. So far, he'd delivered on his end. We hopped in the van and almost immediately passed at least 20 black Escalades with their swirling blue lights and wailing sirens speeding to the scene.

On our drive to Dulles Airport, no one said a word. What had happened was beyond our experience and comprehension. Eric, as tough as he was, stared blankly out the windshield as he drove us to Dulles. Bella, sitting in the back seat, her hands clasped tightly on her lap, had tears in her eyes. This was the second person she'd seen killed in the past few months. The first was driving the van. We never expected Tamara to be killed. *Dammit, Tamara, you were supposed to surrender.* We were still processing what had happened even as we checked in for our flight to San Francisco—with three minutes to spare before boarding.

As we boarded our American flight, one flight attendant was unusually chatty. "Well, look at this handsome group." Attempting humorous conversation with Bella as she scooted to the center seat between Eric on the aisle and me staring out the window, the woman commented, "I'll bet you were here for the Miss America tryouts, and these two handsome guys are part of your entourage."

Although the flight attendant seemed like a nice southern belle, Bella was in no mood for chitchat. She tried to close the conversation pleasantly and humorously. "Yeah, they're part of my entourage, but we skipped the Miss America tryouts to pull a bank job."

"Well, I sure hope it turned out all right for y'all," the woman said.

Yup, definitely from south of the Mason-Dixon line.

Eric saved Bella the response. "Oh yeah, really well. We're loaded. Next time it's first class."

The flight attendant winked at Eric and moved on down the aisle.

On the flight home, we finally started to open up. We were psyched, nervous, frightened, and relieved—all at the same time, but because of all the people around us, we couldn't say much. Besides, we were exhausted. The three of us fell fast asleep and awoke five hours later as we were landing in San Francisco.

SEPTEMBER 18 IS A DATE THAT WILL STICK IN MY MIND FOREVER. Sure, I was rid of Tamara, but seeing her killed haunted me like a continually recurring nightmare. And this nightmare was worse while awake than while asleep. It was going to take some time to get over it. It's one thing to see this kinda thing on TV, but another to experience it in real life.

I wished it could have ended better, but Tamara sure did dig her own grave. She knew the risks of treason, and those risks clearly were acceptable to her—except at the very end when the possibility of death became a better option than being caught. As I thought about what had happened, I wondered how anyone ever adjusts to this spy stuff. It was too much—a constant game of fear and anxiety, and many of the players disappeared or died or both. Truly scary.

We waited anxiously to hear from Major Dallant. There had been nothing in the news for nearly a week. The CIA had sealed off the area surrounding the Russian Embassy and Consulate tighter than spandex on a 200-pound ballerina.

I finally got a text message from the major that he wanted to meet the SPI Team two days later at 9:00 A.M. at the office in Palo Alto Square. He was flying out just for our meeting. It was a relief to know that answers would soon be coming, but Eric, Bella, and I were even more stressed, not knowing what those answers would mean for us. I had high hopes that Major Dallant had figured out how to eliminate—bad choice of words . . . free—Bella and me from the CIA, and from the Russian and Chinese web of conspiracy. It was more than a hope, really. I was counting on it.

WE ARRIVED AT THE PALO ALTO OFFICE EARLY. Bella and Eric had never been there before. They were impressed but could care less about getting a tour. They were more than distracted about our meeting with Major Dallant. The elevator opened right on time at 9:00 A.M. He gave us a quick hello and then walked immediately into the conference room. We followed behind him. No one said a word.

He opened the conversation. "So, you guys think you're super-heroes? Which one of you is Batman, or are you all Jokers?" This wasn't a joke. The expression on his face said it all. He was serious.

No response.

"I realize you helped immensely, but you should be well aware that you could have all been killed. I would rather have died than put that on me or on you."

No response. We had no idea what to say. The three of us were as frightened as little kids during a stormy night, alone on the top floor of an old house, hearing noises in the attic above them.

"Sure, I'm deeply grateful to you for saving my life. But I live my life by certain rules, and when they're violated, I'm very unhappy. I don't know how to live any other way. I hope you understand that." He paused. "Now, then, I have some good news for you."

Instantly, we were all smiles. I spoke up. "We're sorry, Major Dallant. We just wanted to help. But I know I speak for Bella and Eric—we understand your point."

"Thank you . . . now, what is it you call yourselves?"

Bella, still smiling, quickly responded, "The SPI Team."

"Meaning?"

Eric interjected, "Super Paranormal Intelligence Team."

Major Dallant was fast. "That certainly has a nice ring to it—and a memorable acronym—good DC speak. How'd you come up with that?"

I didn't want to get into that whole bit. "Please, it's a long story. Don't even go there."

"Well, okay. But it does seem like an appropriate name. And honestly, if I disregard my initial concerns and look squarely at what the three of you did in DC, I gotta say that you did a terrific job in helping your country and saving it from a catastrophic outcome, had Tamara gotten away. I'm sorry she chose to end things the way she did, and I regret you had to witness it. But your contribution to global security is more significant than you'll probably ever know—and yes, you saved my life."

He stopped for a couple of seconds. I swear he was choking up. "That I will not forget. As you know, I have a wife and two young children who have a lot of years ahead of them. I want to be there for them." This was a side of Major Dallant I'd never seen before, nor did I even think existed.

He continued. "I've taken care of things at the Agency. Your names—and Luc, your dad's name—have been expunged from all internal documents."

I couldn't believe it. *"Madonna mia!* So that's it? We're free now? Just like that?"

"Just like that. You're all free."

Bella couldn't contain herself. "Fantastic!"

Eric echoed it. "I'll say. Thank you so much!"

The three of us were more than curious. I had to ask, "So what happened at CIA headquarters because of our actions? There's been nothing in the news."

"Yes, I know. That's by design. I really can't share any more on that with you. Luc, but some changes have been made. For one thing, your security clearance is gone. But it's for your own good, and believe me, it does have a happy ending."

Bella exclaimed, "I hope so, after all we've been through, including you, Major!"

"Thanks, Bella. And I must say that I'm deeply sorry about what happened to you. I had no idea what Tamara was up to. I hope you believe me. But here's the thing, with what I personally initiated and completed, as far as the Agency is concerned, you don't exist. So, you're all in the clear and can go about your lives like nothing happened."

"Hallelujah! *Thank you*, Major. What a weight off our shoulders." I thought Bella was going to give him a big hug.

"Luc, there's something I also want to share with you that wasn't possible for me to do when you were working for Tamara."

"Really, what's that?"

"When she was contacted by Dr. Ross about your capabilities, she became highly motivated to get you on board to work for her. And when Tamara made up her mind, there was no stopping her. She and I both knew there was no way your parents would allow it, so she had me dig into your dad's war record, and of course, you know the rest. I told her I thought it wasn't a good idea to forcibly recruit a 16-year-old high school student, no matter what unusual skills he had. But she was adamant, so I had no choice. I had to follow through in the chain of command. I'm sorry."

"Thanks, I appreciate hearing that."

I had a question. "When will you close down this office and remove all of the top-secret information?"

The major replied, "I've already had our people eliminate all information on the computer's hard drive and telephones, and so on. But the lease was paid for one year and, as you might guess, we invested quite a bit of money securing the place. I think we'll just hold on to it until the lease runs out. In any case, it would involve too much work to get out of it, and we don't have the time to deal with it. There are much more pressing matters now."

"I get it—right."

Major Dallant smiled. He was suddenly in a good mood—I'd say, even cheerful. "Well, can I take the three of you out to dinner before I head back tomorrow?"

Bella answered for all of us: "Wow! That would be super!"

"Great. I hope you like Vietnamese. I made a reservation for us at 7:00 P.M. at Tamarine on University Avenue."

Bella lit up. "Seriously? I took my parents there for their anniversary. It's their favorite place. Great desserts! You wouldn't believe their Molten Chocolate Lava Cake!"

"See you there at seven."

As the three of us left his office, I thought, *This near-disaster finally has a happy ending*—at least that's what I thought at the time, never thinking to take a peek into the future.

Chapter
Thirty-Five

CLOSURE

Dinner with Major Dallant and the SPI Team was a great way to celebrate a happy ending to what had been a harrowing summer for all four of us. We talked about everything but Tamara and the CIA. It was an opportunity to learn more about the personal side of Major Dallant, and he seemed to feel the same about us, although he probably knew more about me than I did.

I was also looking forward to furthering my relationship with Bella and my newfound friendship with Eric. The three of us were excited about working with Thay as an honorary member of the SPI Team, kinda our *consigliere,* to steal a term from *The Godfather.* I could also finally focus on basketball, school, and hopefully, getting into the best college possible.

As Thay was fond of advising me, "Every challenge is an opportunity in disguise and is necessary for the cosmic dance of the universe." Although I'd never completely understood this, after the events of the past summer, I was beginning to get more than an inkling of what he meant. I could easily tick them off. My relationship with Bella had never been better, I'd found a wonderful new friend in Eric. my father was becoming increasingly disconnected from the disaster that haunted him since his time in Iraq, and he and Mom—and for that matter, he and I—were closer and happier than I could recall. Life was great and seemed to be getting better.

Having learned something from the spy game, I promised myself that from now on, everything would be open and aboveboard—with one exception: there was no way I would say anything to my parents about what had happened in DC. What could I say? It wouldn't do anyone any good. It might even cast an even bigger shadow on our future.

THEN IT HAPPENED—THE CAT JUMPED OUT OF THE BAG. It was Saturday, and most unusually, the whole family was together at breakfast. Mom, Laura, and I were talking about a family vacation to Europe the following summer. Dad was buried in the *New York Times*.

Suddenly, he let out with a huge "Wow." Like he couldn't contain his excitement. "I'll be damned! Luc, listen up! It's a cover story by an investigative reporter for the *New York Times*. About a week ago, there was an incident in front of the Russian Consulate in DC. The reporter has been working since then trying to put the pieces together. Listen to this—it looks like it involved a CIA agent switching sides from the US to Russia.

"Here, I'll read it to you: 'Bystanders walking near the consulate were hustled away by a military intelligence officer later identified as Major John Dallant from the CIA and NSA. Witnesses report seeing three kids with ray guns and a dead woman lying in a pool of blood in front of the entrance gate to the consulate.'

"Dallant, of course, is our dear old 'friend' who finagled an invite with Cap to our barbecue. Remember?"

"No way! Really?" What else could I say?

I grimaced. Was this gonna open up a whole new can of worms, or should I say, snakes?

"They say the scene was quickly overrun by the CIA and FBI, and all streets and walkways within a two-block radius were sealed off for 12 hours. The next day, the reporter went to the Russian Consulate and spoke with a security guard. She didn't get much out of him since he spoke almost no English. He kept saying something that sounded to her like, 'Three kids with ray guns.' She then spoke with an administrator at the consulate, who disavowed any knowledge of the incident.

"The journalist finally tracked down Dallant and contacted him at his office at Langley. When asked about three kids with ray guns, the major laughed dismissively. 'Right, I heard they were extraterrestrials who landed in front of the Russian Consulate in a spaceship!' The CIA refuses to provide any more details. Strange, huh?"

Laura asked, "Are we being invaded by aliens?"

Mom brought her back down to reality. "Not a chance, sweetheart! But that's really something about John Dallant."

What could I say? "Sounds like he and the CIA have much bigger fish to fry than a teenager in Palo Alto. And that's fine with me."

"Yeah, that's really something, all right." Dad looked at me with an afterthought. "Thank God *that thing* went away." It was clear *that thing* was code in front of Laura for my mix-up with the CIA. "But, as Mom always says, 'Everything happens for a reason.' Some good did come out of that whole mess."

Dad, if you only knew.

"I reconnected with Cap, and thanks to both of you, my nightmares are less frequent, and the healing process is beginning to work," he said.

Nosy Laura couldn't resist butting in. "What are you guys talking about? The CIA, bigger fish, nightmare stuff, and a healing process? I don't get it!"

Mom quickly distracted her. "Honey, Dad ran into an old army buddy who introduced him to a government friend of his—nothing out of the ordinary."

Keeping the distraction going, Mom smiled and said to Laura, "But I've got a special thought for tonight. How about we have one of those old-fashioned pizza parties in the garden? Dad could fire up the wood-fired oven in the garden. I'll buy dough, and you and I can make the pizzas. How does that sound?"

That got her attention. "Fantastic! But how come Luc never has to do any of the work?"

"Honey, he does plenty around here."

"Well, he gets a bigger allowance than I do, so he should do more."

I couldn't believe it. This couldn't be my mom, who always obsessed over preparing fancy gourmet dishes. I'd noticed a change in her over the past several weeks. She'd seemed less anxious, but this was amazing.

I jumped right in. "Great idea! Laura, I'll be happy to help with making the pizzas. You'll just have to tell me what to do."

"I like that—being your boss."

Dad was almost as excited as I was. "Fantastic idea!"

Laura asked, "Mom, can I invite Astra? I'm always at her place."

"Absolutely!"

"Luc, you have anybody you'd like to invite? I don't know, maybe Bella?"

"Come on, Mom! Lay off. I'll ask her, but I'll also ask Eric and Thay. You and Dad haven't met them. They're good people. You'll like them."

Laura was confused. "What's that mean? Bad people don't like pizza?"

What could I say? "Oh, Laura, you are one heck of a sister. Life would be boring without you."

"Thanks—I guess . . ."

And with that, we went our separate ways to do our part to prepare for the party.

This was going to be a special night for all of us. With Mom and Dad's recent busy travel schedules, we hadn't sat down to dinner as a family for weeks. And we had so much to celebrate. So what if only three of us knew all the details? Well, make that four—the SPI Team had met with Thay and had filled him in on what had happened in DC. As our *consigliere*, he helped us understand how to accept what had happened and to celebrate the good that came out of it.

DAD HAD THE FIRE GOING, and Laura and Astra had set the circular garden table, which by some miracle was just big enough for all of us—oh, right, no such thing as a miracle. Mom had the table built a couple of years ago. She said its shape made for better group conversations. I guess that's the psychologist in her.

Oh, and another thing about Mom that day—she showed up in sneakers, jeans, a University of Chicago sweatshirt, no makeup, and her hair in a ponytail. It was the first time I'd seen her dress like that. *Mamma mia! What in the world had gotten into her?* She looked more beautiful than I could remember.

Everyone, especially Laura and Astra, were captivated and entertained by Thay's Bronx accent and the fact that he didn't act like a monk. Laura whispered to me, "How can a Vietnamese monk speak like that? What part of Vietnam is he from?" I learned another crazy thing about him that day. He was a great juggler. He entertained us like a circus performer. I never knew what might be next with Thay.

After a few pizzas were out of the oven, we all sat down to eat. As usual, Mom had the first words. "You all know that I'm not a particularly religious person." She stopped for a couple of beats. "Oh, I'm so sorry, Thay. I wasn't thinking. I didn't mean to disrespect your calling."

"That's quite all right, Valentina. I'm not a particularly religious person either. People often forget that original Buddhism was not a religion, it was a philosophy of life, so please, go on."

"Thanks, Thay. But I do want to express my feelings of gratitude—I guess I could say to the universe—for bringing all of us together this evening for dinner—both family and friends—particularly after what we've been through these past several months, and especially you, Luc. I'd also like to say to you, Bella, that we are so grateful you made it through that terrible accident."

"Thanks, Dr. Ponti."

"Bella, please—Valentina. Let's leave the formalities for the university."

"Okay, sure—Valentina."

Mom was on a roll. "You know, for us Pontis, it's been too long since we were together like this. It reminds me of something important I learned from my mom and dad in our Italian household—something that was a big part of our heritage and culture. One of the special things in life is celebrating it as often as possible at a simple dinner with friends and family. Let's see what we can do to make this a habit. And let's have dinner often with our friends who are with us tonight."

Dad loved the idea. "Amen to that, sweetheart. I'm going to cut down on my travel schedule and late-night meetings."

"That's wonderful, Carlo."

Bella complimented my sister. "Wow, Laura, these pizzas are fantastic! What's your secret?"

Laura can sometimes be a charmer too. She replied, "My mom." Everyone laughed.

Then, Mom unknowingly threw out a grenade. I hoped to hell it was a dud. "Eric, how did you and Luc meet?"

But Eric was quick. Without losing a beat, he said, "Oh, we met on the hiking trail over at the Ravenwood Preserve. I bumped into him and Bella there, and we had an interesting conversation. Right, guys?"

I was glad my mouth was full of pizza. I'm not sure what I would have said. Bella saved the day. "Right, quite an experience."

"Oh, that's so nice," Mom said with a smile.

I swallowed. Gulp!

As everyone was enjoying pizza and chatting, Mom decided to share another thought. At first, I thought it was crazy. "You know, when you kids were younger, we used to play that *Share a Secret* game at the dinner table. Remember?"

I almost choked on an olive. "You're not suggesting we play that silly game tonight, are you? Mom, we have guests! *Madonna mia*, please!"

"Luc! Watch the Italian! We're all Americans around this table. And yes, I am suggesting we play it. And they can join in if they feel like it . . . or not."

Thay let out with his exaggerated Bronx accent, "Oh, oh, ya mean I gotta give up one of my deep dark secrets? Fugettaboutit!"

The table broke into a roar of laughter.

"Thanks, Thay, for breaking the ice. Look, if it makes you feel better, Luc, let's modify the game a bit and call it *Share Some Good News*. And since I suggested it, I'll go first."

Dad, who'd undergone the biggest change in our family, and slowly but surely was becoming the Ponti family enthusiast, had become Mom's top supporter. "Great idea! Go for it, honey."

"Okay." Mom skipped a few beats, thought about it, and began. "Yesterday I was deeply honored and, I must say, surprised, when the department offered me the prestigious Lewis M. Terman Professorship."

Dad cheered, "Valentina, that's fantastic!"

Laura chimed in, "Mom, that's amazing. Can I tell the kids in my class?"

I was so happy for her. "That's terrific, Mom. Tell us more."

"Well, it's a prestigious position with all kinds of perks, including a hefty raise in salary. But it's likely to require more travel and additional responsibilities that will take more of my time away from the family, so you guys may have to do more pizza parties or whatever without me. But I think it will be good for my soul, and I was hoping you all would agree."

Dad was right there. "Honey, we'll do everything we can to support you and certainly understand if sometimes you have to be away. Right, kids?"

Laura and I replied in unison, "Right!"

"Thanks, I appreciate your support." Mom continued. "What about you, Laura? What's *your* good news?"

"Well, I know that I'm always giving Luc a hard time, but I've been thinking lately that I wanna spend more time with him. I noticed that over the past few months, he's really gotten pretty smart, and I think I can learn some good stuff from him."

Mom smiled. "Aw, that's sweet."

I added, "Thanks, Laura, I appreciate that."

Eric just couldn't contain his wise-guy self. "Watch out what he teaches you, Laura."

"Sure will." She looked at her friend Astra. "Would you like to share some good news?"

Not a bashful girl, Astra went right into it. "Okay. You know I'm an only child. Well, I'm so happy every time Laura stays at our place. I make believe she's my older sister, and that makes me feel great."

Mom was touched. "How precious. Astra, we'd love to see you stay more often at our place—with your 'sister.'"

Laura and Astra looked at each other, giving each other big smiles. Laura then asked, "What about you, Luc? What good news do *you* have?"

I didn't have to hesitate. I knew exactly what to say. "I guess you all know it's been a challenging several months for me. But I'm starting to learn a lot about life from Thay. And as he often tells me, 'Things are always the way they're supposed to be. The universe makes no mistakes in its cosmic dance.' It's kinda like Mom's 'Everything happens for a good reason.' I'm beginning to understand that even though there are times when the way things are supposed to be can really hurt inside, there can often be a good outcome. I don't want to give you a list of all the great things that did happen to me these past few months, except for one."

Laura again jumped the gun—definitely showing some of Dad's traits. I guess that's genetics. "Quick, quick, what is it? What's the good news?"

"It's two opportunities I learned of in the last couple of weeks, but I had to think about them for a while before I made a decision. This dinner has made the answer really clear to me."

I looked at my father. "Dad, I didn't tell you any of this. I had to go through it on my own to make the decision I thought was best for my future. But here's the thing: I got two scholarship offers. A free ride for four years at Duke, and a free ride for the first two years at Princeton, and then possibly for the last two years as well, depending on my grade-point average and my performance on the basketball team."

Laura was all rainbows and unicorns. "Luc, you're gonna take Duke, right? That's fantastic, and it's free for four years! Guaranteed!"

"No. I'm gonna accept Princeton's offer."

Even though Bella and I knew it would mean separation anxiety for both of us, she couldn't help but let out a cheer. "Way to go, Luc!"

I looked at her, and she sent a passionate wink. God, what a woman. I was sad and happy at the same time—is that possible?

Mom was so thrilled that she unknowingly broke the Ponti Rule of Linguistics, "Oh *mio passerotto*—fantastic!"

"Mom, watch your language!" Everyone had a good laugh.

Dad came over and gave me a hug. "Congratulations! I'm so proud of you. Great choice!"

I smiled. What could I say?

After the ruckus died down, Dad said, "I think it's my turn. I'm sure most of you know that it's not my nature to open up about myself. But the last few months, as challenging as they've been for our family, have done some wonderful things for me. Thanks to Valentina, I've found a way forward with my life that feels good—really good—and I finally decided to do what she's been suggesting ever since I came back from Iraq. I've been getting counseling from the VA, and it's working. I feel better than I have in a long time."

I could see Mom starting to choke up. She was so happy.

Dad, still full of surprises, said, "And, by the way, I sold my membership in the Palo Alto Hills Country Club—no more Mr. Big Shot! I want to spend more time with you guys. Oh, and Luc, with some of the money we'll get from the country club, Mom and I are going to buy you a car—not a new one, but something to get you around town."

Of course, I couldn't tell my parents that I had more than enough funds in the bank to buy my own car, but I knew that I would not only pay them back someday but also use the money to do good.

"Wow! That's super, Dad, Mom—a car! Many, many thanks. That'll put a real positive dent in my life—pun intended! Listen, I have some other good news to share. Is that okay?"

Dad responded, "Absolutely!"

I could see the anticipation on everyone's face. "But I have to say, it's not mine. It belongs to Bella and to Eric. And I know they won't tell you. They're too modest."

Bella piped up, "Luc, stay out of my stuff!"

And Eric, "Come on, dude."

"Not a chance! I think most of you know that with the loss of her older brother, Alejandro, to multiple sclerosis, Bella was inspired to become a research medical doctor and help find a cure for that disease. Well, guess what? Last week she was awarded a full four-year scholarship to Johns Hopkins University to study molecular biology as a premed student."

Everyone congratulated Bella with a loud "Way to go!"

As the noise quieted down, she made a face and let me have it. "I warned you. You'd better watch your back for the next few days." She turned to the others and said, "Thanks, everyone, I really appreciate your support."

I went on. "I'm not finished. I'm not gonna say anything more about Bella because I see her grabbing the knife next to her plate. But I do wanna say something about Eric."

Eric gave me a dirty look. "Oh, c'mon, give it a break."

"Can't do that, Eric. I know you're mostly a quiet guy, and a good guy, so I gotta look out for you." I turned to everyone. "Some of you may not know that Eric dropped out of school in the middle of last year. But he had a change of heart." Dirty looks like daggers that could kill were coming my way from Eric. I was glad he wasn't pointing his electrokinesis fingers at me. "In any case, he entered a high school equivalency program, and based on the results of his entrance exam, he was chosen to take a special tutoring program for gifted students. He's done so well that Mrs. Becker, our student advisory counselor at school, found a way to get him admitted to Paly to finish his senior year with Bella and me."

Cheers and applause again filled the garden.

"Wait, there's more. Mrs. Becker also got him into a special program at Georgetown University where he took a full day of challenging tests, something like the SATs, but more difficult. He got a perfect score! The first time they've ever seen that."

More "Oh my Gods" and loud applause. "And if he finishes his senior year at Paly with an excellent grade-point average and does well on this year's SATs, he's essentially guaranteed a full four-year scholarship to Georgetown. The three of us will be together on the East Coast! Isn't *that* just the best?"

Everyone was applauding and congratulating Eric. What a great party! I hadn't felt like this since Bella had come out of her coma. Life was great!

When things quieted down, observant Laura declared, "Hey, wait a minute. Thay didn't share any of *his* good news."

Mom to the rescue: "Laura, don't be rude!"

"No, it's okay, Valentina. She's right. It's only fair. So, let's see. What's my good news? Okay, I have a story for you," Thay began.

Laura's eyes opened wide. "Wow, this is gonna be really juicy! I can tell."

Thay smiled. "I don't know if it's juicy now, but it sure as heck was juicy when I was a teenager."

Laura was so excited. "Great, I love growing-up stories. Let's hear it."

"Well, it begins when I was a teenager living in the Bronx. I started to hang out with the wrong crowd and got into some trouble. My parents were deeply concerned, so they sent me away to do my schooling at a monastery in the mountains of Nepal. At first, I hated it and wanted to go back to New York. But a wise monk named Anjo, my adviser, you might say, saw that I liked hiking in the mountains, so he got me into climbing. I loved it immediately. After a while I couldn't get enough of it."

You could see that everyone was captivated by Thay's story.

"Then one day—I guess I was 15 years old—against the advice of Anjo, and without him knowing, I went climbing alone. It started out as a beautiful day, but the Himalayas can be as treacherous as they are majestic. The weather changed abruptly. I encountered unexpectedly heavy snow—what climbers call a whiteout. I was trapped on a two-foot ledge with more than a 1,000-foot drop. I couldn't go up and I couldn't go down. For the first time in my life, the big-shot brat from the Bronx was afraid, very afraid. And I was freezing. If I would have had to stay there overnight, I would surely have been dead from hypothermia before morning."

Laura was entranced, as we all were. "Oh my God, Thay. What did you do?"

"I did what I was taught by the monks to do when fear was upon me. I took a number of deep breaths—we call it *pranayama*—and faced my fear. I looked at it in my mind, said nothing, and then meditated, trying as best I could to stay focused on the present, living with the fear, while asking the universe for a way to save my life. The monks had taught me that when you're in a bad situation and you want a way out, the first thing you must do is practice acceptance—acknowledge that this is the way things are supposed to be. If you fight it, then you're fighting against the whole universe. The second thing, in a meditative, calm state, is to envision a solution, a way out. I did just that.

"A couple of hours passed, and I began to feel warm and started to fall asleep. That's the last conscious thing that happens when a person is freezing to death."

Laura couldn't contain her anxiety. "Oh, Thay, you obviously didn't die, so tell us what happened!"

"Suddenly, I heard a voice: 'Pham, Pham, Pham.' Who was that? At first I thought it was a spirit calling me from this life to the next. Was I about to die? But then I realized it was coming from up above me. I yelled back. It was Anjo. He was worried about me and had tracked me through the snow. Fortunately, the blizzard began to stop, and he was able to lower a rope and pull me to safety.

"On the way down the mountain, he admonished me and said that it was a very foolish thing to do. I told him I was unhappy with my life and didn't know what to do about it. It was then that he disclosed two of the most important secrets: the *Meaning of Life* and the *Purpose of Life*, and that's what eventually changed everything for me. They didn't make a big difference at first, but the more I thought about them, the more they made sense and eventually made a huge difference—they defined my life and my future."

Thay was quiet, as we all were, except, of course, Laura. He, as you might guess, was baiting her.

She couldn't hold it in. "Well, aren't you gonna tell us what the secrets are?"

"You really want to know?"

Her eyes and mouth couldn't open any wider. "Oh my God, yes!"

"Okay, I'll share them with you. But, promise me that if, like I was at age 15, they don't awaken your heart right now, that you won't forget them, and you'll think of them often, because someday they will open your eyes and your heart to a magnificent future, and your journey will be as it should be—special, meaningful, joyful, and fulfilling."

Laura responded, "Yes, yes, I promise!"

"Fine. So, here are the secrets: The *Meaning of Life* is to look inside and find those special gifts you came into this world with. Everyone has them. Sometimes it takes a while to find them. But never give up.

"The *Purpose of Life* is to find a way to share those gifts with others in ways that makes this a better world, even if it's just a little bit better. In doing so, you'll experience gratitude and happiness like you've never felt before, and you'll prosper beyond your wildest dreams—emotionally, spiritually, and often, financially."

Mom was nearly in tears. "Thay, that's an amazing and beautiful story with profound and valuable secrets. It's really got me thinking about my life, about my children's lives, and also Carlo's. Thank you so much for sharing."

Dad, Bella, and Eric followed with their thoughts and gratitude. What a happy bunch!

I suddenly went into a deep reverie that somehow filtered out the joyous commotion around me. Over the past several months, I'd delved inside and had done some profound thinking about my future. Finally, my life purpose was clear to me. I could continue to contribute to the greater good and still follow my dream to attend college and play ball. I don't know why it took such a rocky road to realize that simple fact. Bella and Eric were also excited, because they could do the same as members of our SPI Team. Following our dream wasn't inconsistent with helping others. In fact, the two were very much connected. Life was great. What could be better?!

I don't think I'd ever been in a better place than I was at that moment. I looked around and absorbed the positive energy and laughter my family and friends were creating. As everyone was talking and joking among themselves, I heard a cell phone ringing. I'd forgotten mine next to the barbecue when I was carrying pizzas out to the lunch table. I got up to turn it off. As I reached down to grab it, I noticed the caller ID. It was an all-too-familiar DC number. *No, it couldn't be.* Reluctantly, . . . I answered it.

My demeanor did a rapid 180.

"Hello."

"Luc, it's Major Dallant."

"Why are you calling me?"

"Something's come up. And it's critical."

"You're right, my life's come up. And yes, it is critical."

"Luc, this is beyond urgent."

"Sorry, can't help you."

Mom called over to me, "Luc, c'mon, hang up the phone. Your family and friends need you."

Trying to be as normal as possible, I replied, "Be right there, Mom . . . I gotta go."

"I know I promised you—"

"And I expect you to keep your promise."

He was quiet for just a few beats. "Luc, it's Seagull. And it's not good. I'm deeply concerned—no, frightened—not just for our country, but for the world. I desperately need you and the SPI Team. I don't know where else to turn."

We both went silent. Finally, I choked it out. "What about Seagull?"

"Just this one time, Luc. Not over the phone, I'm flying to Palo Alto tomorrow. I'll call you from the office. Fill you in there." He hung up.

I stood there in a stupor, the dead phone plastered to my ear, staring blankly at my family and friends laughing it up at the table, the people I cared most about in my life, all happier than I'd ever seen them before. *No, this can't be. Not now.*

Everyone saw me standing there in a semihypnotic state, but they were oblivious to what had just happened. They started merrily shouting, "Luc, Luc, Luc!" just like the fans in the stands at our games. Except, this was nothing to cheer about.

I stood there trying my best to regain my enthusiasm and energy. They kept yelling, "Luc, Luc, Luc!"

The only one who wasn't smiling or saying a word was Thay. His eyes were glued to mine. We'd developed such a deep connection over the summer. He knew everything—exactly what I was thinking—*Oh, Great White Light, please, please! What is it you want from me?*

I stood there, fearful and concerned about what the future was placing on my doorstep. But then I felt a warm feeling, and I heard *That* voice deep inside of me:

"*You are no longer just Luc Ponti. . . . As your consciousness grows as well as your powers that be . . . you must do your part to help heal the world. . . . It is written in the Cosmic Plan. . . . Namaste, Luc.*"

I stood up straight, swallowed hard, and smiled. I walked over to join my family and friends.

"The purpose of life is a life of purpose."

—ROBERT BYRNE

336

AFTERWORD

The premise of *I Can See Clearly* is—as challenging as it may sometimes seem—that each of us must find and follow our life purpose. It's the only path to long-term fulfillment and happiness. The secondary premise is that consciousness eventually defeats deception and duplicity.

Luc Ponti's journey is telling us something that has important implications for everyone struggling to find and follow their life purpose: *Consciousness is an infinite, eternal, powerful, universal force, present in all matter, and most highly developed in the human species. It has the power to change the world for the better. And with practice and dedication, anyone can access this power through altered states of consciousness—most notably and effectively through meditation.* For millennia, we've been in the Dark Ages concerning its nature. But that's changing.

Consistent results from modern quantum physics have forced us to reconsider findings we didn't want to deal with in years gone by because they smacked of metaphysics, and that ran counter to the practice of the Scientific Method. Our recognition of the infinite and eternal nature of consciousness and its potential for creating a peaceful and sustainable future for us, our children, and generations beyond is beginning to do more than dawn on us. It's at the heart of the emerging science of spiritual physics. Sure, this field has a way to go before it's accepted as "The Next Great Thing" for humankind. However, many physicists and philosophers no longer look at this data as a metaphysical quirk outside the realm of science.

Spiritual physics *is* the next scientific paradigm, and although it is in its infancy, headway is being made to develop and understand the laws of this science.

This change in our worldview started slowly, decades ago. Change makers such as physics Nobel laureate Wolfgang Pauli working together with psychiatrist Carl Jung saw the light. Jung's understanding of the roots of consciousness enabled him to develop the concept of the collective unconscious, not to be confused with Collective Consciousness.

Jung's concept of the collective unconscious maintains that we're programmed from birth by the cultural mores and values that permeate the society into which we're born and raised. We now know that this shadow effect occurs even before that through the forces of genetics and epigenetics. This sociocultural hypnosis controls our worldview and how we develop our lives. It screens us from experiencing Personal Consciousness, our true reality, to its very fullest.

However, because the collective unconscious resides in our subconscious mind, we now know that it is reprogrammable through altered states of consciousness, most ostensibly through meditation, to concepts and values we feel serve us best. We are the first species on planet Earth—ever—capable of doing this. It's our choice—your choice—to make.

"The path within is one that many may travel, but few do journey."
—GEORGE WILLIAM RUSSELL

GLOSSARY

ITALIAN PROFANITIES AND PHRASES

Profanities

- *A fanabala*—Go to hell!
- *Bastardo!*—Bastard!
- *Bovis stercus!*—Bullshit! (Latin)
- *Cavalo*—Holy crap!
- *Cazzo!*—F*ck! Shit! Hell!
- *Che cazzo!*—What the hell/f*ck!
- *Che diavolo?*—What the hell?
- *Che palle!*—What balls!
- *Cullo saggio*—Wiseass
- *Dolor nell'as*—Pain in the ass
- *Dannata*—Goddamn
- *Figlio di puttana!*—Son of a bitch!
- *Gesu Cristo!*—Jesus Christ!
- *Grand palle*—Big balls
- *Incazzato!*—I'm pissed!
- *Lecca mia culo!*—Kiss my ass!
- *Lecca mia cullo, bastardo!*—Kiss my ass, you bastard!
- *Merda!*—Shit!
- *Merda santa!*—Holy shit!
- *Minchia!*—Shit! Damn! Hell!
- *Minchia, che idioti!*—Shit, what idiots!
- *Puttana!*—Whore!
- *Stronzo/a!*—Asshole!
- *Vaffancul, bastardi!*—F*ck you, you bastards!

Phrases

- *Adesso!*—Now!
- *Basta!*—That's enough!
- *Bella donna*—Beautiful woman
- *Bella regazza*—Beautiful girl
- *Buon dio!*—Good God!
- *Buon dio, mia bella regazza*—Good morning, my beautiful girl!
- *Caso pazzo*—Crazy case
- *Che bella che sei!*—How beautiful you are!
- *Che fai?*—What are you doing?
- *Fatti una vita!*—Get a life!
- *Godere!*—Enjoy!
- *Incredibile*—Unbelievable
- *Loco en la cabeza*—Crazy in the head
- *Madonna mia*—Oh, my mother!
- *Madra mia!*—My mother!
- *Mamma mia! Toute e perfecto!*—Mama, everything is perfect!
- *Mi cachorro*—My puppy
- *Mille grazie!*—A thousand thanks!
- *Mio figlio disubbidiente, adesso!*—My disobedient son, now!
- *Molto pazzo!*—Very crazy!
- *Oh mio Dio!*—Oh my God!
- *Passerotto*—A sparrow learning to fly
- *Porca vacca!*—Holy cow!
- *Purtroppo*—Unfortunately
- *Quando finira questo?*—When will this end?
- *Sei pazzo?*—Are you crazy?
- *Shifezza*—Crap
- *Si, lo sono*—Yes, I am
- *Veloce per favore!*—Quickly, please!

SUPPLEMENTS

This section provides supplementary information that you, the reader, may wish to study concerning concepts discussed in the novel. It is not essential to the storyline but expands on the meaning and implications of these concepts.

1ˢ   An interesting and practical part of Pham Tuan's lecture concerned how to bring into your life things you desire. There are five steps to such manifestations: *intention, attention, imagination, belief,* and *detachment.* He explained how each of these steps worked and how they were all interrelated. The most difficult of these steps was *detachment.* Think about it—after you've done all of the work in the first four steps and you're excited about success, you must detach from the outcome and trust that the Cosmos will handle all of the details, even the small ones. Not easy.

Pham Tuan said that it was possible to bring nearly anything you wished into your life. There were only two cosmic rules for success. Your manifestation must bring no harm to anyone, including you. And second, it should, in even the smallest way, make the world a better place. These two rules assure that each manifestation increases the consciousness of the cosmos toward greater Unity Consciousness. He said that **a continuous, eternal increase in Unity Consciousness was the sole purpose of the universe. He called it the *Cosmic Purpose.***

Pham Tuan emphasized that you didn't have to be a Gandhi, a Mother Teresa, a Nelson Mandela, or an Abraham Lincoln. You just had to be your deepest authentic self, which he said was not your physical body, mind, or ego, but your Personal Consciousness, which is infinite and eternal—some might call it your soul. And the best way to access your consciousness is through the power of meditation.

2ˢ He said, "I want you to let go of all thoughts and begin to focus on the inflow and outflow of your breath. With each inhalation and exhalation, allow yourself to become more relaxed, more comfortable, more at peace. Now, introduce into your meditation the following Sanskrit mantra: *Sat, Chit, Ananda*, which means *Existence, Consciousness, Bliss*. Repeat it mentally and allow it to flow with effortless ease. Then let the mantra go as you focus on the gap between your thoughts—that is, on the absence of thought, sheer nothingness, which may seem like nothingness, but actually contains an infinite number of possibilities for anything you or anyone else can conceive of and wish to manifest into your three-dimensional 'reality.'"

There is, Pham Tuan said, an analogy in quantum physics. When an atom is acted upon by physical forces, the nearly infinite number of possible final outcomes for that atom can be described in precise mathematical detail by an equal number of specific statements of the famous Schrödinger equation. It is only by the experimenter's observation at the instant those various forces are acting on the atom that the numerous possibilities instantly "collapse" to one equation that precisely defines the final condition and form of the atom. This is known in quantum physics as the Observation Effect and is the basis for the statement that the physical universe would not exist as perceived if it were not for an observer's observation.

Pham Tuan advised that during my meditation, whenever I'm distracted by thoughts or feelings that may creep back into my body or mind, I should return to repeating the mantra. He said to continue meditating, and at some point, he would gently touch my forehead to indicate it was time to release the mantra and become physically present.

3ˢ Meditation plays a critical role in this novel. Its potential to help create a balanced and successful life has been demonstrated scientifically. Unlike for the ancient Wisdom Seekers, its incredible power is most often misunderstood and unappreciated. In our hectic, sometimes chaotic modern world, many people find meditation a challenge and often give up on it after a short time when they feel they cannot clear their mind of all thoughts. A good way to ease into meditation is to start with the practice of mindfulness. A source for training in mindfulness can be found at Headspace.com. Deepak Chopra's healing center (www.Chopra. Com) offers numerous introductory programs for learning the effective practice of mindfulness and meditation. I like the one on abundance.

4⁵ I said to Thay, "I don't understand what you mean by pre-conceptions."

He explained, "I'm sure you've heard the saying 'You're known by the company you keep.' This simply means that over the years, we all tend to inherit the beliefs of those people with whom we spend the most time—our parents, relatives, friends, teachers, the media, and so on. Their ideas and philosophies tend to become part of our subconscious mind. And it is well known that we function primarily through our subconscious mind, which has been programmed unwittingly by these sources.

"But, as humans, we have an incredible and amazing advantage over all other species on the planet. We can change or erase any of our past conditioning or preconceptions if we choose to do so. We can also release negativity.

"One way to achieve this is by interacting with like-minded conscious people—people who expressly believe and practice our values and the new way in which we choose to function. We can also engage in uplifting activities—music, the arts, yoga, sports, theater, and more. In doing so, we can develop new and more positive ways of living and clear the subconscious of all that does not serve us in the new way in which we choose to live. The most effective and expedient means to make this shift is to support your engagement in any of these activities with a complement of earnest and frequent meditation."

I expressed my surprise at what he said. "It sounds to me as if all of us have been brainwashed since birth!"

"In a manner of speaking, you're correct. But some of this so-called brainwashing has had personal benefits—but often not all of it."

5ˢ Thay elaborated. "Buddhists like to say that *the physical universe and everything within it are a way for its Source, namely, Cosmic Consciousness, to eternally know and be intimately aware of Itself*—'I was a hidden treasure and wanted to be known'—reminiscent of the famous maxim from the Delphi Oracle of ancient Greece: 'Know thyself!' You see, Luc, that's how important we are in the grand scheme of things. *You, I, everyone, all material things, enable Cosmic Consciousness, what many would call God, to become fully aware of Its very presence and essence. Just as our five senses provide our awareness of the three-dimensional physical world, the consciousness of beings is the means for these beings, including God, to be self-aware.*"

6ˢ Thay said, "Perhaps, even more challenging for you to digest, is that there are three forms of consciousness: Cosmic, Personal, and Collective Consciousness. Personal Consciousness is consciousness associated with a specific entity, like you. It enables you to be aware of everything, including yourself. 'Personal' is perhaps not the most accurate description in the English language, as all material things, people, animals, plants, and even inanimate objects such as mountains and the sea—all the way down to the atom and beyond—have some level of consciousness associated with their existence. However, consciousness is most highly developed in the human species and perfectly developed in Cosmic Consciousness. As is the case for Cosmic Consciousness, Personal Consciousness is omnipresent—it's infinite and eternal. Luc, your consciousness is infinite and eternal—it's everywhere. It has always been and always will be!"

"A part of me is infinite and eternal? You've gotta be kidding me."

"I'm not, and I will prove it to you in a few moments. And by the way, it's not a part of you, it *is* you—the real you. It's who you really are, your very essence, not your physical body, which is something you assume at conception and birth to embrace the real you, just like you put on your clothes as part of your body."

7ˢ Thay looked directly at me and asked, "Think about this inquiry—do animals, plants, and other nonhuman organisms really have any semblance of awareness or consciousness? And if so, how 'far down' to the cellular level does this awareness proceed? That's *the* question that has been asked over hundreds of years by numerous scientists and philosophers. A scientific answer may have been uncovered during research carried out over three decades, beginning in the 1960s."

Thay then told me about the amazing work of Cleve Backster. Backster, a former naval officer during World War II, was a polygraph interrogation specialist, having founded the CIA's polygraph unit shortly after the war ended. He founded a reputable school in New York City that taught lie-detection methodology to the FBI and other law-enforcement agencies. Backster ultimately moved the school, The Backster School of Lie Detection, to San Diego, California, where to this very day, it has been the longest-operating polygraph school in the world.

In February of 1966, Backster's secretary bought him a Dracaena cane plant to dress up his starkly decorated office in New York City. Early one morning, after working throughout the night on some polygraph experiments, he decided to see if his instrument could detect the instant when water fed to the roots of the plant reached its leaves. He reasoned that there could be a signal since the polygraph device functioned by measuring galvanic or electric skin responses in humans, a phenomenon highly sensitive to, and affected by, water content. Those individuals not telling the truth emit more moisture through their skin than those telling the truth. The technology is more complicated than that, but that's the general concept.

Backster was intrigued by research he'd read that was carried out in 1900 by a highly regarded Indian polymath and physicist named Jagadish Chandra Bose. Bose found that plants actually responded to certain kinds of music and grew faster.

Backster's reported research findings were amazing. He found that the plant *did* respond, and in fact gave off a signal similar to that observed in humans. He was intrigued, and this set him on an entire new tack for exploring the use of polygraph technology. His findings were increasingly profound—actually, unbelievable, to most scientists at that time.

Even more baffling—on the morning of February 2, 1966, during his very first experiments with his Dracaena cane plant, as he sat at his desk after watering the plant, impatiently waiting for a response from the electrodes that were attached to a leaf, he thought, *I wonder what would happen if I put a flame under a leaf on this plant.* But before he could get up from his desk chair, the signal from the polygraph instrument went off the recorder chart. This result was reproducible. Perplexed, Backster thought, *This can't be. Can the plant actually read my thoughts and in turn respond violently to my vicious intention?*

These initial experiments and many others subsequently motivated Backster to begin a detailed research program over a period of 36 years concerning the concept of consciousness and awareness in plants and other living organisms. Backster found that all forms of living organisms have the capability to respond to one another, from plants and bacteria to live foods such as yogurt and animal cells. For example, he carried out extensive research with leukocytes, the white blood cells of the human immune system, and found that they communicate with each other. He published the results of all of his research in a book released in 2003: *Primary Perception: Biocommunication with Plants, Living Foods, and Human Cells.*

Although early on, Backster's work was dismissed by many scientists, recent efforts have found substance in his research results. An article in the *New Scientist* (December 6, 2014, p. 34) had this to say:

In the past decade, researchers have been making the case for taking plants more seriously. They are finding that plants have a sophisticated awareness of their environment and, of each other, and can communicate what they sense. There is also evidence that plants have memory, can integrate massive amounts of information, and maybe pay attention. Some botanists argue that they are intelligent beings, with a "neurobiology" all of their own. There is even tentative talk of plant consciousness.

The same article describes the work of Professor Anthony Trewavas at the University of Edinburgh, who was one of the first scientists to seriously study plant "intelligence." He cites the example of the parasitic vine *Cuscuta*, also known as dodder. In time-lapse photography, the dodder seedling appears to "sniff" the air looking for its host, and having found one that it "desires," lunges and wraps its tentacles around the host as a boa constrictor would around its victim. The dodder also shows a distinct preference for tomato plants over wheat. Trewavas remarks, "You'll stop doubting that plants aren't intelligent organisms, because they are behaving in ways that you expect animals to behave."

Backster's pioneering research was not taken seriously by the scientific community, primarily because he was not a scientist, and often his work was not carried out with the best scientific standards. This is unfortunate, as the body of his research was so large that a significant portion of his findings are likely to have been directionally correct.

However, Thay said that if I had any doubts about nonhuman consciousness, such as plants and their ability to communicate with humans, with animals, and with other plants, and would like to see a much more scientifically sound analysis, I should consult *Brilliant Green: The Surprising History and Science of Plant Intelligence*, by leading plant physiologist researcher Stefano Mancuso and science writer Alessandra Viola. He pointed out that I could also learn of similar findings from *Plant Sensing and Communication* by Richard Karban, professor of entomology at the University of California, Davis.

Although we may have evolved to a higher level of conscious-ness than nonhumans, there are indications—perhaps precipitated by the driving hunger of our egos for wealth and recognition—that unlike plants and animals, we've lost our way in our Collec-tive Consciousness and its intimate connection to nature.

Thay said that author Eckhart Tolle makes the point that "nature exists in a state of unconscious *Oneness* with the *Whole*. This, for example, is why virtually no wild animals were killed in the 2004 tsunami disaster in the Indian Ocean, which claimed more than 230,000 lives. Being more in touch than humans with the totality of nature's consciousness, they sensed the tsunami's approach long before it could be seen or heard and so had time to withdraw to higher terrain."

This Collective Consciousness is present in all species, and to the greatest extent in human beings. Thay said all we need to do is to "wake up, lower the noise level of chaos in our lives, and listen carefully."

8ˢ   Then Thay said, "Excellent. But then, how do you under-stand this apparent paradox? All three forms of consciousness are separate yet one."

"That doesn't make any sense to me at all."

"I thought so. Maybe a metaphor would help. Consider a con-tainer of water, where the water droplets or molecules represent Cosmic Consciousness. Now, let's stir in a fine white powder, the particles of which represent Personal Consciousness. You now have a pure white liquid. Correct?"

"I guess so. Seems right to me."

"Next, we slowly stir in fine black-powder particles that rep-resent Collective Consciousness. As I'm sure you'll agree, as I add the black powder, the white liquid will turn gray, and the inten-sity of the gray color will increase as I add more black powder. Now let's look at this gray liquid under a strong microscope. What will you see?"

"I don't know. I guess you'll see the black particles, the white particles, and the water droplets or molecules, if the microscope is strong enough."

"Exactly. The three entities, white and black particles and the water droplets, are still separate, yet they are one when you observe the gray liquid."

9^s I was starting to phase out but was trying to stay with him. Thay pushed on.

He explained, "Consciousness within your mind is a much greater force and extends infinitely beyond the mind. It's your spirit, your Personal Consciousness; and it's eternal, unchanging, and imbued with pure, unlimited potential. Tapping into this potential is what enables us to create what some would call miracles. The world 'out there' may seem to be objective, but in fact, it is subjective, something we create by our own interpretations, by our words, our thoughts, and our beliefs. Sadly, most people are unaware of this incredible power within them."

10^s I asked, "But can't we control the valve, and open it up for greater access to Personal and Cosmic Consciousness, to the infinite knowledge that's available 'on the other side'?"

He answered, "You can, but it requires some work. You must reprogram your subconscious, and that you can do through meditation."

"Is that a difficult thing to do?"

"Absolutely not. But it does require a modest and continuous level of effort, and the benefits, as we will discuss later, are huge."

11^s "But why do many scientists still disregard this information?"

"Because they have a difficult time understanding NDEs. Their scientific instruments don't work for NDEs. They are unable to measure any conventional physical properties during an NDE. The reason is that the science of NDEs falls in the realm of spiritual physics, and a different approach to analysis is required. At this time, the only instrument that is sensitive to detecting and measuring the effects of spiritual energy is a conscious entity, and most especially a human being. The laws that govern this area of physics are different from those that govern classical physics or even quantum physics. But we're getting ahead of the story. We'll come back to spiritual physics another time.

"Another purpose of all life is the continuous and eternal evolution of consciousness toward Unity Consciousness. This is an infinite process. It had no beginning and will have no end. The current time domain began 13.8 billion years ago with what has become known as the Big Bang birth of our current universe—a rapid expansion of a single subatomic-size entity physicists call a 'singularity.' Well beyond our comprehension, this microscopic point actually contained all of the energy and mass of our universe. This energy and mass was responsible for the formation of everything in the universe—galaxies, stars, planets, and all living things—meaning you, Luc, as well."

12⁵   Thay said, "Allow me to continue. Even though most, but not all, physicists currently believe that our universe will expand forever, spiritual physics maintains that once we understand the true implications of what are called dark matter and dark energy— in particular, changes in their immense gravitational forces—the future of our universe is much different. We will then see that over billions of years, the universe and everything in it will not continue to expand, but instead will eventually collapse on itself, re-forming that singularity, which in turn will again expand over billions of years, forming another universe.

"This process of formation and collapse of the universe, sometimes called the Big Bounce, will continue *ad infinitum*, and each time the three primary elements of consciousness will evolve further toward Unity Consciousness—moving toward greater perfection of expressions of love and harmony of all things, unconditionally."

I shared a thought with Thay. "What you are telling me is a lot to digest, but I have a thought. Maybe what you've said can explain my understanding of the idea of karma. If we're all connected as parts of a whole, then what's good or bad for one must be good or bad for the whole. If I do something good or bad to someone, since both of us are part of the whole, it affects not only the one, but the whole and therefore, me, as well."

"Brilliant! As the ancient wisdom thinkers taught, we are all connected. What is good for the One is good for the Whole, and conversely. Therefore, both individual and collective existence benefit by bringing every aspect of creation into a state of complete unity and harmony. It is the primary principle of spiritual physics—namely, *only the continuous evolution of consciousness toward Unity Consciousness can bring about an increasingly peaceful and mutually cooperative world, just as our continuous physical evolution has brought about a more advanced physical world.*"

13⁵ "I'm getting dizzy with all this spiritual physics stuff. I'm not sure I understand a thing."

Thay said, "Be patient. It will soon make sense to you. But to make you a bit dizzier with this new information, it is possible for certain gifted people to experientially identify or communicate with other people and even with animals, plants, and inorganic matter, where normal five-sense communication is impossible. This becomes understandable if you accept that connection occurs and is controlled by information that you can access from the Akashic Record, which is prevalent over what we in our world would call all space and all time—in physics we say all space-time. This spiritual, physical principle is at the heart of synchronicity, telepathy, clairvoyance, and astral projection. Have you ever heard about the man called the 'horse whisperer'?"

"Right, they made a movie about him."

"He can communicate with horses simply by thought. That's spiritual physics in action."

"I see, I think."

14⁵ https://www.scribd.com/document/122441287Near-Death-Studies-and-Out-of-Body-Experiences-in-the-Blind.

15⁵   "Let me explain. If we look back at the entire physical evolution of the human species, there have been approximately 7,500 generations since *homo sapiens* appeared on the face of the earth about 200,000 years ago, and about 500 generations since modern civilization started some 20,000 years ago. Several times throughout that history, a special person was born, whose mission it was to correct the evolution of human consciousness and guide it in a way that kept it on track for its primary purpose—to facilitate the evolution of all consciousness toward Unity Consciousness. These changes, which created more efficient and effective conscious species, appear to have occurred instantaneously by geological time standards. To scientists they looked like unexplainable evolutionary quantum jumps in consciousness, but they were simply necessary corrections in our journey together toward Unity Consciousness.

"Evolutionary scientists have discovered similar creative leaps in the physical evolution of species," Thay said. "They called them *Punctuated Equilibria*. They were huge changes in species that occurred almost overnight in a geological time frame and then stabilized with minimal change over a long portion of their future geological history. For example, ancient fossils of both amphibians and birds exist, but we have never found any solid evidence of a fossil record of a connecting creature between amphibians and birds, even though we know from DNA and other data that birds evolved from amphibians. This suggests a quantum leap where certain amphibians needed to create the necessary physical features to enable them to fly, and birds evolved nearly 'instantly' as a result of that intent. The same is true for the evolution of consciousness, but in that case, it requires a wise, highly conscious person to help facilitate such an 'instantaneous' jump in consciousness. Some have actually been Avatars."

16⁵   Thay explained even further. "Consider the known history of one whom you may be most familiar with: Jesus."

I said, "To be honest, I don't consider myself a member of any religion. I've never thought deeply as to whether or not I even believe in a God as associated with any organized religion."

Thay said, "Maybe that's one of the reasons you were chosen. But please, allow me to continue. If you study the history contained in the existing Judeo-Christian literature, especially that which was hidden, destroyed, or dismissed as heresy by the Church of Rome—for example, the Lost Gospels, the Dead Sea Scrolls, and numerous ancient codices—you can easily conclude that Jesus had no intent or interest in forming a religion. The Christian religion was formed at the Council of Nicaea in A.D. 325, more than 300 years after his death, and solidified in A.D. 337 with the convenient political conversion to Christianity of Constantine the Great on his deathbed."

"Is that well known?"

"Yes, it is, and it's also well known that modern Christianity was founded by men—and I do mean men, not women—seeking wealth and control over people through their use of fear, based on rules they created that were allegedly from the mouth of Jesus. Not so, and it's been proven over and over again. When he finally found and accepted his spiritual path, Jesus, as the Buddha before him, was simply interested in teaching a philosophy of spiritual values so that all people could live more purposeful, passionate, and peaceful lives and fulfill their destiny of enabling Cosmic Consciousness to become aware of Itself and for all creation to move toward Unity Consciousness. He taught that 'Heaven is within you,' meaning the knowledge and reward for living a fulfilled life can be found 'inside,' not 'outside,' as so many of us are taught from birth.

"Please understand, I am not criticizing religion. Over millennia, organized religions have given millions of people a sense of hope in the future and in life after death. However, the physical structure and dogmatic philosophy of organized religion was never intended by its alleged founders."

"You seem to emphasize that men are the culprits," I said.

Thay replied, "Yes. It's well documented that men throughout the ages have feared the feminine energy of women as well as the natural, innate feminine energy within themselves, so they have suppressed it. As Eckhart Tolle states in his book *A New Earth*: 'It seems certain that during a three-hundred year period between three and five million women were tortured and killed by the "Holy Inquisition," an institution founded by the Roman Catholic Church to suppress heresy. Leaders of the Church feared women and their intuitive feminine energy as a threat to the religion they were building.'"

Thay continued. "But staying with the ideas of Jesus, this was not his way. It is reasonably well established that Mary Magdalene was arguably his favorite and most effective apostle. The recently discovered Lost Gospels note that the 12 apostles were jealous of Jesus's attention to her, arguably the 13th apostle. There are some writings in the Lost Gospels that suggest they eventually married and had children."

I said, "I think that would have been so cool, an Avatar with a wife and kids, just like other men. People could really relate to that."

Thay said, "I agree. This perspective highlights a critical principle in dealing with challenging global issues such as poverty, climate change, nuclear proliferation, terrorism, and human inequities—these problems require the appropriate balance between masculine and feminine energies."

"I don't understand what you're getting at."

He responded, "As social units progressed and evolved over millennia, an increasing ratio of feminine to masculine energies has been required, but men, out of fear, have not allowed that to come about. This evolution has been a transition from a primary focus on protection from predators and provision for food and shelter to an intimate sensitivity to social and cultural complexities. The former necessarily required high levels of masculine energy—men were important—but the latter required high levels of feminine energy—the primary domain of women. Feminine energy focuses on compassion; win-win negotiations; rapid and intuitive assessments of complex systems; and a deep sensitivity to multidimensional social factors such as culture, gender, race, and emotional intelligence. This is the domain of what some have called the *Sacred Feminine*, which is always committed to the success of the whole."

"Are you telling me our modern world needs more women leaders?"

"To some degree, yes. But equally important, I'm also saying that our culture needs to encourage men to express their feminine energy in leadership and in making certain critical corporate and political decisions."

"There are a lot of women in this world who would love to hear that—Bella, for one!"

ACKNOWLEDGMENTS

Writing a novel is a solitary journey. However, the final product would often never see the light of day without the input of talented "giants" working behind the scenes.

Early drafts of *I Can See Clearly* benefited from important constructive critique by several of these giants—Tinker Lindsay, Dara Marks, and Marie Rowe. The novel was substantially improved by the editorial skills of Stephanie Westphal and Kenneth Kales. My daughter, Polly Cole, and her husband, Joe, provided significant guidance on getting the voice of Luc to what I envisioned for his persona. I am grateful to my dear friend Marco Sipione for checking my Italian.

My literary agent, Bill Gladstone, helped me successfully navigate a sometimes tortuous path from the very inception of the book's concept to its endpoint. To these talented people, I am deeply grateful. However, any errors of omission or commission are strictly mine.

I am especially grateful to my wife, Inez, for her emotional support from the moment I sat at my computer and typed the very first words of *I Can See Clearly* until its publication. She has always known better than I, my strengths on which to focus and my shortcomings to recognize and manage. To her I continue to send my unconditional love and the Spirit of Light, here and hereafter.

ABOUT THE AUTHOR

James A. Cusumano (www.JamesCusumano.Com) is chairman and owner of Chateau Mcely (www.chateaumcely.cz/en/homepage), chosen in 2007 by the European Union as the only "Green" five-star castle hotel in Central Europe; and in 2008 by the World Travel Awards as "The World's Leading Green Hotel." Chateau Mcely offers programs that promote the principles of inspired and conscious leadership, finding your life purpose, and long-term fulfillment.

Jim began his career during the 1950s in the field of entertainment as a recording artist. Years later, after earning a PhD in physical chemistry, studying business at Stanford, and being a Foreign Fellow of Churchill College at Cambridge University, he joined Exxon as a research scientist and later became the company's research director for Catalytic Science & Technology.

Jim subsequently cofounded two public companies in Silicon Valley: Catalytica Energy Systems, Inc.—devoted to clean power generation—and Catalytica Pharmaceuticals, Inc., which manufactured drugs via environmentally benign, low-cost, catalytic technologies. While he was chairman and CEO, Catalytica Pharmaceuticals grew in less than five years from several employees to 2,000, and became more than a $1 billion enterprise before being sold.

Subsequent to his work in Silicon Valley and before buying and renovating Chateau Mcely with his wife, Inez, Jim returned to the entertainment industry and founded Chateau Wally Films (www.chateauwallyfilms.biz), which produced the feature film *What Matters Most* (2001: www.imdb.com/title/tt0266041), distributed in more than 50 countries.

Jim lives in Prague with Inez and their daughter, Julia.

Website: www.JimTheAlchymist.Com